The Universe Before Us

Marc B. DeGeorge

MuseMarc Studio, LLC

Contents

Acknowledgments

I may say the same thing every book, and thank the same people, but I am grateful that some things never change.

To my completely dedicated reading group: Tracey Canole, E. Marie Robertson, Michelle Darnell, Joe Creech, and J. Logan Rice. Thank you always for your critical commentary, positive support, and friendship.

My amazing editors, Joanne Machin and Ariel Anderson. Your skills have kept my stories from becoming a total disaster. Thank you for working with me.

Also to my wife and family, for your support and love.

ACCIDENT

—— • ——

CERI

WE ARE A CREW by half. Decimated by sickness and war, only those who were strong enough—or lucky enough—to survive remain. Thirteen kids, plus two more: Fana and Raey, though only Fana is a permanent member of our shrunken crew. And I could not be gladder for her presence. Without her, the *Stratford* would still be lost.

And so would I.

Still, there's much to celebrate. Our passengers are back on course to their new homeworld. My parents, when they wake, will only know they'd made it, as the directors promised they would. Of course, neither I nor any of the other crew will be there to watch them emerge from a thousand years in stasis, but many others will, and we have Fana's brilliance to thank for that. I will forever be grateful to her for making my one wish a reality.

I still can't believe she tried to kiss me. Sometimes I wish she had.

"Be careful, Ceri," Fana says over the comm in my helmet. *"That tether the two of you have is seven hundred years old. I doubt it's as strong as it used to be. Keep some slack in it and stay together*

when moving. Hold hands if you need to...and...oh, you're not feeling dizzy, are you?"

Fana warned us about disorientation. She was right to. The moment Seren and I stepped through the airlock, the near-total black of our surroundings, combined with the unending spectacle of billions on billions of points of light, brought me to a full stop. It was as if they washed over me, submerging me inside an ocean of forever. It took ten minutes before either of us could focus on accomplishing our task.

Somewhere inside of that infinity is a single bright point—a star, Seager-Ghez 1267b. Around it orbits a planet. Asteria. That's the *Stratford*'s, and our passengers', destination. They will build a colony there, and eventually a new civilization, free of hate. Free of war. Free of everything that destroyed Earth. That's their dream, and it's mine, too. Everything I do here is so they can have that chance.

"Ceri?" Fana queries again, her voice pitched higher than normal.

"No. I'm fine," I reply, perhaps not sounding as convincing as I should. Too late to correct it. I've already turned to focus on the task in front of me.

Seren glances at me worriedly as we stand, separated by a few paces, with our boots locked to the outside skin of the *Stratford*. I respect her courage for coming out here with me to repair the damage around the airlock, left when the *Devant*'s crew leeched their ship on to ours.

That they drilled holes into my ship to secure their connection grates me hard. That they then used it to abduct and murder members of my crew is more than unforgiveable. Fana's former ship floats in space in its oddly rounded configuration, close enough to see with my eyes, yet too far to hit. If I had a weapon powerful enough to reach them, I would put an end to their journey.

"If you do, get back inside right away," Fana says, her tone reminding me of my mother's. She's far from that age or level of maturity. Some things she does make me wonder if I'm not the one who's five years older. Still, until Commander Azazhi disowned her, she was chief engineer of the *Devant*.

I reach a hand out to Seren and motion for her to join me. Fana may be immature, but she's also right. This is our first time outside the ship, and the tension in my body is already seeping fatigue into my muscles. Add the constant feeling of being pulled toward the *Stratford*'s aft, and my legs are already burning.

"Let's get started," I say to Seren, handing her a welding tool. "We've only twenty minutes of air in these tanks."

"I know," Seren replies. *"Where should I start?"*

"There." I point to a spot near the top hinge of the outside airlock door, the one closest to us. I'll let her try the first hole while I supervise, mostly because I'll worry less about her. If it takes longer and we have to come back to finish this, I will be fine with that.

Seren drops a metal plate over the hole and secures it with a pair of magnets not unlike the type keeping our feet secured to the hull. Except a processor controls the ones in our boots and senses when we move our feet. Walking is simple. Running isn't recommended.

Once she's satisfied with the positioning of the repair plate, Seren lifts the bulky welding tool over the plate and powers the device on. Without hesitation, she engages the device and moves it down one edge of the plate, making what appears to be a solid join. I press my lips together and nod. How she became so skilled with it in such a short time is more than impressive. She must have spent the last week doing nothing but practicing with the machine. Her dedication, while admirable, likely frustrated Rhys to no end. Their off-and-on relationship is currently in an affectionate phase. Until it's not. Perhaps one day he'll learn to let her do what excites her. Then he might find he becomes one of those things.

"Looks good," I say as Seren finishes another side.

"Of course it does," she replies, continuing to the next edge. *"Now let's see what you got."*

I huff and shake my head, moving to the opposite side to cover the damage there. If we can repair all five holes in under ten minutes, we'll be back inside the ship with plenty of air left in our suits. That'll make Fana happy. She was already near panic when I told her we were planning to do this.

"First section complete!" Seren chirps. *"Moving to the next one!"*

"Make sure the welds are clean first!" Fana chides.

"Don't worry. They are."

Seren's making the process seem easier than it is. When I place my welding tool on the plate, it bumps a magnet and the plate slides out of place. I curse and let go of the welder to reset it, catching the device before it floats away. It wasn't possible for me to find much time to practice, and I knew I'd have some trouble. Sayer should be here. He's got more experience with the welder. I just wanted to experience being outside of the ship.

And now that I have, I'm ready to return. Nausea is causing me to swallow constantly to keep anything from coming out of my stomach. For the sake of caring for my ship, I'll bear it. We've got to get this done; otherwise, Fana says it could cause a rupture in the hull.

"Second one down, moving to the third!" Seren calls.

"It's not a race!" Fana replies. *"If the weld is bad, are you willing to go back out and fix it?"*

"Absolutely. I could do this all day."

I smile at their banter. The two of them have gotten close enough to publicly declare each other as sisters to the rest of the crew. Some jealousy may have resulted, but only a little.

"Oh bish!" Seren shouts as she shoots to her feet and swipes at something floating just out of her reach. A magnet. She bends her legs and hops to try again. I gasp, the breath getting caught up in my lungs as the tether between us goes taut. Fana better be very wrong about the strength of it.

I shouldn't have worried. The moment the tether reached its maximum length, it snapped her back to land on the hull again. Seren's boots secure themselves, and I won't be telling Fana what just happened.

"Let it go," I say. "I'll give you one of mine."

"It's okay. I've got it," Seren replies.

"What happened?" Fana's voice is tight. *"Is everything okay?"*

"Fine." I press my teeth together, forcing myself only to tell her what's necessary. "We almost lost a magnet, but we're just about done."

With a sigh, I return my focus to the first side of my plate, which has yet to be bonded to the hull. By the time I've completed this one, Seren will have done the rest. That could be for the best. This is far more dangerous than I'd considered it to be. If there's a next time, I will make sure we've got more safety measures in place.

There's a tug on the tether, likely Seren returning to her spot on the other side of the airlock. But then there's another, and my body jerks back as if someone just let go of—

Seren screams. My head flies up.

My chest goes tight as Seren floats aft, just off the hull. Her arms flail about, trying everything she can to stop herself. But all it does is send her tumbling, the speed of her rotations increasing as she heads toward the white-hot glow of the engines.

"Hyuk!" I'm on my feet in a heartbeat, sliding my feet across the *Stratford*'s skin faster than is safe. It doesn't matter. Seren's in a situation that's far above my need to feel comfortable. "Seren?" I call. "Can you hear me? Stay calm. I'm coming."

"What?" Fana says. *"Ceri! Do you need help? Seren? What's going on?"*

"Not now," is my reply. I regret it instantly.

Fana snarls a few curses, then gets back on her comm. *"I'm telling Sayer and Tegan to suit up."*

"No! No one else comes out here!"

Seren is moving at a steady pace, but I'm struggling to close the distance between us. And she's rising off the hull. If I don't get to her soon, she'll be out of my reach. The horror of that thought pushes me harder. I can't lose her. Seren's special to me. I've always looked out for her, and for her to go like this...

No. She's not dying today.

"Seren! Just relax!" I shout. "You're pushing yourself away from the hull!"

"*Relax?*" Seren's voice pitches high. "*How the hyuk am I supposed to do that?*"

My jaw tightens. I don't know how to calm her. Seren can't save herself and she knows it. Panic must be rushing through her body like an inferno. I'm the one chasing her and that's how I feel. All I can do is get to her as fast as possible.

But I'm already running out of strength. It's a massive effort to move in this thick suit with the weight of another person on my back. I'd take the air tanks off if I didn't need them. Each step makes me cough and wheeze, my sides aching with the force I'm using to push oxygen into my lungs. I must be gulping down a ton. My breathing time just dropped by minutes.

"*Ceri!*" Seren pleads. "*Where are you? I'm getting really high. Hurry!*"

I spot something: an extension jutting out from the sheer smoothness of the rest of the hull. It could be a vent or a heat exchanger—I don't care. All I know is that it could be my one chance to save her.

But it means releasing my feet from the ship. If I mess this up, we're both lost.

"Ceri?" Fana says. *"Talk to me. Please! What's going on? Seren? Are you alright?"*

My finger finds the comm button in my glove, and I inhale. I might regret saying this to her, but she needs to know. The crew is everything. Not me. Without them, our passengers won't survive.

I speak as I exhale. "I don't mean to frighten you, Fana, but if we don't come back, tell Efa she's in charge."

With that, I disconnect the comm and prepare to take what might be the biggest risk I've ever taken. If I survive this, I might just reconsider what it means to be the leader of this crew.

In three seconds, Seren will be nearly in the right position. I can't calculate speeds or vectors or any of that, so I'll just push off the hull at my top speed and hope it's enough, because it has to be.

"Okay," I say. "In five seconds I'll be there."

"How?" Seren asks. *"No. Never mind. Just save me. Please."*

Two seconds...one...

With as much power as I can force into my legs, I launch off the hull, shooting straight for the extension. Seren's path—if I've judged it correctly—will cross mine just at the right moment. Everything is up to my best guess now. And luck. If there was a time for our Ancestors to lend a hand, now would be it.

My arms rise, my fingers stretching out, pointing toward Seren's rotating body. She's stopped reaching for the hull.

Maybe she's realized the pointlessness of it. Or maybe she's just accepted her fate.

I'm close. Just a few paces away. The hull passes below me in a near blur. Only then do I realize how dangerously fast I'm going. I flex and clench my hands. There will only be this one chance.

"Brace yourself, Seren!" I call.

"What?"

She twists her body to look. It only makes her spin worse. *Bish.* Grabbing her with my hands will be impossible. I spread my arms wider, praying that's enough.

I suck in a breath. Oh hell. My guess was too on it. We're going to collide. I brace, fearing the pain of impact. This will hurt.

My body slams into hers with a hard thump, Seren's arm smacking into my helmet. She yelps, her body jerking.

"Don't move!" I cry, my arms wrapping around her and holding tight. Seren rotates in my grasp to hold me in return.

But now we're both tumbling, the ship's hull flashing past my vision nearly every second. The rest is terrifying blackness. We could be headed into it. Or we could be safe. I can't tell.

Dizziness is overtaking me. I shut my eyes as Seren cries out. We're together. That's all I can ask for. If we're dead, at least we won't die alone.

Pain flashes across my vision as my shoulder crunches against a hard surface. Seren yells and twists, reaching out for something. My eyes are rolling back into my head. We drop. There's a clank of metal on metal.

And as everything goes dark, my boots click as they reconnect to the *Stratford*'s hull.

ENIGMA

—— • ——

FANA

I WAS DESPERATE NOT to leave her side. She nearly disappeared from my life. But Efa, with that gentle smile of hers, took my hand and promised me Ceri would be okay. It put me enough at ease that I could return my attention to some much-needed work. There was certainly enough that needed doing.

So here I am on one-thirty-five, sweaty, filthy, and tired. This level has most of the processors for the ship's water and sewage. It's not a pleasant-smelling space. Even the respirator I wear lets through enough of the stink to make me not want to take it off, despite it turning my chin and cheeks into swampland. I can always shower, but I don't know if I'll ever get this stench out of my nose.

I should have brought help. Someone down here to share in my misery would've been welcome. And the overhead lights, even at full blast, only cover the main walkways. Shadows blanket every nook and crevice between the machines, turning as dark as the voids of space and leaving someone with an active imagination—like me—more than a little creeped out.

At least I'm almost done. Just a few more adjustments on the last group of flash distillers, and I'll be smacking the call button to take me up to medical so I can see how Ceri's doing. Hopefully, Raey and Efa put her shoulder joint back in place. Maybe they also found out what sort of crazy thing occurred to dislocate her left arm from her body like that. Even chatty Seren kept her mouth shut while Raey looked her over.

My chest hurts when I think of Ceri. Those beautiful, hard blue eyes that have seen so much tragedy. Her firm hands and powerful arms that make me melt every time they wrap around me. And those lips. Her sultry, full lips I'm dying to press against mine. There's no doubt in my mind that I've got it bad. Raey warned me about falling for her, yet I'm more than ready to jump right off that cliff.

Ceri may be denying herself the joy of a relationship, but I'm determined to show her what she's missing. It's not fair that she has to live in self-imposed loneliness while the rest of her crew is pairing up. Even Efa, her second-in-command, is already talking about babies. Ceri can lead and be in love. I'll prove to her it's possible. If she'll have me.

I flick the access hatch shut on the number-three distiller unit, satisfied that it's working the best it can for a seven-hundred-year-old machine. Two more units to go and—

What the hell was that?

Trembling, my body spins around as I search for the hissing sound that came from behind me. That was not a noise made by any machine. It almost sounded like someone speaking. Maybe it was.

Is someone down here?

But just as quickly as the sound brushed against my eardrums, it's gone. Now all that I can hear is the *drip-drip* of the condensers and the low drone of the pumps pushing water up to the recyclers and tanks on the levels above. It's possible I imagined it, yet I heard it clear against the background noise. If it was a voice, what did they say? And if someone wanted to talk to me, wouldn't they just call me on the comm? Unless...

No. The kids are too busy to be playing jokes. And I would've heard the rail car stop on the level. Besides, only Seren knows me well enough to mess around like that, and these days she's so focused on learning as much as she can from me. Serious is her only mode when we're together.

With a sigh, I continue to distiller number two. Likely the sound was my imagination. A lack of sleep will do that, and ever since Commander Azazhi ordered his security agent to shoot a hole in my hand, I've been struggling to rest well. I should tell Raey about my nightmares. She'd understand, yet—

Something flashes through the shadow. I scream, fly into a dark space between the distillers, and drop into the deepest corner, my pulse pounding hard. I try to keep still, but it's difficult. Every breath comes faster than the next.

I saw it. I know I did. Whatever *it* was. A person? Something else? I'm reluctant to come up with an answer. That definitely wasn't my imagination playing tricks on me. So what was it then? Poisonous gas messing with my eyes? There's always that possibility, but I doubt it. Even on an ancient ship like the *Stratford*, the designers would have accounted for potential leaks in the recycling system. Water's too critical to let it drip all over the place. And I've checked all the obvious places for signs of a problem. There's none.

Which means…

My first instinct is to run straight to the rail car and shut the doors behind me as fast as they'll move, then shoot up to Ceri and tell her what—no, wait. She'll just think I'm worrying too much, like I did when she was working outside the ship. I was, and I have no problem admitting it. EVAs terrify me, and the thought of something happening to her while she was out there nearly froze me. It doesn't matter my fear was justified this time. That was just pure chance.

What would Ceri do in this situation?

She'd track down whatever she saw and determine if it was a threat or not. And if it was, she'd remove it with as much force as she needed to make sure it never came back.

I can't do that. I'm not a soldier like she is. And if she were here, I'd be clinging to her for fear of being dragged away by the monster in the shadows, which is likely nothing more than a puff of steam or something like that. Then again, I'd be just as afraid to admit how scared I was. Ceri'd tease me for acting like a child.

As the pounding in my chest dies down, I slink forward, peering across the walkway into the dark on the other side. I press against the distiller with my hands and body, as if it would protect me from danger. It's silly, and heat comes to my face, imagining Ceri, the person of my desire, laughing at me.

With no reason to do anything other than finish my work, I step out of the nook and pick up the digital spanner I dropped the moment I ran.

But even as I grab it and stand to return to the distiller, I get a chill that makes me shiver. Like someone's watching me. There's no way anyone is. I'm the only one down here. Still, I can't shake this feeling.

Wait. My imagination is way too overactive here. If I run up top and make a big deal out of this, I'll be the source of jokes for an entire month. Everything I've done to gain their respect will be gone, and I don't want to spend the rest of my time here being made fun of. I had enough of that on Earth.

I reach into my pants pocket and pull out a light, powering it on and blasting the black space where I saw movement. It illuminates every open area within its beam's reach. The entire area glows brighter than even the lamps overhead. Of course, the space is empty. Not a single hint of movement. I should feel as stupid as I know I am, yet this chill that's putting bumps across my forearms won't go away.

I have to check the rest. If only for my sanity.

There are three other spaces I need to inspect. The first is easy. Just a quick shuffle to the left and repeat what I did a second ago. I clear it of suspicion in less than ten seconds. The only reason it took me so long is because I became sidetracked by an interesting piece of equipment I didn't know the function of until I took the time to examine it. The three escape valves on the top are an odd choice for the design of it and make it way more complicated than it needs to be.

I remember I'm on a ship designed several centuries before the *Devant*, my former assignment. That ship would never need emergency protections. The intelligence in its systems does all the redundancy by itself. But the *Stratford*, handicapped by programs that can't make abstract choices on their own, would.

All of that is less than important at this moment. I should be searching for the ghost that made me scream like a four-year-old. And when I don't find one, I'll finish my work and go see Ceri so I can put a smile back on my face.

Right. Next one. Let's do this.

My body gets tight as I shine the light into the next space. I have nothing but tools to defend myself with, and the only time I've used any of them for violence was when a stubborn machine was defying me. Even then, I was swinging to release my frustration. I don't know if I could hurt someone, even if my life depended upon it.

All clear. I exhale and thank whomever or whatever I need to thank that it wasn't in there. There's just one spot left, and I am seriously wishing I'd never seen a horror movie in my life before now. The last spot is always where the monster is.

I take a breath, step forward, and prepare to flood the space with light, hoping whatever might be in there is harmless. Aside from the crew, there's nothing here that should be capable of harming me. At least, not on purpose. Right?

Another breath, and I steady myself for whatever might be there. Of course it'll be nothing. But my hands are shaking. I'm shaking. What if there's some vicious beast in here preparing to claw me to death?

So glad I just thought of that.

Two gentle steps, and I come before the utter darkness of the space, leveling my light as if it were a pistol. My thumb slides forward, slowly, carefully. I don't want to miss anything. I count down from three. Two...

My comm buzzes. I jump.

"Fana." It's Sayer. A little disappointing, but not totally. *"I think something's going on up here on forty-eight. Can you come up and check it out?"*

Fix something? Up there? How could I not accept an invitation like that? So what if I'll need to come back down here—with someone—and finish my work on the last unit? They're just backups, anyway. And the system's designed to work with way more of a load than we're giving it.

It can wait.

"Sure," I say, rushing to the rail car. "I'll be right there."

EMERGENCY

FANA

Sayer frowns at me as I blink at him. We've been standing like this for more than a few seconds, and it's making my stomach churn. I came up here to level forty-eight to check the stasis beds that he's concerned about. And now, with a sea of units before us, he won't let me touch any of them until I fix the problem. And that's the problem. I don't know what's wrong.

"Okay," I say to Sayer as I pat the air in front of me. "I heard you. You can calm down. We'll get to it as soon as I do some—"

"These are our families, Fana," Sayer replies, folding his arms. "You may fix the ship for us, but you don't care about these people like we do. Something is definitely wrong with the readings on most of the pods here. That's all you need to know."

A pang hits my chest. He didn't need to remind me of my outsider status. Or how I'm the second-oldest person, after Raey, awake on this ship. I know I'll never truly be one of them, even when I'm trying hard to fit in. We may have fought a battle together, but I missed the entire war. There's no way for me to earn that connection and no way for me to experience what they suffered through. Even if I wanted to.

Still, the least he could do is show a little appreciation.

"Sayer, I need to know what to fix before I can fix it," I say, motioning to the stasis units. "The systems diagnostics on the pods say what's wrong on that pod and *only* that pod. If they all show errors, then it's a bigger problem. Give me a few minutes to take some readings, and I'll have a better idea about what's going on."

"And what if they don't have a few minutes?"

I sigh. I get he cares so much it makes him crazy, but Sayer should realize it, too. Especially after Ceri, Efa, *and* Merek have warned him about it. Time to put on my grown-up pants and make what I need happen.

"We're just wasting time talking like this," I say with my hands open. "If you help me, we can get every reading I need in a handful of minutes. I promise you, nothing bad will happen in the next thirty minutes. At least."

He chews on his lower lip, his body relaxing. "Are you sure?"

I nod. "Absolutely. The pods are stable. None of them—"

Everything goes black. A chorus of alarms blare out from the stasis pods, their power units blinking in warning—a power failure! My mind races as I force myself to think. *What to do? Right. Find the power source. Locate the fault. Get around it and repatch.* But how much time will it take? Two hours at most. It's not enough.

And just as quickly as the power went down, it returns.

I let out the breath I'd been holding for the last thirty seconds. So does Sayer. Our gazes connect, and for a moment, I relax. But only for a moment.

"Well, now we know what the problem is," I say. "All we have to do is locate where we're losing power."

"How fast can we do that?" Sayer's voice is tense.

I shrug. "We won't know until we start."

He motions toward the pods with a nod. I give him one in reply. At least he's calmer. Or maybe he's just holding it in. I don't care which, as long as he puts the effort in to help me. This won't get done without him.

I grab a pair of voltmeters from my tool set and hand one to Sayer. He examines the device with mild curiosity, clutching it as if he were about to stab someone. He probably could, trained to kill like he was. I bet that kind of muscle memory never goes away, and he's had years to perfect it.

The thought gives me chills.

"Start at the end of one row and run it across every one of those thick wires going into the pods," I say. "If the power in the line is dead or way off, you'll see a red light. Let me know about that right away. Green or yellow is fine."

"What's yellow mean?"

"That you're on a seven-hundred-year-old ship."

Sayer's done scanning the first two pods in the row before I even consider where I might start. Though if he's that quick, I should head to the primary distribution system and check that first. It's more complicated than the pods, and he might get confused with which wires he already tested. Hell, I might get confused, too.

No, I definitely will.

The distro system is housed in a bulky metal cabinet at the far end of the level, away from the stasis pods. That's because the magnetic field created by the massive coils inside of it could mess up the delicate electronics in the pods and shielding them would just add unnecessary weight. The coils step down the voltage from the *Stratford*'s main generators, so they need to be big—about the same size as me, and they probably weigh ten times what I do. Wound around each core hundreds of times are thick black cables nearly as wide as my forearm. Each runs a powerful charge through it that'd kill almost anyone. I'll need to be careful.

The lights drop out for a second, wavering in intensity as they return. I tighten my jaw as I stare up at them, expecting the worst.

A second, brief flicker is a forceful reminder we need to get this solved now. A few more hands would help. But who? Seren, my first choice, is on a mandatory double rest cycle, as recommended by Raey and ordered by Efa and Merek. Those two will make excellent parents one day. Right now, though, I need someone who can do the job of three of her. I won't get anyone like that, so I'll take whoever I can get my hands on.

"Rhys...no, scratch that," I call through my comm. "Tegan, Aidan, and Beka. Please drop what you're doing and come down to forty-eight. Sayer and I need a hand."

Sayer glances at me with a raised eyebrow. But I don't have time to discuss it. He should have no complaints, anyway. These three have family in stasis, too.

"Copy that, Fana," Tegan replies. *"I'm here with Beka. We'll be down as fast as we can."*

A little more than five seconds later, Aidan shows up, climbing up from the floor below as he breathes hard. I grin and thrust a finger at Sayer, and once Sayer nods in understanding, I return to my testing of the coils. These kids will drop everything to help one another, and that puts me at ease. I may be an outcast, and an adult, but I can rely on them to treat each other well.

I finish scanning one coil—it's fine—and move onto the next one. Almost immediately, the meter flashes red. I pull it away and try again, just to be sure, then check the reading. Not way off, but enough of a variation to cause issues. I'm still impressed that this device worked for as long as it did. Even when we were building the *Devant*, we couldn't be sure how long things would last, so we made the ship accelerate as fast as possible.

The engineering team I once supervised is still over there. I wonder if they miss me. What I wouldn't give to have even one of those talented people here working with me. It hurts my chest to think I'll never see their faces again.

"Done!" Sayer says.

"No problems," Aidan adds. "What are we looking for, anyway?"

I lift my head up to see him, Aidan, Tegan, and Beka all looking at me expectantly. Wow. I must have been so focused on testing, I didn't hear them arrive. They're here now, and that's all that matters.

"Okay, well"—I nod to the distribution system—"I've likely found the issue, but we've got to decide the best way to fix it."

"Can't you just replace the part?" Sayer asks.

"Yes, we'll replace it, as long as we've got another to replace it with. That's not the question. Removing one core will put a severe strain on the other, and given the age of these things, it could be too much for it to handle."

As if hearing my words, the power does one long blink, prompting a gasp from Tegan and Beka. They both stare at me, wide-eyed, watching to see my response. I'm getting used to it happening, so I don't have one other than to keep talking. It's better if they don't see me worry.

"So to avoid that happening, we could power down everything for a little while and hope we get the replacement done before the pods' batteries go out. Or we could just leave everything on and hope that's safe enough for us to work around a high-voltage line."

"How much time would we have?" Tegan asks.

I shrug. "A few hours maybe."

"No way," Sayer says, shaking his head. "We won't have enough time. Let's keep the power on."

I purse my lips as Tegan shifts and crosses her arms. As if the air wasn't tense enough. I should be patient, however. Let them talk through it and come up with an answer. That'll get everyone working toward a solution they all agree upon. Teams work better that way.

"Is your brain fried or something?" Tegan looks at Sayer with disbelieving eyes. "Because it will be if you touch a live circuit."

"Forget that!" Beka says.

"Anyone you know on this level?" Sayer challenges, thrusting a finger toward the back row. "My uncle is right there. I'm not taking any chances with his life."

"So you'll take one with your own?" Tegan shoots back.

"Okay! Okay!" I raise my hands to cut them off. So much for productive discussion. "We'll try it with the power on. There's a safe way to do that, but everyone needs to be hyperalert. Accidents can happen just like that if we're not careful."

"We'll be alert," Beka says. "We had that skill beaten into us."

I offer her a sympathetic smile. Beka's not exaggerating. I can see the truth of it on their faces. Each one of them is reliving a horrific moment where the adults took their anger out on the body of a child. That'll never happen again on this ship. We've already made sure of it.

"So what's first?" Sayer asks.

"First, we create a bridge between the two cores in case that one goes down," I reply. "Then you'll go find us a replacement core, and if everything goes smoothly...which is never the case, but we'll manage...then everyone on this level, including your uncle, will be safe."

For the first time since I arrived here, there's hope in Sayer's eyes. The edges of his mouth are even curling up a little. Maybe that's all he really needs.

"Great, let's do it," Sayer says.

Then, darkness.

"Oh bish," Beka says as the pod alarms scream, and I sigh through gritted teeth.

She said my thought exactly.

DISASTER

CERI

EFA SITS NEXT TO me in my recovery bed, her legs crossed as her dirty boots rest on the white sheets. I'd say something about it, yet she'd just remind me of who broke the rules first and dislocated their shoulder, and my complaint would fall flat. Besides, I'm enjoying her company—something that doesn't happen very often with everything we have to do. We need this time together. There are a great many things to discuss that concern only her and me.

The medical bay has taken a turn for the worse since our battle with the *Devant*'s crew. We may have beaten them, but we couldn't defeat the scratches and stains ground into the bay's walls and furniture. And we've yet to replace the glass of the isolation room after I smashed through it.

This place and I have a tragic history, all of it far too clear in my mind.

"Still thinking about a baby?" I ask, just to make conversation. We both agree it's not the right time for her and Merek to have one, though I'm surprised she let me have any say about it at all.

A wistful smile appears on Efa's lips as she tilts her head and drops her gaze to her hands. "You'll understand one day," is her soft reply.

"Will I?"

Her smile mutates into an impish grin as she presses her face close to mine and waggles her eyebrows. "You're dying to be in love, Ceri. I know it. And you would be if you stopped denying it to yourself."

I huff. "I've got passengers and crew to look after. And between you and Merek, there's already love dripping everywhere."

"Ew." Efa wrinkles her nose and giggles. "Why'd you have to put it like that?"

"Besides, you're not the only couple. Seren and—"

Efa's comm buzzes. She holds up a finger to me and taps the speaker button to receive the call. I settle back into my pillow, content for the moment to let her handle it. She never had her own squad or crew to command, yet I would trust her decisions more than my own. In the two days I've been in here, nothing's fallen apart and no one's gotten hurt. As much as I struggle to, I can relax a bit with Efa in charge.

"Efa, it's Fana."

Fana. The space between my eyebrows gets tight, along with my jaw. There's a problem with the ship. A big problem. Fana wouldn't bother Efa otherwise.

So much for resting.

"Go ahead, Fana," Efa says. "What's up?"

"I need you down on forty-eight. Like, right now. Please."

"That's a stasis level," I say.

Efa glances at me, tight-lipped. The moment she disconnects the comm, I'm going to get fifty reasons why I'll be staying here while she goes. Efa also knows I'll protest every one. Perhaps for her sake, and our passengers, I shouldn't. But that'll be difficult when my stomach is already twisting.

"Okay, I'm coming." With that, Efa slips off the bed and sighs, taking a long, slow breath before turning to me. "I won't stop you from going," she says. "Because I know I can't. That doesn't mean I don't think you're a bish-head for doing it. Rest is what you need. Not heroics."

"Who's being heroic?" I ask.

She thrusts a finger at me. "Don't make me strap you to this bed. You'll hate how tight I make it."

I just smirk.

Despite her threat, we're walking out of the rail car doors on forty-eight two minutes later, with Efa in the lead. She's still in charge until she and Raey release me from medical. If it were up to me, I'd make that happen right now, but Efa deserves a chance to handle the problem. She's more than capable.

"Power's about to go," Fana says as we approach. She throws a concerned glance at me before returning her attention to Efa. "I need to replace one coil in the distribution system. Faster than I expected I would. So I need as much help as I can get."

Efa shrugs. "You could have just told me that over the comm. We'd all be here by now."

"Well, I didn't want to..." Fana glances at me again and goes silent. I'd cross my arms and glare if one of them wasn't in a sling. Everyone had better cut the delicate act around me before I get really irritated.

There's a flash and a powerful boom that knocks most of the floor panels in the center of the level off their tracks. A puff of smoke rises from the far end of the level. Beka cries out. Aidan throws his arms up in surprise and backs away. I go still. There are few emergencies that will send ice through my veins. One's a hull breach.

The other is fire.

In the next second, Efa's clicking her comm. "All crew, this is Efa. I need you on forty-eight as fast as you can get here."

"No! Don't!" Fana shouts at Sayer as he charges toward the brightening glow behind the smoke. "It could explode!"

Sayer stops short, staring at her with an open mouth. A breath escapes my lungs. Fana just saved him and I'm grateful, but I realize something, and panic strikes me: my parents are on the level above, and just like the stasis beds here, there's no way to move them.

"And you want me to bring everyone here?" Efa eyes go wide, and she taps her comm. "All crew—"

Fana holds her hands up. "It's okay! They can come! We need them!"

"Need them to what? Die?" Sayer counters.

"No!" Fana's brow gets tight. "I mean, yes. Of course it's dangerous, but the more crew we've got to put the fire out, the less chance it'll explode."

Hyuk. Fire could cause a hull breach. It might go out from the sudden depressurization of the level, but we'd need to get off forty-eight in a hurry if we wanted to stay alive. But our escape would only be temporary. After that, we'd be on a serious time crush to shut the emergency hatches before we all suffocated.

A crackle and a hiss from the core gets my attention, and I turn. Flames flicker up from the distro system cabinet, reaching higher than my head as the wall behind them blackens.

My throat gets tight. That wall is part of the inside hull.

"Efa!" I shout and point.

She spins, following my finger, cursing as she sees it. But then she turns back to me, her mouth half open. I gasp. How does she not know what to do? We've all had fire-suppression training drilled into us. And a boy died. None of us will ever forget his screams. Or what to do in such an emergency.

"Get the fire chokes!" I say, motioning with my good arm toward the pair of red canisters at the back of the level. Sayer and Tegan rush to them, grab one each, and turn to Fana for direction. She freezes but shakes herself out of it and instructs them to stand on either side of the cabinet.

"Pull back as fast as you can once you spray the charge," Fana warns. "The gas sucks all the oxygen from the air."

"Do they work?" Efa asks.

I shake my head, unsure. The adults have maintained little of anything for fifty years. All we can do is pray and hope the devices kept their charge.

"Ready?" Sayer looks to Tegan. She nods, and they take aim. Sayer counts down from three and grits his teeth, squeezing the canister's trigger.

Nothing. Absolutely hyuking nothing.

"Bish," Efa growls. "Ideas?"

"Efa, we don't have time for discussion!" I say. "Take action!"

"I'm thinking!"

I sigh and run my good hand through my hair. This is hard, but she shouldn't be hesitating to give orders. Everyone is waiting.

"Maybe shut the power off?" I try. "Would that help?"

Fana shakes her head as she watches the flames on the coil grow. Tegan and Sayer back away, their eyes widening.

"We can get canisters from above!" Aidan suggests.

"Yes. That's good." Efa gets back on her comm and tells the crew to grab as many fire chokes as they can on their way here.

"Someone get the fire chokes from forty-seven," I say.

"I'll go," Tegan replies, racing toward the ladder.

"But we can't just stand around and wait for her to come back," I say to Efa.

"I know," Efa replies, staring at the rising flames. "Sayer, get buckets and fill them with water."

"No!" Fana cries. "We can't throw water on an electrical fire! We'll fry the entire system!"

Sayer freezes and turns to Efa, but she only stares back as she grasps at her shirt collar. There's panic forming in her eyes, threatening to lock her in a vicious cycle of fear and indecision. She'll hate me for it, but if she can't give an order in the next five seconds, I'm taking charge before we've got a disaster. She'll forgive me eventually.

"Efa, we need to do something now," I say, pressing.

"Like what?" Efa shoots back. She throws a glance at the rising blaze, her face going pale.

"All we need to do is smother the core and deprive it of oxygen. The fire will go out then," Fana says, prompting Efa, but Efa only stares into space, her jaw going slack.

I gasp, a memory from when I was young flashing into my head. My father spilled something on the stovetop, and it caught fire. He put it out with—

A blanket.

Yes. That'll work. The stasis recovery level is just below. There's bound to be hundreds down there.

"Tegan, wait!" I call after her. "Forget the canisters! We need blankets! There's plenty on forty-nine!"

Fana's face lights up. "Yes! Blankets! But wet them first!"

"You just said water was bad!" Efa's hands fly up. "How am I supposed to make decisions when you don't give me the right information?"

I'd comfort her if I could, coax her back into thinking straight so she can direct everyone into knocking this fire out. I can't. There's no time to be considerate of her ego any longer. I'm stepping up and solving this. Now.

"Efa," I say as calmly as I can. "I've got this, alright?"

Efa's face falls, understanding hitting her. Relief follows. Her shoulders slump and she nods. I hope the smile I give her is enough of an apology. It's hard to tell when she's dropped her gaze away from mine. Great. Yet another thing we'll need time to talk through. But first, the *Stratford* has to survive.

"Aidan, get as much water as you can." I motion to a nearby cabinet. "There are buckets in there. Tegan, get going!"

"I'll help," Sayer says, bolting after her. Beka and Fana follow, hopping onto the ladder and sliding down it.

When Aidan struggles with opening the cabinet, I move to help him but get held up when Efa grabs my good shoulder and yanks me back.

"You want to lead? You stay here and do that." Efa aims her finger at me, then rushes to help Aidan. Of course I don't. Aidan will have his hands full, and even one more hand, if that's all I can provide, will help.

A red-orange glow seeps down the front of the coil as smoke billows out of the cabinet. The flames are stabbing at the ceiling. Amazing that the coil still works. Which makes me worry about what happens when it fails. Fana didn't want to shut it off. I'm sure she had an excellent reason not to.

If we can't suffocate this fire, we might just find out.

Aidan hands me a bucket and jets off to one of the recycler spouts. Efa only glances at me before shooting off to the other. I follow Aidan at my best pace. This had better work. I've not nothing else we can try other than to seal the level and flush the air out of it. Who knows if our passengers would survive that?

The rail car rings, and Merek, Deryn, Mari, Rhys, and Dru come piling out, skidding to a stop when they catch sight of the fire. Tegan flies up, blankets strapped to her back. Sayer is just behind her with a bundle on his shoulder. Aidan and Efa meet him as he and Tegan drop their bundles on the deck and spread the blankets out.

"What should we do?" Merek calls, running toward Efa. She glances at me, but I just motion for her to answer.

"Grab a blanket!" Efa replies.

I dump my bucket of water over the blankets and back away, letting the crew handle the rest. Under Fana's direction, they cover the cabinet with a mass of wet fabric.

Everyone cheers when the flames are reduced to a cloud of steam and smoke. We'll have to vent that somehow. I think Fana's already on it. That should give me plenty of reason to celebrate, but when I glance at Efa, my desire to do so fades.

She's got her arms around Merek, pressing her head onto his shoulder and closing her eyes as he returns the embrace. The edges of my lips curve upward. They truly are meant to be together, and I'm glad he can comfort her when she needs it.

Efa's eyes pop open, and her gaze finds me. I sigh when she separates from Merek and approaches. I guess she doesn't want to wait to talk.

"Don't feel bad," she says, stopping in front of me. "I messed up, and you made the right call. That's why you're the leader."

"You're doing fine," I reply. "Don't be too hard on yourself about it."

She looks away. It'll take time for her to get over this. I only hope she can before I need her to take over again. The crew will struggle with both of us gone. And the thought of that terrifies me to no end.

IMPASSE

CERI

"You should go back to medical," Efa says as she helps the rest of the crew clean up after the fire's out. It's the last thing I want to hear and absolutely the last thing I'll do.

But every time I try to help, someone stops me. I can't even lift a wet blanket without Mari or little Dru or Tegan snatching it from my hands. Nobody wants me doing any manual labor, and the more they get in my way, the angrier I become.

Fana comes over to me and does her best to lead me away from the action. I'm resistant, but she doesn't push, and half a minute later, I give in and sit down at a control desk with a hard sigh. Fana stays near me, watching me with a half-guilty, half-sympathetic gaze. I accept neither, though I understand her desire to do so.

"I'm fine. Really," I say. "I'm just as capable of cleaning as anyone else."

She glances at the others, watching them for what is longer than necessary. She's about to tell me something, I think. And she doesn't want the others to hear it. I tense, preparing for whatever she's about to say, and hope it isn't about something worse than a fire.

"I'm sure," Fana says and faces me, her lips pressed. "But I need your help with something else."

I would have just shrugged and agreed. I won't now. She's got me too suspicious of her, and Fana had better come out with it immediately or I will shake it out of her with my one good arm.

"Sure, but—" I stand. "What is it? Efa recommended I go back to medical and rest. So unless it's important, I should probably do that."

Fana shakes her head with a little too much force for me to walk away now.

"Don't do that." Fana glances back at the others. "You've got to be the one who decides. Efa—"

"Is more than capable. And why are you acting like this? If it's critical, just say it."

"Everyone doesn't need to know." She swallows hard and glances at everyone again. Twice was already too much. I grab her shoulder and swing her back around.

"Know what?"

She bites her lip, taking a few seconds to get her words out. "That second coil won't last more than thirty minutes. We don't have enough time to switch it out."

I can't blame her for being worried about that. We all are. There's no telling when the power could fail again. And it will. Sayer's already down on the lower levels searching for a replacement. He'll call as soon as he finds it. Then we'll switch out the bad one as fast as we can.

"You don't need me to decide anything about that. It's getting done, and we'll all help," I say, doing my best to smile. "Let me get back to medical so Raey can clear me to work. I want to be a part of the repair, too."

But when I go to walk away, Fana grabs my arm and presses her face close to my ear. "If it fails, the entire level goes down."

I stare at her, expecting more, but when it doesn't come, I resist the urge to grab her by the collar and shake it out. Maybe it's my fault for not understanding. It wouldn't be the first time Fana's talked well over our level of technical knowledge without realizing it. And her hand's trembling on my arm. I should be gentle, or I won't get anywhere.

"Okay," I say and nod. "So what's your idea? What is it you need me to decide?"

Fana exhales. "If we drop the load on the coils, we can keep the one good one powering most of the pods."

Air rushes from my lungs. *Most* of the pods? Hyuking bish. How could it be so bad? We just stopped a fire from destroying the entire power system. Everything is working. Our passengers are safe, just like they've been for hundreds of years. We're caring for them the best we can. They'll make it. All of them will make it.

My chest gets tighter. I press a hand to it and force myself to breathe. This isn't what happens next. I refuse to believe it.

"Forget it!" I cry, my anger building. "Nobody else dies on this ship!"

Efa throws a curious glance at us, and I wheeze, struggling to get air back into my body. It's good Fana didn't go to Efa with this. No one should have to make this choice. Not even me. I could no more kill our passengers than I could end any of my crew's life. And I know less than one percent of the people in stasis. I love my crew with no limits.

"How many?" I ask, tensing for her answer. "How many pods will we need to shut down to save the rest?"

Fana shrugs and looks up, doing her best to be brave. "A row. At least. Maybe more."

Faces flash into my mind. An elderly woman. A child maybe five years old. I remember them all from my time down in the stasis levels. All real. All deserving to live to see their new home. Just like I promised them they would.

"That's twelve people, Fana," I say.

Fana's face grows pained. "I know."

"Is there no way to save everyone?"

"No." Her head bows as she shakes it. "We just don't have enough time."

Time. How could we not have time? We've the rest of our lives, and our passengers have hundreds of years to ensure they get to where they're going. Only those who've already died will never make it. I'm to blame for many of those deaths. I've killed more people than I ever should have, all of them children, like me. I did it to survive and to protect my friends. It was still wrong, and I have to live with that, but I will never kill another person. Not while I have a choice.

I snatch the comm off Fana's belt and press the mic key. "Sayer! Sayer, pick up!"

Efa glances at me and frowns. I grit my teeth and turn, pretending not to see her. Likely it's already too late. She'll be here in five seconds, demanding I explain my outburst. And then I'll have to tell her.

"Sayer!"

"Relax your panties," Sayer replies. *"I'm here. What do you want?"*

"Did you find it?"

Sayer's sigh through the comm sounds like an airlock cycling. *"Nooo. There's twenty levels to check and only me looking! If you want to speed things up, maybe you can send Tegan and Beka down here to help?"*

"What's going on?" Efa says, folding her arms as she looks between Fana and me.

"I'm going to check on the coil," Fana says, snatching her comm back and dashing off. She probably didn't mean to abandon me like that, but I still curse under my breath a few times before I'm ready to face Efa. Sayer should know, too. He's the one who's got family on this level.

"Give me your comm," I say to Efa and hold my hand out.

"Tell me what's going on first."

"I'm about to. Sayer needs to hear this."

Efa unclips her comm and drops it into my hand as she continues to stare at me with narrowed eyes. I'd smile at her if I thought it would ease her suspicions, but there's no reason to. This is as bad as she thinks it is.

With a slow breath, I get Sayer back on the line and describe the situation, keeping the most gruesome detail to the very end. Efa and Sayer remain silent throughout my telling. I'd expect them to. I didn't know what to say at first, either.

"*I'm coming back up,*" Sayer says.

"No," I reply. "Stay there. Keep looking. I'll send help."

"*What's the point? Even if I found the spare right now, Fana already said we can't replace it in time.*"

"But wouldn't we have to take the damaged one offline to replace it, anyway? How was she planning to do that?" Efa asks.

I'm lost on how to reply. And Efa should know I can't answer a technical question like that. Certainly not in any detail. But I trust Fana has a plan. She's likely thought it through ten times already and only came to me when she realized there was no other way.

The lights flicker, and an alarm goes off on the console behind us, the sound stabbing at my ears. Efa and I spin toward it, searching for the source to shut it off.

Fana comes rushing back, her eyes wide. "Whatever you're going to decide, you need to do it now. We're out of time."

Efa and I share a glance before she snatches her comm back and tells Sayer. My throat feels like it's closing, and I'm getting dizzy. I should've stayed in medical, just like Efa advised. No. Then all of this would be on her, and I can't let that happen.

"*We've got to wake them up,*" Sayer says. "*That's the only way we'll save them.*"

"Do you know how to do that?" Efa counters. "Because I don't."

"*Raey does.*"

"Raey's not here."

"Well, hyuking call her!"

I scan the control console again, searching for the master alarm switch. There's no way we'll think straight with this constant screeching in our ears. All it's doing is making my muscles tight.

A thump on the console cuts the siren off. Fana's hand is there, covering over a section of the console that I must have checked three times.

"Ceri," she says. "You've got to make a choice, or all the pods will switch to their internal batteries."

"How long do they last?"

Fana's eyes widen. "On pods this old? They might not work at all."

"How long if they do?"

"I don't know! A few hours at most?"

I try to recall the last time I watched someone come out of stasis. Their skin was blotches of red and blue, turned thin by the hibernation process. They dry heaved for an hour before a doctor came and gave them something to help. It turned my stomach to watch, so after that hour, I left, but that person was awake by then. Maybe Sayer's got it right. I'll accept anything that isn't murder.

"Efa, call Raey," I say. "We'll wake them up. That could be the only way."

Efa nods and makes the call. Raey listens as she explains, then sighs hard.

"Ancestors, is that what you need to do?" she says.

"We're out of options," Efa replies. "Can you come down to forty-eight and show us how?"

"You can't wake them up in two hours," Raey says. *"It takes half a day just to let the body come up to a temperature where the pod can administer the medications to bring them back to consciousness. It's still another twelve hours after that before anyone even moves for the first time."*

I wrench my hands until my knuckles turn white, ignoring the pain it causes in my damaged shoulder. I'd suffer a universe of agony if I could save these people. And which ones do I choose, anyway? What if I kill a top scientist? Or an engineer? What if I save someone who becomes a criminal?

"Understood. We'll keep you updated," Efa says, disconnecting with Raey as she smashes her lips together. A second later, she's keying the mic again to call Sayer, her hand squeezing her comm so hard the case flexes. "What about moving them to a different level?" Efa asks as she waits for Sayer to call back.

"Then you risk unbalancing the power there," Fana replies, looking down. "Trust me, I've thought of everything."

I twist the fabric of my shirt until the buttons threaten to pop off. Every bit of me is aching for hope. I might as well be trying to walk back to Earth.

"Ceri," Fana says softly as she strokes my arm. "Even if Sayer found the spare, it takes hours to replace. And that's with an experienced crew. On the *Devant*—"

"I don't give a bish what happened on the *Devant*!" I snap. Fana jerks back, and Efa flashes me a concerned look as the shame hits. I shut my eyes, exhaling to calm myself. "I'm sorry. This isn't your fault."

Their silence only makes it worse, and my chest is already hurting enough. I push past them as they watch, shuffling to the nearest row of pods. My good hand scrapes the frost from the pod's port, and I peer in—a middle-aged woman. I go to the next—a boy, maybe ten years old.

"Don't, Ceri," Efa warns. "Don't do that to yourself."

By the time I've covered the row, everyone has stopped to watch me turn to the next one and start over. But before I can even get past the first in the row, Efa gets in my way.

"It doesn't matter who they are," she says. "Everyone here deserves a new life on Asteria. Us included. We're just not going to get it."

"But at least I got to know you," I reply.

I gaze across the mass of stasis units, and my vison goes blurry as salty tears sting my eyes. Perhaps it's for the best, as I can no longer separate one pod from another. They become anything but what they are, and my ability to decide grows. I stumble toward what looks like a pod and lay my hand down on it.

"This row," I say.

"Are you sure?" Fana whispers. Someone gasps. Maybe Aidan. Another murmurs something. I don't care what's said or thought about this moment. No matter which pods I chose, they were always going to be the wrong ones.

"Of course not," I reply. "Just...turn them off."

The pods' alarms clang as they switch over to their internal batteries, a lament for those inside. With Merek's help, Fana rushes down the aisle and powers each one down, the alarms fading out into a distorted wail as they go silent.

"How long before they're…" Merek starts.

"Pretty long, actually," Fana says. "The pod is so well insulated that—"

"Fana." Efa throws her a glare, and she immediately clamps her mouth shut, an apologetic look in her eyes.

I drop myself into a chair as my body gets weak. Efa comes to stand next to me, and I lean on her, hoping that our touch connects me back to reality. But it doesn't. I'm lost, and I won't be able to find a way back until I know these people's sacrifice was worth it.

This is the first time I've failed to save my passengers. That doesn't hurt as much as realizing it likely won't be the last.

REVELATION

FANA

I SPEND HOURS IN bed, restless and unable to see past how I failed to come up with a solution. There had to have been a way to get power to that row. If only I'd had more time. Instead, Ceri and Efa had to stay up all night and prepare the bodies for their last rites. How sick I was when I heard that. I begged them to forgive me, but Ceri refused to hear it. No one else would, either, and it drove a stake through my gut. Sayer or someone should've yelled and said how terrible of an engineer I was to fail those people. At least I would've accepted that.

Despite everyone's grief, there's still work to be done. I could have a thousand years and not get to everything on the *Stratford* that was broken. Some things can wait, like the doors and walls that took a beating during the battle with the *Devant*'s security agents, or all the broken lights that are on nearly every floor. Others, like the ship's navigation system, need immediate attention.

Which is why I'm up on level four, shuffling down the corridor in a half sleep toward the towering bank of processors that we repurposed from backup to become the new navigation computers. My little quick fix of a device is doing a fine job, but it's impractical, and freeing it up from duty that other machines can do will allow it to be put to better uses.

Like making sure the power doesn't go out on any other stasis levels.

"This'll be a challenge on no sleep," I mutter to myself as I slip into the room to face the four towering racks of processing equipment. Right now they're just a bunch of dumb processors with no directions, so I'm going to write a bunch of new code that'll make them do all the work the multiprocessor is currently doing.

With a sleepy groan, I open up my keyboard and attach it to the first machine. Once I've got this one working, copying the instructions over to the other three will be easy. And the coding should be straightforward, though I thought that about the instructions I wrote to connect the multiprocessor to the old navigation system. Those—

I tilt my head and listen to a curious noise. *Footsteps? Who would be up here now?* Everyone's either stuffing breakfast into their mouths or working to get the twelve lifeless bodies out of the pods and prepared for a proper farewell. Nobody really wanted to do that, so maybe they're dragging their feet more than I did.

But when I try to listen again, all is silent, save for the humming of the coolant pumps in the back of the racks. There are quite a few of them in each unit.

I shake my head, remembering the noise I heard down on one-thirty-five. It's got to be my sleep-deprived imagination playing tricks on me.

Then someone's voice floats into the room from down the corridor—no. Not someone. Raey's voice. I would never forget her sultry tone in an infinite number of years. Even deeper as it is now, I recognize it.

"Raey?" I call.

When there's no answer, my curiosity wins over my interest in work, and I slide back down the hallway, guessing the direction from which I heard Raey's voice. Maybe she's looking for me and someone told her I might be up here.

There. Her voice again. That definitely came from the other direction. Raey's likely in one of the storage bays.

But...wait. Why? I'm easier to find than that. She could have just called me on comm. We all have one now. I would have met her anywhere she asked.

As I approach, I listen to the rhythm of her words and frown. There are sizeable gaps between when she speaks—she must be talking to someone. So why can't I hear them? Are they on comm? Why would she need to go into a storage bay to talk to someone who's not next to her? Privacy?

I need to find out.

"Yes sir," Raey says as I get closer. "Yes...Understood...No...No, sir. Everything is going as we discussed. I expect our next call should be much sooner than this one...Thank you, sir...They've been treating me fine."

We've been treating her...Wait...Sir? I gasp and quickly cover my mouth. She's talking to Commander Azazhi! What does she have to say to him? Raey has regular communications with the medical team, but she doesn't hide in a cabin to make those calls. And after what that bastard did to me, how could she show him any respect? What is she thinking?

I sneer and stomp toward the sound of her voice. Raey needs to know she can't just be buddies with our former leader while she's living comfortably on the *Stratford*. Ceri and the others treat her well, making her meals to eat, giving her a place to sleep that's likely better than anything the crew is sleeping on. Helping her when she needs it. And how can she do this when she knows Azazhi wants me dead?

Hold on. If she's talking to him, then what are they discussing? Is Raey returning to the *Devant*? She never really told me what she was planning to do. Commander Azazhi hasn't called her back, either, though.

My pulse quickens. Now I really want to know what's going on.

Raey's voice is close. Maybe just a few doors down from where I am. She'd cut her call if I threw the bay door open and gave her the most beastly glare I can.

But then I wouldn't know what's she's talking with him about.

I slip closer, pressing my body against the wall, then stop as I realize how silly that is. She can't see me and likely won't hear me if she's listening to what the commander has to say. That's why she's hiding in a closet—so she doesn't have to worry about anyone overhearing.

Except Raey is judging the sound-dampening qualities of this ship based on the structural technology of the *Devant*, and the two couldn't be further apart. The *Stratford*'s designers expected way fewer crew to be awake at one time, so with the ship's 147 levels, it was unlikely many of the four dozen crew would be together at one time. Privacy is far from a concern. I can stand ten paces away and hear everything she says.

"Well, yes sir," Raey continues. "There's a good chance that they'd still be willing to trade for the surplus pods. There was a power failure on a stasis level yesterday, and they had to shut twelve machines off...What's that? Yes sir...those passengers died. It was a tragic moment."

Trade? Right! There's a bunch of unoccupied pods in the *Devant*'s cargo hold. I'm not sure why she thinks we'd need them here. Our problem is power, not the units themselves. And trade for...*oh!* But Ceri would never agree to trade away the excavation equipment. Whatever Raey is thinking, it won't happen.

Despite my earlier decision not to, I take two steps forward, my will to remain in place faltering as my curiosity rises. What does she expect? Has she discussed it with Ceri? Probably not. I need more data to understand what's going on. The best way to do that is to go right to the source.

Before I realize it, I'm standing outside the storage bay, my hand on the door handle. Inside, Raey is silent. I freeze—did she hear me? No. She would have come out to check. Right?

I snatch my hand away, holding my breath. I can't be selfish here. All I should do is, as Ceri calls it, gather intel. Then I can tell Ceri everything I've heard and hope she doesn't throw Raey in a cell because of it.

Bish. What if Ceri actually does that? I should give Raey the chance to explain first. After all she's done for this crew, she deserves that much. She's probably just doing what she thinks is right. And if she's not, I've got to talk her out of it.

"What?" Raey shrieks, and I jump. "How many? How could it have spread like that? It burned out over here, and everyone who showed symptoms has fully recovered with no side effects...Do you need me back, sir? Of course I could do that. Perhaps even in...No? Sir! You can't ask me to do that! I promise I'll find another way...just give me time. I won't need long...Yes sir...Thank you, sir...I will...Specialist T'ena signing off."

There's an outbreak on the *Devant*! But that's not possible! Everyone on the medical staff over there would have been careful not to spread infection. How did that happen? Some security agent got too close to one of the kids when they were sick? How many people are sick?

The door slides, and I spin to press myself against the wall as Raey rushes out, wiping her sleeve across her eyes. I so want to reach out to her, to let her know she's not alone, but my body won't move. My mouth won't open, and two seconds later, she's gone, disappearing down the hall to who knows where.

And I'm left alone, trembling from what I just heard. I should have stopped her. I should have gotten her to talk to me. She must be desperate to tell someone.

Because everything just changed for her.

CHANCE

— • —

CERI

"You can't blame yourself," Efa says as she sits shoulder to shoulder with me on level eight, against a wall that faces an empty spot on the deck we used to call Delta position. All the sections of ductwork, old machinery, and crates we used to build a secure area are gone, removed and recycled even before the adults abandoned us. What remains are memories of violence and death I very much want to forget.

No one ever claimed this level as their own, and yet both sides did. Tarakh and Fahrasi. Those names have become just words to us. There's only one side now: the crew. The battles are over.

And yet, people are still dying.

"Everyone on this ship is my responsibility," I reply. "So I will blame myself. No one dies under my supervision. And twelve people did. Twelve people who believed they'd wake up on a new planet."

Efa sighs and shakes her head. If she thought she could change my mind, she'd be giving me an earful right now. It's only because she worries about me. I could tell her not to, but she wouldn't listen. Efa rarely does when she knows she's right. And despite her performance as leader in our last crisis, I need to let go of any doubts I have about her. No one else has more of a level head or a wider understanding of our crew. That includes me.

"Ceri." Efa lays a hand over mine as it rests on my leg, free now of its sling. "Punishing yourself every time something goes wrong isn't healthy. Bish is bound to happen every day on this wreck of a ship. You'll make yourself sick if you keep it up."

I huff. "Who says I haven't already?"

She squeezes my hand. It's more than enough said. We've known each other long enough that a single look or touch can say more than words ever could, though I've missed being close to her as of late. I'd tell her how I feel, but Efa would deny anything had changed between us. Still, it's Merek, not me, who she thinks of first.

Letting them be together is also my fault.

"You know that's why I worry about you," Efa chides. "Bish, someone has to. If it wasn't for—"

"What are the two of you doing here?" Raey asks as she walks toward us. I frown as she approaches. Not only is she interrupting my time with Efa, which is irritating, but her eyes are shiny, like she'd just been crying. And that sparks my attention.

"Nothing," I reply. "Why? What does it look like?"

"Exactly what you said." Raey stops before us. "May I sit?"

I shrug and motion to the space before us. "Plenty of room to do so."

But even as I attempt to act at ease, I'm squeezing Efa's hand past a comfortable level. She squeezes back, but she's squirming. I should stop. Or perhaps I should bury my face in her shoulder. By the sober look Raey's giving us, she doesn't have good news.

"What is it?" Efa asks, all business. She respects Raey enough, but her tone is almost threatening. Raey is trespassing in our moment, and if it's not important, Efa will let her know just how unhappy that makes her.

"I never thought of it much before, but after the tragedy on level forty-eight, I wanted to know how the other stasis levels are faring." Raey rests her hands on her thighs as she kneels. "So I asked…Deryn, I think it was…to help me run some stress tests on a few stasis pods in each unit. It took a day, but I've collected enough data now to understand what's going on."

A weight drops into the pit of my gut. I should have expected another problem. This ship must be cursed. Or maybe it's me. I'm the one who's jinxed, and I've damned everyone on this ship to a hopeless fate along with me.

"What do you understand now?" I growl.

Raey ducks her head before speaking. My tone was harsh for a reason. Efa may trust her, but I don't. She stole Fana from us and tried to take advantage of our desperation for her own needs. I should have tossed her back to her ship. The only reason she's still here is because we need her skills.

"There's a good number of units that are on the verge of malfunction," Raey says. "Their fluid recyclers are failing, and if we don't shut them down, they'll poison the people inside."

"Is this because of the power fault?" Efa asks.

"No. It's more likely because these machines are seven hundred years old. With the rush to get off the planet, I doubt there was much long-term testing done. Computer simulations, sure, but I'm not an engineer. I don't know how reliable that would be." Raey shrugs. "We didn't test the *Devant*'s pods very long, either. Years, maybe, but there wasn't a need to. By the time we left, stasis technology had been around for centuries. Our pods are the best humanity could create."

My body feels heavy. We've struggled so much, sacrificed so much, yet we're still just two steps away from failure. The desire to surrender is building inside me, and I can't fight it. Losing so many of my crew and passengers has left me wanting to do nothing but curl up in a corner and shut my eyes until it passes. But it won't. I must find the strength to withstand it. I just don't know where to search.

"Which is the other reason I'm coming to you," Raey adds. "I think I may have a solution to this."

"And what would that be?" Efa asks. She's trying not to show interest, but I can feel her body sliding forward.

Raey raises her hands. "This is just an idea at the moment. I can't guarantee that it'll happen, but if you want to try, I will do everything I can to help."

I prompt her to continue with a nod. If she's offering ideas on how to save our passengers, I'll listen.

"The *Devant*—" she begins.

"No." Efa shakes her head. "No hyuking way are we dealing with them. I don't even understand why they're still riding alongside us, except to get you back."

"Please, Efa. Just listen for a moment. They—"

"They murdered half our crew!"

"And you killed half of theirs." Raey's sober stare silences Efa, who drops back against the wall.

My shoulders sag as I think about that last battle. The *Stratford* would stink of dead bodies if the *Devant*'s crew hadn't taken back their fallen comrades. We had our funeral rites, too. Many of those we said goodbye to were far too young to fight, much less die. We pushed the *Devant* invaders off our ship, but at a loss too great to bear. I can only imagine what effect the death of fifty of their crew members must have had on them. Raey hasn't forgotten the losses, nor what her commander did to Fana. If she's bringing her ship up, she must think there's a good possibility of helping everyone.

I sigh. "Let's just say Commander Azazhi would be willing, which I doubt he would be. What is it they have that would help us?"

"Ceri, no," Efa warns, squeezing my arm. I cover my hand over hers, asking—perhaps begging—her to give me a chance. It twists my insides something fierce to consider even looking at Azazhi again, but desperation is nipping at my back, and I need to hear what she's offering.

"Excess pods," Raey replies. "Perhaps you won't believe this, but people remained on Earth. Their reasoning is beyond me. We had planned to take everyone, so when they remained, we ended up with more than we needed."

"Not everyone is looking to escape their situation," I say. "Some of us are right where we belong."

When Raey tilts her head in confusion, I continue, "Your commander won't be so generous as to just give us all of his surplus pods. Especially the ones that no longer have an occupant."

Raey curls her lip in and drops her gaze, looking stung. Perhaps some of those who died were her friends. I didn't mean it, but it was still effective. She needs to understand just how uncomfortable we are dealing with child killers.

"You're right, of course," she says. "It'd have to be something compelling."

"I know where this is going," Efa interjects. "And we already said no to the excavation equipment."

"What good is excavation equipment if there's no one to drive it?" Raey counters.

I tighten my grip on Efa's hand, warning her to keep calm. Odd that our roles are reversed here. She would normally be the one holding me back from aggression. But as I hold her hand, my energy to resist her hostile posture is waning. Neither of us wants more death, yet I can't find it in me to fight back. I'm almost content to let things slide.

It's not like anything Raey is suggesting will ever become reality. Azazhi wants to avenge his decimated security teams, and when he realizes how desperate we are to save our passengers, he'll push hard to make us pay. It'll be all of our excavation machines or nothing.

"Ceri," Efa pleads. "Talk some reality into her, please."

"I am being realistic," Raey insists. "This'll be hard for both crews. Our people lost life partners, Efa. Spouses and friends they were planning to start a new life with on Asteria. And the crew you've lost—"

"The *children*, you mean."

"Yes, Efa." Raey nods. "The *children*, who will never grow up to have dreams like that. I haven't forgotten them. I can't. My only charge, the one I've been training you to do, is to save as many lives as possible. With everything that's happened, I've failed that oath, and I need to right my path. So please, consider this as a way for all of us to protect those in stasis and those awake."

Efa slips her hand off mine and drops both her hands in her lap. For a quiet moment, she stares at her upturned palms. Raey only watches, waiting to see if her words have had the right impact. They have with me. I may be feeling like I'm ready to quit, but for Efa's sake, I'll pretend I'm about to do anything but that.

My gaze connects with Efa's as she turns her head toward me. There's concern in her eyes, but also the desire to help everyone. She was born to do just that, and for the strength of that determination within her, I will always be grateful.

"I'll do whatever you want," Efa says. "Just give the order."

I frown. "Since when have I ever given you an order?"

"Since always."

That comment deserves an eye roll. It's not the moment to be childish, however.

"I won't order you, Efa," I reply. "Tell me what you want to do."

"Save our passengers. That's what I want, but that bastard"—Efa thrusts a finger in the *Devant*'s direction—"will try to hurt us again. And there's no way in hell we'll let him."

"No, but remember we hurt them bad, too. And Azazhi will never forget a bunch of kids beat him. All he's trying to do is recover, just like we are. He'll take as much as he can to get there, but we'll never let him have even that much, right?"

Efa's shoulders slump, and I reach out to touch her arm. She may be subdued, but she's far from done. We have faced far worse than this. And survived.

"I don't know, Ceri," she says. "Any deals with the *Devant* are bound to be dangerous. What if they trick us at the last second? Break the pods somehow..."

"They would never do that," Raey interjects. "No more than you would sabotage the excavation equipment."

But Efa just glances at Raey, then lowers her head when she returns her attention to me, more dejected than she was before. If Efa knew in this moment how dark my heart was, she'd walk away from this conversation. I owe it to her not to let her see that, even if it's hurting me to do it.

We need those pods. I don't know how big of a price I can tolerate paying, but to do nothing is to condemn our people to death or a horrible life, and there's nothing left within me to withstand another tragedy.

"You have to report in anyway, don't you?" I ask Raey. She nods. "Then mention to your commander that the time might be right to make a deal. Don't, and I absolutely mean *don't*, tell him we're having a problem with our pods. There'll be no deal and no discussion if I find out you did that. Got it?"

"Of course. Lives are depending on this." Raey smiles. "You can trust me, Ceri."

I tilt my head as I lock gazes with her. "Can I?"

SUSPECT

—— • ——

FANA

Damn.

I share a frown with Seren and Rhys as we watch level forty-eight's new transformer coil fail for the third time. We've been at this for hours and have little to show for it. This entire grid needs to be ripped out and replaced. That could take a month, or longer if all I've got for help is these two part-time lovebirds.

"Hey, why don't you take a break?" I say to Rhys. "Come back in twenty minutes and bring something to eat with you."

Rhys' brow gets tight. "Why me?"

"Because I know you won't leave two ladies here to starve, will you?"

Seren chokes a giggle as Rhys rolls his eyes and walks off. But it's the best thing he could do for me at the moment. When the two of them get attached like a pair of polar-opposite magnets, they do less work than a single person. And Rhys, as handy as he is with tools, can't problem-solve like Seren can. She gets circuit flow as if she was born knowing it. But she's awkward with wire stripping. I guess that's why the two of them make a good pair.

Right now, though, I need brainpower and no distractions.

"Okay." I exhale and put my hands on my hips. "Let's think this through one more time. There's got to be something we're missing. Now, assuming the source is properly balanced, which we can do because we've measured it like ten times, we can isolate the failure to the local—"

Why isn't she paying attention?

The moment I follow her far-distance gaze to the opposite side of the level, my heart skips a beat.

Ceri.

Her face is all business, a total reversal of the hopeless look I saw when she ordered me to shut the power off. I gulp down my discomfort as she winds her way through the rows of pods, and I do my best to put on a welcome smile.

"Hey," I say, forcing the edges of my mouth up. "Everything okay?"

She stops a few paces away and eyes Seren before focusing on me. "I need to talk with you."

"Sure. What is it?"

Seren hums and moves to walk away.

"No," Ceri says, pointing a finger at her. "You can stay."

Seren nods, but her pursed lips and diverted gaze say she's far from interested in doing that. Maybe she thinks Ceri and I are about to have some kind of private chat, but Ceri's active stance tells me this'll be about the *Stratford*. Still, the conversation likely won't include Seren's input, so it'd be best to give her a means of escape.

"Why don't you trace the secondary lead again and put the field gauge on it to make sure current's still running through it?" I suggest. It's just a redundant task, but Seren nods enthusiastically, and in less than a second, she grabs the device and heads off at a fast clip.

"Seren enjoys spending time with you," Ceri comments. "She's learning a lot about the ship."

"Well, she's good at it." I shrug. "I've only taught her a few simple concepts. She's figured out how they relate all on her own. I'm glad to have her."

A long moment of silence follows between us. The longer it goes on, the itchier my skin feels, like it's got bugs crawling all over it. And then my insides twist because all kinds of pests are running through my head. I cringe and shake it off, remembering I'm supposed to be the more mature of the two of us.

"So...how are you feeling?" I ask.

Ceri stares at me for another comfortless few seconds before she speaks. "What do you think Raey wants here?"

I blink, the skin between my eyebrows pulling together. "To make sure everyone is healthy here...Why?"

"Do you think there's more of a reason than that?"

Hyuk, did she find out about Raey's call? I really hope she's not about to tell me she just arrested my ex-partner and is about to put her on trial. If Ceri's investigating her, I need to think twice before I say anything. A single wrong word could put Raey in serious trouble.

"Well, I mean, Raey is interested in studying the effects of long-term stasis on the body. She hasn't mentioned it much, but gathering that data will be critical to understanding what passengers will need when they're reanimated."

Ceri steps forward, closing the distance between us so quickly my breath catches in my throat as I pull my hands tight to my chest. Then she leans in, her mouth getting close to my ear. I'm already tingling with anticipation. *Were those questions just an excuse to get close to me?*

Nope.

"I think she's got an agenda," Ceri whispers, "one that only benefits her. You can figure out the rest."

I pull away, my jaw going slack. *She has to know.* I don't understand why she's intimidating me like this. *Does she think I'm involved?* No. That can't be. Ceri'd be more direct, and she'd be mad. She's not. At least I don't think so. Could she be holding her anger back? Why? I'm shaking at the thought of her suddenly knocking me on my back and binding my wrists together.

Or maybe that's just me being paranoid. More than likely. Panic is my natural state of mind. So is curiosity.

"What makes you think that?" I ask.

"Fana!" Seren calls as she races back to us, her hands waving over her head. "There's some big surge in the system! The cables you put in are smoking hot!"

Oh hell! Now I know why everything we've tried today has failed. With the new core, all the power runs have the wrong impedance load! That needs an adjustment now, or we risk not just a fire but losing power to the pods again.

"Bish," Ceri says, getting that hard-eyed stare like she's about to go into battle. "What do we do?"

"Don't worry, it's only a problem if the cables connect." I gulp, imagining the damage that'd do to my makeshift repair. "I can get this done quickly. Just hold a few tools for me."

"Of course. Anything."

I grab my tool kit, and we rush to the open hatch where Seren waits, then drop down next to the wide circular nest of wires and cables leading to the cores. It's a shameful mess, and guaranteed, this is half the problem.

With a quick survey of the connections, I drop to my knees and get to work while Seren and Ceri watch over my shoulders. In two seconds, they'll be bugging me to help. It might just be easier to do it all myself. Giving them explanations and instructions will only take time I can't afford to waste.

Like I'm doing right now, staring at the multi-tool in my hand.

Think Fana! What's the best way to lower the load? It's hard to concentrate. My heart is thumping harder than it should, even while I tell myself this isn't a major crisis. Something is eating at me, pulling my focus away from the job in front of my face.

"Tells us how to help," Ceri says, crouching next to me.

And then it hits me. After I solve this problem, there'll be another to face. Ceri will want to know where I stand with Raey, since I did my best to squirm out of giving anything away. I'll have to tell her something, though, or she'll suspect my loyalties. She must have forgotten how I've all but asked her to marry me. Ceri must be seriously stressed. I'd love to help her relax, but I'm probably the one creating most of her tension.

"Just hold on," I reply. "I need to figure out a process."

"Well, let us know. Whatever it is."

Okay. The proximity of the cables to each other is creating an electromagnetic field that's causing the increase of resistance in the power flow. Untangling them and coiling them properly should lower the load and stop any risk of fire. Easy enough.

"I need something to handle the wires," I say. "Gloves. A blanket. Whatever."

"On it," Seren says and dashes off, leaving me with Ceri's eyes burning a hole in my shoulder. I'll try to ignore that feeling, as I know she's only worried about the safety of her passengers—*our* passengers. This is my ship now.

Does Ceri realize that? She must. She made me an honorary member of the crew. And she should know I'd never betray her or her crew to the *Devant*. Not after Commander Azazhi ordered my execution.

But I just spoke up for Raey, and Ceri won't easily forget that. *Oh no. What if her anger is building against me as I play with a bunch of cables?* Raey is innocent of anything Ceri might consider accusing her of. Mostly. She did just take a call with the commander while she was hiding in a closet. And Ceri won't ever forget how Raey had me arrested and returned to the *Devant*. Maybe she thinks Raey is planning to do that again.

"Careful," Ceri says. "I can feel the heat coming off those."

"Yeah, yeah, it's okay." I wave her concern away and return to my thoughts.

"How bad is it?" Ceri asks, her voice tight. "Are we in serious trouble?"

I go still. That's the same question I asked Raey before she ended our relationship. But no. Ceri isn't talking about me and her. There is no me and her, and if I don't figure out what I'm going to tell her about Raey, there may never be a me and her.

Hell, untangling wires is so much easier.

Seren rushes back, three sets of gloves in her hand. I give her a grin and a nod and accept a pair as she distributes them to Ceri and me.

"Okay, Seren." I point to the far edge of the wire mess. "You're there. Ceri, about two paces left. Move nothing until I say, and don't touch any cable until I tell you. If we work fast, we can have this done in twenty minutes."

"And that'll avoid another fire?" Ceri asks. "Will we lose power again?"

"Yes, and no."

Ceri frowns. "Which is it?"

"Both. Yes, there won't be a fire, and no, power's still solid."

As we lay the cables in a proper anti-EMR configuration, my mind returns to Raey. It'd be a big problem if she wasn't here. Efa's learning as fast as she can, but it'll still take lots of time for her to become as skilled as Raey. Until then, we can't let Raey return to the *Devant*.

It takes seventeen, not twenty, minutes to get the cables untangled. I only get two burns on my bare arms. Seren gets one. And if Ceri was hurt at all, she didn't wince or make a sound. That's not really a surprise. She's had worse happen to her.

"Good job," Ceri says as we complete our work with a sigh, then shakes her head. "I don't know what we'd do without you, Fana."

Seren takes that as a cue to escape, making some excuse about being thirsty and going to find Rhys. He didn't come back when I asked him to, so her reason is valid, even if she's using it to remove herself from the conversation. I'm itching to do the same. I know what's coming, and I don't want to upset Ceri. She's not looking well, hunched over and rubbing at her eye like that. I'd lie to her just to make her happy.

Maybe I should.

"Ceri," I say, touching her arm. "Trust Raey. Her loyalty is in her oath."

She angles her head as she looks at me. "To her commander?"

"No. Her oath is to her patients. To do no harm and care for them. That's what's always been important to her, and that's why she's stuck around. Your crew and your passengers are her primary concern right now. And yes, she'll go back to the *Devant*, eventually, but for now, she's here, and her commander is allowing it. So don't stress yourself wondering what motivates her."

As Ceri drops her gaze to the deck, I inhale quickly and hold it. I force a smile, even though my lower lip is trembling. *Can she see it? Does she know?*

Regret is building up into every fiber of my body. It wasn't such a big lie. Was it? Maybe I should admit everything and beg forgiveness. If I'm lucky, she'll just accept. But I did it, and that means I've got to take whatever comes from it, even if that means I lock myself away in the engine room for the rest of my life.

"Alright," Ceri says and gives me a small smile, reaching out to touch my arm. "I'll take your advice. Thanks again. I'm really glad you're here."

For a moment, her gaze lingers on mine, and I nearly melt. I look away, pretending and not pretending to be embarrassed by her words.

"No, you saved my life. Nobody here owes me anything," I reply.

Except for Raey, as I just risked my relationship with Ceri to protect her. It had better be worth it. Maybe I should ensure that it is.

Time to find you, my former lover, and get some answers.

COMMITMENT

CERI

Raey watches me expectantly as we stand on level two, preparing to connect her comm with the *Devant*'s system. In less than a minute, I'll be talking to a man who only a month ago ordered the murder of my crew. I will put my personal feelings aside and do what's best for my people, though I truly wonder if I can form any agreement with someone I consider my enemy.

I must be desperate to do this. Any other leader would have found a better way.

Efa, Merek, and Sayer are here, too. I asked them to be. They would have come even if I hadn't. Fana also asked to join us. *For support,* she said. But hearing Azazhi's voice again might upset her, and I gently suggested we needed her to do more important things. I don't know if she believed me, but she accepted it, and I'm grateful. Perhaps when this is over, we should show our appreciation to Fana. A party, or something entertaining. We need more of that on this ship.

"Ready?" Raey says.

I nod, and she places the comm device—a small black box with a screen, a microphone, and a speaker on it—on the table, flips over the cover, and initializes the call. Everyone gathers closer as the air in the room gets thick enough to cut.

"This is Commander Azazhi." My opponent's gruff voice, free of emotion or goodwill, comes through clearer than I've ever heard a comm sound. If a fire wasn't burning under my skin, the tech might impress me. *"Specialist T'ena, do you read?"*

"I'm here, sir." Raey clears her throat. "So is Ceri, the leader of the crew, and her second, Efa, and two senior crew, Merek and Sayer."

"Just first names? And no ranks?"

"Our first names are all you need," I reply, stepping closer to the comm. "So that's all you'll be getting."

"I remember that voice," Azazhi states, his tone taking on an edge. *"And you. You're the leader. Still defiant, even when you're begging me to trade?"*

Efa rapidly gestures for Raey to mute the mic and turns to me. "Not a good idea to anger him before you've even made an offer."

My mouth opens to respond with something harsh, but I think better of it and take a breath. I'm doing this for our passengers. Some humility might go far.

I nod to Raey to unmute the mic. She watches me a moment before she turns back to the comm and presses the button. I do my best to show my appreciation with a smile and motion for her to step back. I don't need to worry about her manipulating the conversation while I'm focused on getting the best deal I can.

"All I'm interested in, Commander, is to discuss an exchange," I say, watching the comm's screen as small green lines flash against an orange grid. "I have no other agenda here."

"*Alright, then,*" Commander Azazhi says. "*I understand you are offering excavation equipment in exchange for stasis pods.*"

"That's correct," I reply, inhaling slowly before continuing, "We are willing to—"

"*Then listen closely, because I'm only going to say this once.*"

We all share a glance. Why would he start out like that? Perhaps Efa should give him some advice, too. He wouldn't listen, but this is still unfamiliar to me. This is only my second time having a negotiation. The first was also against Commander Azazhi, after we defeated his agents and captured him. This time, however, the battlefield tilts in his favor.

"Yes? What is it?" I try.

"*As long as I'm in command of the* Devant, *you will never get even a single piece of scrap from my ship, you little brats.*"

Raey's eyes go wide, and she throws her hand over her mouth to hide her gasp. Merek slumps and turns away. Efa's hardening gaze must be the same as mine. I'm already reaching for the switch to disconnect the call. I should have known this would be a complete waste of time. He has no interest in dealing with—

"*Not unless you give me every last thing I ask for. That includes all of your excavation equipment, twenty tons of solid fuels to power them, and ex-Chief Engineer Fana Neridi.*"

Sayer's face gets twisted. "Go to hell, you—"

I thrust a finger at Sayer before he destroys everything. He glares but clenches his jaw to keep it shut. I acknowledge his restraint and exhale relief. Commander Azazhi only wanted to shock us. It's his revenge for our victory, and it's far from the first time an adult has done that to a child.

Now our negotiation really starts.

I look at Efa for advice. She gnashes her teeth and shakes her head. Merek and Sayer won't even meet my gaze. So I'm on my own. I hope my crew will forgive me when I screw this up.

"You already know we won't give you all of that," I say. "So just tell what you'll accept and how many stasis pods we'll get for it."

Efa waves both hands and motions to mute the mic again. When I hit the button, Efa says, "Don't let him tell you how many. Give him the number! Then he'll know who he's dealing with."

"No," Merek interjects. "Tell him a higher number than we need. Then we can let him talk us down."

I glance between them as my hands clench. They're both making sense. Who should I listen to? And what if neither of them are right?

"Commander Azazhi will see through your tricks," Raey says, holding up her hands when Sayer starts at her. "I'm just offering you some advice because I'd like to see you succeed. I'll stay out of it, otherwise."

"Good," Efa growls. "Make sure you do."

"I'll be giving you nothing," Azazhi says. *"Not until you agree to what I asked for first, and then I'll tell you what you'll get. Not before."*

I won't react to that. He wants me off-balance. I can't be. Our passengers deserve my best. I just wish I knew what that meant in this negotiation. I'm no master of words. One wrong choice and this could be over. As much as I dislike it, I need to stay humble.

Wait. Azazhi has only dealt with me once. Maybe he expects me to be aggressive, just like I was when I offered him nothing but his freedom. Maybe he's just throwing that back in my face.

I click the mic back on. "I want five hundred pods, minimum. Then you can have half of what you asked for, except for Fana. She only goes if she wants to, and my guess is she'll never set foot on your ship again."

Raey grimaces and tilts her head. But I'll remain confident. Commander Azazhi is just testing me. He's seeing how much he can get away with. I think.

A burst of static comes from the comm, hissing and crackling for half a minute. I shift when it goes on for longer. Did I guess wrong? No. This is just more of his game. By the frowns on their faces, Efa and Sayer are falling for it. I can't blame them. Hundreds of lives are at stake here.

"No." The firmness in his voice breaks through the noise. *"You'll get nowhere near that number, and you'll agree to every-thing I want immediately, or I disconnect this call."*

"I don't think so," I fire back. "You'll—"

Efa's hand claps over my mouth, and she grabs my arm before I can back away. I struggle until we lock eyes and I catch her silent message. She just wants to talk. I let the tension slip from my body and nod my confirmation.

"Give us a moment, Commander," Raey says, flashing a worried glance toward us. "They just want to discuss something."

"They have one minute. Then I expect an answer. It had better be yes."

Efa lowers her hand from my mouth and slides it down to my shoulder, moving her other one up to match it. My stomach is tight as I wait for her to speak. She has a way of cutting through the bish and getting to the truth. Often, it's not what I want to hear. It's still better than us throwing punches.

"You need to try a different approach, or he's done with us," Efa hisses, emphasizing her words by squeezing my shoulders.

"Yeah? And what do you suggest?"

"Give him a peace offering."

My brow goes tight, and like that, my entire plan evaporates. Wasn't I on the right path? And wasn't his response what I expected?

"Have you lost your mind?" I ask, shaking my head and slashing my hand down at the comm. "He doesn't want peace! He almost took our entire crew!"

Azazhi is still fighting a battle with us, one that doesn't require guns but is deadly all the same. If he wins, I lose more passengers. And there is no way I will allow that to happen.

"He does," Raey says. Efa turns to silence her, but I grab Efa's arms and hold her in place. She looks away, and I motion for

Raey to continue. "The commander's mission is the same as yours, Ceri. His crew and his passengers are precious to him, and he'll do everything he can to protect them."

I shrug. Of course he would. But Raey's words hit my heart harder than I expect. Does she mean that there's something honorable about that man? How could I ever believe that? Then again, who would make him leader if he wasn't? What kind of leader fights to protect his people? Or tries to get everything he can for them? Or makes Fana chief engineer?

One who cares about their people.

Azazhi is battling us right now, but he's been in another fight for far longer. Perhaps it's time that I showed him, leader to leader, that I understand.

"Time's up, Ceri," the commander says. *"What's your answer?"*

I inhale and share one last glance with Efa, Merek, and Sayer, saying, *Trust me.* Efa curls one side of her mouth up. Sayer nods. So does Merek. I gain strength from their support. Perfect. Now I've got the boost I need to make this happen.

"We've all suffered, Commander," I say. "Your crew is going through a difficult time, I'll bet. So is mine. There are no winners in war. I know you get that."

A pause from him, then, *"What's your point?"*

I smile a little. He's not the unfeeling bastard he's pretending to be. And my words have struck their mark. Things are tough over there, as Raey said.

With a deep breath, I say, "If you would provide us with four hundred pods, I'd be open to giving you the most critical excavation equipment and enough fuel to power it."

Sayer nods and pumps a fist. Efa squeezes her hands together. It could be enough. I'm not expecting it to be my last offer, but it's got to be close. My pulse speeds up. This has to be the right approach.

"Did you expect a few words about suffering would make me give in to less than we deserve?" Azazhi replies, the edge in his voice returning. *"Just for that, I should take your crew and leave you isolated."*

"But that's not what you really want, is it?" I challenge.

"Fana Neridi in permanent stasis is what I want! You will give us justice, or you will get nothing!"

Efa and Raey catch me as I panic and stumble backward. A pain like a hot knife cleaves through my heart. I press my hand to my chest. Why is this affecting me so much?

"No!" I shout. "You can't have her! I won't leave four thousand passengers stranded with no one to fix this ship."

"Then you have no deal. Goodbye."

Ancestors. What have I done?

"Wait!" I pound my fists down on the table. "Is revenge that important to you? Is it? Then take me!"

"Forget it!" Efa tightens her grip on my arm as she and Raey come alongside me. "I won't allow that!"

"Neither will I," Sayer growls, just behind her. Merek shakes his head. I twist to stare at them, wondering why I responded like that. The thought of Fana...No. There's no time to dwell on it. I just hope I haven't ruined everything.

Azazhi snorts. *"I don't want you or any other of your germ-infected crew on my ship ever again. And if that's all you're offering, then we're done."*

Raey's face turns pained, and I frown. Why? She's hiding something. Maybe Azazhi is, too. If nothing else, considering that grounds me again. I take a moment to stop my shaking. This isn't over until he disconnects the call, and he hasn't done that yet.

"Commander," I start, my tone more at ease. "We have a mutual interest in ensuring our passengers get to their destination. So let's try to come to an agreement. Okay?"

"There is no we. *Every ship is on their own. It doesn't matter to me if you make it or not."*

My teeth clench. I'm about to put my fist right through the comm unit. I won't. Azazhi's shown he's no better off than we are, and he's provoking me to hide it. He won't get me to explode at him again. I'm steady now. I've got to focus.

This is where I win.

"You're wrong," I state. "We'll survive if we work together. That's why we're talking now. That's why our destination is the same. And we *must* support each other, even if that means forgetting what happened in the past. I can do that. Can you? Otherwise, there's no point in going on if all we do is destroy each other on a different planet. That will end us for sure. *All* of us."

I'm panting by the time I'm done, the passion in my words surprising me. My gaze locks on the comm's screen as I wait for his reply. And he will. Azazhi won't let his hate of me or my crew get in the way of protecting his. Nor will I.

"I can't give you four hundred pods," Azazhi says, almost apologetically. *"I don't have that many."*

A shiver runs through me. I don't know where I came up with all of that, but the power in my appeal is still energizing my body. Even Sayer's watching me with his jaw slack. I smile.

We're on the verge of an agreement. An actual agreement.

"How many can you spare, then?" I ask.

"Two hundred seventy-five for your excavation equipment and the fuel. That's my last offer." Commander Azazhi returns to his true self, his voice losing any hint of the softer tone it just had.

I turn to Raey, hoping that'll be enough units. She bites the corner of her lower lip and looks up, calculating. Two seconds later, she returns her gaze to mine and confirms. I shut my eyes, releasing the fiery unease in my body with cool relief.

"We'll accept," I say.

MONITOR

FANA

I didn't do as I was told.

Though, Ceri had asked me while completely distracted by the upcoming call to the *Devant*. She'd even used her most gentle tone on me. But I didn't want to leave her. I knew she'd be in for a rough time with the commander. Even before he became completely selfish, he was unyielding to all but the strongest appeals.

So instead of playing emotional support person, I shuffle around the dim corridors of level six, my hands jammed into the pockets of my work overalls. Silver doorways line the passage, spaced with an even rhythm as I pass them by. This level is one of the few with real cabins on it. Real beds, too. But they all remain empty. All I can guess is that there's some history here none of them want to repeat. After learning what happened on this ship, I can't blame them for their reluctance to relive the past.

I picked this level because I'm far enough away from them not to be annoying but close enough that I can be the first to hear what happened once they're done. And I need to know. No matter what the result, Ceri's bound to be upset. As much as I shouldn't, I want to be there for her, even if she says she doesn't need it.

Ceri's stronger willed than I am by at least an order of magnitude. Likely more. But inside, Ceri's always concerned about something or someone. She can't help it. For every life on board the *Stratford*, there's a part of her that hurts when they do. Even if they're not awake to feel it. It rubs me hard to see her suffering, and though she's resistant to my touch, I can't help but want to comfort her.

I wonder if Ceri worries about me, too.

She does. She absolutely does.

Just the other day, Ceri had come to machine access with a pile of rations, wearing the face of an irritated parent. I guess repairs had buried me so deep in work I'd forgotten to take a break. She made me stop until I finished everything she'd brought. It took a long time. I had a hard time chewing my food with such a huge grin on my face.

No, wait. I have to stop thinking like that. She's already made it clear she doesn't have time for a relationship. And Ceri says what she means. No games with her, unlike the torture I went through to date Raey. There's no comparison, though. I won't be dating Ceri. And that's my problem to deal with.

I stop at a door, tempted to enter. There's more history on this ship than anyone will ever share with me. I'll need to piece it together, collecting one bit of information at a time and combining it with what I already know. It's bound to be harsh, but this is my crew now, and I need to understand what happened to them.

Footsteps echo from down the hall, ones I'd recognize any-where. Raey. Why's she here? Unless...No. She better not be doing that again.

My body goes still enough to hear my heartbeat pounding. I do my best to listen past it as I try to determine her direction. A door's actuators hiss. *Dammit.* That's it. There's only one reason she'd be sneaking into a cabin on this level.

She's calling Commander Azazhi.

I shoot toward the sound of the cabin door sliding shut. There's no way I'll let her complete that call. She just talked to him. With Ceri. And now alone? Whatever they have to discuss must be something devious. But Raey won't get the chance. This time, I'm putting a stop to it.

I skid around a turn and find myself at a closed passage with just one door at the end. Perfect. That's where she went. Time to confront her and make her confess her treachery. I won't allow her to be a spy for Azazhi, not when she's supposed to be here helping us.

Ten breathless steps, and I'm at the door, pounding on the access button. Once she realizes I know what she's up to, she'll be begging me for forgiveness. Then she'll tell me everything she's done for that bastard.

But the room is dark inside. Is she hiding? I tap the light control near the door, and the cabin brightens—no Raey. *Shoot, did I check the wrong room?*

The sound of Raey's boots down the hallway turn me around and get me rushing after them. But bish, they're far. I speed up, doing my best to remember Ceri's training on how to stay quiet.

Raey better not be playing games with me, or I'll really give her an earful about my disappointment. I'd call out to her if I thought she'd wait. That's not likely. Raey won't want to answer questions about what she's doing here. She won't be able to get any lies past me. I know her too well.

I cross an intersection and double back. *Bish, I went too far!* The tap-tap of her boots on the deck is coming from behind me, like two passages back. I pivot and turn, bouncing off the wall with an awkward twist, then I'm back on her trail.

Hopefully she didn't hear that. I won't know until we come face to face. I didn't expect her to be so sneaky. That was usually me, even if I was bad at it. *Now what did Ceri say again about silent pursuit?*

I pause. Everything is quiet, save for the pounding of my pulse in my ears. *Where's Raey going?*

There! Just past the turn. I'm up on my toes and scooting after her. Raey's picked up her pace. Maybe she's looking for another place to make her call. Another level, even. She's not going anywhere until we have a few words.

My anger doesn't erase how odd this is. Raey and I never chased after each other. Our relationship was never so playful. At least it was loving. But something happened to her in the seventeen years that I was in stasis. I wish I knew what. Then maybe we could have an honest talk about how things are different.

If I've changed at all, it's because of Ceri. She's made me braver than I ever was before, if only so I can help her. It explains why I'm creeping around this level, stalking my ex-girlfriend.

Whoa. A sweet scent hits my nose. It still makes me shiver. Raey must've just showered. I press against the wall and listen as she fumbles with something. Then she taps at a furious pace—Raey's sending messages on her data comm. To Azazhi, I'll bet.

The click of her heels makes me drop into a crouch, ready to spring. I'll surprise her and grab her comm. That's all the proof I'll need. Then Raey will have to confess, or she'll spend a very long time locked up in some tiny closet. I don't want that for her, but if she refuses to cooperate, she'll only bring trouble down on herself. And I'm through defending her.

I tense as her footsteps echo down the hallway. But she's taking longer to turn the corner than I'd expect. Should I check? What if she's right there and sees me? Do I stick to my plan?

Of course I will.

With a deep inhale, I press myself along the wall and lean forward. Ceri said this lowers my visibility. I hope I'm doing it right.

As my eyes come around the corner, I search for Raey, hoping to spot her before she spots me. If she does, I've got to be as quick as Ceri. Raey may be seventeen years older than me now, but her stamina hasn't suffered from age.

"Dammit, where is she?" I mutter to the empty corridor—then freeze. *Oh hell, I just said that out loud.* Raey's making her way off this level for sure now—but she won't make it. I won't let her.

With my pulse pounding, I rush back the way I came, headed for the ladder. Raey won't risk waiting for the rail car. But we're in a race to get there. Forget stealth. I pump my legs hard as acid pushes against the top of my stomach, threatening to burst up my throat. I don't want to vomit while I'm running, but I can't stop. My lungs are burning. My head's spinning. I push myself harder. She can't get away with this. She can't.

A skid around the corner nearly sends me slamming into the far wall. I slip by with a spin, stumbling once as my eyes cross. I clench my fists and dig into the deck, racing faster than I've ever gone. Raey's got no chance now. I'm certain of it. She'll be shocked to find me there.

My confidence is so high, I miss a person stepping out from a side passage and slam right into them. The impact knocks them backward, their white coat snapping taut as it spreads. My inertia keeps me shooting forward, out of control. I trip over their body and go flying.

The person shrieks as I go near horizontal, my arms and legs splayed out. The deck comes fast. I'm far from prepared for it. The shock knocks the breath from me. My sight goes black. I tumble and roll, ending up on my back, feeling like I just got run over by a spaceship traveling at the speed of light.

The other person groans and moves. *Raey!* I've got to get up before she escapes!

I grunt and push up, but Raey's on me, shoving me back down as she leans over me. Her gaze is hard as she glares. I swallow. She's got me helpless.

REGRET

FANA

I STARE BACK AT Raey, struggling to catch my breath. Her chest rises and falls with the added burden of trying to regain her senses, just like I am. One of us will be first, and that's who will be asking the questions.

"What are you doing, Fana?" Raey's voice is acidic and deep, a tone all too familiar. She often used it when we were together. Nearly all the time at the end.

This isn't how I expected to catch her, but she's not running, and that's what I wanted—never mind the minor detail that I'm currently her captive—so I should use this chance. I should be on the offensive here. We'll see how she responds.

"What do you mean?" I ask and immediately gnash my teeth. *Focus, Fana! She'll eat you alive if you don't turn things around.* Raey was always the more mature and direct of the two of us. Now she's added seventeen years of experience on top of it.

I could be in trouble here. No. I am.

"Do I really need to explain?" she replies. "You're following me and trying to be sneaky about it. And it's not the first time. You were after me the other day, too."

"I wasn't after you."

Raey presses her lips together. "Yes, you were. I could hear your feet pattering all across the level."

Wow, I really failed Ceri's tactical training, didn't I? "I wasn't!"

"Stop being a child and admit it."

I can't hide whatever guilty look is on my face. And I know it's there. There's way too much history between the two of us for her not to be familiar with every response I give and for me not to understand every reaction she has in return. We couldn't keep secrets from each other before, and now they're all about to be revealed.

"What are *you* doing here, Raey?" I spring up to sit before she can stop me. "It's not like this level has anyone on it for you to care for."

Raey jabs a finger into my shoulder. "Except you. If I wasn't here, I—"

"If you weren't here, I wouldn't be here either!"

Whoops. I just gave away too much.

"Well, now we've got that cleared up." Raey smirks, leaning toward me. "Why are you following me?"

This is it. If I don't challenge her now, she'll walk away and I won't be able to keep an eye on her. Maybe I shouldn't. Clearly, I'm much better at maintenance than surveillance. Seren, or Tegan, or any of the crew who isn't me would do a better job.

Still...

"Were you about to call Commander Azazhi?" I demand.

The muscles in her jaw go tight as her body stills. The lines on her forehead are deeper than I remember them. And the redness in her cheeks conveys a fire that makes me shiver. I don't recognize this woman. Whoever Raey has become, she's not the same person I loved.

"That's what you're doing? Spying on me?" Raey hisses between her teeth. She stands, breathing flames out of her nostrils. "After everything I've done for you and this crew? Fine! I don't need to be here."

"No. I..." I shoot up—too fast. My head spins, and I reach out to her to steady myself, but Raey pushes me away. I stumble as my feet collide, my shoulder smashing against the wall. Pain explodes through my body as I stagger back, my hand covering the sore spot.

Raey turns to walk away, and suddenly it's not just my shoulder that hurts.

"Wait!" I cry. "Won't you give me a chance to explain? You didn't even ask me why!"

She stops and glances back. "I don't care why."

No. She's lying. To me, definitely. Maybe to herself, too. Ever since I woke up, we've been trying to redefine our relationship, and we still haven't come to an agreement. Friends? *Maybe.* Colleagues? *Not anymore.* She's loyal to a maniac and a murderer. And that's been getting in the way of us forming a new bond. I have a big problem with anyone supporting the man who wants to kill me.

Still, we've got more in common than Commander Azazhi and our lost relationship. We share a powerful need to help the passengers and crew of the *Stratford*. If Raey only cared about her duty, she'd already be back on the *Devant*. It's her love of these people that keeps her here.

I go to her as she waits, her head still turned to watch me approach. When I'm close, she pivots to face me, arms crossed. I'm warmed by her willingness to hear me out. Maybe I should do the same. Sure, she's working for someone I've got serious hate for, but what if she really is just doing what she'd told Ceri she was doing? Maybe she is trying to help us.

"So?" Raey says. "I'm waiting for your explanation."

"That hurt, you know," I reply, rubbing my shoulder for effect. Raey only glances at it before she rolls her eyes. *Yes, I know it's bad acting.* I never said I was good at it. That's why I'm an engineer.

"Talk or I walk away."

I sink a little. No kindness left in her to humor me with. I guess that's all for the best. Now I've just got to figure out how to approach this.

"I want to believe in you," I say, taking a measured cadence with my words. "You've done so much for this crew, I would find it hard to believe that you would ever want anything other than to treat them well. But you're still part of the *Devant*'s crew, and that's got to be tough. Especially if Azazhi gave you orders that conflicted with your medical oath."

Raey shifts, one arm dropping while her opposite hand grips it. "Do you really believe I would ever do anything to hurt these children?"

My jaw drops. *Oh hell, I just backed myself into an airlock.* "No! I'm not saying that at all!" But even as I deny it, I realize she's trying to manipulate my thoughts. But how do I respond? I can't just call her on it. Or...can I?

"All I want is for them to succeed," Raey adds. "They're in a dangerous position with the ship damaged as it is. And this situation between them and the *Devant* only makes things worse. If I can—"

"Is the virus spreading over there?" I press closer. "Because that could happen, couldn't it?"

Raey inhales sharply. "You've been listening to my calls?"

"No, I only—"

Her hands slam into my body. I stumble backward. She does it again. And again. I cry out. *She's really trying to hurt me!* But my heart aches worse. Am I nothing to her now? Is what I've done so terrible that she's willing to break her oath just to get back at me?

"Did Ceri put you up to this?" Raey shouts, stomping after me, her fists raised. "What does she think I'm doing? Huh? I just helped her negotiate nearly three hundred new stasis pods for this ship! Three hundred of our best pods! And here *you* are sneaking around, scrounging for evidence to give to your precious girlfriend so she can use it against me!"

I keep my distance, my body trembling at her rage. "Why are you hitting me? Didn't you just say you've done nothing wrong?"

"Why?" The blaze in Raey's eyes is almost blinding. I back away, fearing more violence. "Why? Because *you*, someone I trusted—someone I've loved—are accusing me of betraying this crew! And how dare you! All I've ever done is care for them! And you!"

Loved? As in no longer? The idea of that is like Raey grabbing my heart and yanking it from my chest. We may not be lovers anymore, but for her to say that shakes my entire being. A mental wall forms around me, hardening my emotions and numbing me to her words.

"Except when you had me arrested," I spit back, "and locked me up in a closet. That's when I realized you only cared for yourself."

The gasp that escapes her lips is real. Good. She deserves to get hurt, too. Raey's the one who started this, stabbing with her declaration first. It's only right that I strike back. And as her eyes widen, I'm filled with satisfaction for my action.

Raey's hand across my face comes faster than I can react. My head snaps to one side, the sting of her slap burning into my cheek. I inhale a shaky breath as my eyes get wet, a sob building inside me.

She watches me bring my hand to my cheek, the skin hot to the touch. I wipe at my eyes, staring back at her. Raey's face bares her guilt. I'm struggling not to be happy about it, but after what she just did, I'm not sure I want to try too hard.

Suddenly, the reality of the moment hits, and I'm over-whelmed. As much as I try to fight it, my tears flow, even as I become numb to the pain that caused them. I cried when Raey dumped me, but I knew that was coming. This hurts way more than I can stand.

"I'm sorry," Raey says, reaching out to clear the tears from my face, like she used to. I turn my head, refusing her touch, and after a few seconds, she drops her arm and pulls away.

"Ceri didn't put me up to anything. She trusts you," I say, sniffling. "I heard your voice from down the corridor and got curious. You know how I am."

It's all a lie, of course. Raey's acting too out of character for me to trust her. No matter what she says after this, I won't believe it. It's fair. She's already made it clear that she doesn't believe me.

Raey's face turns pained. "Fana...I—"

"Why do you still obey him?"

Raey drops her gaze, finding some edge of the floor to stare at. "I don't have a choice. It's the only home I have."

Her words rattle my resolve, even as I bet everything on it. It's only because she's telling the truth. Before now, she'd always been straight with me. *How far we've split in such a short time. It's like there's an entire galaxy between us.*

"You could stay here," I say. I don't know if I even mean it. Likely I do. After being so close with her for so long, saying goodbye to Raey would be like tearing my guts out and throwing them away. I'm not sure that even Ceri could bring me back from that.

Raey shakes her head. "No. He'd never let me. And they wouldn't welcome me here like they did for you."

They. She's already distanced herself from the *Stratford*'s crew.

"How do you know?"

"It doesn't matter, Fana. I can't stay. And you don't really want me to, either."

I sniffle again and hug my arms to my body, keeping silent. No way I could lie about that and make it sound truthful. Not while my cheek still burns.

"How long will you stay, then?" I ask.

"I'm here until they bring the pods over from the *Devant*, we set them up, and I'm confident Efa can manage them." Raey tries a hopeful smile. "That's a long while from now. And during that time, I promise I am here for Ceri, and Efa, and everyone else. I won't leave them unprepared. You, out of anyone, should know I'd never do that."

I nod, my eyes falling to my feet. "I do."

"Then"—she bends, trying to catch my gaze—"I'll see you around?"

I lock my eyes on the deck, ensuring I see nothing but my feet. "Yeah, you will."

Raey heads toward the ladder then, taking with her any feeling of connection to her I've ever had. And this time, I know it won't return.

RIVAL

—— • ——

CERI

I'VE NEVER BEEN ON level ninety for more than a minute at a time. I was always just passing through. There's nothing here but a pair of thick walls separating the massive airlocks, one on each side. Even the deck is spotless, and the walls are free of stains. It's as if we're the first people to step onto the *Stratford* after it was completed nearly seven centuries ago.

I don't get the sense that any of us are as ancient as that. Really, we're not. Save for the last eight years, Efa, Merek, Sayer, and I have all been in stasis. I try not to think about how we still should be. There's no point in lamenting a future denied to us when the one we've chosen for ourselves is as clear as the stars outside the airlock.

And I could see them, if only the *Devant*'s dark mass wasn't blocking the view.

In less than five minutes, that ship will dock with ours—again—this time to make the agreed-upon exchange—pods for equipment. We can move most everything through this cargo lock, save for some of the larger crates, which will be jettisoned directly from their levels for the *Devant* to pick up.

Then there's the equipment on thirty-eight that Commander Azazhi doesn't get to know about. I won't leave my passengers without tools to build their new colony. Fana was only too happy to delete them off the manifest. And Raey will never be allowed on that level. It's a risk, but so is opening my ship to these murderers again.

Efa bumps against me as the *Devant* powers on its docking lights, flooding the area with a fiery glare. I raise my hand in front of my face as I squint, hating how we'll be blind well after they make the connection.

"It'll be fine," Efa says. "They've got no interest in spending more time with us than they have to. As soon as the transfer's made, they'll be gone."

"How I can't wait for that moment," I mutter.

The *Stratford* shudders as the two massive crafts connect. It's as if my ship fears what's about to happen. Or knows.

At least they've shut the lights down, leaving only the residual afterglow in my sight. It'll disappear, eventually, but until then, I'll be keeping my hand near my pistol. The memories of battle are all too fresh in our minds. Likely in the heads of the *Devant*'s crew, too. No one wants to repeat that slaughter, yet despite our mutual understanding, there won't be any level of trust between our crews. We will get this trade done as quickly as we can and disengage with their ship even faster than that.

A succession of thumps rings out from the hull, created by something much heavier than a fist. Those bastards better not have damaged my ship.

"Open the airlock," I say.

Sayer steps up to the controls and taps in the command. As the outer door slides up, four bodies step onto our ship, and for the next few minutes, we can do nothing but stare each other down until the system finishes cycling the air.

Commander Azazhi is in the center of his group. His scraggly hair and long beard are obvious. The man behind him, with the rifle held in an aggressive position, must be a security agent, as is the other on the opposite side. They've also got two more inside of their airlock to cover their escape.

But the man to Azazhi's left is familiar. His bulky frame sends a shiver through my body, not unlike what the *Stratford* just did. And I have good reason to feel tense. That man almost killed me. Twice.

So Captain Yelekal has recovered, and he wants to shove that in my face. He should have kept hidden on the *Devant*. Now I'll be watching his every move, ready to put him down if he so much as sneers.

"Rhys, Tegan, and Deryn are in place, right?" I whisper.

"Right where you told them to be," Merek replies. "And they've all got those beam weapons we took from their wounded."

"No firing until Ceri gives the order," Efa says, her tone firm.

"And what if she can't?" Sayer asks.

Everyone knows what to do if a leader goes down, though, if I did, Azazhi would drop half a second later. I expect they're aware of that. I also expect they've made a plan to stop that from happening.

My hand slides closer to my holster.

The high squeal of the airlock cycle alert chirps five times before the massive door slides out at a pace ten times slower than I could shove it open myself. All it does is add to the tightness in every muscle of my body, dragging out the tension with each hair's width that it moves. Merek and Sayer stiffen, their casual demeanor evaporating. They know better than to place hands on their weapons, but I flash them a warning glance, anyway. These adults are our enemy. Just because we're making a deal with them doesn't change that.

Once the door clears Captain Yelekal, his eyes swing across the deck, searching for threats. It's as if he can see through each bulkhead and layer of the hull to observe what's behind them. Then, when he's satisfied there's no immediate trouble, his gaze lands on me, becoming narrower as he evaluates my condition. I'll give him nothing to be happy about. My old wounds may still ache, but they don't stop me from moving as if I have none.

I shift my weight forward. Captain Yelekal inhales sharply. Good. I want him to know I'm watching him, too.

"Requesting permission to come aboard," Commander Azazhi says with a nod.

A smirk hits my face—it's a canny move. He's trying to make me lower my guard. I won't. Despite us being on safe ground, I've no illusion of dominance in this situation. Azazhi wouldn't have agreed to this moment if he didn't have some level of control. And if he thinks I would fall for a few pleasant words, he's not as crafty as I thought.

"Granted...for you, the captain, and your cargo crew," I reply and point to the two men behind him. "But your security team needs to return to your ship. I won't allow armed adults to invade my ship again."

Commander Azazhi returns my grin with one of his own. "And leave my people vulnerable? Come now, Ceri. Someone with your level of military tactical skill would know I'd never accept that."

"That may be so, but no weapons come aboard the *Stratford*. That's final."

He tilts his head. "Are you that willing to let this deal go? Because that's what will happen if you keep insisting."

Azazhi's bluffing. He just wants to provoke me. Yet even as I tell myself that, my stomach twists. I can't fail my passengers again. Twelve people can't have died for nothing. I must get what we need, even if we've got to take it by force.

My hand slips behind my back. I signal, *Get ready.* This exchange may not remain peaceful for long.

"And what about you?" I fire back. "You're about to walk away from a deal you will never find again."

He chuckles but glances at Captain Yelekal, seeking advice. Narrowed eyes and a tight jaw are all he gets in reply. It's a welcome sign that they fear us. And a dangerous one. I need to stay sharp.

Azazhi returns his focus back to us, his gaze landing on Efa. Then Sayer. And then Merek. All of them remain still as the air surrounding us. If he only knew how ready they were to end him, he wouldn't be so casual with his observations. Nor should I. There could be twenty agents hiding just out of sight.

I scan for signs of movement, my fingers itching to wrap themselves around my gun and feel the comfort there. He wants this deal. He needs this deal. We both do.

"Those two boys have to go," Azazhi says. "You and the other girl can greet my crew. Then I'll have my security agents return to the ship."

The breath I held in my lungs releases. I press my lips into a grin to hide it. It helps that he just said something amusing.

"You think your chances are better with her?" I motion toward Efa in jest. "She's the first one of us to have killed someone."

Captain Yelekal eyes Efa as his eyebrows raise. Perhaps he's found a level of respect for my slender friend. Or fear. A knife in the belly will do that. I'm impressed he's even here. Maybe the medical tech on the *Devant* is just that good.

"I don't care what she did," Commander Azazhi says. "My condition remains. So either you tell them to go, or I'm ending this."

My gun hand clenches. *So much for de-escalation.* "I don't order them to do anything," I say.

"Okay." Azazhi tosses his hand. "We're done here, then. Let's go."

Bish. I didn't expect him to walk away so easily. Now what? Is the only option I have left to attack? I will if I must. Our passengers must survive. My hand drops to my pistol. If this is it, then so be it. They'll regret turning their backs on us. I will fight to the death to get those pods.

A gentle hand touches my shoulder.

"It's alright," Sayer whispers close to my ear. "You'll be fine, and you know it. Let's just get this done."

Merek nods when I look at him. Efa does, too. But by now, even Captain Yelekal has turned to leave.

"Hold on!" I call. They glance back, faces still. They're hiding their satisfaction as I duck my head, hating myself while I do it. I just gave in to adults, breaking the one promise I swore to myself I never would. No matter how much it grates on me to do it, I must. This is for my passengers and my crew. "They'll go."

Commander Azazhi makes a show of pivoting back around, taking longer to move back into position than it did to dock his ship. I hold my words back, fearing any small comment will make him walk away again.

So this was part of the negotiation, after all. I'm the fool for failing to recognize that. He won because he was willing to walk away, or at least get me to believe it. I will be wary of him doing that to me again.

Ease up, Ceri, Efa signs on my back, then flattens out her hand to keep her connection to me. I'm grateful. It'll be hard to forgive myself for this beginner's mistake. I can't afford to make any more of them.

As the four security agents leave, Captain Yelekal retrieves one of their rifles and slings it over his shoulder. He's making statements again. At least this is one I need not worry about.

Sayer and Merek would have informed Tegan, Rhys, and Deryn of the situational change.

"Now, this is how the exchange will go," Azazhi says, taking a few confident steps forward. "Listen up so your little child brains remember it."

I let my lips curve upward. Let him think he's won this battle. The commander may believe we're evenly matched now, but they're on my ship, and I write the rules here.

"We're listening," I say. "Just make sure you speak clearly."

WARNING

— • —

FANA

I DON'T KNOW HOW I became involved with this.

I've got a lot more important things to do than to play guard here on level ninety, standing watch as the *Devant*'s crew floats stasis pods into our ship while Merek, Seren, and Rhys push bulky crates of excavation machinery out of the rail car and slide them over to awaiting members of the *Devant*'s team. Everyone moves in routine silence, unwilling to say a word to the other crew. It's dull enough to make me want to leave. If I could remember how I got caught up in such a routine procedure, I might figure how to squirm my way out of it.

Wait, I do remember. It was my stupid curiosity that prompted me to come down here and see what was going on. Merek spotted me standing around, so he handed me his comm and put me to work. I should have run away.

Maybe I'll get to see one of my old team, and we'll have a conversation. Catch up or something. I've got a small pang of homesickness in my chest, and a quick chat might cure it for a while.

Time to get a little closer.

I pluck a small crate off the top of Merek's cart and head toward the drop-off point at the center of the airlock, nearly halfway between the *Devant*'s hatch and the dividing wall of the level. As I plop it down on top of another crate, two people exit the airlock, pushing a pair of stasis beds between them.

Ooh, that's Baati! I should go say hello and thank him for his help. I bet he's wondering how I'm doing.

"Hey! What are you doing?" Merek hisses as he pulls up behind me.

I point at Baati. "Just going to say thank you."

He shakes his head. "No way. You shouldn't be this close to them. They could grab you, and two seconds later, you'd be back on the *Devant* with no way for us to save you."

My nose wrinkles at that thought. But I know it'll be safe. Ceri made Commander Azazhi agree to no guards and no weapons anywhere near the hatch. So far, the worst that's happened is a few glares between the crews.

"Don't worry, it's just a quick hello. I'll be mindful."

Merek rubs a finger along the side of his eye and sighs. "Please, please be careful."

With a wink, I skip over to where Baati is handing off his pod to Seren. He keeps his eyes on the unit, and she does the same. It's a shame, really. If Azazhi wasn't such a selfish man, these two might have gotten along. Ah well. Maybe I can at least introduce them to each other.

"Baati!" I wave as I approach, then frown when he doesn't respond. I'm sure I was loud enough for him to hear me. Seren's curious glance is proof of that. Yet, even as I get closer, he just pivots to return to his ship.

I try again as Seren slides the pod away. Now he just stops because he's got nothing to hide behind. The least he could do is look at me.

"Hey, Baati, how are you?" I say, coming around his side.

"Step back," Baati growls.

My heart jumps, thumping hard at the aggressiveness of his response. *Whoa*. Okay, so he's stressed out or something. I try to keep the mood light.

I grin. "Is that any way to talk to a chief?"

Baati's jaw quivers as he inhales. So Azazhi ordered him to keep his mouth shut. That could be the first wise thing he's done since we received the *Stratford*'s distress call, though he's probably worried about secrets getting out more than anything else. Not that I care. I don't take orders from him anymore.

"Don't worry." I pat the air in front of me. "No one will tell on you for talking to me."

Baati huffs and pushes past me, keeping his head down as he heads for the *Devant*'s hatch. I put on a playful smile and get in front of him, holding up my hands to stop him. Baati grits his teeth and attempts to keep me from locking gazes with him, even as I weave and duck to get him to glance up.

"Get away from me...Chief," he hisses, throwing his hands up so I can't grab his arm.

"Oh, come on," I plead. "All I want to do is say thanks."

"Go away!" He takes a wide step to go around me, but I'm already there.

"Why won't you talk to me?"

Our gazes connect then, and the breath goes out of me. His face is hard. Angry even. If I didn't know better, I'd say there's hate for me buried in that glare. Actual hate.

"Because you're a traitor. That's why," he hisses.

My hand covers my heart then, because it's the only way to stop it from falling out of my chest. Baati's reply almost hurts more than the shot through my hand. Is this how the entire crew of the *Devant* thinks of me now? As a backstabber and a defector? Do they even know the truth about what happened? I doubt it. Azazhi would have made up a hundred lies to justify his actions. He would have made a criminal out of me, and every *Stratford* crew member, too, just so there'd be no chance of anyone questioning why they kidnapped a bunch of ragged-looking kids.

Maybe if I pulled the glove off my hand and showed him the huge hole in it, he wouldn't judge me so harshly.

"I'm not," I say. "And I know why you think that, but give me a minute to tell you what you don't know, and then you'll understand."

Baati just stares, his forehead creased with anger. But he's struggling to maintain it. A sliver of hope drips into me. And in it is all the energy I need to reach him.

"You want to believe me, don't you?" I try, and as soon as I speak, it snaps him back into his smoldering disapproval of me.

"It doesn't matter," Baati growls under his breath. "You made your choice."

"My choice?" I throw my hands out. "I'm following the regulations *our* organization created to deal with situations like this! Maybe you should ask your commander why he chose not to follow them!"

"He's protecting us. You're just trying to defend a bunch of murderers."

Oh, that just grinds my teeth hard. In two seconds, my level of angry will match his. In the next, I'll be ready to explode like a pressurized gas cylinder.

"Are you hyuking kidding me?" I shout.

Disgust crosses his face. "You even talk like them now."

"What's that matter?"

Baati shakes his head and side-steps a second time to get around me, but I block him again. He moves left, and so do I. Then right. Every time he tries, I'm there to get in his way. He doesn't get to insult my crew like that and just leave.

"Move. Now," Baati says, his voice full of warning.

"Not until you answer me."

Baati mashes his lips together and grabs me. I yelp as he throws me aside, stumbling and crashing onto the deck, banging my knee. It's more shock than pain. If I was still a chief, he'd never dare to touch me like that. Azazhi would toss him out of the nearest airlock.

"Hey!" Merek shouts, rushing toward us as he thrusts a finger at Baati. "You don't touch her!"

Seren and Rhys drop their crates and race forward, startling the two *Devant* crew, who spin and race back to their ship. Baati stomps after them, his chest forward and arms back. My chin quivers as I watch him go, knowing that I'll never see him again.

Merek stops in front of me, creating a wall of protection with Rhys. Their hands linger near their lower backs. *They've got guns!* I press my fist against my mouth to stop the gasp from coming out. *How stupid could they be?* It's a good thing Baati walked away. This could have gotten dangerous.

Then again, it was probably a smart thing for them to maintain a hidden defense. I think Ceri tried to teach me something like that in her tactical training. Maybe I should have been less focused on her and more on what she was teaching.

"You okay?" Seren asks as she crouches next to me.

"Fine," I sigh. "I just didn't expect him to do that."

"What happened?" Merek asks, turning around to me.

I drop my gaze to the floor. What happened? Commander Azazhi made me the villain. That's what. That's no surprise. But for Baati to be so upset with me, when he isn't even sure who to believe, that was just...I don't know. Maybe it is all my fault.

"I guess I need to work on my anger management a little," I reply.

"By the look of it, you've got plenty to be angry at." Merek offers me a hand. "And that doesn't excuse him for pushing you like that."

I let him pull me up while Seren puts a hand on my back to make sure I'm stable on my feet. I am. Just barely.

"Maybe not," I reply. "But it's clear I need to be careful around them now. Even the ones I thought I could trust."

"Yeah," Rhys says. "It's like a completely different planet over there."

Different planet. Huh. Different universe more like it. And Azazhi is the god that rules over it.

MURDER

CERI

WITH MY ARMS CROSSED in front of me, I observe the pods the *Devant*'s crew pushes through our airlock, keeping a running number of how many they've given us. So far, I've counted ten. Those, plus the ones already delivered, give us fifty-one units—not anywhere near enough to replace the ones in danger of failing. I've asked Merek to push them to move faster, and he has. Their resulting increase in speed is still far from acceptable.

Merek assures me he's got everything under control, and despite what happened to Fana, I believe him. It's our opposition I can't trust. Who shoves someone down just for saying hello? I'm glad she's alright. Fana is delicate compared to anyone else on our crew. I regret not being around to protect her. Maybe I shouldn't have been spending all that time on the stasis level, watching my mother in her pod. Something compelled me to be there. I don't know what it was. I just knew I had to be there. But I won't be making that mistake again. From now on, my eyes are on Fana.

Seren smiles at me as she wheels a heavy crate out of the airlock, grunting as she forces it forward. Yet it barely moves. She leans into the handle and tries again. The crate rolls forward, but her foot slips on the deck, and Seren's caught hanging off the bar. She chuckles and mutters a curse under her breath as she pulls herself up to try again.

She'll refuse me if I ask to help, but I can't just stand here and watch her struggle. And she'll feel ashamed if I tell her to let me do it. So, with a glance at Merek, warning him not to stop me, I stroll over to Seren as I do my best to seem embarrassed about something.

"Hey," I whisper. "Could you do me a huge favor?"

Seren exhales and stands up, dusting herself off. A smirk comes across her face, and she jests, "What? Tell Fana you broke the navigation computer?"

My eyes narrow and she shrinks, even as the grin on her face remains. I'm already fighting against myself not to laugh.

"I won't be asking anymore," I growl and nod to the rail car. "Go back to fourteen and get the clipboard and stylus there."

"Come on! There's got to be one closer than that!"

I thrust my finger at the ladder. "You want to climb all the way up? No? Get going then."

She huffs, rolling her eyes and pivoting to shuffle back toward the rail car.

"You're still my favorite," I call after her. Seren responds with a rude gesture I wasn't aware she knew. I laugh and watch her walk away before dropping my hands on the crate's handle and thrusting hard to get it to move.

For a moment, there's an ache in my chest as I think of her. Seren is the closest thing to a sister I've ever known, and every time I remind myself that she's not, it only makes me want to cling to her more. If there was ever a way for either of us to return to stasis, I'd make sure she'd be the one to have it.

"Hello? Commander Ceri?" a man calls and waves at me as I roll the crate into place. He's tall, lean, and muscular and walks with a casualness that lowers my suspicions. Not a soldier, but someone who's used to physical work. I'm curious about his tight curly hair.

"Not commander, but yes, you found who you're looking for," I reply. "Who might you be?"

"Chief Taye, head of maintenance on this rotation. My team is responsible for getting the stasis pods to your ship."

I nod, though this seems like a distraction ready to happen. If it is, I might have to give this man a rude reminder of how we are not on friendly terms. But if it's not, then maybe I can turn it to my advantage and ask him to speed up their delivery of the pods. Better to play nice for now.

"Thank you and your team for their hard work," I say with a smile. "What can I do for you?"

"Well." He sighs. "I'm not sure you can help, but I have to ask, just in case. You see, one of my team is missing, and he either can't or won't answer his comm."

My forehead gets tight. "And you think *we* can help you find him?"

"Possibly. He doesn't seem to be on our ship, and—"

"Hold on." I throw up a hand. "You think he's here?"

Chief Taye presses his lips together, and my gut tightens. This could easily be an attempt to cover for this crew member as he does surveillance on my ship. He'd pretend he got lost and, in the meantime, be gathering intel of as many levels as possible. If this missing crew member discovers the level with the excavation equipment we're hiding from Azazhi, our trade with the *Devant* could be over.

"Alright, I'll get a few of the crew to search for him," I say. "Likely, if he's here, he wouldn't have made it far. There are a lot of ladders to climb on this ship."

"Thank you, Commander—er, Ceri. Thank you. We'll do another thorough search on our ship, and I'll pull another two of the team off the standard routine to make sure the pods keep coming."

It's only the second time I smile, if tightly, at one of the *Devant*'s crew. Perhaps not all of them are as bad as their commander. Or their security agents.

"Aidan, Mari, Beka, Tegan," I say into my comm as I put distance between me and Chief Taye. "Drop what you're doing and get down to ninety right away. We may have a situation."

"Do we need weapons?" Tegan asks.

"Negative. Bring lights, though."

"You need me, too?" Seren asks.

"When you get back, yes."

"Coming also," Efa adds.

"No," I reply. "Merek's here. We're covered."

"And I miss you, too." Efa makes a rude sound through the mic. *"Merek's mine, remember."*

I snort, though I'm glad she's at ease enough to joke. I can't say the same for myself. Dread pricks at my skin, giving me the feeling this will end badly. We'll find this *Devant* crew person on a level where we absolutely don't want him to be, and then I'll need to interrogate him before we hand him back. Chief Taye won't appreciate me returning his team member bruised and battered, but for the safety of my crew, I might have to.

It only takes twenty-three minutes to find him.

"Ceri." The regret in Tegan's voice is clear, even over the comm. *"Come to ninety-nine. I've found your missing* Devant *crew person."*

"Good. Hold him there until I arrive," I reply.

"That won't be a problem."

Seren and I share a worried glance as we rush to the rail car. Is there anything on ninety-nine that could get someone into trouble? Broken machines? Dangerous equipment? Weapons?

And then I remember. No. That's our morgue.

I only find it curious until I arrive and see the lifeless body crumpled on the deck. Poor kid. He's close to my age—*was* close to my age—and had features similar to Chief Taye. He won't be getting any older, that's for certain. Not with his throat sliced open like that and the top of his work jumper covered in blood. Tegan had the decency to shut his eyelids, and I doubt he would have shut his mouth before he died.

Bish, I hope he isn't related to the chief.

"This is the boy who shoved Fana," Seren says, staring down at him. Perhaps there's pity in her voice, or maybe it's satisfaction that some kind of extreme justice has been served.

"Hyuk," I mutter, knowing how much trouble this will cause. Azazhi will raise hell for sure and demand all sorts of things, none of which I'll comply with, but there's a much more immediate issue at hand.

"One of us did this," Tegan says through clenched teeth, stating exactly what I was thinking.

Seren's eyes widen as she stares at the body, the possibilities racing through her mind, just like they are in mine. The potential suspects are few and even those—Dru, Deryn, Sayer—are highly unlikely candidates.

"Efa," I say over comm. "Looks like I'll need you after all. Come to ninety-nine. Bring Raey." I turn to Seren. "Go back to ninety. Let Merek and Rhys know what happened. Make sure you keep weapons hidden but handy. I'll follow soon enough."

Seren glances again at the body, then nods and rushes off. One less problem I'll need to concern myself with for the moment. But eventually I'll need to build a plan for defense. We're at risk of Azazhi ordering the remainder of his agents to overrun our ship. And I fear what happens if he does. We're in no condition to hold off another massive attack.

"So what do we do?" Tegan asks. "I mean, finding who did it..."

I wave my hand dismissively. "That's the least of my concerns. We need to protect the crew first. Then we can talk about justice."

"Maybe one of their own did it to trap us."

"For what?" I shake my head. "Besides our equipment, we have nothing they want."

"They wanted to turn us into their slaves. Or sacrifices. Whatever." Tegan shrugs. "We were nothing to them before, and we still are nothing now. Hyuking adults."

True enough, but it doesn't give me any idea of how I should approach this with Azazhi. There's no way to hide it. Anyone who goes missing on a ship gets found eventually. Faster if they're dead. Word would get out. Hyuk, the person who did it could leak it to the *Devant*'s crew. Or even try to frame one of us. There'd be war if that happened.

"Can you stay here and wait for Efa?" I ask. "I've got to tell Chief Taye about this."

Tegan nods. "Don't give them anything. It's their fault they can't keep track of their own crew."

Ten minutes later, I stand face to face with a speechless Chief Taye, who stares at me with his mouth wide. There might even be tears in his eyes. He wiped his sleeve across them when I first broke the news.

"For whatever it's worth, I'm sorry," I say. "I know it's difficult to lose someone you care about."

"You'll investigate, won't you?" Taye implores. "You'll find who did it so we can have justice?"

I tighten my jaw. What he's asking for makes my skin crawl. If what Tegan says is right, Azazhi will demand we turn over the guilty. I might as well shoot them myself, as it'd be less painful for them. There is no reason in this entire universe to return one of my crew to the hands of adults. None whatsoever.

"Honestly, I don't see a reason to," I say, shrugging.

Chief Taye shakes his hands at me. "But you just said some-one murdered him! You have to find the killer! They've got to be punished!"

This is dangerous. I've already stumbled in my last negotia-tion with him, and he used it against me. This could put us at his mercy, and I know Commander Azazhi has none.

"I said it seems like that could have happened," I reply, folding my arms to hide my shaking hands. "You told me he roamed off on his own. There's no telling what happened. This ship isn't safe for those who aren't familiar with it."

"Let me see his body, then! I'll be able to tell what happened to him."

No. In a million years, no. He's just looking for a way to blame us. And that'll be almost as bad as finding out one of my crew slit the throat of a non-combatant. My gut twists something fierce when I consider that, and I shove it out of my head as fast as possible. We all have blood on our hands, but I refuse to believe any of us are capable of murder.

Yet my will to disbelieve it is weakening. Our anger at the *Devant*'s crew's abuse is far from forgotten. And Fana's mis-treatment only rubs that wound harder. Anything is possible, especially if this dead boy provoked our rage.

"One of your own is already examining it," I say. "I'm sure she'll be providing results to you as soon as there are some. Again, I'm sorry for your loss."

His face goes dark. "Yeah, I'm sorry, too. Because until we find out who did it, I'm ordering my team to stop delivering pods."

"Now wait—"

"No." He shakes his head. "You'd do the same for your people, I'm sure. This is the way it's going to be."

Bish. I pushed back too hard. But I had to. Any hint of guilt on our part and he would have been all over it. I need to stay confident. There'll be a way to solve this. There has to be.

"Now excuse me. I've got to report this to my commander."

Merek steps to my side as Chief Taye exits, calling to his team members and motioning for them to leave with him.

"That didn't go well, did it?" Merek asks.

I shrug, playing at indifference even as I stifle a scream. "As long as it doesn't get worse," I say.

But I have a feeling it will.

SABOTAGE

— • —

FANA

"This is it?" I ask as I survey the small herd of stasis pods pressed together on forty-nine. Even one level below the accident, the oily scent of burned electronics hangs in the air, irritating my nose and stinging my eyes. If Merek hadn't asked me to be here, I'd likely be sleeping, as I'd had little of that in the last fifty-four hours.

Though, Ceri let me crash in her office while she was there, and that was the best hour-long nap I've had in a while. If only it could have been just a little longer.

"It's what your crew...sorry." Merek scratches his head. "What the *Devant*'s crew delivered while they were in operation. Sixty-one units, if I counted right."

I eye the units again. Most of their white shells are pristine, with a few still covered in their transparent blue overwrap. A few on the right side look scuffed, but it's unlikely to be any actual damage. Still, I wouldn't put it past Commander Azazhi to break a few. His quest for vengeance is infinite. Ceri wouldn't have dealt with him if she hadn't needed to.

"So you just want me to test them all?" I ask as I circle around the mass of pods.

"No, not all," Merek replies. "We'll only need to do that if we find problems. Let's just pick a few and see if we're safe."

Not we, Merek. The most you'll do is push a few heavy things around.

I'll be the one jamming my hands into the wires and circuits, likely scraping my hands and fingers as I always do. It goes with the gig, so I won't complain. Out loud.

"Alright." I motion to the pods as I find a bright, open spot on the level. "If it's to be a random sample, pull five of them and bring them over here. Make sure it's truly random."

The first two units Merek brings me pass any test I can run through them with all the awards and accolades possible. They're ready to be fully powered and have people put inside. Whoever's lucky enough to have that opportunity will wake up after a thousand years feeling better than they ever did, no matter what their current age is.

There are no issues with the third unit, either, and I feel a little foolish for suspecting Azazhi. Maybe he has every intention of keeping his word, or he couldn't find the time to damage these units before he sent them over. The fourth pod has a few dents and a long scrape on one side, but it's not deliberate. No one's so creative that they could have scraped the pump in such a way that is so unnoticeable. I found that out accidentally, after working way too many hours. Kind of like this.

"Here's the last one," Merek says, sliding a near-pristine example of a stasis pod up next to the damaged one.

I exhale and wipe the sweat off my forehead. I bet I stink. Merek's just too polite to say anything about it. It doesn't matter. I'll run this unit through the checks, maybe tighten a few things up if it needs it, and make my way to the nearest shower. Maybe I'll get to crash in Ceri's office again. The mattress on the floor isn't all that comfortable, but it smells like her, and that might help me fall asleep. Then again, it might not.

Oh hell, what's this?

I frown when an error flashes across the diagnostic screen. It's saying it can't find the medical stabilizer module. Not a problem if it's broken or missing, but it's the main benefit of using these newer pods. That unit healed my wounds from the acidic rain back on Earth. It still functions fine without it, yet I wouldn't put Niah in this pod if I wanted her wounds to get better.

Maybe it's just a poor connection. I'll reseat the plugs and test it again.

It only takes a few minutes, then I'll be shower-bound and refreshed before I hit whatever mattress, or nest, or bed I find myself in. Bish, if I wasn't so dirty, I'd just crawl into one of the recovery beds here.

My lips mash together as the same error appears. *So much for the quick test.* There's something wrong with this unit, and now I've got to get inside it and figure out why.

"What's that mean?" Merek says, leaning over my shoulder to peer at the screen. "How can something be missing? It looks intact, doesn't it?"

Oh gosh, imagine if he was down here by himself. This poor boy would just kick the side of the pods and call it a day. At least Sayer or Ceri would open these things up and check their insides. Not that they'd know what to look for.

"That's what we're going to find out," I reply as I rub the corner of my eye. "Hand me that tool case there, would you?"

"Huh?" Merek searches around until he spots the small black satchel I brought with me—one of five kits that I took from the *Devant*. It wasn't stealing. They were already mine.

I open up the case and grab a pair of precision pliers, which I use to pluck a pair of clips from the unit. I pull the panel off and dive deep into the guts of the pod, searching for the bundle of slots and cards that make up the medical module. Maybe a communication cable came loose while they were moving it around. It'd be far from the first time something like that happened.

"Dammit," I seethe.

"What's wrong?"

"Nothing, just scraped my hand. It's normal. I've got to sacrifice a little blood to the tech god so I can make a good repair."

Merek blinks as he nods. I don't expect him to understand. It's something I made up a long time ago, and since I cut myself nearly every time I work, it made sense. Only to me, of course.

It's not long before I find, or don't find, what I'm looking for. The diagnostic is correct. The module isn't there. Now I'll have to get in there to examine the slots. If they're bent, there's a good chance someone ripped the cards out. And there'd only be one reason to do that.

"So?" Merek asks, kneeling next to me.

"Yeah, it's not there," I reply as I squeeze my hands into fists. I shouldn't get mad just yet. One broken unit isn't representative of the rest. I hope.

"What does that mean?"

"Hold on."

Merek pushes himself to his feet and walks away. Out of stress or boredom, I don't know or really care, but I've got nothing to tell him until I know what's going on in this machine.

I reach for my headlamp and slide it over my hair, wincing as I do. The straps on these things don't like braids very much. I've already lost a few hairs because they're designed for the silky-maned or the bald. But their usefulness outweighs their annoyances. And I can handle a little pain. Most of the time.

Pulling myself deeper into the machine, I get my head as close to the card slots as I can. It's more than cramped in here. Razor-edged circuit boards and hastily cut wire stays threaten to gouge any bit of my bare skin that is unfortunate enough to slide across them. These things may be cutting-edge technology, but they built them as fast as possible. As long as they worked, they passed inspection.

I'm so glad I'm not claustrophobic. Ow! Dammit!

With a few curses and a lot of frustration, I get my lamp on the card slots. And...they're wrecked. One half of the slot is bent so far out, nothing could ever stay in there as long as there's gravity. Even if there wasn't, they'd likely float away. A few contacts are blackened, too—someone who didn't want the module to ever work again did this.

I grumble as I slide myself out of the inside of the pod, rolling onto my back as I clear the last panel. I really don't want to do this again, but I may have no choice.

"Find something?" Merek queries as he comes around from the opposite side of the pods. What was he doing over there? Looking for a place to nap? His eyes widen when he sees me. Or rather, when he sees whatever annoyed look is on my face.

"Severe damage," I reply, sitting up and wrapping my arms around my knees. "No way the medical module would ever work without a bunch of part swaps."

"So this pod is defective?"

"No. It's been sabotaged."

His brow gets tight. "Why would anyone want to do that?"

I just stare. He can't be serious, can he? But Merek just returns my stare with an expectant gaze. I really want to roll my eyes at him. Really, truly, honestly do. But he only wants to understand. I just can't explain right now. I don't have the energy.

My forehead drops to my knees, and I sigh. So much for sleep.

"I'll need to check the rest of them," I say and push myself up. "But first, I'm going to talk to Raey. This could put a real bug in her plans."

He nods and walks away as I grab my comm unit from my belt holster and flick it on, rotating the channel to one I know Raey is always on.

"Raey, it's Fana, come in."

"This is Raey. Go ahead." Her words are so distinct, I can hear the flatness of her tone. For a moment, I hesitate, recalling how our last conversation ended. There won't be anything other than business discussed on this call. Or in any other future talk with her. And that really stabs me hard.

With a slow exhale, I key the mic. "Listen, I just found some damage in a pod we received from the *Devant*'s surplus. The entire medical module is missing, and it's not a mistake. Some-one ripped it out and damaged the card slots bad enough that they've got to be replaced. Now I've got to check the rest of these units and make sure the same thing hasn't happened to them."

The acid in my stomach churns as I wait for her to reply. Why is she taking so long? She doesn't need to think about this!

"Okay. So? Do that."

What the hell? Do I need to ask her to be outraged? There's so much we could do for the passengers and crew with those modules.

"Raey, don't you get it? If I find more, that's a serious issue!"

"Not really. We don't need the pods to have the medical module installed."

Merek stares at me as I throw my hands up and scream, shaking my fists at the ceiling. Raey better have heard that from wherever she is.

"Hyuking hell, Raey! The human body doesn't work right if you rip the liver out of it! And I mean like physically tear it out, because that's what someone did to this pod!"

"Fana, the medical module is nowhere near as critical as the liver. If—"

"The damage to this pod is not repairable! That's what I'm saying! And it will definitely cause problems as this thing ages. Do you really want to put someone in it knowing it'll break? Possibly in a really awful way?"

Silence again. I hated when she did this to me before, and I'm seriously considering how to murder her now.

"So, what do you want to do?" Raey asks.

"Why is this on me to decide?"

"You're the one making this into an emergency."

I connect gazes with Merek as my mouth opens. He shakes his head at me as his eyebrows crunch together. I can expect him not to have any suggestions. He doesn't know the consequences of broken tech. I don't know all the risks, either. But Raey has more than some background knowledge about how stasis pods work, and she's even less help.

She better not be getting back at me for spying on her.

I click my comm mic on. "I'm quarantining these pods until I can check them all, top to bottom."

"Understood," Raey says. *"Sorry, I've got to go. We're transferring Baati's body back to the* Devant *now. Raey out."*

She signs off, and I slip down the side of the pod, shutting my eyes as I lean against it.

Merek leans down to check on me. "Everything okay?"

"No," I reply, knocking the back of my head into the pod. "Nothing's okay. Not at all."

WITHDRAWAL

CERI

I DON'T CARE FOR Fana's droopy face. It's a serious contradiction to have such a sad look on someone who's cheered me up on so many occasions. Her head's slumped, too. Or maybe it's her entire body. It's difficult to tell from our cross-legged position across from the airlock on level ninety. She reminds me of a child in need of a parent's embrace. While I'm no parent, if it helps to pull the gloom off her shoulders, I just might be willing.

"What makes you think it's deliberate?" I ask. Merek and Efa join us, sliding forward to take a spot on each side of Fana. "Wouldn't they realize we'd find out?"

"Maybe it wasn't planned," Efa suggests. "Like one of the crew did it on their own. I'm sure there's a lot of them upset over what happened."

"We are, too," Merek adds. "No one wanted to kill that kid. That I'm sure."

"How many pods do you think could be broken?" I ask.

Fana shrugs and hangs her head. Her silence is bothering me to no end, and it won't stop until I do something about it. I reach out and take her hand, giving it a squeeze. Fana jerks, her eyes widening before a small smile appears on her face, along with a bit of red on her cheeks. She covers my hand in both of hers and gives me an apologetic look.

"You can't blame yourself for this," I say.

The rail car chimes, and Sayer exits onto the level, taking a quick glance at the airlock—open but quiet—and strolls over to us, hands in pockets. For being the one who's often raging mad over the slightest trespass, he's a bit of a contradiction right now.

"Nothing from them, huh?" he asks, stopping a few paces away from our huddle.

"No," I reply with a shake of my head. "Why? Are you expecting them to come apologize for making assumptions about us?"

Sayer snorts. I expected as much. Perhaps he was hoping, as we all were, that some miracle would happen. Or that Azazhi would realize it would be better to continue the exchange. I'm hopeful about the fact that our ships are still connected, but it's the only time I would be.

"Everything okay there?" Sayer asks, motioning toward Fana and my clasped hands with a nod of his head. Fana disconnects, pulling her hands into her lap, and I glare at Sayer. If he was so worried about her, he might have just asked her directly.

A klaxon screeches through the level, pounding our eardrums and sending us rocketing to our feet. We share a confused glance and scan the area for some sign of trouble. But other than the siren, everything seems fine.

The ship shudders, knocking us to the deck. My heart jumps as my hands fly out to stop the impact. But the *Stratford* rolls, unbalancing me. I crash hard on my side with a cry.

Five seconds later, an automated voice booms through the area: *"Warning. Warning. Warning. Separation routine halted. Check all ship-to-ship locks and close all hatches. Warning. Warning..."*

"The *Devant* is pulling away!" Fana shrieks, vaulting to her feet. "We've got to stop them!"

My head spins. My shoulder throbs in agony. Even the wound on my side aches fiercely. Instinct and training takes over. I fight to get to my feet as I throw a glance toward the ladder. It's the only means of escape if we need it. And I fear we will.

Merek yanks Efa up from the floor, pulling her to him. Her eyes roll back in her head as her body goes limp. Sayer goes to help, but Fana grabs him and shoves him toward the other ladder.

"Shut the hatch!" she yells. "We've got to seal the level off!"

My heart drops out of my chest. Fana's worried about decompression? Bish! Of course she is! How much time do we have? It can't be much. I reach for my comm unit, only to find it missing. I scan the deck until I find it several body lengths away. A quick dash and I retrieve it, keying the mic the moment it's in my hand.

"Raey, come in!" I shout. "Raey! Pick up now!"

"Ceri? What just happened? What was that?"

"The *Devant* is disengaging! Call Azazhi! Get him to stop!"

She gasps. *"That can't be! Okay. Okay. I'll do what I can."*

It's as much as I can ask. I lift my thumb off the mic key. Now I've got to focus. Two ships as large as the *Stratford* and the *Devant* maneuvering this close to each other isn't just dangerous. It's a disaster in the making.

My breath becomes short as my accident outside the ship flashes before my eyes. This could be a million times worse. But I can stop this from happening. I can solve this.

"The *Devant* can't leave unless we power down our magnetic locks, right?" I ask Fana. "Could we keep them engaged and stop them?"

That'd force Azazhi to talk to me. And now that I know he gave me broken pods, I'll be pressing him for more. Much more.

Fana shakes her head, the whites of her eyes showing. "Don't forget how fast we're going. Just a minor change to their vector would rip the entire side of the ship off."

Bish. My gut twists just thinking about it. "Merek, take Efa, and secure everyone else," I say. "Get them to shut every major bulkhead door all the way up to level one. No exceptions."

"Okay, but," Merek protests, "you've got to evacuate this level, too!"

"I will, I will! Just go!"

"What's next?" Sayer shouts as he comes rushing back, his chest rising and falling in half seconds. He sticks his hands out as if he's ready to run with whatever someone shoves into them.

I glance at Fana for an answer, my head spinning with the overload of emergencies hitting me at once. She shrugs and shakes her head as she turns away from me, peering across the level. For what? What is she thinking? And why isn't she telling me?

Dammit. We need those pods, even if they're missing parts. But as I search my mind for a solution, I come up with nothing. It'd be so much easier if this were a battle. I wouldn't have to think. Neither would my crew. We'd just move, trusting each other to know what to do and where to go.

A lump forms in my throat. This might be the moment where all of my hopes of being a good leader collide with the reality of my inexperience.

"Uh…" Fana scratches her head. "Are there any pressure suits on this level?"

"No. Why?" I step closer to her, my hands wide.

"Well…"

My gaze connects with Fana's, searching for more. Fear races deep within her eyes, and it shakes me. We need action. Now.

"Warning. Warning. Warning. Serious hull breach is imminent. Shut all airtight doors and evacuate the level immediately. This is not a drill. Warning. Warning…"

My heart skips a beat. Or maybe the tightness in my chest just felt that way. Bish. Azazhi's making a huge mistake. Raey better make him realize it before he rips a hole in my ship.

Raey. How hyuking stupid I am! Why didn't I make her connect me to him? I should be the one forcing him to stop. She'll only do what she needs to in order to survive. That doesn't include getting the pods we're owed.

I take off, racing toward the airlock, hoping I can get there in time. Or at least that I don't get blown out of the ship. Maybe I deserve to for failing my ship and its passengers.

"Where are you going?" Fana calls after me. Sayer must answer her, as a second later, their boots slap the deck, trying to catch up. I can't let them. There's no time left to wait.

I key my comm as I run. "Raey, come in. What did he say?"

"He's not replying!" Raey says. *"I don't understand why he'd do this."*

No. She can't be that naïve. She's working with him. I can almost sense it. Maybe this was their plan all along. Hyuk. I'm such a fool to have trusted her.

"Yes, you do," I shoot back. "You know what kind of bastard he is. He'll space us all and come back to salvage the *Stratford* for more equipment."

"What will you do?"

"Save us."

The airlock status lights are flashing at a frantic pace. I scan the panel, searching for a way to disengage the locks. Once they're off, the *Devant* will float free, and the *Stratford* will be safe from damage. It's the last thing I want to do, but I'm out of options.

The ship bucks again, throwing me into the wall. My face hits first, smacking my cheekbone with a resonant crunch. I bounce off, waving my arms to stay upright as I struggle to keep my sight on the panel.

Found it! The sequence to disconnect the locks is on the keypad. I reach out and tap in the security authorization code. Memorizing it was good for something, after all.

The airlock hisses. A chill colder than death penetrates my body. Needles stab everywhere on my skin. I gasp and tremble, stumbling back. My breath explodes out of me. I struggle to inhale, even as I curse myself for being such an idiot.

Wrong. I did it wrong. Hyuk. I may have just killed us.

My teeth chatter so hard I might bite my lip. I can't breathe, I can't move. I'll suffocate if I keep standing here. It's cold. It's so hyuking cold. Even as my body screams to run, my brain's stuck on that one thought.

Cold. Stop the cold.

"The airlock! Shut it! Shut it!" Fana cries, but I can't respond. In the pulse of a heartbeat, she crashes into my back, her hand shooting out from under my arm to slap the door and pound the airlock door control. Her arms wrap around me and yank me away from the door. Sayer's there helping. Thoughts return as my mind thaws.

"Bish, she's freezing!" he hisses.

They rub my limbs until the stiffness disappears. My knees buckle when they're loose enough to bend again. Fana and Sayer catch me and let me down easy.

Out the airlock window, something stirs. A shimmer forms over the *Devant*'s hull, and for a split second, the airlock port blurs. The two ships separate, and stars fill the void where the *Devant* just was. I stare into the open space, a lump forming in my throat. This vision that once sent my pulse racing has turned frosty, a hard reminder of the distance that now separates Commander Azazhi and me. It was always there, but for a brief time, I believed I'd bridged that gap.

What a fool I was.

PAYMENT

—— • ——

FANA

"WHAT ARE YOU DOING here?" I ask Sayer as he slips down the latter to forty-nine, hopping once when his feet touch the deck.

When he approaches with a big grin, I get tense. Maybe I should've hidden before he saw me—just ducked behind the stasis pod I've been examining and avoided any potential conversation. Not that I would have had a chance. Sayer can be as stealthy as Ceri, and now I find myself face to face with a person I'd rather not be talking to because I've got a lot of work ahead of me.

"Looking for you, actually," Sayer replies, leaning on the pod. "How come you're not up with the others in the meeting?"

"It's not a meeting. Yet. And I need to check this pod before I go because it may have some clues."

Sayer frowns. "Clues? What are you looking for?"

Oh hell. There I go, opening my mouth and letting out potential conversation starters. I don't have time to explain something highly technical to someone who stopped their education at twelve years of age. Though, Ceri's in the same situation, and she's sharp. Maybe a quick answer won't hurt.

"These pods are damaged. I think it's deliberate, but I'm trying to get proof, one way or the other."

His eyes widen. "Deliberate? Like sabotage? So they threw us a bunch of destroyed pods and then took off?"

"That's exactly what I'm hoping didn't happen, but I need to do some tests and find out." I dig my head into the guts of the pod in hopes I won't have to answer any more of his questions. Ceri could be waiting for me. The sooner I finish here, the sooner I can get up to her.

"Hyuk." Sayer drops next to me and goes quiet. Maybe he's thinking through the reasons why the *Devant*'s crew would do that. That's easy—Azazhi ordered them to. The better question is what the commander had in mind.

"Wouldn't they know we would check?" he asks, getting closer.

"Of course they would." I shine my light on the medical system's card slots. *Yep. Just like all the others.* Someone with a flat tool bent all the connectors way far out. There's some blackening on each of the finger slots, suggesting the damage was done when the machine was powered. *Stupid.* No one on my old engineering team would have been so reckless as to risk death by electrocution.

"Raey better not have known about this," I mutter.

"What? Raey's involved?"

Bish, I shouldn't have said that out loud. Again with my over-sharing of speculation. At least he can't see my face and the massive amount of regret that's likely all over it. I'll just pretend I didn't hear him, and he'll drop it.

Sayer grabs my arms and pulls me from the stasis pod. I yelp as I hit my head on the bottom of the pod's tub. But flinching away only makes it easier for him to get me out.

Did he just read my mind?

"Hey!" I shout as he twists me around to face him. Amazingly, he's done this from his cross-legged position next to the pod, with only his torso moving. I can only stare. He didn't mean to hurt me, but he's more than capable of it.

I swallow hard. He still hasn't said what he wants from me. It'd be just my luck that it's something minor, like asking me for advice about girls or getting me to build him some kind of game. Whatever it is, it'd likely be less stressful than what he's about to put me through. Maybe I should scream and run. But that might be an overreaction. And given my terrible running skills, I wouldn't get far.

"Tell me what you know," Sayer demands.

"Nothing." I duck my head. "There's no evidence of anything. That's why I'm doing this."

"But you suspect Raey," he says, lifting a finger. "There's got to be a reason for that. Why?"

I press my lips together, forcing myself not to speak. I've already gotten myself into a black hole that I won't escape. Raey's my problem, and no one else's. And we still need her help, especially if these pods turn out to be useless.

"Why did you want to see me, anyway?" I ask.

Sayer pokes my shoulder and sneers, "Don't change the subject!"

"Ow!"

He does it again. I pull back, smacking at his hand. But Sayer's too fast. And persistent. I swipe at him again as he threatens to dig his fingertips into me. He evades and needles me once more. My eyes narrow, and I threaten him with my fist.

He just does it again.

"Enough!" I reach for a heavy tool to drive my point home, but my distraction earns me a pop right in the forehead. "Alright! Alright!" My hands fly up in mock surrender. "But I'm telling Ceri what a jerk you are."

"She already knows." He grins, then motions peace between us and prompts me with a nod to continue.

"I overheard a call between Raey and the commander of the *Devant*," I say. "It sounded suspicious, but I could be jumping to conclusions. She's been helping us. A lot. So there's no reason to think she's up to no good."

"Yet, here you are, checking the pods to see if she's had a hand in this, right?"

I shake my head. "Raey'd never do this. It'd be against everything she believes. She wouldn't know how to unless someone told her, and even then it'd be a lot of work for one person to disable sixty units."

Sayer's eyes narrow. "But there is a question in your mind about her, isn't there?"

I look away. There's no denying it. All I'll be doing is dodging his verbal pokes if I try. And he'll get mad at me for doing it. I don't need more enemies. There's an entire ship of them not that far away.

"I want to believe she's on our side, too," Sayer says. "So let me help you figure it out. Let's investigate together and find out whose side she's on. We can get more done if we work with each other. Raey knows you well, but she won't suspect me. I can watch her when you can't."

I blink. *Wow, that's unexpected. He wants to help me?* And after he crossed the line by poking me? I'm not one of his crewmates. Well, I am, but not like that. Still, he should respect someone who's older than him. And not a guy.

But he's also making sense. A lot.

A long sigh escapes from my lungs. I can't be in two places at once, that's for sure. And Raey would never suspect him of spying on her. He might even be better than me at it. No, hold on. He'd absolutely be better than me.

I nod. "Okay. I accept."

"But!" Sayer holds up a hand. "If I'm going to help you, I'd appreciate you doing something for me, too."

My forehead gets tight. "What?"

"Those beam weapons the *Devant*'s security agents have. I bet you understand how they work."

I shrug. "Of course I do. Theoretically, anyway. I've never worked on one."

Sayer gets a wide smirk across his face, and I shrink a little as I prepare myself to hear his request.

"I want you to build one for me." He raises a finger. "Just one. Then, when we've got it perfected, we'll make more for the rest of the crew."

My head is already moving back and forth in refusal. I don't even want to consider the reason he wants that or what he's planning to use it for. Sayer has a strong need for justice, and he may think powerful weapons are the means to that end. I should remind him why he's on this ship and why his family left Earth. Maybe then he'll stop believing he can achieve everything with force.

"The *Devant* won't attack us again, no matter what," I say. "You gave them too much to be afraid of last time. Commander Azazhi just wants the excavation gear, and he'll be gone. We'll never see him again."

"And what if he decides he wants everything on this ship, including us?" Sayer makes a fist. "Or what about another ship? Yours can't be the only one that heard our distress call."

I wrinkle my nose. I want to tell him no other ship has me. *Had.* Others might be curious, but not all of them will have the authority and capability to make their ship commanders change vectors. And most won't be anywhere near close enough to try. The *Devant* did it because we weren't that far away and the ship was fast enough to catch up. No other ship could match our speed.

Our. I've got to stop thinking that. I'm part of the *Stratford* crew now, and very glad for it. I want to protect every person on this ship, but that doesn't mean I want to arm Sayer with deadlier weapons. It's bad enough the *Devant* left any of theirs here.

"No other ship can do what the *Devant* did," I say. "I doubt they'd even want to try. Once the *Devant* is gone, we'll be on our own again. Forever."

Sayer leans in. "You say that as if you know what it's like to be alone. We've always been alone here, Fana. It's only ever been us. It only ever will be us for at least another three hundred years."

No, Sayer. I get it. "Your argument is out there," I say, pointing toward the last known position of my former ship. "Yes, we're alone, but we've been preparing for that. Every day. You've been part of all our efforts. The chance—"

"Chance? What was the chance of your ship finding this one?"

"Fairly good, actually. Don't forget how advanced the *Devant* is."

Sayer flips his hand in the air. "You know what I'm saying. Don't complicate it with minor details."

"You're right. I do," I reply. "Which is why I feel the need to correct you."

He scoffs and tosses his head. "Do you want my help or not? All I'm asking for is a bit of your time. I think you can manage that."

Doesn't he realize time is the one thing I don't have?

My fingers slip through my braids, feeling the grime pressed in them and realizing how much I really need a bath. I haven't had one in a week. I will, once I finish the thousand other things I need to do. Or maybe I should just quit now and soak myself for the rest of the day. I can ignore all my problems that way.

Still, Sayer's waiting for an answer, as impatient as any teenage boy can be. I really need his skills. If Raey's truly innocent, the only way to prove it will be with his help.

"If I do this for you," I say, wagging my finger at him, "you're backing me up until I'm satisfied with Raey, okay? And we clear her before I even consider opening up one of those guns to have a look inside. Got it?"

"Absolutely. I trust you." Sayer grins and puts his hands behind his head. "It's not like you're going anywhere."

I wish I knew what he means by that, because it's making me shiver.

EXACTION

—— • ——

CERI

THE BLANKET AROUND MY shoulders does little to remove the chill in my bones. To push it away, Fana feeds me something warm and sweet, but it only sits heavy in my stomach. Efa suggests a hot shower, but I decline. It won't help. After my total failure as a leader, this feeling may be permanent.

Right now, all I prefer is the coziness of level two and the closeness of those I trust most: Efa, Merek, Seren, and, not least, Fana. We huddle together near the warmth of the navigation console, each of us staring at our feet in silence. No one wants to be the one to break the fragile stillness.

There's no question we'll make the exchange happen again. But there are zero ideas on how we might do that. The *Devant* hasn't answered our calls, not even when Raey uses her comm. They're going to string this out for however long they can because they know we're desperate. Likely Azazhi thinks the longer he waits, the more we'll be willing to give in to whatever new demands he comes up with.

He could be right.

Fana slides closer and rests her head on my shoulder. I flinch, only because it's unexpected, but she takes it as rejection and pulls away, turning her head toward Efa. She gives me a small glare as if I was doing something wrong. Likely I am. Fana was only trying to comfort me. I should tell her that's an impossible task.

Instead, I nudge her with my elbow and motion for her to rest her head again. She smiles but demurs, her cheeks reddening a little. At least Efa nods approvingly at my actions, though when she became my mother, I can't be sure. Still, it settles my stomach a little to know I chose the right response.

A buzz comes from the console. We all share frowns until Seren pops up to look, her lips crushing together as she searches the controls.

Seren's entire face lights up as she dives toward the console, frantically tapping out a command, then going still for an uneasy moment. I hold in a breath, waiting for her to speak.

"It's a call," she says, then gasps. "Azazhi's calling!"

I shoot up, tossing the blanket off and flying to Seren's side. The others press in against us, each clamoring for a chance to see and leaning to peer over our shoulders.

"Answer it!" I urge.

Seren's already set up the mic and speaker, and three seconds later, Azazhi's gravelly voice fills the level, a low-pitched distortion added to it by our half-functional system.

"I'm sure you're there, Ceri. Acknowledge," he says.

"I am. What do you want?"

"Anyone else there?"

Efa shakes her head, motioning to Fana. I nod. We don't want to destroy this conversation before it starts. The commander's opinions of any member of my crew are suspect. He could end this call simply because someone he doesn't like is here. I'm very far from taking chances with this.

"Yes. One of my crew. She can hear whatever you're about to say."

Silence on the other side. He's received my reply. I guarantee it. Azazhi's just making me wait so he can claim control of this negotiation. Only he knows if there's to be one or not.

"Specialist Baati Girma was murdered on your ship," he says, his voice empty of emotion. *"You and that group of brats you call a crew allowed it to happen. I'd be justified in demanding you surrender every passenger and every bit of excavation equipment to me immediately. If you refused, I'd also be justified in taking control of your ship."*

My insides twist. If he meant that to force a reaction, he'll get one. How dare he threaten us? Doesn't he remember how he lost a full-on battle to my crew of *brats*?

"Of course I would refuse," I growl. "You don't get to—"

"But I'm merciful. I won't leave children with nothing, even if you deserve it. All I want is one person. And you'll hand them over if you want any more of my stasis pods."

Fana wraps her arms about her body and ducks her head. I reach out to squeeze her shoulder. She needs to understand I won't allow her to be used as a bargaining chip. Once she looks up and our gazes connect, she relaxes, the edges of her mouth curving upward.

I turn to the communications console again, ready to make a few demands of my own. Efa grabs my arm before I do, her eyes pleading caution. As much as I know she's right to, the fire inside me only wants to burn Azazhi with as many words as I can come up with. And just like he says, I would be justified in doing it.

Though, wait. Am I just making an assumption it's Fana he wants? What if it's me? No. He already said he's not interested in any of my crew.

Bish. Could it be one of our passengers? Never. But I've got to remember this is a negotiation. Every demand he makes is just a test to see what I'll give in to. I won't fail my people again. Not while I'm still the leader here.

"Who do you want?" I ask.

"*Who?*" Azazhi scoffs. "*I want that assassin. The one who butchered my crew member. I don't care who it is or how old they are. If they did it, then you'll hand them over.*"

My fingers dig into the composite of the console's armrest, so hard the material pops and cracks. Efa whispers something in my ear. I don't hear it. I hear nothing other than that hyuking monster's words. He's lucky he's on his own ship. If he were here, my hands would squeeze the life from his throat.

"I won't be turning over a member of my crew so you can execute them," I growl.

Silence. His intentional pauses are grinding me hard. I know he's trying to irritate me, yet I can't stop reacting. Any more of this and I'll explode.

"*Yes, you will. You'll bring that murderer to me so I can blow them out the airlock one body part at a time if I wish, because that's what they deserve. To suffer and die like the filth they are.*"

"Damn you! I'm going—"

Fana and Efa slap their hands over my mouth and tear me away from the console. I twist, throwing Fana off. Merek joins in, locking my arms behind me and dragging me to the far corner of the level. Efa follows, leveling a narrow-eyed stare at me.

"You're going to what?" Azazhi taunts.

"Sorry," Seren says. "Ceri stepped away from the comm for a moment. She'll be back in a minute."

Azazhi chuckles. *"Is that so? Does that put you in charge now? Maybe you're more cool-headed than she is."*

"And maybe I'm not."

I'd smile if Efa wasn't in my face, warning me to keep silent. I'll obey. For now.

I glance at Fana to make sure she's okay. She should know better than to surprise one of us like that. If Efa hadn't been helping her, I might have hurt her. But she only watches me with that watery gaze of hers. I'm glad she's alright, because now I can refocus on finding the best way to tell Azazhi to go die.

"You need to step it down," Efa hisses. "Or he'll end the call and we lose."

"Like hell!" I shoot back. "That bastard needs to be put in his place."

"Yes, but not now!"

"Then when, Efa? We already know what he'll do to our crew! We're nothing to him! He would just as soon execute us all as he would turn us into his slaves! There's no way—"

Efa smacks my cheek. Not hard, but enough to get my attention. It's fair. I'd do the same to her if she was out of control, too.

"Pods," she says. "That's what we're after. Agree to whatever you want. Or not, but you've got to get him to reconnect the ships and transfer more of them, or we lose."

I exhale, taking the moment to return my mind to rational thinking. Efa's kept her calm; otherwise, this would be a very different situation. Though, I can remember not a few times when it was reversed. Neither of us needs a reminder of that. Those desperate moments are still all too clear in our minds. This may be another, but it's one I can still salvage.

"Okay." I nod and exhale. Merek releases me, and I return to the console, reaching out to touch Fana's arm and share my best look of apology with her. Her lips curve upward in understanding as she finds my hand and squeezes it. I return her smile, gaining strength from our connection.

Now to get what we need for our passengers.

"I'm back," I say.

"Done with your tantrum, then?"

His attempt to provoke is entirely expected, and I'm well prepared to deflect it.

"Say whatever you want," I reply calmly. "But you will never forget how my little crew of brats destroyed nearly a hundred of your adult agents. Now, will you reconnect the ships so we can get back to this exchange like we've already agreed, or will you let your need to punish children get in your way?"

This time, his silence is different. I've found a vulnerability on him, and he's reeling from my strike. I'll thank Efa and Fana for stopping me later. Merek and Seren too. Everyone played a part in keeping me focused.

"No," Commander Azazhi replies. *"That won't happen. Not until you produce the killer and hand them over."*

A flame ignites inside me, growing slowly as it travels up my body. I grind my teeth to keep it from engulfing me. Then I breathe—simply breathe—to remain in control. I've got every option in the universe to choose from right now. That only disappears when I let him provoke me. It's too easy for him.

Maybe I should show him how quickly I learn.

"You can go to hell, then," I snarl.

Azazhi chortles. *"Are you sure that's what you want to go with?"*

"I'm sure you can blow yourself out the airlock, you hyuking piece of bish. I will never turn over any of my crew for you to abuse, even if I thought any of them were guilty. And they're not. Your specialist deserved what they got for wandering off. I'm far from sad over your loss."

Fana's mouth drops open. Efa sighs. I can almost imagine the look on Azazhi's face. Good. I hope my words stab him deep and hard. He needs to understand the crew of the *Stratford* can do everything he can.

"Then this conversation is done," Azazhi says after a few seconds—a moment where he needed to regain his humility and realize he can't control us, I'm sure.

The connection goes silent as I wait for his offer of compromise. More posturing. He should realize by now that he's overused this tactic. It's no longer effective. I'll just fold my arms and wait for his patience to give out.

And wait.

And wait.

"Bish," Merek says, after what seems like an hour. "He's not going to reply, is he?"

I hold up a hand. "Just be patient."

Seren frowns and leans over the comm screen to check. A second later, she gasps, her hand flying out to tap commands into the comm system.

"Forget it," Fana says. "We've lost connection."

My forehead gets tight. The comm system is more than reliable. At least that's what Fana assured us. It has to be working. It would have given us an error or something. Wouldn't it?

"Well, get it back, then!" I say. "We're not done!"

Fana turns to me. "He is. For now, at least."

Hyuk. That's what she means.

"You had to go on the offensive, didn't you?" Efa shakes her head and sighs, walking away. Merek glances between us, his gaze troubled.

"No. Come on," I say. "He'll be back. Just wait."

But as I say it, realization hits me square in the gut. I overdid it. I pushed back too hard and gave Azazhi power over me. Again. But as long as he insists one of my crew is guilty, the battlefield is uneven. It doesn't matter if it's false. I can't surrender my crew to execution. Azazhi wouldn't either, but he cornered me with it, and I reacted.

And that's what Efa is mad at. As usual, I've messed up everything.

HUNT

CERI

I SHUFFLE TO THE side of the wall that is deepest in shadow and slide down it to press my back against its chilly surface. The cold numbs me, and I welcome it. There's freedom in the void of emotion that comes, even if it's only temporary. A few seconds of feeling nothing reminds me I'm still capable of rational thought.

When Chief Generys locked me away in that closet, I could either accept my situation or succumb to it. The choice was obvious. I would never allow the adults to win. It took time, but I learned to appreciate the oppressive space I was in and make the best of it.

I wouldn't mind returning there, if only for a little while. Those four walls are more than familiar. I have mastery over them. Out here, in front of my crew, my friends, my passengers, there's a universe of problems to face. Foes to fight. I'm losing those battles and solving nothing. As much as I want to run away, I know I can't. So this dark corner must suffice until I can figure a way to fix things.

Azazhi didn't beat me in a negotiation. I beat myself. I let my overconfidence in my thinking rule my decisions, and I must do better. As long as the *Devant* is nearby, I'll have that chance, though I suspect there's little time left to make corrections.

"Come out," Efa says, crouching before me with a hard gaze. "We've got decisions to be made."

"I will," I mumble. "I just need a moment."

Efa tilts her head and eyes me, lips pressed. She wants to say more, but she can't. Not while there are others here. I'm already compromising my leadership by pouting in a corner. If any more of the crew were here, it could become an issue.

Seren and Merek join Efa after a minute. Fana lags behind, her shoulders down. I hope it's the situation that's troubling her and not me. I'm already the source of one of her problems. At some point, we need to talk about that, because I...I'm...not sure what to think about me and her. And I don't have time to consider it.

Still, it aches to see her kneading her hands like that. I motion for her to come sit by me, and after a moment of hesitation, she takes a place between Seren and me along the wall.

"We could still work this out," Merek says. "Maybe give him something real enough that'll convince him to reconnect the ships."

"Like what?" Seren asks.

Merek shrugs. "We can say anything, really. It doesn't matter. We could make it up. As long as it's appealing but still vague enough that he'll want to know more. Like, you could tell him we might have found clues about the attack."

"Or you can really look into what happened," Efa counters, "and prove to him everyone on our crew is innocent."

"That might uncover something we don't want to know."

Efa's mouth drops open. "Do you really think one of us would murder someone like that?"

Merek puts a hand on her leg. "Don't forget who we are. Or what we've done."

"We're different now. Everything's different now!"

"Is it?"

She pushes his hand away as they collapse into bickering, neither giving the other opinion even a second's worth of consideration. I lower my head into my hands, my fingers rubbing my temples as their words stab needles into my ears. Is this what happens to two people in love?

It's too much. I pound the deck with my boot, the boom echoing across the level.

"I am not investigating my crew!" I shout. They clamp their mouths shut and stare, eyes wide at the intensity of my voice.

"Is there anyone else awake on the ship besides your crew?" Fana asks, leaning closer.

I blink. "What?"

"Could there be anyone else awake?"

"No," Efa says. "Everyone else left."

I frown. "Why are you asking?"

Fana takes a breath and swallows, the fear in her eyes all too clear. I reach for her hands, but stop myself. She's here with us, so she's okay. I'm sure she realizes that. Maybe it's why she thought to bring up the question.

But what the hyuk does she know?

"Last week," she begins, "before the fire on the stasis level, I was down on one-thirty-five fixing the flash distillers, and I thought I heard something. Then, I saw something! It could have been someone. I'm not sure, but it scared the hell out of me."

Fana's face pales as she replays that moment in her head. Whatever she saw or imagined terrified her. It wasn't one of us, definitely. None of the crew would do that to Fana. We've already had enough terror for a lifetime.

"Hold on," Merek says and bites his lower lip. "Rabbit said…Don't you remember? He said there were others like him. They wouldn't have gone with the adults. Could it be one of them?"

Rabbit said that alright. I remember. And it puts a tightness in my chest. Did we fail to discover a threat on this ship?

"How could we not have come across them in all this time?" I ask.

"Maybe the fight with the *Devant* forced them into hiding," Merek suggests.

"Then why would they come out and kill someone?" Efa challenges. "Rabbit wasn't violent. Why would they be any different?"

A chill hits me, and I shiver. No one like Rabbit could have sliced someone's throat so effectively. This is pointing to someone with the training to kill. And I know everyone on this ship like that. They're my crew.

"Maybe they lost their minds," Fana replies. "Isolation can mess with people's heads. Make them see things. If Baati was the first person they saw, they could have panicked."

"Maybe we should clear the lower levels," Seren says. "It's the only way to be sure."

Merek scoffs. "Don't you remember how many of us Captain Daga needed to do that? He had nearly a hundred soldiers plowing over every little space. We've got less than a quarter of what he had. And we've got to keep the ship running. It's an impossible task."

Merek needs a reminder of how many impossible tasks we've already pulled off. And it might not be nearly as difficult as he thinks. Just the idea of some rogue adult sneaking around in machine access could be enough for Azazhi to reconnect our ships. We'd need to find something or someone quickly, though. He's hungry for vengeance, and I must keep him from just grabbing one of my crew to extract his justice.

"Seren might be right, though," I say, standing up and pushing myself out of the darkness.

"What?" Efa blinks, then shakes her head. "You can't be serious."

"Listen." I raise a hand. "We've only assumed it's just us here. That could be very wrong. Maybe there is a killer down below. We can't take the risk of not checking. Do you want to let Fana go down there alone again and find out the hard way? And from now on, no one goes below ninety without armed escort."

"There's only fifteen of us, Ceri," Efa says. "Properly clearing every floor on this ship could take a month. Or more. And that'd be at the expense of everything else we're trying to accomplish."

"We don't need to check every level," Merek says. "I don't think we need to check any at all. If there are others like Rabbit still here, let them be. They haven't caused us any problems."

"Except the one who lost us our chance to get replacement stasis pods," Fana corrects. "And the more I think about it, the more I'm sure I saw someone. No way will I go down there by myself again."

Merek rolls his eyes and looks to Efa for support. But she's looking at me, a grimace forming on her face. It was so much simpler when it was just the two of us and our squad. Yet now that we've traded oppression for freedom, every choice we make gets more difficult. I'll never wish to be under adults again, though I would give almost anything just to hear a little advice from my parents. Not that I'd ever want them to know how big of a mess the *Stratford* has become.

"What happens if we find someone?" Seren asks. "Would we turn them over to the *Devant*?"

I run a hand through my hair. When I said no one else dies on this ship, insane old men were not in my thoughts. Perhaps they should have been. It's a guarantee anyone who's turned over to Azazhi is dead. I'd hate myself for doing it, but if that was the only way to protect my crew, I would do it every time. Maybe I could plead with Azazhi for mercy. There wouldn't be much satisfaction in executing a mindless old man.

"Let me make that decision when the time comes," I reply. "If the time comes."

Huh. Here I am, considering the death of someone who may not exist, just because desperation is coursing through me. But I've failed my crew and my passengers too often. That ends now, even if I have to scour every level on my own to pull up a clue.

"I'm going," I say. "Who's coming with me?"

"Ceri, no! *You* run this ship!" Efa counters.

"We all run this ship. I only try to keep everything together." I crouch before her so she can see the intent on my face. "I've been bish at that lately, and I need to fix that. This is something I can do, so I'm doing it."

Efa nods and lowers her gaze. She may not like it, but I'm glad she's accepted my decision. I hope she understands how important that is to me.

"We don't need everyone," I add. "I want a small squad only. Four people maximum. Everyone else has work to do."

"I'll go!" Seren volunteers.

Efa folds her arms. She's staying out of it. Merek too. With how connected they felt to Rabbit, I'm not surprised. And I get it. I'd rather they run things in my absence, anyway. Likely they'll do better than I would.

"I'm sorry," Fana says to me, her eyes full of regret. "But this doesn't sound like my kind of thing."

"It's not," I say and smile, glad she's decided for herself. I turn to Seren. "Who else do we want?"

"Tegan," Seren replies with more than a little certainty. "And Niah."

I shake my head. "As much as I'd want her experience on the lower levels, Niah's not in any kind of battle-ready condition, and after what she's sacrificed, she shouldn't ever have to raise another weapon ever again. Niah deserves her retirement as a soldier."

Everyone gives a grim nod. I'm thankful they understand Niah has more value to us than her combat expertise.

"Then Rhys," Seren says, completely expectedly. "Maybe Sayer, too."

"No," Merek says. "He's got to organize the upper-level defense in case Azazhi does something stupid, like attempt to repeat the last battle."

"He won't," Efa says. "He's not that stupid."

"He's not stupid at all," I add. "All the more reason to prepare for anything. That includes ensuring our ship is secure, from the engines to command and control. If we say we own it all, then that should be true."

"So when will you go?" Merek asks.

I connect my gaze with them and gain strength from their confidence in me. Likely I'd need as much as I can get for the coming days. My battle of words with Azazhi is far from over.

"We go now," I reply.

SCRUTINY

FANA

Sayer and I meet on thirty-one, where Deryn, Aidan, and Mari are organizing supplies. They're our first stop in gathering information about Raey. We're not telling them that, of course, which is why I'm nervous about this. If one of them tells Ceri what we're doing, it's all over. It's a good thing she'll be focused on finding a murderer.

"Hang back," I say to Sayer as we approach the three of them.

"Why?" he asks.

"Because you might intimidate them, and then they won't give us honest answers."

Sayer frowns. "Why would you think that?"

"Because you intimidate me."

Sayer huffs and moves to lean against a pile of sacks, crossing his arms while he watches me walk away. I smile at him to show my gratitude for his cooperation, but he only rolls his eyes and looks away. I'll let him have his chance to ask questions. Rhys especially seems to get along with him well. I'm sure they'd have a lot to discuss. For now, I prefer a softer approach.

"Hey," I say to Mari, who turns to stare at me with a raised eyebrow, a heavy sack on her shoulder. I motion to her to put it down, and she lets it slide back onto the pallet it came from.

"Hi," Mari replies. "Do you need my help or something?"

"Yeah, kinda." I stuff my hands into the pockets of my coveralls. "I'm just trying to remember where I put my tools. Raey said she saw them around the new pods we just received. I checked and couldn't find them. Do you remember seeing a few black satchels with a pink lining?"

I hope Sayer catches on quickly to what I'm doing. It won't be hard to get the answers we need this way, as none of the crew will suspect I'm after something very different than tools. They might even offer information about Raey I wasn't aware of. That's where my plan becomes highly effective. At least I hope that's what happens.

"Um," Mari replies as her eyebrow drops and crashes into her other one, her forehead wrinkling along with it. "You know I wasn't involved in moving pods, right?"

Oops. Of course she wasn't. How'd I forget that? The only time Mari was down near the exchange was when she was searching for Baati. Now to ungracefully bow out of this conversation.

"Yeah." I chuckle. "I knew that. I was just hoping you might have seen them while you were down there."

Mari stares again, as if she's trying to figure out if I'm serious or not. All I can do is stare back. And after a minute of our staring contest, she just shrugs.

"Sorry," she says.

I give her a smile and reply, "Don't worry about it."

With nothing left for me to say to her, our awkward silence ends with Mari hefting the sack onto her shoulder and me shuffling away with reddening cheeks. If I want to make the best out of this investigation, I'd better get my head together; otherwise, we'll gather no information at all.

I move over to Deryn next, since he's close by, though I take my time and pretend to wait until he's done transporting a heavy crate to a stack over by the rail car. The thing is so large it doesn't seem possible for him to see where he's going. Yet he's at his destination in a much shorter time than I estimated. *Okay. So what's my reason for talking to him?* Deryn wasn't anywhere near level ninety. I have no clue what he's been doing.

Damn, I really should have considered this before we got here.

"Hey, Fana, what's up?" he says as he returns, his face dripping in sweat. He's also a bit...*yuck*...as if he hadn't washed himself in a few days. I've got a bad feeling that's true.

"Uh..."

Great. In the time it took him to drop that crate off and come back, I could have overhauled three air filtration units and changed their filters. How I can't come up with more than a single syllable to utter is ridiculous.

"Let me guess," Deryn says. "You want to ask me about the tests I helped Raey run on the stasis pods, right?"

I blink. How come I didn't know that?

"Well, that wasn't the main reason." I toss a hand to the air. "But that can wait. What tests?"

Deryn slicks back his hair to get it out of his face. Sweat shoots from its tangled ends and sprays the air with deadly droplets of teenage boy nastiness. I shift to dodge it but wind up getting pelted by another blob.

I turn and cover my mouth to hide my retching, but Sayer, in his unhelpfulness, points and laughs at me, catching Aidan's attention. Since Aiden always seems to want to be involved in anything Deryn's doing, he plods over, face curious.

"What was that about Raey?" he asks.

"Nothing," Deryn replies. "Fana was just asking me about the tests I did with her."

Aidan's shoulders droop. "Why'd she ask you? I'm the one who knows all the manifests. She's only ever asked me to do one thing, but I could be of so much more use to her than that."

"What'd she ask you to do?" I'm just vaguely curious, since I don't see Raey and Aidan bonding. Ever. He'd annoy her in the first five minutes of them being together, and then it'd be downhill from there.

"Oh, she just wanted to borrow some crew medical records, so I gave her access."

Before I can even inhale, Sayer springs from his position and thumps his way toward us, his eyes set with an intense focus, as if he was hunting for something. I frown at him butting in, especially with that terrifying look on his face. He'll scare sensitive Aidan, who'll shut down, and then we'll get nothing out of him.

"Whose medical records?" Sayer demands.

"Well, all of ours," Aidan replies, regarding Sayer with widening eyes. Aidan shrinks, his hands clamping together.

All of them? Why would she want access to all of them?

Raey hasn't focused on the crew's health since everyone recovered. What would she need everyone's medical records for now? If she was worried about something, wouldn't she share that with Ceri? Or did she?

And then it hits me. Raey's request would seem normal to anyone on the crew. Even Ceri wouldn't suspect anything from it. It'd only seem strange if she'd asked for data on one specific crew member.

"Did she say why?" I ask.

Aidan shakes his head and shrugs. "To make sure we're all doing okay?"

"No, that wouldn't be it," Sayer counters. "No one's updated those records since the adults left."

Aidan bites his lower lip, his forehead wrinkling in thought. If he was naïve of Raey's manipulations before, he's waking up to the possibility. I was already under her spell, so she never needed to control me in that way. I would have done anything if she had asked in that gentle way of hers. But then the *Stratford* appeared, and it, and Ceri, broke her spell.

"Is this what we're looking for?" Sayer asks me. His narrow-eyed glance shares another question: *Is it time to go find Raey?* But that's tricky. Raey could have been completely honest in her request of those medical records. Maybe she found something she's worried about but doesn't have enough evidence to present to Ceri and Efa yet. Or maybe she's hoping there's something in that data that'll help the *Devant*'s medical team with their outbreak. If there actually is an outbreak.

Maybe asking her about that is the reason we go talk to her now. I'd need Sayer to back me up, and that's risky, like an overvoltage in a processor—it'll increase the computation speed, but it could also explode in a shower of sparks.

I swallow hard at the thought.

"Not sure," I reply. "We should do some more searching."

"Are those tools such a big deal?" Mari asks, coming over. While she was still lugging sacks, she'd seen her companions standing around talking to us and likely wanted a break, too. I can't blame her for that. I'd need a break after the first round.

"We can't fix anything without them. So yes," Sayer replies, in the worst possible attempt at a lie. Yet another reason to make him stay away from my attempt to gather intel, as Ceri calls it. "Come on, Fana, let's keep looking."

He throws an arm around my shoulders, all buddy-like, and moves me to the rail car. I go stiff but do my best to turn back and wave at the three kids watching us with confused looks on their faces. Sayer redoubles his efforts, and I jerk forward with a yelp.

Once the doors close on the rail car, I rip myself away from his grasp and glare.

"What?" Sayer asks. "That went well, right?"

"Of course it did," I reply, my voice dripping with sarcasm. "They won't be suspicious of us at all!"

"Relax," he says, waving a dismissive hand in my direction. "They'll forget we were even there as soon as they get back into their work."

He does his unbothered lean on the wall and folds his arms. I continue to give him a narrow-eyed stare, though it seems to be completely ineffective on him.

"When have you known any of the crew to forget anything?" I demand.

Sayer shakes his head. "That's not the question we need to be asking."

"What is?"

"What Raey wants with our medical records."

It's a question I fear the answer to. Raey could be doing what she's pledged to: caring for others. But she could still be Azazhi's eyes and ears here. And his hands, ready to take advantage of this young crew and steal everything they have. Maybe it's both. Only one way to get an answer.

"Let's go to medical and find out," I say.

Sayer smirks and nods. "Good plan."

Hyuk, here we go.

PREDATOR

—— • ——

CERI

ONE-THIRTY-SEVEN IS A PLACE only engineers could love. Huge machinery—pumps and vents twice the height of other normal levels—fills its core. Massive tanks, full of fuels and other necessary chemicals, are trapped in a web of steps, ladders, and walkways, each leading to platforms above and below the tanks. That this is one of three such locations in machine access near the aft of the ship only emphasizes the massive size of the *Stratford*.

We may be at ease in the dark and unafraid of the shadows, but this close to the engines, the heat is oppressive. Condensation drips off every surface, making the walls and deck slick. Then there's the smell. Caustic and choking, as if we were standing in a pool of acid. We cover our faces with masks to keep from breathing in poison. It's more for our peace of mind than any real danger. At least that's what Fana's promised. Still, I would never come down here if the lives of my passengers weren't at risk.

Fana. The skin on my forearm still tingles where she brushed her fingers across it as she reached to embrace me. The moment was innocent enough. I think. She was just begging me to be careful. Yet I can't help but wonder at the confidence in her voice. And how she held me close.

And how I let her.

Perhaps I needed a minute to feel...I don't know. Something. I've no way to name it. At least not yet. But in that moment I was free to just exist. Fana removed every emotion that does me harm. I want nothing more than to relive it. If there was a way to—

Tegan's fist shoots up. We drop to the deck, powering weapons and sliding blades from their sheaths. My heart thumps hard, drowning out the hiss of steam, and I curse myself for letting my mind wander. We're in patrol mode. Ears are alert, listening for any unnatural sound. Eyes search for movement. Hands and feet at the ready. To do anything else means death.

How I forgot all that is beyond understanding. My head is still half stuck on Fana's gray irises and the warmth of her smile. I blink hard once to clear her from my thoughts, feeling instant regret for having to do it, and motion for Seren and Rhys to cover our flank. Only then do I sit back into the ease of battle awareness and slide up to Tegan, putting a hand on her shoulder and getting close.

"See something?" I whisper in her ear as the two of us stare across the walkway and into the black on the other side of the level.

She shakes her head, just enough for me to notice. No reason to tip anyone off who might be there.

The sharp whine of a weapon sends the two of us diving for cover. Two bolts of white flame rocket past, slamming into the wall behind us. Tegan responds, hurling a volley of darts toward the source of the attack.

"*Devant* agent!" I yell. "Spread out!"

Our attacker is across the platform. Somewhere. I level my pistol—a stolen *Devant* weapon—searching for a target. It's got to be one of Captain Yelekal's, a stray who abandoned their position, too terrified to fight us. Until now.

I take cover behind a control console and glance at Tegan. Just as I expected, she's watching me, waiting for an order. Seren and Rhys have their gazes burning across the level, covering our backs. For the moment, we're in secure positions. But the lack of fire from our attacker keeps my body tense. They better not have run away. I'm not in the mood to give chase.

Two bolts come from the right, striking a rail near Seren's head. She shrieks and drops flat to the deck. Rhys yells and fires back, then races to Seren's side.

"Dammit! Don't break formation!" I shout as Tegan floods the area with covering fire. I join in, fanning my shots across hers. Tegan pivots and crosses behind me, taking up Rhys' position and returning him to a supporting-fire role.

I level a glare at him with a shake of my head. Rhys should know better than to let panic get the better of him. Seren's fine. The shot only surprised her, and he risked us all by leaving us vulnerable to an attack from behind. It's my fault, though. I should have chosen Deryn instead. He may make bish decisions sometimes, but he won't forget his training if Seren gets a scratch.

Seren pushes up, breathing fast but signaling her readiness. I query Tegan with a flip of fingers to see if she's spotted our opponent. She shakes her head. Strange. The *Devant*'s agents aren't this proficient. But I'm sure it's just one of them, so there's no need to wait them out.

Time to go on the offensive.

A quick tap on my ear gets everyone's comms set for silent communication. Once they signal readiness, I take a calming breath and key the mic on my throat.

"Seren, wide left, behind Tegan. Rhys, you're wide right after me. This hostile knows how to shoot and move, but we're better. Go on my signal and call out your positions so we don't wind up shooting each other in a bunch of crossfire. Clear?"

Three single clicks in confirmation. I tap three in response, and we move, spreading out, two by two. Either we'll trap them or force a retreat, and then we've got them.

I keep down to a walking crouch, muscles taut and lungs tight as I advance on the last location our attacker fired from. They'll have moved on from there, and soon enough, we'll run into them. One mistake from them and—

Three shots come from behind. Rhys cries out. I drop and spin, panting hard. Bish. Where is he?

A thump comes from my left, followed by the clang of something metallic bouncing off the machinery as it plummets into the depths of the level.

"Rhys!" Seren screams. Two more bolts fly at her, hitting high on a truss above her head. Seren flattens herself to the deck, her face covering over in fear.

Tegan and I launch a torrent of fire at the agent's position, lighting up the space with sparks. A shadow darts away from our attack. I pivot and fire, but it's gone before I even get one shot off.

"Reform!" I call. Too late. Seren dashes across the level to crash down next to Rhys. She grabs him and drags his body into cover.

Rhys isn't moving. At all.

"Tegan, pull back," I say, my throat getting tight. "Rhys is down."

"No!" she hisses. *"I saw him. There's just one. Press the attack!"*

But I hesitate as unease fills me. They've tricked us. There are at least two. Likely more. They only want us to think we're up against a single agent. Hyuk. I should have brought a full squad to handle this. Now we could be at serious risk.

Is this my fault? Was I distracted? Why? Because I experienced a few seconds of excitement being close to someone? Efa and I have shared a thousand such embraces.

Stop. Situational awareness. Battle focus. That's what I need. Anything else gets us killed.

Seren's sobs come through the comm, and I'm pulled back to a vision of Efa's lifeless body in my arms. Seren could be going through the same thing. I can't let her. In a heartbeat, I'm up and scanning the area as I ready myself to dash across the platform.

"Ceri? What do we do?" Tegan's query gives me pause. I drop and check for threats again.

"Pull back to cover Seren," I reply, then shake my head. "No. Hold up."

As much as I'm desperate to help her, Seren doesn't need it. I'll bet she's already got both Rhys' and her med kits out and is rifling through them to cover up his wounds. It's natural to want to help her. It's also foolish. Tegan and I need to secure the position and keep any hostiles far away from her and Rhys. That starts with clearing the area.

"Okay," I say. "Pincer movement. Our target is that boiler minus six points off center. See it?"

"Got it. You think that's where they are?"

"It's a guess. They've been moving counterrotation to confuse us. I think."

"Copy. Going on your signal."

Wait. How do I know that's what they're doing? Because their tactics seem familiar? They do, don't they?

A chill runs through me. Yes. We learned that tactic. Captain Daga taught it to us to keep the Fahrasi guessing about our direction of attack. It was effective.

I gasp. Are we fighting one of ours?

No. The *Devant*'s agents could have come up with it, too. They wouldn't expect us to know it. But they realize we're onto them, and now, our opponents are coming up with a new plan.

I won't give them the time.

Three clicks from my mic and we move, keeping down and going wide. I reach the wall first and follow it past a bulky distillation unit to the back wall, heading toward its center. Tegan's nearly in position when I arrive.

I push off, moving quick and silent, straight toward our target. My pulse quickens. I clamp my jaw tight. My finger covers the trigger as my combat skills take over. My senses are hyper-alert. I'm aware of every speck of dust floating across my vision. The near-silent tap of my feet on the deck is like thunder in my ears. I ignore it and focus on my approach. Only one thing matters.

Ending my enemy.

There's a noise. Just ahead. I signal Tegan. She's nearly there. We're almost on them, I can sense it. Just a few steps more, I'll drop into a firing position. They're guaranteed to make a mistake. These *Devant* agents aren't skilled like we are. One shot is all I need.

I bend my knees and steady my weapon. My pulse is racing now. I inhale and hold the air in to keep calm. I've done this a hundred times before. More. One more time doesn't matter. It'll be over in half a second.

Ready?

Go.

"Thought you had me, didn't you?" A man's voice, deep and sickly, wafts into my ear. I know it.

Daga.

I spin, my mind screaming denial while my body explodes in panic. I squeeze the trigger over and over to destroy this nightmare. The space lights up with weapons fire. A bolt glances off my shoulder, knocking me over and throwing my pistol from my hand. I cry out as hot metal sprays across my skin, my arms flailing wide to stop myself from crashing.

Too late.

The back of my head slams into something hard. I twist and collapse on my side, my head spinning, my hands desperately sweeping the deck for my gun. I know it's in vain. Daga's boot finds my gut and slams into it, flipping me onto my back as he looms over me. He's blackened his face with dirt and oil, just like his uniform. He stares down at me with wild eyes and a grin that's missing two front teeth. My breath gets caught in my throat. I'm staring at death itself.

"You can't. You can't be here," I groan as I struggle to push myself up. Daga only digs his heel into my chest and shoves me down again. I cough, spitting blood from my mouth. My eyes are rolling back into my head. *Impossible.* This is impossible. Yet he's there. How? Why?

"You're not the only one they abandoned," he hisses.

"They...We...weren't abandoned."

Daga frowns and tilts his head. He had no idea. But it's been nearly a year. Where has he been? And why would Chief Generys leave him here?

There's no reason to know. Not now. Daga's leveling his gun at my head. It's over. I'm dead.

The screech of a dart gun fills the air. Daga barks in pain and rushes off, his hand covering his arm. A second later, Tegan appears, dropping next to me. I close my eyes as my head rolls to one side. Consciousness is fading. My shoulder burns like it's on fire. The pain spreads through me, making it hard to breathe.

"Where are you hit?" Tegan asks, doing her best to pat me down gently. I cry out when she touches my wound. Her light flashes on to check it, and she draws a sharp breath through her teeth.

"Sorry, Ceri," Tegan says. "You're going to live, but you'll be in a lot of pain."

"Efa. Call Efa," I say through hard grunts. "Get reinforcements."

Tegan nods and reaches for her comm, then pauses, locking gazes with me. "Ceri," she says, her voice quivering. "Tell me the person I shot wasn't him. It couldn't be...right? There's no way Daga can be here."

As much as I want to deny it, I can't. The hyuking bastard confirmed it, and as he spoke, I saw the viciousness in his eyes. This is a nightmare we will never wake up from.

"But he is," I reply.

CHASE

—— • ——

FANA

Level fourteen. I take a full, deep breath, inhaling and exhaling slowly, before stepping out of the rail car and onto the level. It's protection against the unknown, or at least from my overactive thoughts. Something is about to change, and it shakes me. My knees feel weak, and my feet shuffle across the deck as we make our way to medical.

It doesn't help that the corridor lights are dim, set for the dusk of second shift, though I doubt anyone is sleeping. Not successfully, anyway. I couldn't. Not until I uncover whether Raey is up to something. And at this point, I'm almost certain that she is.

I dread having to confront her about it. My record of beating her in a discussion is horrible, and that was only the first year we were together. I've failed to win every argument since. Sayer might back me up, but he can't defeat her with words, either.

How the hell am I going to do this?

Every potential outcome of this encounter—all of them negative—flashes through my head. My gut's tightening with each step, and I'm struggling to manage it. Raey won't forgive me for accusing her yet again, even if I'm right. And if I am, she'll get locked up. I don't want that for her. But if there's a better option, I can't think of it. Not that I'll have any control over the matter.

We turn the corridor to the medical bay. Light spills out from the interior, washing the corridor in a sterile glow. It reminds me of how much I fear needles. And scalpels. And subdermal applicators. Basically, pain in all forms and conflict in general. All of it will happen if we're forced to arrest Raey. I'm not sure I can. She may have locked me away, but it wasn't right. Still, I've got to consider it. It could happen. Justice, for whatever that might count, will be done, and...and...

And I stop, my gut twisting so hard I'm ready to vomit.

"I'm sorry," I say, as I press a hand against the wall and double over. "I can't. I just can't. You check the records. I'll wait here."

Sayer blinks and stares. Irritation is building in him, and I expect in the next two seconds he'll be yelling at me, just like Raey has always done. Maybe I deserve it, but I cower at that thought. My eyes squeeze shut as I fight hard not to lose my lunch.

Then Sayer sighs and says, "Why don't you find a place to sit down or something? You look like you're about to puke all over the deck."

"I might," I moan.

"There's a ladder just down the corridor. Go to fifteen and get...I don't know. Whatever'll stop you from doing that. There's four storage bays of medicines there. You'll see."

I retch and lean forward, my eyes watering. Sayer backs away, but I hold up a hand to show him it's okay. Not that he was about to come to my rescue. I stand up straight and nod to him as bile tickles my throat, jerking my thumb toward the ladder. Sayer only stares. Maybe he's concerned. Maybe he's just a little freaked. Either way, he's getting his wish to be away from me.

I take an entire five minutes to get down the ladder. With my stomach ready to burst, I'm not taking any risks. Slow and steady is a solid plan. I can focus on moving my feet and not on what happens when I meet Raey next.

Before I touch the deck on fifteen, though, my eyes are already scanning for the storage bays Sayer said would be here. I know exactly what I need. Sort of. Metoclo-something or lorry-something or, I think, alpacazolam? Any will do. Raey's given them to me before, sometimes in combination with other things. I'm not sure I could trust her with administering stuff like that to me now. I've already fallen for her switching out medications once, though it might have been more than a few times.

Never mind. I'll just take the first thing I find. There's a bay across the landing. I'll start there.

But as I approach, I hear a noise from inside—the hiss of drawer seals opening and shutting at a fast pace. Someone's in there, and they're in a hurry. I smile to myself. Maybe they've got an enormous headache. It's probably Niah searching for her treatment. I should say hello. She might need help to get back into her bed. I shuffle forward with a smile, leaning to peer into the bay.

And freeze.

It's Raey. Her hands are flying through a host of open drawers, snatching packets and stuffing them into a bag. A few slip through her fingers and fall to the deck. She keeps going, slapping open each section of the storage crates and digging into them as if they were candy.

What is she doing?

But the moment I open my mouth, I remember why I'm here and pause. I'm not ready for a fight with her. It'd take very little for me to lose my last meal all over her lab coat and boots. Then Raey'd really never talk to me again, because that'd be the second time.

Instead, I find a doorway covered in shadow with a clear view inside the bay to hide in. Raey keeps glancing outside of the bay as if she's expecting someone.

My stomach rumbles. No. She's not waiting for anyone. She's keeping watch in case someone shows up. Which means she's doing something she shouldn't be.

My jaw drops. *Raey's stealing medication!*

But why? She could take anything she wanted, and no one would ask a single question. Likely no one but Efa really knows what any of those medications are, so she wouldn't need to steal anything.

What's she taking?

The only way for me to find out is to get closer or go find a pair of vision amplifiers, and those would take time to hunt down, if the *Stratford* even has them. There's no need to see long distances inside of a ship!

I could just go ask her. We're still on speaking terms, at least since our last talk. But my twisting stomach quickly vetoes that idea. And if she's doing something she shouldn't, the last thing she'll want to do is talk to me.

Maybe I should go get Sayer. He'd stop her. But then we wouldn't find out why she's raiding the medicine supply for things she could just take anytime.

I need to get closer.

The corridor is well lit—as it should be. Ceri could easily avoid detection as she slinked across it, but my awkward gait would get me caught in a microsecond. Then my lunch would be airborne, for certain. Attempting to follow her isn't the best idea, either. I already failed at that once. There won't be a second time where she's concerned.

Sayer. I need Sayer. He could follow her. All I need to do is get back up the ladder and get him. And do it before she runs off. Then maybe—just maybe—my stomach will ease up on me.

I wait to move, crouching down like I've seen Ceri do, though I don't know what I should wait for. I'll go right after the next time Raey peeks her head out of the bay. Then I've got to make as little noise as I can.

There. Raey puts her fingers on the doorframe and leans out. Her narrowed eyes scan the corridor, sweeping every inch. I go still when she stops and stares at the ladder. *Bish!* Does she see me? Did I make noise? My pulse is pounding so hard, Sayer could hear it. Its thumping drowns out everything. I think I can even hear the blood rushing through my veins.

A millisecond later, her scan slides by, ending at the last corridor. Her gaze lingers for a second, then she retreats again.

As Raey ducks back into the bay, I tiptoe to the ladder. After pulling myself up, I twist, checking to make sure she's still preoccupied. My toes tap the first rung. I press down, then push up.

And my foot slips off.

I swallow my gasp, spinning to the back side of the ladder, to shadow and safety, letting the darkness envelope me. My lips smash together as I hold my breath, fearing even a single inhale will give me away. She's going to catch me. I know it. Raey always does. She always does. *Oh hell.*

But if Raey heard, she has yet to react. Maybe she's too busy reading the labels on the medicine packets and throwing them back as she struggles to find whatever she's looking for.

Okay. Here's my chance. If I'm going to go, I'm going...
Now!

I climb the back side of the ladder, keeping to the dark until I can't. Then, with a feat Ceri should be proud of, I swing around to the front to grab the handrail. My hand slips, and for half an exploding heartbeat, I panic.

Until I catch it and scramble up the rest of the way.

"Sayer!" I hiss between gulps of air. "Sayer!"

Why doesn't he hear me? I shuffle closer to the medical bay and try again.

"Saaaayeer!"

"For hyuk's sake, who is that?" Niah growls. "Just come in already."

"Hold on," Sayer replies. "I think I know."

He pops his head out to check, spotting me in the next second. By the roll of his eyes, I can guess he'd be happier to be interrupted by me any other time. I won't worry about it. This is important.

"What?" he asks as he shakes his head.

"Raey!" I hiss.

His forehead wrinkles. "What about her?"

I stab my finger at the deck, the best indication of the floor below I can come up with. When he raises an eyebrow, I know he gets it.

"And?" he asks.

"I think she's stealing medicine!"

Sayer's face goes dark. Now I regret breaking the news to him like that. He's ready to drop down the level and slice her head off. But I can't let her get away, either. We're already wasting time.

"Let's get her," he growls.

"No!" My hands fly up, waving back and forth to stop him from doing something rash. For a second there, my nausea was gone. Now it's back with a vengeance. I stagger to the corridor wall and lean on it. Hard.

"No?" Sayer twists his head and narrows his eyes. "What do you mean?"

I open my mouth to swallow a load of air, then take a moment almost longer than his patience to exhale it out before speaking. "Let's follow her and see where she goes," I reply, feeling a little better. "No way she's taking it for the *Devant*. They've got plenty and can make more. I think she wants to use it here."

"For what?"

"I don't know." I shrug. "There was no way to see what kind of medicine it was."

He drops his gaze, trouble coming over his face as he considers what I've told him. I clench my hands together, my thumb rubbing my knuckles in anticipation of his answer.

"So, what do you want to do?" he asks.

I swallow and breathe again. This better be the right choice. "We follow her."

Sayer only stares. The possibilities here are troubling him as much as they are me. We want to accept her for what she's done for us, but if she's about to drug one of us, then that'll put a serious damper on our welcome. I'd feel much, much better if we can stop her from a making a poor decision.

After a moment, Sayer nods. "Okay. But let me lead."

I smirk. That's exactly what I was hoping. My stomach is still a total mess.

RESCUE

— · —

FANA

Sayer's down the ladder to level fifteen in three seconds, swinging himself onto the back of it halfway down to slip into the shadow of the landing. For a moment, I lose him and I gasp. I've seen the *Stratford* crew do it a hundred times, yet it still amazes me. These kids have survived through war for way too long. They're never getting it out of their blood. And for that, my heart breaks for them.

I lie on the deck, peering over the edge of the ladder portal, searching for him. Just as I'm ready to give up, Sayer's hand shoots out of the darkness and beckons me down. But I shake my head and motion to the first bay where I saw Raey. No way am I going to mess this up.

"She's not there," he whispers, his voice floating up to me. "Come down. It's clear."

I'm hesitant. How the hell can I be stealthy like him? If Raey hears me stomp down the ladder and escapes, I won't forgive myself.

"Hurry," Sayer hisses. "We've got to track her down again."

"Maybe she's just hiding nearby."

"Trust me, she's not."

"What if she is?"

"Then I'd know."

I sigh. Sayer's likely right. I bet he could probably hear footsteps on the other side of the level. One level down, even. I guess I'll take the chance. Raey could be fifty levels down by now, anyway.

But I'm not sliding down like he did. I take each rung one at a time, making sure my footing is solid before proceeding. No way I'll mess this up by slipping and landing flat on my face. We'd have to abandon our pursuit and return to the medical bay.

Though that'd be one way to get Raey to return.

The moment I'm down, Sayer emerges from the dark, motioning to a side corridor. How he knows she went that way, I can only guess. Maybe he's guessing, too. I'll take his estimate over mine and follow along, doing my best to be as silent as he is. I won't come close, but it won't stop me from trying.

Instead, I'll contribute to our team by figuring out where Raey is going. If I knew what medicine she took, I might make a better prediction. All I have is what I already know. That might be enough.

Raey had that call with Azazhi. He gave her orders. I don't know what they are, but I've got a strong feeling they're related to the outbreak on the *Devant*. Maybe she's trying to develop a cure here, or do some tests to support the doctors over there. But they don't need her help. For all of her experience, Raey is just a medical technician. There are more than a few on the *Devant*'s medical team with deeper knowledge than she has.

When she was caring for the *Stratford*'s crew, they're the ones who advised her.

She was desperate to get that medicine, though. There's no mistaking that pained look on her face. I've seen it plenty. Usually it was when she was struggling to get me to understand her point. I always did, of course. My difficulty was in remembering it.

"Keep up!" Sayer warns. He's only halfway down the corridor. How close do I need to be?

When I shrug, he shakes his fist and beckons me forward. All I can do is comply. But as I shuffle forward, he speeds up and my chest gets tight. Sayer's onto something, and I'm keeping him from honing in on it.

We race to the next ladder and slide down. He does, at least. I do my best to get down in record time. For me. My heart is already pumping as much blood as it can through my body, and my lungs are struggling to keep up. Fatigue is sinking into my muscles, and soon I'll just collapse. Sayer must think I've got as much endurance as he does. Is he in for a surprise!

As we dash down the corridor on sixteen, he suddenly stops, spinning to catch me before I rush past. My knees collapse as I crash into him. But he drops to hold me upright, pushing me up against the wall with one hand while he puts a finger to his lips.

When I frown, he leans close and whispers, "Raey," then nods to a doorway just down the passage. My breath gets caught up in my throat, but I nod and motion for him to continue.

With his hand on my back, we slink together toward the door. There are voices inside. One is Raey's. The others...

Little Dru. And Beka. I can guess that much. Both are chatting casually with Raey. It's innocent enough. Girl talk. Raey never enjoyed doing it, but she could, if needed. Why she's entertaining these two is beyond me. Especially after hastily raiding the medicine supply.

"What's that?" Dru asks.

"Just some supplements I want you to take," Raey replies. "I'm worried the two of you aren't getting enough vitamins."

"But the stuff we eat every day has vitamins," Beka whines. "Those things taste like bish."

I slip forward and kneel so I can peek into the room without being seen. Sayer does the same on the opposite side of the doorway, but he pushes himself up on his toes and goes high. The corridor remains dark for second shift, so we should be hidden well. Or Sayer should be. I can only manage a feeble version of his spying.

Inside are four beds. Dru and Beka each sit on their own. The two others are Mari's and Seren's. I remember them moving in here after the battle with the *Devant*. They were so excited that Ceri and Efa had approved it, they wasted no time in organizing the space to suit their needs. The orange and blue tarps on the walls and ceiling make it more like a place where teenage girls would enjoy living, though it's a far cry from the soft pink walls and bright white curtains of my bedroom when I was that age.

"But the two of you have been sick," Raey answers in an advisory tone. "So you've lost some of the nutrients you need to protect your body from further illness. These pills include things like zinc and selenium, which aren't in your food. If you wash them down quick with water, you'll never taste them."

Sayer and I share a frown. I've never known her to push nutrients on anyone. Not even me. Though Raey's never really had to deal with children. Physical-age children, that is. If she wanted me to take something when I didn't want to, she would have just forced me down until I submitted.

Dru and Beka take the pills from Raey's hand and pop them in their mouths, then follow up with a big gulp from the canteen she provides. They look up at Raey expectantly as she smiles back at them. I don't know what they expect to happen. If they're just vitamins, there won't be any effects, and I'll feel the fool for suspecting her.

Until Dru and Beka collapse.

I throw a hand over my mouth to hide the squeal of my shock. She's poisoned them! Why? After all she's done for this crew, how could she betray them like that? I wouldn't believe it if I didn't just watch it happen. Acid pushes up into my throat. My breaths come so fast, I struggle to get air. I'm going to faint, I know it. I lean hard on the wall, forcing myself to stay up. But my head is spinning.

Raey wastes no time laying them down on their beds and wrapping them up in their blankets, throwing one end over their heads. She reaches for a cart, pulling it closer so she can lift Dru onto it. Beka's more of a challenge, but Raey grabs her legs and drags her onto the cart. Beka's head thumps onto the hard metal surface, and I gasp.

"I will hyuking kill her," Sayer growls, pulling out his blade.

"No!" I hiss. "Wait! Let's see what she does!"

"I've seen enough!"

Sayer rushes in with a shout. I'm just behind. Raey spins, shrieking in surprise as we thunder in. Her hands fly up, and she stumbles back, tripping over the cart and falling onto a bed.

"No! They're fine!" she cries as she flies up. Sayer shoves her back down and slams a knee into her stomach. He raises his blade above his head. "Please! I didn't hurt them! I swear!"

My pulse is pounding in my ears. He's going to kill her!

"Sayer! Stop!" I shout. "Don't!"

I plow into him, reaching up to pull his arm down. Sayer shoves me away. I fall onto a bed, but I'm up in a heartbeat, grabbing his wrists with both hands. His blade hand drops. The point catches me across the arm. I yelp and jump back.

"She assaulted our crew!" Sayer shouts, pointing his blade at me. "*Our* crew, Fana. She's the enemy!"

My hands fly up. No way am I going to fight him. He could cut me down with his bare hands, much less a blade. He only glares at me and spins back on Raey.

"Get up, murderer," Sayer says, grabbing Raey's coat and yanking her to her feet.

Raey whimpers as she flinches and ducks her head, her hands covering her face to protect it. "No! I'd never hurt them!" she sobs. "They're just asleep! I swear!"

"You better hope that's true, or I will gut you," Sayer growls. "But you're done here. Forever."

I clutch my bleeding arm as I stare, fighting with my conscience to believe Raey's words. I don't know if I can. She's changed so much, I'm not sure I recognize her anymore. Sayer's right about one thing: we will never trust her again, and for that, I won't ever forgive her.

"Fana!" Raey cries, her eyes pleading with me. "Let me explain! I'm just following orders. That's it. No one will be harmed. I—"

Raey yelps as my hand comes across her face, her head jerking to one side. She staggers and gasps, taking a moment to catch her breath. When she recovers, she stares at me, her jaw going slack. But I won't regret what I did. I have no sympathy for how she's betrayed us.

Raey has become our enemy.

"You made me feel like I was wrong!" I spit. "I hate you for that."

"Forgive me. Fana, please. I'm sorry," Raey whimpers. "I'm only trying to help."

"Keep your excuses for Ceri. You're her prisoner now. I can't even stand to hear your voice."

I spin and walk out, hoping to exit before my outrage wears off. She can't see me cry. She doesn't deserve to.

SORROW

CERI

We stumble to the rail car in a sloppy retreat, my legs threatening to buckle with every step. Just ahead of me, Tegan and Seren carry Rhys' body. His pants and shirt are soaked with blood. And Seren's constant tears. She grimaces, fighting to stay strong, but every time she looks at his face, her despair begins all over again. It crushes my heart to see her like this, but fear of another attack keeps me focused on our defense. I will do what I can to help her when we're off this level and safe. Right now, I must keep us alive. If I can.

Then, when Rhys is secure, I will have to slay a monster we all believed was gone.

Daga. It'd seem the obvious choice to gather arms and hunt him down. But more of my crew will be wounded on that mission. Or killed. That bastard made it clear we're as worthless to him now as we were before. He will end any of my crew who get in his way, and now that we know he's here, Daga will go on the offensive. There is no hiding for him any longer.

The rail car dings, and the doors open. Tegan slaps the controls for level fourteen as we tumble in. I crash onto the back wall, sliding down it to pull my knees up so I can rest my throbbing arm on them. Once Tegan helps secure Rhys, she comes to check the coagulant and field dressing she put on me. I shut my eyes, unworried. My body has taken so much damage, I half expect to be joining Niah in permanent retirement after this. Funny to think of it, really. Retirement, at twenty years of age.

I hardly could. Not with a threat like Daga walking around my ship. My gut twists just hearing his name. Why did he have to appear now? I wish we'd never seen him, and he could just slink back into the depths of the ship, no one the wiser. But that's not a plan. That bastard will have to be dealt with before we can even consider talking to Azazhi again. I'll need Efa, Merek, and Sayer's input on how to do that, and I'll have to stop my head from spinning, too. For now, I should just focus on the problems inside of this car.

"Seren. Come here," I order. She won't, but it might at least take her mind off of Rhys for a split second. The hoarseness in my tone doesn't command much attention, anyway. Perhaps I should get up and drag her over here, though that'd take more effort than I can manage.

"Can—can you feel his pulse?" Seren asks Tegan, her voice breaking. My fists clench, warding off the ache in my chest. Better to feel the pain in my shoulder than that. I can forget how my arm hurts.

"Yes, it's weak, but it's there," Tegan responds, though I doubt her answer. Rhys' face is pale, and his mouth hangs open. At least she's closed his eyes.

"But he's cold," Seren replies.

"Yeah, that's normal."

"There's nothing normal about that!" Seren pounds a fist on the deck. "Bish! Can't we move any faster?"

"Hey," I hiss. "Noise discipline. And no, it only goes one speed. Come here and keep me company."

She goes quiet after that. Too quiet. I'd rather have Seren's emotions flooding over us than her burying them deep inside. I just don't know what to say to her to stop that from happening.

Damn. I'm getting drowsy. It's the shock of the wound. My body's shutting down, and I can't let it. Rhys is already enough of a burden to them. I'll walk myself into medical, even if that means I collapse the moment I pass through the doorway. I force my eyes open and inhale sharply to keep myself awake.

We've just passed level thirty-one—almost there. Raey'll take us in and do her best to heal us. Then the real work will begin. I expect Efa to sideline me, but we're too short on crew for that. And nothing will stop me from being there when we put Daga down.

"Bish," Tegan says, intensity growing in her gaze as she presses two fingers into Rhys' wrist.

Seren shifts, her eyes growing big. "What? What's wrong?"

Tegan shakes her head. "I can't get his pulse."

"Try the jugular, then!"

Their hands shoot toward Rhys' neck in the same moment, pressing and prodding in multiple spots, but the more they try, the more their breaths quicken. I grind my teeth, doing my best to keep calm. Rhys will live. We've just got to stay focused.

"Five more levels," I say. "Get ready to move him to the operating room. I'll make sure Raey meets you there. Don't worry. We've got time. We've got time."

But Raey doesn't answer when I call on comm. I try again. Nothing. My throat is getting dry. I reach for my canteen, then remember I didn't bring one. This was supposed to be a quick hunt, not a full-on battle.

"Efa, pick up," I call.

"Go," Efa replies. *"What's up?"*

"You have a location on Raey?"

"No. Why?" A pause. *"Are you wounded? You sound strange."*

I open my mouth to speak, then shut it. This isn't about me—I'll survive. But Rhys' chances are dropping quickly. It'll haunt me forever if he dies. If I have to, I'll give every working organ inside me to keep him alive. But we need Raey for that. And likely Efa too.

"Can you get to medical?" I reply. "Rhys is down. It's bad."

I catch Seren's worried glance, then sigh. No sense in hiding it. We'll only save him if we're clear about what he needs. Everyone's feelings will have to wait.

"Going now with Merek," Efa says. *"Get him into surgery one. We'll be there."*

Seren bites her lip and drops her gaze onto Rhys' hand in hers. With a shaky breath, she tightens her grip on it, as if fearing what happens if she lets go. Not good. I've got to get her to relax while they're working on him, even if that means knocking her out, which I hope I really won't have to do.

One level to go. Raey better be there. I better ensure it.

"Fana, come in," I say.

"Ceri?" There's noise in the background as she holds her mic open. *"Go ahead…What? Oh! Go ahead, Ceri."*

"You know Raey's location? We need her."

"Uh…"

Sayer gets on comm. *"Get Efa on it. Raey can't help us anymore."*

"No! Wait! I—" Raey says in the background. *"I can help!"*

Tegan and I share a glance.

"Clarify that statement, Sayer," I demand. "Rhys' condition is serious. We need her."

"We caught Raey poisoning Dru and Beka. They're unconscious but breathing. Fana and I are bringing them up to medical. Raey's not our friend, Ceri. She's been pretending this entire time."

Time freezes. Everything becomes a blur. Sayer's words float inside my mind, isolated from the rest of my thoughts. If I touch them, then they become real. And they can't. They absolutely can't.

Hyuk. Hyuk. Hyuk.

"All crew. This is Ceri. Drop everything and come to medical immediately."

Seren and Tegan gather up Rhys' body, tensing and ready to move the moment the rail car arrives on fourteen. They glance at me, concerned. I shake my head, motioning them to go. As soon as the doors open, they fly through. The med bay is just down the corridor. I'll get there, too. I just need to get myself up.

Efa's voice blasts from the bay, barking orders as Tegan and Seren arrive. *Move this! Get that! Keep it sterile!* Feet pound in from every direction. Table legs squeak against the deck. A thunderstorm of sound rumbles through the bay entrance.

"And where's Ceri?" she yells. "Well? Go find her! Check the rail car!"

I can tell by the slap of their boots on the deck it's Deryn and Mari. They're both panting hard by the time they get to me, their gazes scanning me over as I do my best to force a weary smile.

"Oh bish!" Mari says and elbows Deryn. "Quick! Get a stretcher!"

"No." I shake my head. "Just give me a hand up."

I stretch out my good arm, but they bypass it completely and lift me from under my shoulders instead. I draw in a breath through my teeth as I fight through the pain. I've had worse, though my body doesn't agree. My knees go rubbery as the two of them lift me and slip down the corridor, my feet dragging on the deck.

Every conscious member of the crew race around medical, getting the operating room prepped. Even Niah, unable to stand on her own, does her best to help, unwrapping tools and bandages from her bed in the main bay.

I've hoped I'd never had to see them hustle like this. I've made my pledge to keep them safe. Their oath to each other is just as strong. We'll become liars if we can't save Rhys, Dru, and Beka. And we never tell lies to each other. Not where life is concerned.

Merek is yanking on sterile gloves and a mask with Tegan's help. Aidan and Seren move Dru into a bed. Fana's doing her best to help Efa don a sterile suit for surgery.

And there, in the isolation room, Raey sits with Sayer looming over her. He's bound her legs and feet, though by the way she hangs her head, I doubt she'd move even slightly. Sayer's hand on his gun reinforces that.

"In a bed. Now!" Efa shouts as she spots me. I only approach her as she glares.

"I'm standing, so I'll be fine," I reply.

"That's total bish and you know it." She jabs a finger into my good shoulder. "Don't you dare be a problem for me right now!"

I shut my eyes and nod, too tired to fight her. The best thing I can do is stay out of Efa's way and let her do what she needs to.

"Have you seen Rhys yet?" I ask.

Efa's face falls. I need nothing more to know she's in over her head with this. I saw his wounds. Two in his chest, another through his leg. Done by one of those beam weapons from the *Devant*. Daga got his the same way we did. I curse myself for not securing those hyuking death rays sooner.

"Has Raey seen him yet?" I ask.

Efa huffs, her eyes widening. "So she can kill another one of our crew?"

My eyes narrow. This isn't the time to be concerned with dispensing justice. Rhys' life comes before any of that bish. And even if she's guilty, I'd let her help him or force her to do it. Then we can lock her up.

"I don't get that Raey's anything other than what she's said she is," I reply. "And we've got little choice if we want Rhys to live."

"We've got plenty of choice." Efa motions to the isolation room. "And good luck getting Sayer to agree to it."

"Rhys doesn't have time for all of us to come to an agreement." And fighting him won't help, either. I need a softer approach than I've got the patience for.

"Fana will get him to cooperate."

Efa huffs. "How about you go lie down before you fall on your ass?"

"Fana!"

Efa sighs and shakes her head as Fana rushes over.

"Are you okay?" Fana asks, glancing at my shoulder.

"Fine." I'm short with her because I have to be. "Give me your first instinct on Raey. Doesn't matter what it is, just say it."

Fana watches me, searching for a hint of what I expect her to say. But there's no trick here. All I want is honesty, whatever it is.

"Please, Fana, just say it," I press.

She presses her tongue across her lip, then says, "She's an idiot for listening to Commander Azazhi. Not that she had much choice, but Raey's no killer. She never even hurt me when I deserved it."

"There you have it," I say, turning to Efa. "Take her in there with you. Let Sayer play guard if he's going to be a bish-head about it."

"Is that an order?" Efa charges, folding her arms.

"It is if you're about to refuse. Now go!"

Efa rolls her eyes and motions to Merek, who jogs into the isolation room. He returns with Raey and Sayer in tow. Sayer only glances at my wounded shoulder, then presses his lips tight and continues on as Merek leads them into the operating room.

"Can I help?" Fana offers Efa, who glances between the two of us.

"Yes," Efa replies, sarcasm deep in her tone as she gestures at me. "I bet you'd have a better chance of getting her into a bed than I would. Make sure she stays there."

Fana's mouth drops open as her cheeks turn rosy. I think I missed something, but Fana doesn't seem likely to share her thoughts. With a nip of her lip, Fana motions to the nearest bed, doing everything she can not to look at it.

I shuffle over to the bed and rotate to deposit myself on the edge so I can face the now-closed door of the operating room. Fana sits next to me, our shoulders connecting. It's welcome, and I find I need more. My hand covers hers, and she responds, taking her hand in mine and brushing her thumb over my wrist. Her touch smooths the edge off my fears and lifts my lips into a near smile. Even if my heart still pounds, I can now think clearly without collapsing into a panic.

Though, replaying each terrifying moment of our encounter and searching for my failures isn't the best use of this new calm. I should have treated the situation with more seriousness. It's my fault for not riding Rhys and Seren harder. Not just down there. Maybe I was happy to see them smile together. Maybe I was even a little jealous.

But how could I have ever expected Daga? We went down there to pull some half-sane elder out from the depths. That was what we prepared for. That was what was on my mind. Not someone who could easily take out most of my crew should it occur to him to take advantage of our current disarray. All he'd have to do is show up here in medical, weapons out, and it'd all be over.

Fana tightens her grip on my hand as I shift, my gaze landing on a spot near the entrance into medical. My skin goes cold as I remember something from not long ago I'd hoped to forget. Niah and I were rushing out to find Efa, fearing she had done something bad. Of course, I now know she had. But that was far from the only horror of that day. There, on that spot, I ran into Seren, her face soaked with tears as she dragged Rhys' bloody body in. By herself.

That wasn't today. That was nearly a year ago.

There were doctors here then. Adults, but still doctors. Doctors who could heal him. I don't know if that can happen this time, but I'm praying hard that it does. It will destroy Seren if Rhys doesn't make it. And I will blame myself.

You better make it, Rhys.

Minutes go by. Perhaps hours. And still we wait for them to open the operating room door. My head sags. Fana encourages me to lie down as she strokes my hair. I decline, but I don't stop her from running her fingers through the mess on the top of my head. She's keeping me grounded like nothing else could. If only I could give in to sleep.

Ten minutes later, Efa and Merek exit the operating room, followed by Sayer with a tight grip on Raey's arm. She keeps her eyes on the deck, perhaps afraid to connect her gaze with anyone else's. She doesn't need to. One glance from Efa and the acid in my stomach eats away at my insides.

Forgive me, Rhys.

He is with the Ancestors now. I hope they'll look after him. I can't spend another moment to do so. Someone else needs my full attention.

I scan the room, searching for her. But the moment I turn my head, Seren's there, staring through me as if she can't remember where she is. I release Fana's hand and open my good arm to Seren. She crashes into it, burying her face in my shoulder as I lay my cheek on Seren's head and gently rock her.

This is all I can do for her. I've failed at everything else.

WRATH

CERI

This silence I'm experiencing is near perfection. I feel no pain coursing through my body. No angst crushes my mind. All I have is the cool quiet of semiconsciousness. If it wasn't for the sound of someone's anxious feet shuffling past my bed, I could imagine I was anywhere but on a rotting interstellar ship.

I remember Efa and Merek pulling Seren off me, their soft groans and sighs as they eased her into the next bed, brushing by my state of calm. I remember the edges of my lips curling upward, imagining Seren as a young child, her listless body carried to bed by her parent. She must have been completely gone not to notice. I hope, at that moment, she was dreaming of something peaceful, far away from here.

I remember, too, a gentle kiss on my cheek. The spot on my skin still feels warm from where her lips touched it. She smiled at me. Fana did. It was all I needed to fall asleep.

But the constant crackle of fingers handling packages and the tinkle of metal touching metal has wrecked my peace into a heap of smoldering thoughts. Whoever's making this much noise has forgotten every skill on stealth that was driven into them. I plan to remind them of them all. Right now.

My eyelids crack open. I blink as I twist in the bed, waking up immobile limbs and returning responsiveness to my body. When I've gathered enough strength, I push my eyelids the rest of the way up.

Seren stands at the foot of my bed, her face drawn tight in focus as she stuffs a package of bandages in her bag. So she's the source of my disturbance.

"What are you doing?" I ask.

"Packing." Seren grits her teeth as she forces one last package in and snaps the cover shut. "I'll need all of this. But I'll stash some in a few of the regular spots and only carry a few things at a time. Travel light. Right? Like you always taught us."

Her words are slow to register in my half-awake brain, but the advice I've given her comes back in a flash. *Travel light. Stash supplies.* I learned those lessons the hard way. Why Seren needs to remember them now is unclear. Still, an unease I've yet to understand is building in my body.

"No one packs like that unless they're going to war. And we're not. So why are you doing that?"

"I'm going to end Daga."

I shoot off my pillow, my unease exploding into alarm. How could she be so foolish? Is she even thinking at all?

"No hyuking way," I say. "You put that bish away right now and get over here."

Seren continues to pack. Likely she expected me to say that, which is why she was planning to sneak off. She knows I'd tell her she's letting her emotions rule; no one with a level head would let an idea this stupid pass through their thoughts more than once. With all the noise she's making, there can't even be one shred of reason in her head right now. Perhaps she hoped I would wake up and somehow give her my support for the insane thing she's about to do.

"Are you listening to me?" I growl.

"I heard you."

"Then stop."

She mashes her lips together and grabs a handful of painkiller ampules to stuff in a side pocket of her pack. But her hand doesn't fit inside. She's got more medication there than anyone would need in a lifetime. Seren's following my lesson to stash them everywhere—though that's far from the lesson she should be heeding.

"Seren," I try, keeping my voice soft. "Stop. Come here and let's talk, yeah?"

"I'm done with talking. That bastard has to die."

I twist toward Niah's bed, but she's gone. In therapy with Efa, likely. No one else is here. No one else alive, anyway. I'll have to be the one to talk her down—I'm fine with that—I'm just worried about what happens if I need to use force. One of my arms is useless.

I slip my legs off the bed and slide to the edge. The deck seems farther away than it should be, and my head feels lighter than it should. Bish. Someone dosed me with a sleep agent. That had to be Efa. Her good intention is dulling my ability to react when I need to be sharp.

"Hey," I try again. "You know I care about you, right? I don't want to see you get hurt, and you will, if you do this."

Seren huffs. "If you care about me so much, you'll come with me."

For half a second, I consider it. We know it's Daga down there, so we can adjust our strategy. He may have taught us a lot, but he's never fought against the *Devant*'s crew. That beam weapon he's got only gives him so much advantage when he's unfamiliar with the tactics.

Who am I kidding? If I go down there now, I might as well shoot myself in the head.

With an exhale, I slip off the bed, using my one good arm to steady myself. And I'm not steady. At all. My legs are so wobbly they could give out at any moment. Likely they will.

"Not now," I reply. "We should take the time to honor Rhys' sacrifice and put him to rest. That's what—"

"Hyuk that!" Seren slaps her hands on her backpack and glares at me. "If he was still alive, Rhys would be down there right now hunting for Daga!"

"But he's not, is he?"

Seren shuts her mouth, her lower lip trembling. I didn't mean to attack her like that, but if it makes her reconsider, I'll push as hard as I need to and hope I can pick up her pieces when I'm done.

"Of course he's not," she replies, her tone flat. "That hyuking bish shot him. And I'm about to return the favor a hundred times over."

I take a few unsteady steps toward her as she eyes me warily. I press my leg against the bed and raise my hand to show her

I'm no threat. But now that I'm this close to her, I notice her hands shaking as she fits the last of the painkiller into the pack.

My stomach twists, thinking of her somewhere deep in the ship. Alone. Having to resort to jabbing herself with an ampule so she won't collapse under the pain of her wounds.

I reach out and touch her hand. "I can't lose you, Seren."

She pulls it away and returns to packing. "You won't."

I grind my teeth. She has no idea what she's saying. I need to make a move.

"You can't promise that," I say.

"I won't fail."

"It's the wrong move, and you know it."

Seren spins on me, her eyes getting wet. "No! *You* don't know it! I'm a better soldier than you give me credit for! I can beat him, and he'll never see me coming!"

For a moment, I just stare, stunned by her sudden rage. Seren's got a thousand thoughts going through her head right now. I know, because I've been where she is. But she far from deserves to be trapped by her feeling like this. It's not fair that she has to go through this. I hyuking hate that she ever got to this point.

"Dammit, just stop this fake courage bish!" I hiss. "You go down there on your own, and you're dead. That's all there is to it. You want to be with Rhys that badly?"

Tears drop onto her cheeks, turning them red and puffy, even as her jaw tightens, the anger building inside of her. Tightness strikes my chest, knowing I'm responsible for that. But better she's here, where I can comfort and care for her, than alone and in a danger I can't pull her out of.

"And what am I supposed to do? Huh?" she sobs. "Just wait around while that hyuking bastard rules the lower levels? He killed Rhys, Ceri! Rhys didn't even do anything to him! He didn't deserve to die!"

She breaks down, and I go to her, wrapping my arm about her and pulling her close. I can't stop myself from tearing up. I'm so terrified of losing her. Not just to Daga, but to everything. Seren's changed. She's becoming her own person. And it's a fierce one. She may still need my protection for now. But not for much longer.

And when it happens, I will miss the little sister she's become to me. Dearly.

"He'll get what's coming to him," I say. "You know I won't leave a threat like him walking around our ship. And I can't watch you die like Rhys did."

Seren pulls back, wiping at her eyes. "What makes you think I will?"

Bish. After all this, did I fail to convince her?

"Seren." I reach out for her. "This is Daga we're talking about. *Captain* Daga. The one who learned how to fight by killing more Fahrasi than any Tarakh ever has. You're not his soldier anymore. You're his enemy."

"I know that."

"Seren," I growl. "We're waiting. That's final."

Her head lowers, and the breath I had locked in my lungs releases. I pull her to me again, making as best of a peace offering as I can with a single arm. Seren leans her head against my shoulder, staring down into nowhere, perhaps accepting, for the moment, what is possible.

"Thank you," I whisper. "Thank you for listening to me. We'll get this done. I promise. Just give it time."

Seren's head shakes, building in intensity. I tense as her body goes stiff. What is she doing? She presses against my arm. I tighten it to pull her back. Seren only resists more. My chest gets tight. Oh hell. I thought she was going to listen to me.

"No," Seren says, pushing away from me. "No! I'm doing this!"

"Seren, stand down! That's an order!"

"No!"

Seren breaks free of my hold. I snatch at her shirt, but she twists and ducks, getting under my grasp. She grabs her backpack and throws it on, headed for the door.

"Don't!" I shout.

With a last attempt, I rush after her, my hand flying out as I leap. It's not enough. My legs fail. I crash into a cart and go down, pain radiating from the scar on my side and the wound on my shoulder. It doesn't matter. I've got to stop her. She can't die.

But it's too late.

Seren's gone.

APPEAL

—— • ——

FANA

With Seren put to bed and Ceri successfully dosed, I turn to my other problem and head across the level to a room with a large closet, all too familiar to me. Ceri's told me all about it. Described each malformed notch and point in the walls, ceiling, and floor in minute detail to the point of insanity. She told me about how she'd get bumps all over her skin the second someone shut the light off, how she would tap out the rhythms of each piece of machinery she could hear. I don't know what unnerves me more: that they locked her in there for so long or that she appreciated it.

Raey's in there now, likely not handling it as well as Ceri did. Then again, she's had a pampered life compared to what Ceri's been through. Maybe that's to my advantage. I might get more out of her if I dangle the possibility of her release.

Wow, when did I get to be so evil?

I knock on the door before I tap in the code to unlock it. Raey may be sleeping or something, and I wouldn't want to surprise her.

"Who is it?" Raey asks as the door slides open. When she sees it's me, she relaxes back into her seated position, knees up against her chest, hands on her knees. There are deep pockets under her eyes, and the edges have gone from a bright white to a muddy red. Her braids hang from her head, tangled and bent. I can't believe that only one night has broken her usually neat appearance in half.

"Come on. I'm allowed to let you walk up on eight," I say, offering a hand. Raey only glances at it until I drop it back to my side. With a grunt, she pushes herself up and dusts herself off.

"Let's go, then," she replies, motioning to the rail car. But I shake my head.

"We've got to climb," I say.

Raey sighs. "Fine."

She might appreciate that I'm letting her stretch her legs and get some exercise. Ceri got nothing but a trip to the toilet once a day and a shower once a week. *If* she behaved. I bet she didn't. Often.

"So why are you doing this?" Raey asks as we step up the last rung onto eight. "Don't you have more important things that need your attention?"

I take that to mean I should be repairing the ship rather than being here with her. As if our past relationship has nothing to do with it. Raey's severed the last connection we had, though I'm responsible for wearing it down to its last threads.

"The others are in a meeting," I reply. "And I was hoping to talk."

Raey stuffs her hands into her pockets and glances around the level. "Does that mean I don't get my exercise?"

"I can multitask. You know that."

She snorts, scuffing her heel against the deck as she looks down at her foot. I put my hands on my hips and wait. A moment later, she picks a path along the hull and eases into a casual pace down it. I'm caught off guard and have to scramble to catch up, but by the time I do, we're moving side by side in a familiar gait.

"So talk," Raey says, keeping her eyes forward. I'll take that as her attempt to keep things calm between us.

"Dru and Beka woke up a few hours after you did whatever you did to them," I state, doing my best to make it sound like an apology.

Raey nods. "Of course they did."

I blink and stop, turning to her. Raey notices and looks back at me.

"I told you I didn't hurt them," she says.

My mouth drops open. There she goes again, trying to take control of the conversation. Then she continues walking, stopping me from coming up with any kind of thoughtful response and forcing me to catch up instead.

"Raey!" I throw my hands up. "Don't you realize how that looked to us? How could we know what you gave them?"

"You could have just believed me."

"Believed you? How can any of us do that when you're making it hyuking impossible to even try? I want to believe you, but"—I point to my heart—"it's like you stabbed me with one of your scalpel things. Right here. Deeply."

Raey spins on me then, her arms folded and her gaze lowered. She studies me, watching my face as if she was examining it for some sign of illness or reaction. It's not an unusual look for her, but there used to be care and love behind it, and now there's only a wall.

"You talk like them now. Did you realize that?" she asks.

She's lashing out, doing her best to wound me. She's the one who's hurt. I've got no reason to feel like I've been abandoned. Not any longer. My loyalties lie with the *Stratford* crew. They're the ones who saved me, protected me, and welcomed me.

"I am *them* now," I quip. "Did you realize *that*?"

I hide my smirk as her body deflates. No need to gloat over her defeat. Raey touches a hand to the base of her throat, looking down at the deck, sullen, as she works through something in her head.

I hope she's about to confess. If only because it might heal some of the damage we've done to each other. Then we might try to stitch up the rest of the wounds we've made.

"My orders were to bring two subjects to the *Devant* for diagnostic tests," Raey says. "Blood and tissue samples, maybe a few body and brain scans. That's it. They'd be back here before they ever woke up."

I watch her for any sign that she's lying. I know her tells. But if there was one, it's gone now. She's either gotten good at hiding them, or she's telling the truth. I really hope it's the latter.

"Or anyone noticed," I add.

She nods. "It'd be best that way. No misunderstandings."

My eyes widen. "Misunderstandings? What could we have misunderstood about you kidnapping two of our crew?"

"*Your* crew." Raey huffs and looks away. "Can't you understand I'm only trying to save mine?"

When I only stare, she turns around and keeps walking. But her pace has slowed. It's easy for me to match her in just a few steps. And then we amble along, down to the end of the wall, and turn left. We pass a cluster of chairs arranged in a semicircle. There's three sets of office chairs, pristine and new, likely taken from the colony's equipment storage. Four I recognize as stolen from the workshop down on one-hundred-sixteen. A handful are blackened and filled with holes, perhaps once used for protection in battle. *Likely, they were no help at all.*

I don't want to give her sympathy, but I feel the strain of it tugging at my heart. There are people on the *Devant* I still care about, though it was clear from Baati's response, it's far from a mutual feeling. I can only hope that's not everyone over there. It'd make me happy to know one or two of my old team still think about me. Not that I'll ever see them again.

"I'll admit it wasn't the best plan," Raey says quietly, after we get halfway down the next hull section. "But you know I'm telling the truth, Fana. And you know most of these kids will never believe that. Especially Sayer."

"You're not wrong," I reply. "They trusted you. And then you proved how stupid they were for doing so."

"And you?"

"You heard what I said before."

We get to the end of the wall and turn the left again. I notice a few blackened spots near the ladder's landing. Dark holes where fire got so hot it melted metal. Good thing this ship has three hulls.

Raey stares at the damage, slowing more without even noticing she's doing so.

"If you don't want me locked away in that closet like Ceri was, then you've got to do more than want to believe me, Fana." Raey glances at me. "And you know these kids could forget that I'm in there. On purpose."

I shift on my feet, suddenly feeling as if something's crawling across my skin. She wants me to defend her or, at least, stop them from exacting revenge. My crew may be focused on living better these days, but there's still a very base instinct in them that terrifies me.

"Ceri won't let you be harmed," I insist, even when it could be a lie. I'm not sure if I care—*No. That's wrong.* I'm angry, that's all. I don't want to see her tortured and executed. But she needs to face justice for what she's done.

"Ceri's got her own problems to deal with," Raey says.

I frown. "What do you mean by that?"

Raey's answer is to return to her stroll. Once again, I follow as my insides tear themselves to shreds. What does Raey know about Ceri? Or am I overreacting? Maybe she only meant that Ceri has to worry about finding that killer. Or getting Azazhi to deliver the rest of the pods. Ceri's got no more bandwidth to spare, which could be why Efa's been managing the crew.

"I know I've got no right to ask, but I'm begging you for your support, Fana," Raey says, her voice wavering. "You're the only one I can turn to."

My jaw goes stiff at that thought. Why me? Can't I be angry, too? Her betrayal affected me the most.

"Ask Dru or Beka," I say, doing my best to keep my voice calm. "You saved their lives once. They might be more understanding."

"Be serious." Raey wags a finger in the air. "They're children. And even if they're willing to forgive me, they don't know me as well as you do."

A *tsk* slips off my tongue as I fold my arms and look away. *Does she never stop?* What gives her the right to corner me like this? As if my feelings have no importance. As if I'm just expected to bow down and do as she asks and forget how my chest aches at her selfishness,

"Who says I'm willing to forgive you?" I demand.

Raey tilts her head and watches me with one eyebrow raised, and I smolder. Let her play this game and see how far it gets her.

"Are you?" Raey counters.

I won't answer that. Or maybe I don't want to admit I already know what I'd say. It took time for both of us to get over our breakup, though we never lost touch. Maybe, in some ways, we helped each other through it, and that's how we remained friends. To forgive her is like reconditioning an engine. I may not enjoy it every time, but I still do it because it's who I am.

But just because I might forgive her doesn't mean I'll risk my relationship with the crew to defend her.

"I'm sorry. I can't help you. Find someone else," I say and turn away.

"No! Wait. Fana." She reaches out to touch my arm. I pull away, but it stops me. "Please, there's no one else. Can't you understand that?"

I can't let her get to me. She's guilty and deserves to be punished.

"I understand you should take responsibility for what you did," I say, my voice flat. It's a fight to keep it that way. I'm about ready to burst with all the pressure I'm feeling. It's a mystery why I don't hate her right now.

"Is that it?" Raey comes around to put herself in front of me, her mouth hanging open. "Am I judged guilty already? Don't I have a right to a defense?"

No way did she just ask that.

"Did you give Dru and Beka the chance to choose if they'd be tested on or not?" I fire back.

Raey's face turns pained as she sighs and drops her head. A twang of guilt raises my hand, and I reach out for her.

And then I pull it away to place over my heart, my fingers twisting the fabric of the pocket there. "Time to get you back," I say.

As we return to the ladder, the crew, or most of it, comes up. Raey and I pause.

"Oh," Efa says, looking between me and Raey. "You're here. Good. We need to have a vote."

I tilt my head. "On what?"

Efa turns to Tegan and Deryn and motions to Raey with a nod. They approach her as Raey watches them with widening eyes. But they only take her by the arms and move her toward the rail car, Raey throwing a glance back at me as they depart.

When I raise an eyebrow at Efa, she answers, "It'd be wrong to have her sit here while we discussed it."

"Discussed what?"

"Her fate."

EXECUTION

FANA

"Shouldn't we delay until Ceri gets here?" I ask as everyone, other than Ceri and Seren, takes a seat in the meeting area. Had I known when Raey and I walked past it this would happen, I might have suggested we just sit and wait.

"She won't be coming," Efa replies. "She needs rest. So does Seren."

My hands tighten as I remember what Raey said about Ceri having her own problems. I really hope that's not related to what Efa just said. When this meeting is done, I'll go see how she is. She could be hungry. Or thirsty. Or maybe she'd just like some company. It's been a while since the two of us just talked. *Okay, we've never really talked.* Not like that.

And we never discussed my failure of an attempt to confess how I felt about her. That's more on me, of course. I've been far too embarrassed to speak of it to anyone, even Raey, who, before she became a spy, might have approved.

"Hey, attention everyone!" Efa claps her hands, pulling everyone's eyes to her. And me.

Oh, no. This isn't about me.

I find the nearest chair and drop myself into it, turning it toward Efa and Merek, who joins her as I vacate the space. Deryn and Aidan pull their chairs up next to mine, while Sayer takes up a spot in the back, leaving the four girls—Mari, Beka, Tegan, and Dru—to watch over Niah. Not that she needs or wants their help.

It cheers me to see her up and about, though. Color has returned to her face, and she moves with a flexibility she hasn't had in a long time. Her hair, cut to a near bob, hangs loose from her head, framing her face in a way that gives her a more mature appearance.

She'd punch me hard if I told her that, though.

"We have some crew business to attend to," Efa says and glances at me. "I know some of you would prefer we all be here for this, since it's really important, but it can't wait."

"It's okay," Niah says, her voice hoarse until she clears it. "Let's just get it done."

Efa smiles at her, then connects her gaze with everyone, her face growing troubled, and as it does, the others turn gloomy, except Sayer, who folds his arms as his leg bounces. He narrows his eyes as if he's expecting trouble. If anything, he'll be the one bringing it.

"We need to decide what to do about Raey," Efa continues as she paces. "Now, we all know how she's cared for us, and even after all that's happened, I think she still wants to. We should take that into account and give her a fair chance to speak for herself."

"Forget it!" Beka says. "She was planning to do something to me! Who knows what? Now we know whose friend she really is. Anything she says will just be a pack of lies."

I know what she was going to do, and everyone deserves to hear it, but they might not be ready to hear the truth of it, if they'd even care. Still, if they found out I was keeping it from them, they might suspect me as being a spy, too. I'll be careful about what I say, even as I say it.

"She was going to bring you and Dru to the *Devant*," I answer. "For medical tests."

A host of curses, gasps, and hisses fill the level. Beka screeches her disgust, but Dru only shrinks in her chair, moving closer to Niah, who stares at them both with a frown. I feel the tension in my gut. *I hope I just did the right thing.*

Efa's face turns troubled. "Why? Dru and Beka are fine. We all are. What more tests do they need? The virus is gone."

"Not on the *Devant*, it's not," I answer.

Murmurs float through the crew. Mari whispers something to Beka, who now looks like she just ate something bad.

"Wait," Merek says, holding his hand up. "Raey was going to abduct Dru and Beka so she could experiment on them?"

"Just how bad is it over there?" Efa asks.

I shrug. "Bad enough to make them want to steal a few of our crew, I guess."

We all hang our heads. No one wants the *Devant*'s people to suffer like we did. At least, not the ones who are innocent of causing us harm. And there are a lot. Only the security agents attack us. Everyone else likely has no negative opinions about the *Stratford*. At least they didn't until their commander poisoned their thoughts. I bet most of the *Devant*'s crew would have been excited to meet people from another ship.

As the others agonize over this, my mind wanders through the possibilities, until Sayer slaps his hands on his legs so hard it echoes across the level and returns.

"And she was planning to expose Dru and Beka to that hyuking disease?" he shouts. "Was she ever really helping us? Or just herself and her crew?"

"Easy," Merek warns, motioning with his eyes at Dru and Beka. But it only agitates him more.

"And we want to give her a chance to talk?" He stands and shakes his hands in the air. "Hyuk no! Toss her out the airlock! That's what she deserves."

"Sit down, Sayer," Niah growls.

"No!" He jabs a finger at me and Efa. "You'd better straighten your heads out so you can understand this. Raey is the enemy, and the only thing we do to the enemy is execute them!"

The crew collapses into chaos.

Shouts come from all sides, the noise so loud I clap my hands over my ears. Even then, I still catch a few words from everyone.

"...out the airlock!" Deryn cries.

"...our friend..." someone else fires back.

"No...the *Devant*...war!"

My stomach threatens to launch my dinner onto the deck. Maybe there was no stopping this. Sayer could have been planning to provoke everyone into action from the moment he watched Dru and Beka collapse under Raey's deception. I should have known this would happen with him. Sayer was the only one of the senior crew who was captured by the *Devant*'s security agents. I'm sure he resisted every chance he got, and they made him as miserable as they could in retaliation. That's something he'll never forget. Or forgive.

"Shut up!" Merek shouts, throwing his hands over his head. "Everyone shut up!"

Once the crew calms down, he nods to Efa, and they turn their attention to her. Efa circles once around the chairs as she ponders something. After a minute, she pivots to face all of us, resting her hands on her lower back.

"We'll put it to a vote, just like we do everything important. Take a moment to think about this. In battle, we killed others because we didn't want to die. None of us ever want to relive that. But Raey isn't a soldier. She's not a threat to us like that. So make sure you take that into consideration. We don't execute someone who doesn't deserve it."

The hair on the back of my neck rises as Efa speaks. How ridiculous is this? We're about to vote on whether to murder someone? To take their life? On purpose? They're actually going to consider killing Raey! Over what? *Being a spy?*

"You…you can't be serious!" I shout before I realize it, shooting to my feet as my chair tips over and crashes to the floor. Aidan jumps away with a yelp, ducking behind Deryn before he realizes how foolish that was.

"Of course we are," Merek replies. "That's why we're taking a vote."

"To end someone's life after thinking about it for a minute?"

"I've been thinking about it way longer than a minute," Sayer answers, leaning forward in his seat to rest his elbows on his knees and level his gaze at me. "And you were there, Fana. You saw exactly what I did."

"And I stopped you from killing her then!"

Ceri should be here. She should know what her crew is about to decide. No way would she allow this vote to happen. And she's likely shot and stabbed more people than anyone here.

"Hey," Efa says, putting a hand on my shoulder. "I understand you care about her. I've spent a lot of time with Raey. She's not a bad person. But this...is well beyond anything I'd ever expect she was capable of. I mean, all Raey had to do was up the dose or switch to something more potent, and we'd be saying goodbye to Dru, Beka, *and* Rhys. Our crew deserves to vote on this. Justice needs to be done."

"How the hell is this justice?" I turn to catch everyone's gaze. "Don't you all realize that this only makes things worse? When does it end? I mean, what if you suddenly decide I'm the enemy?"

Merek's brow wrinkles. "Why would we do that? You're one of us, Fana."

"Yeah," Tegan echoes. "You're one of us."

There are gentle smiles and nods all around. Of course there would be. My loyalty isn't in question. Neither is Raey's. It was never a secret whose crew she was on, and she never tried to hide where she belonged.

"Okay," Efa says, turning back to the rest of the crew. "Whoever believes we should hold—"

I shake my head. *This isn't happening. This is insane.* I can't take part in a vote to end the life of someone I was in love with. Deeply. It's so far beyond wrong. *But nobody will hear me. Nobody will listen!*

"No!" I clap my hands over my ears. "No, I can't do this! I won't!"

I race toward the ladder as everything spins around me. There's no stopping. I can't. My feet keep moving, even when I think I'll collapse. I keep going. I must get away.

"Fana! Wait!" Merek calls after me. "Let's talk about this!"

"Let her go," Sayer says. "We don't need her vote."

My blood is pounding in my ears, muting every other sound. I hit the ladder and slide down, rushing across the level to the next one. Ceri. I need Ceri. She's got to stop this madness.

As I drop to level ten, then eleven, it gets harder to breathe. I've got to rest. I find a side corridor and back into it, hitting the wall at the end and sliding down it. I'm gasping hard for air, gulping and wheezing as my head rolls back. Drops of sweat slide down my neck. It's horrible. The entire thing is horrible.

But what if Ceri doesn't listen? What happens then?

Raey was right to beg me. She knew. She knew this could happen. And I ran away from her. I'm a coward. I'm useless. Ceri would never want me.

Tears stream down my face. I bawl. Hard. I cry for the weakling I am. A complete failure.

No. No, I'm not.

In that dark corridor, gasping for breath, I realize I've got to prove myself. Not just to her. I've got to do it for myself, too. I've got to do what I fear I can't.

I've got to defend Raey.

DISJUNCTION

CERI

TEGAN, AIDAN, AND NIAH gape at the mess strewn across the med bay as I struggle to clean it up. They're frozen in that moment before comprehension kicks in and they realize they should help me. Then comes the awkward coordination between Tegan and Aidan to figure out how to get Niah back to bed safely. Niah solves the problem by pushing the two of them away and hobbling to the bed by herself.

I could almost laugh. We're a pair of broken bodies, her and I. Yet despite her difficulties, Niah moves with purpose, driven by the desire inside of her to be free of others' support.

Me? I can't catch a fifteen-year-old girl with my two good legs.

"So you're planning to share what happened here, yeah?" Niah asks as she leans back on a pillow.

"That should be obvious," I mutter as I strain to lift the cart up, both my shoulders aching from their recent wounds. Tegan's there a second later, dropping a handful of IV fluid packets to grab the opposite side. Together, we turn it upright and set it down on its wheels.

As Tegan retrieves her packets to set them on the cart, I shuffle over to Niah, my head lowered. I can feel her watching me, perhaps with some mild curiosity. Whatever judgment I sense from her is in my head, just my conscience chastising me for failing to protect one of my crew.

"Where'd she go?" Niah asks.

"Down. Way down," I answer, leaning against the edge of her bed. "And as soon as I can brief Efa, we're heading down after her."

"Are you sure that's the best plan?"

My head jerks up to stare at her, wide-eyed. I rack my brain to come up with a reason for her challenge—I can't. I'd demand she explain it to me if I didn't think I'd embarrass myself with her answer. Niah taught me nearly everything I know about being a leader. None of it connects with what she's asked me.

"It's Seren!" My hands spread wide. "She's no match for Daga!"

"What makes you think he'll kill her?"

I blink, unable to understand what she's getting at. It took Niah a long time to build the courage to get out of bed. I'd hate to believe she's trying to hold me back because she's scared about what could happen. Yet I can't get that thought out of my head. How did she change so much?

"You know what that bastard did! Seren's loaded a backpack full of ammunition and painkillers. What do you think she's planning to do the moment she sees him? He'll kill her for sure!"

Niah leans her head to one side, exhaling through her nose. My blood is already boiling from her lack of urgency. Any more of this and I'm going to throttle her.

"I doubt that," she says. "Killing her is a poor move, strategically."

I have to turn away. Looking at her any longer will only move me to violence. How can she be talking about strategy at a time like this? There's only one plan here: go down in force and destroy Daga before he harms Seren or anyone else on my crew.

"You're coming with me, right?" I ask Tegan just as she's placing the last packet on the cart.

Tegan goes still, her gaze drifting toward Niah, as if she needs her permission to respond. Hardly. My fists are clenching, and I'm not sure I can remain calm for much longer.

I glance at Aidan. "What about you?"

He presses his lips together, dropping his gaze to the floor. My gut tightens as the rage builds inside me. How could they not want to save their crewmate? Haven't there been enough deaths already? I don't understand it. All that matters is Seren.

"Come on!" I shout. "Don't you care what happens to her? No one else dies on this ship! No one!"

Perhaps I should just go alone. Then I wouldn't have to deal with these cowards. But it would be more than a foolish choice. Daga will target me for sure. And with only one useful arm, there's no way I could defeat him. I'd end up dead, just like Seren.

"Ceri, there's something you don't know," Tegan says, moving to stand before me. I frown and face her, trying to discern what that means. Whatever. It had better be the best excuse I've ever heard. If it's not, I'll grab her by the collar and shake the life out of her.

"Then tell me," I growl.

Tegan looks askance at Niah again, and I fume. But when Niah nods and Tegan's face covers with regret, my chest tightens.

"Raey's been arrested," she says. "She tried to abduct Dru and Beka and take them back to the *Devant* for some kind of experiments. There's an outbreak over there. That virus. Apparently, a few of their crew died."

If I had received this news at any other time, I'd be concerned. Even when I trusted her to care for my crew, Raey has always been under my suspicion. No one can split their loyalties the way Raey pretended to. I only let her heal us because she had made an oath to help others. Of that, I had no doubts.

"And?" I level my gaze at her and cross my arms.

Tegan curls her lips in before responding. "We had a vote. Some wanted to execute her on the spot, but they didn't win. At least not there. Efa's set a trial for tomorrow. And if she's found guilty, who knows what'll happen to her?"

I squeeze my eyes shut. This is a distraction. There's no reason to execute Raey. She has way more value to us alive. And Beka and Dru seemed fine when they were here. That they're already out says a great deal about how Raey didn't want to harm them.

Sayer must be pushing for it. I can be sure of that. But this is just a problem I don't need right now.

"Nobody's killing her," I say. "That is not an option. I don't care what Sayer says. And any dumb bish trial can wait until we've got Seren back with us, safe."

"You'd better talk to Efa about it, then," Niah says.

I spin on her. "Why? Why do I need to talk to her about it? If I'm the leader, then what I say gets done. No discussion! There's no need for a debate about such an obvious hyuking thing! Efa knows how stupid it is. Why's she giving in to that idiot?"

"Efa's having a hard time making everyone understand what you think should be clear. And she tried."

I throw my good arm up. "Well, then she'll have to postpone it! This is far from priority! Lock Raey in a room where she can't do any harm. She'll be fine there until we can deal with her."

Tegan and Aidan share a glance. They'd better share whatever they just communicated.

"I don't know, Ceri," Tegan says.

I huff and shake my head. How difficult is this to understand? Seren could already be dead, and if I can't get help, I'll never know. I'm far from willing to accept that.

"Forget it, just give me your comm," I say, holding my hand out.

Tegan does as requested. I snatch it up and make quick work of getting Efa online to explain the situation. She's quiet as I talk, and that rubs me hard. The first word from her mouth will be to dismiss my concerns. She's just lucky I can't smack her through the comm.

"This isn't a great time for this," she says once I finish.

"When would it ever be?" I shoot back.

There's silence on her end for longer than I'm comfortable to wait. A second is already too much. If she can't answer that instantly, then I'm not talking to the right person.

"Just get some rest," Efa says finally. *"We'll go after her when we can."*

Efa disconnects before I can reply. I grit my teeth and squeeze the comm so hard I shake. How dare she try to treat me like her patient? What the hyuk is happening on this ship?

No, I don't care. This is all total bish, and I'm through with it. I lift Tegan's comm over my head and stretch my arm back to fire the device at the wall. Tegan's mouth drops open, and she launches herself at my arm, catching my wrist to stop me.

We stare at each other, locked in a tense stalemate, until reason reaches my brain again. I sigh and hand the unit back to her. Tegan offers a sympathetic smile, and heat comes to my face. Maybe forcing my will on everyone isn't the right way to go about this. They have a right to be concerned, or worried, or whatever it is they're feeling. And if I am their leader, I should know how to handle my crew.

"I really need your help," I say, catching everyone's gaze. "Please. I don't know if I could handle losing her. We've lost too many already. It's my fault Seren ran. I need to make it right with her, and I can't do that if she's..."

I get choked up and collapse on Niah's bed, folding my hands into my lap as strength evaporates from my limbs. Every thought of Seren shakes me. I can't have regrets anymore. Not with her. They'll eat at me until I'm something far less than Niah. And there will be no chance of recovery.

"Have trust in her," Niah says as she rests her hand on my shoulder and squeezes. "Seren's upset, but she's sharp. She'll survive long enough to wake up from her grief and realize just how stupid she's been."

A shiver races through my body. "And what if she can't?"

"You know she will. You taught her everything she knows."

Aidan and Tegan share another glance, and I tense. Aidan approaches, kneeling before me, his hands on his knees.

"Ceri, we didn't want to bring this up, but you should know something else," he says.

"What?" I can hardly think of anything that's messed with my emotions more than Seren walking out on me, though everyone's refusal of my wishes is a close second.

"Fana refused to vote. She ran before anyone could stop her."

Bish. Of course. She's likely taking all of this hard. She needs someone to talk to if she's feeling alone. But as much as I want to, I can't be that person. Not until Seren's back.

Unless...

Fana could help me find Seren. And I could help her. Yes. That's got to be the best option, because it's the only option I've got that makes any sense.

I push up from Niah's bed and remove the sling around my arm, sucking in a breath through my teeth as I lift my arm to take it out. For a moment I get dizzy, but I recover and toss the sling on my bed.

"Don't be ridiculous," Niah warns. "Efa said you need rest. Sit this one out."

"Impossible," I reply.

"You need to think this through again before you cause a permanent problem to your health."

"I'll think about it along the way."

"Ceri." Niah's voice becomes so gentle it makes my skin crawl. "Do you really want to end up like me?"

Our gazes connect, and I shudder. But in that moment, we share more than we could ever with words. I am to her as Seren is to me. I don't want to cause her distress, but Niah doesn't want me to be tortured by grief, either. And I would be if I stayed here.

Niah lowers her eyes, backing down, even as pain crosses her face. I wish I wasn't responsible for doing that, but if I had wishes to use, I would have wished the adults of the custodial crew had never woken us up.

"I've got to go," I say and move to the door.

"Where?" Aidan asks.

I pivot to look at them once more, my face in apology. I hope they understand. There's a good chance they might.

"To find Fana," I reply.

CONNECTION

FANA

OKAY. THAT'S IT. I'M done with crying.

If I'm truly to save Raey, I need proof. And I need help. Ceri's that help. She's my shining light. My master program. If anyone can uncover the evidence I need to save Raey, it's her. She'll be the one to cut through this execution nonsense and get the crew to realize how wrong their thinking is.

I wipe the wetness from my cheeks, sniffle a few times, and push to my feet. Ceri's still in medical. Maybe. I haven't known her to stay in one place for very long. Though Efa dosed her pretty hard. If she's woken up yet, she'll probably be fighting to shake the dizziness from her head.

But she'll want to help, even if she's in recovery mode. I'm more than confident about that. I felt it before when she held my hand and let me care for her. It was like she wanted to tell me something—*No. Never mind. This isn't the time to think about that.*

But still...

Pressing out of the darkness of the side corridor, I jog to the ladder to level twelve and climb down it. Two more floors before I'm there. Even at my single-processor speed, I'll make it to medical before the rail car arrived on eleven.

I turn down the main corridor, taking the most direct path to the next descent. Maybe I've got enough time to get this done. Maybe I don't, but I won't be wasting it plodding through the corridors as I whine about my plight. I should be thinking about what I need to say to Ceri so I don't stumble over every word like a total idiot. She's got to understand what I'm asking for quickly so we can get moving on it.

Then, as if appearing from out of my wish, Ceri's dark brown head pops through the ladder port. I pause and watch. One step later and she flies through to land on the deck with the lightest of touches.

Wow, that's impressive. No wonder her enemies never stood a chance.

"Ceri!" I call and wave, jogging toward her. She spots me in a heartbeat, standing straight as she waits for me to get to her.

"I was looking for you," she says.

"Really?" I catch my breath and smile. "Same here."

The hardness evaporates from Ceri's face as she slides her hands into her back pockets and tilts her head.

And then silence. I curl in my top lip and wait for her to speak. *Oh! Hold on.* That's what she's doing, watching me with that look of hers—cool and detached, but with a nuclear furnace powering it. I can feel my cheeks turning red as our gazes connect. *Oh boy.* If this keeps up, I'll melt for sure.

"You go first," she says, motioning toward me with her head.

"No." I hold up a hand and shake my head. "It's okay, say what you need to."

"No, it's..." Her lips curve upward then, too sharp to fall into that routine. I smile back, a happy warmth flooding into me. But the intensity of the moment builds so suddenly, I've got to drop my gaze or risk fainting.

She has absolutely no idea what she's doing to me.

"I need to find Seren," Ceri says, and the serious turn her voice takes makes me look up again. "She went after Daga. On her own. I'm going after her, and I need your help. You don't need to come. I just need someone to provide support and notify Efa in case anything happens."

Anything happens? My jaw drops. "Seren's gone somewhere?"

But that's just my brain catching up with my mouth as it runs through the horrible vision of Seren lying wounded somewhere down in a machine room. And Ceri, alone, searching desperately to find her. I swallow back the distress that I feel and do my best to keep myself from dropping into a complete panic.

Ceri shifts when she realizes I've said all I was going to and asks, "You'll help me, won't you?"

"Yes! Of course!" I burst out. "Of course I will!"

I mean, how could I not? I'd tie her bootlaces if she asked me to. Anything she needed I'd take care of in an instant. Ceri doesn't even need to ask, and I think she knows it. Yet she asks out of consideration for me. And that only makes me want to help her more. It's pathetic, but my self-worth increases the more use I can be to her.

She smiles again and gets closer. A breath catches in my throat, and I hold it. How Ceri has this effect on me, I'll never know. Raey and I weren't this intense when we first met. We just—

Wait...Raey. Oh no. What should I do?

How can I ask Ceri to help me now? And how can I do both the things I've chosen to do? I'm a good multitasker, but it'd be well out of my ability to cover everything I needed to and remain useful. I want to help Raey, and I must help Ceri.

Would Ceri understand if I explained my problem? What if I've got no choice but to focus on Raey? Would Ceri get mad? *Bish, what do I do?*

"Ceri, you should know something," I say, quickly closing the distance between us, my hands landing on her arms. "They're putting Raey on trial. If they find her guilty, they could execute her."

The frown that crosses her face is strange. Did she already know? Wouldn't she say so, then? This is more like she didn't care, and that can't be. Ceri may not trust Raey, but she doesn't want her dead, either.

"So?" Ceri shrugs.

I blink, staring at her. Is she just so focused on Seren she's got no time for anything else? No. She's a better leader than that. But the way she just brushed off my concern is making my heart slam against my ribs. Doesn't she realize what will happen?

"So?" I shake her arms. "She'll die!"

Ceri shakes her head. "She'll be fine. No need to overreact. Raey's getting locked up, and that's it."

What? How can she think I'm overreacting? I get she might be really upset about Seren and maybe not thinking as clearly about this as she could be, but that shouldn't make her forget how Raey is a human being and deserves to be treated with respect.

"I'm not overreacting!" I reply. "No one but me was defending her, and they wouldn't listen to a word I said. She deserves a chance to tell her side! Maybe she's innocent."

Ceri takes hold of my arms, her fingers brushing across my skin as her hands slide up to my elbows. I inhale a shaky breath, quivering at her touch. She's got to feel that. I can't stop. I might not want to. But it's wrong. This is about Raey and how to prevent her from dying. But I'm seriously doubting I can stay her execution. At least not on my own.

If I had Ceri's help, I'm sure I can prove that Raey is far from a traitor. Yet no matter what I say, Ceri's going after Seren, even if she has to do it alone. That could mean her fighting Daga again. There's no way she's ready to do that. Likely she's already told Efa her plans, and if Efa couldn't stop her, I shouldn't even try. Should I?

"Is she innocent?" Ceri asks, locking eyes with me again. It's different this time. Ceri's getting fidgety, as if she already knows what's in my mind.

I pull away and take a moment to get calm by pacing around the landing. It's a good idea to distance myself from her, too. I don't want to be close by when she realizes I'm going back on my word.

Oh hell, is that what I'm really going to do? How is she going to take it?

I let a slow exhale. I was always going to defend Raey, wasn't I?

There's no reality in which I could turn Ceri down. And that's not what this is. It's just a delay in saying yes. Or maybe I'm just lying to myself. Still, my reply won't crush her, but it's crushing me to disappoint her even a tiny bit.

"I want to believe in Raey," I reply, pausing my rambling gait and facing her. "Maybe she's just misguided or feeling trapped, I don't know. But I'm sure she had no intention of hurting anyone. That's why I've got to stand up for her. If she's on her own, I don't think she'll survive."

My heart crumbles as Ceri's shoulders droop. Her face grows pained, even as she struggles to hide her disappointment. In me. I can't imagine how alone she must feel. All she wants is to save someone she cares about. Someone who's important to her and to this ship. Yet the others turned her down. And I just slammed the door on her last hope. Me. The one who's supposed to be in love with her.

"I'm so sorry," I say, rushing to her, arms out. But I hesitate to touch her. How can I comfort her when I just crushed her hopes? I don't deserve to. Not at all. I shouldn't expect her to accept anything from me now I've turned her down. "Ceri, talk to me," I say as my voice breaks.

She runs her tongue across her teeth and exhales, pressing her lips tight. Every bit of me aches with regret. I reach out, my fingers landing on her forearm. Should I try to do more? Will she deny me? How can I have done this to her?

Ceri pulls away and shakes her head. "No, it's alright. You're doing the right thing. Raey's side deserves to be heard, so you should help her. It makes sense."

"Yeah, I—"

"I have to go." Ceri moves to turn back to the ladder. But she must see something in my gaze, because she pauses. I should say something. It should be meaningful. Or wise. Or something.

Dammit, just speak!

"Please be careful," I plead. "I don't want to lose you."

Ceri forces a smile and nods. Then, to my surprise, she returns to me, leaning in, but then she hesitates. Her lips are close to my face. Her warm breath brushing across it sends a shiver down my spine. I go still. *Is she about to kiss my cheek?* Why the indecision? Hasn't she done this to Efa before?

As if in answer to my confusion, her lips press against my cheek, holding there for longer than is casual. Her soft touch sets an inferno on my skin. I gasp, soft and light, trying to hide my surprise.

Wait. Does this mean that she...likes me? Is this a promise for something more to come? Dare I hope?

Then Ceri dashes off, leaving me in a state of frustrated elation. How could she?

"Wait!" bursts from my mouth before I can stop it.

Ceri pivots, blinking at me.

"What was that?" I cry, my heart pounding in my chest. An ache forms around it—a need to understand. A desire to hope. My body presses toward her, as if pulled by some gravitational force. I clench my fists and strain to resist getting nearer. I can't. All I want is to know.

She bites her lower lip and stares as if she's considering something. I get breathless, hanging on her answer. If only she were to tell me the words I want to hear. But I don't deserve them. Not after I pushed her away in her time of need. It's too selfish of me. *Oh, why can't I stop messing this up?*

"Yeah, you're right," she replies.

Suddenly Ceri's coming back, fast, rushing toward me, her steady gaze focused on my face. My eyes grow wide. *What's she—*

Panic rushes through me. I step back.

Then she's there, right before me. Her hands come up. She cups my cheeks. *Wow, why am I so hot?* Ceri's head is tilting. I can't breathe. My skin tingles more with every passing second. My body yearns for her. *Oh bish, is this really happening?* I press to her, my lips parting as my head leans back. I inhale slightly.

And then she kisses me.

This is...it's...impossible. But...it is!

Everywhere her mouth meets mine is heaven. Our lips touch with such a passionate tenderness it makes my knees weak. I want more. I need more. My hands slide to her hips. I press up to meet her body again. Then I close my eyes and fall into our connection. Her arms wrap around me, sliding across my back.

I tremble as her fingers slide down, touching my waist with a gentle caress. Ceri presses against me, and I melt further into her. I'm floating. I must be. My feet have left the deck.

And of course, it's over far too soon. Ceri pulls away, searching my face for what she must hope is a positive reaction. It is. It so is.

"I'll be back soon," she whispers, breathless. I just stare, words having left my brain a long time ago.

Ceri rushes to the ladder, then pauses, turning to look at me, her face glowing with pure joy and maybe what might be a little regret.

"Sorry," she says. And then she's gone.

That's when my legs give out and I drop to the deck with a whimper, staring at the spot where our eyes last connected.

How am I ever going to be the same again?

IMPOSITION

CERI

THE ARMORY ON TWENTY-FIVE is dark, save for a row of lights that illuminate the weapons racks, sending tiny beams across the level as they reflect off the worn parts of pistols and blades, scraped clean of the tactical gray we'd painted them with to hide such tells. The potent yet familiar scent of gun oil hangs in the air, drawing me deeper into my self-induced haze.

I don't know how long I've been staring at my pack, lost in that moment. I keep replaying it in my head because to forget, even for a second, the smallest detail would be heresy. It's still hard to believe I did it, though my pounding heart says otherwise.

Did Fana like it? She did, didn't she? Maybe I should've been gentler. Fana was ready to run away.

I squeeze my eyes shut and shake myself out of the dream I've been living for the last twenty minutes. Or is that reality, and everything I've done until then has been a dream? Nightmare, more like. No matter what, I hope our next time comes soon. Very soon.

But first, I've got to rescue Seren.

I stuff my belt pack full of dart clips, my jaw tightening with each one I jam into its slot as I get closer to understanding why she wanted to kiss me that night. I just wish she hadn't been so impulsive about it. She knows better. Still, I suppose if I was Fana...

A vision flashes across my eyes. Daga. His face is contorted. Bloody. He grins as he rips his blade from someone's chest. With a choked cry, they stumble back and collapse. I rush to their side, turning their face toward mine.

And see Fana's lifeless eyes.

My breath gets short. The deck spins around me, and I'm forced to drop myself onto the stool in the space. As I fight to push air into my lungs, I double over, my hands slapping onto the workbench to steady myself.

Then, just as quickly as it hit, the dizziness evaporates, leaving me exhausted, with an ache in my chest that's all too familiar. Death lives in me. It disturbs my sleep and forces my imagination to run wild. It haunts me with the faces of my squad mates lost in battle. Until now, I've managed such horrors. I'm not sure I can if Fana continues to appear in them.

A clank on the down ladder sends me shooting off the stool, a gun and a blade in my hands. Daga wouldn't be as foolish as that, but I won't chance it. He'll use everything we learned from him against us.

I'm overimagining things, however. It's just Efa and Merek. Though, by the tightness on her face, she's another kind of threat altogether. I lower my weapons but keep my guard up.

Efa stops a few paces away. Three, exactly. Enough to keep her out of the reach of a blade and to give her ample time to react to a gun aiming at her. She stands, mirroring my stance but with hands open. When her eyes drop to the weapons in my hands, I holster the gun and put the blade back in its leg sheath, more out of embarrassment than anything else.

Merek keeps close to her, but his posture is more casual, save for the worry that creases his brow. I prepare myself for the trouble that's coming.

"We know everything," Efa says. "Fana told us."

My eyes go wide as heat rushes across my face. How could she? That was a moment meant for us. Only us. I would never have blabbed about it to anyone. As it is, I broke my own rules. Not that I could help it. Something powerful came over me. And I won't regret my actions for even half a heartbeat.

Efa frowns and approaches, watching my face with a suspicious eye. I avoid her gaze as she comes closer, confused what she's on about. For a moment, the edges of her lips turn upward into a half smirk. It disappears a second later as her suspicion returns.

"Are you—" She shakes her head. "Never mind."

Wait. This is about something else. Fana's kept our moment to herself. My shoulders relax and I exhale. This'll likely become a standard disagreement between the two of us. Still, I should make sure of that.

"What did Fana tell you?" I try.

Efa's face turns dark. "Where you were going. And you're not. At least not yet and absolutely not by yourself."

Merek shifts and folds his arms as he braces for the upcoming battle. Looks like he'll be keeping out of it unless it gets bad. With all the problems we've had lately, that's a real possibility. My gut's tightening over the idea of another fight with Efa. I'd much rather be blabbing to her than trading blows.

I truly miss the carefree moments with her. Maybe one day. Right now, I'm about to make my will known.

"No." My tone is firm but not angry. I'm tired of fighting with her. "We've wasted too much time already. I won't risk another moment where Seren could get hurt. Or worse."

I stiffen, but Efa's counterstrike never comes. Instead, her face turns pained as she rubs her thumbs over tight fists. So I've misjudged the situation. I should be glad for that. Yet the tightness in my shoulders stops me from feeling any relief. Maybe I'm afraid of what she'll say. I roll my shoulders to loosen up and relax, but it doesn't help, and I only become tenser.

"Ceri, I just want to talk," she pleads, stepping closer. "I'm worried about you. It's not good for you to be cutting your recovery time short. You did that with that weapon blast you took to your side, and look at what happened."

"I'm fine," I reply. "Better than you might think."

In some ways, that's true, though I'm keeping that to myself for now.

"And where's your sling?" Efa challenges.

"I don't need it."

Efa sighs and looks to Merek, who takes the cue and steps in. He drops his hands and steps next to Efa, taking her by the arm. She presses close to him in a show of unity. Massing forces is all it is. Perhaps this'll be a battle after all. Very well. Despite my reluctance, I'm ready.

"We're all concerned for Seren," he begins. "It's—"

"If you're so concerned," I counter, "why are you holding some bish trial instead of organizing a team to go after her? And yeah, Fana told me everything."

They share a glance. Unprepared to spar with me, I guess. Maybe I should go easy on them. Or not. The sooner I end this conversation, the faster I can head down. All I need is another blade and a canteen, and I'll be ready.

"Then you know Sayer's calling for Raey's execution," Merek continues, "and if he keeps it up, the rest of the crew will join him."

For a moment, I just stare at him. It'd be far from the first time that Sayer tried to rally others to his reckless ideals. Usually after we beat him over the head with reason, he backs down. This time won't be any different.

"So? Put him in his place," I reply, moving to a storage cabinet. "He's your friend."

"He's yours, too."

I level my gaze at him. "And what is Seren to you?"

Efa rolls her eyes. "Come on. We're not choosing anyone over anyone else. We're going after Seren as soon as we settle this situation with Raey. You know we need the entire crew to beat Daga. Especially if we want to avoid more casualties."

She offers me an apologetic smile, and I get the sense that she's asking, rather than demanding, I do what she wants me to. Perhaps I should. But there's something she's not telling me. Not directly, anyway. It'll have to wait unless she wants to just come out with it.

I grit my teeth as I pull a canteen from the locker and give it a quick examination, hoping it will remove the unease growing within me. Efa wouldn't ask me for help unless she really needed it. And she knows how every second that passes is one less for us to retrieve Seren unharmed.

"You can handle Sayer," I say with calm. "I can't think straight enough to solve that problem. Not until I bring Seren back."

Efa watches me as she chews on her lower lip. Her breathing's faster than normal, too. She's definitely hiding something. I might just be about to find out.

"Did you consider how Fana would feel if you went and got yourself killed?" Efa charges.

Bish. They know about our kiss, after all.

How do I reply? I'm not ready to confess anything to them. Not in the middle of this conversation. If I mention anything close to love, they'll use it against me, and that'll be a hard weapon to defend against. I'm not even sure if I'm in love. I don't look at Fana the same way Efa looks at Merek. Though the opposite is obvious. Fana's unskillful attempt to hide her feelings has all but failed. And I've heard Seren and Rhys openly discussing it once, before I stopped them by putting them to work.

And nothing's changed. My moment of weakness, one I hope to repeat often, is making my head spin. I've got no time to consider how I feel. I just know if Fana were here, I'd be reaching out for her again.

"No one is dying," I reply, clipping the canteen to my belt. "That includes Seren. And Raey. I can't be in both places at once. The two of you are better at that kind of thing, anyway."

"But you're crew leader," Merek says. "Only you can make some of these choices."

"So I'll step down." I throw the pack over my good shoulder and buckle the waist straps around me.

As I reach for a blade, Efa grabs my arm. I jerk away, but she holds on. Her touch is soft, and I pause. What could she be after?

"Ceri, you can't fight anymore," she says and locks her gaze with mine. "It's too dangerous."

The fear in her eyes shakes me to my core, and I shudder as I exhale. Now I'm desperate to know what she's keeping from me. I won't get it with this aggressive stance, however. I reach up and cover her hand on my arm with my own. Efa loosens her grip and slips her fingers into mine.

"I promise you, I will avoid fighting if I can," I say. "I'm going to get Seren and bring her back. That's all I want. Once she's back safe, then we'll deal with Daga together, okay?"

"No, you don't understand." Efa's grip on my hand tightens. "I've been reviewing your medical records. You were lucky that shot you took on your shoulder didn't end you."

My forehead gets tight. "What are you talking about? A single shot there can't kill me. There are no major organs or blood vessels there. You know that."

Merek looks away, swallowing as wetness rims his eyes. A sickness hits my gut, and I brace, as if I know what's coming.

Efa turns me to face her. "Been getting dizzy lately, haven't you? And trouble thinking, too, right? Or breathing?"

No. No. No. She can't do this. Not while Seren is down there. I'm the only one who can bring her back. There's no way I'm going to let Efa sideline me now. I'll fight her if I have to. Merek too.

"So?" I pull my arms from her grip and cross them in front of me.

A sadness touches Efa's face, even as she holds her gaze steady with mine. I won't let it get to me. That'd be like accepting whatever she's about to say, and I can't. She can worry about me all she wants, but no matter what, I'm going. I need my little sister back. I need to tell her I'm sorry. And I need to know she's safe.

"Your body's broken from all the damage it's taken," Efa says. "You won't survive another hit. Even a minor one. Do you understand?"

A chill races through me. Now I get why she was struggling to say it. If this was another time, or a different situation, I could care. I don't have that luxury now.

I nod. "But it won't stop me from going."

Efa's eyes get wet as her fists shake in rage, and the muscles of her jaw tighten as she struggles to keep her emotions under control. But the moment I sigh and look away, she breaks.

"Dammit!" Efa pounds a fist into the locker. "I don't want to watch my best friend die!"

I swallow hard to keep a sob from welling up, even as the pit in my stomach grows deeper. I don't fear death. It is already with me. But if I make my friend suffer over my loss, I will curse myself into the afterlife.

"You won't," I say through clenched teeth.

She grabs me by the arms to force me to look at her. "Don't you realize that Daga's the one responsible for doing this to you?"

I look deeply into her eyes, seeking forgiveness for the thing I am about to do and hoping she will understand. Yet when I see the despair that's there, anger builds inside me, and in it a renewed strength to see this through. I won't accept Seren getting killed, and I won't accept Efa's sadness. Daga must die.

"All the more reason to make sure he never does it to anyone ever again," I say.

RECOVERY

—— • ——

CERI

RATHER THAN CLIMB DOWN to machine access, I take the rail car down to one-twenty-three. Better not to take any risks on nearly a hundred levels' worth of ladders. I'm not sure I could make it, anyway. Efa's words have shaken me hard, and now every step I take puts me in doubt. I don't know if I'm a dead girl walking, but as long as I can breathe, I will do what I must to protect my passengers and crew. Even if that means sacrificing my life for them.

What twists my gut is how Efa was so sure of her opinion. As if anyone with only minor knowledge of the body could determine how much life I've got left. Did Raey reveal something to her? Efa was certainly more upset than I've seen her in a while, and she'd only be that way if she believed whatever she's learned.

Still, it's harder to accept than Daga being here. What made him suddenly come out of the shadows is anyone's guess. It would have been better for everyone if he had just stayed hidden for the remainder of his life, however long or short that would be. I have my preference, of course. With Daga gone, I could do the unexciting things required of a leader, like keeping

Aidan and Deryn from strangling each other, or understanding just how I kissed someone when I swore to put my crew before my own needs.

At least the darkness here brings comfort. After so many months of living under oppressive lighting, it's no wonder I've found solace sleeping under my bed rather than on it. The blackness wraps me with a sense of security, and with everything that's happened, I could use a lot more.

I've been out in the light for too long, that's for certain. It takes minutes for my eyes to adjust to the dark. It used to take five seconds. I'm vulnerable to attack, as I'm forced to wait until I can see again. If Daga came by, this small alcove I'm hidden in wouldn't protect me. He'd know to search it, because that's what he taught us to do.

Once my eyes return to their sensitivity in the dark, I move, using the pinpoint illumination of status lights along the corridor to guide me. I pass rooms full of systems-access terminals, data kiosks, and walls of monitors. Most are dark, save for the few we've used—that Fana's used. The air that brushes across my skin is cool, but the deck is warm, even through my boots. It's a reminder of just how hot machine access will get as I descend closer to the engines.

I pull my gun and round the first corner on my way to the ladder. No *Devant* tech this time. Let Daga give away his position. My advantage lives in the blackest of shadows, where even his sight, long accustomed to a lack of light, might have difficulty. And I'm more familiar with my slender pistol than the bulk of the security agent's beam weapon. A poor design, that is, even if it's powerful. Its designer never imagined it would be used on board a colony ship, or they would have made it smaller and lighter.

A hint of white, tucked just behind a kiosk, catches my eye. I pause, scanning my surroundings for a danger. This is a textbook trap placement, and any rookie squad member would best avoid it, as it would lead them to a quick death. But I'm cautiously optimistic about who put it there, and once I'm certain Daga's not waiting in ambush, I'll go check it out and confirm my hopes.

It's clear. I push off the deck and make a silent dash toward the object. My pulse quickens as I strain my eyes to see what it is. A smile hits my face when I do.

It's a pack of bandages.

Seren put this here. Not as a stash, which she would have hidden well out of sight, but a hint. A message—to let me know she's been here. And that she wants me to follow. Efa, Tegan, and Deryn would also have known its meaning. Seren's hoping for reinforcements, and I can't keep her waiting.

With a surge of adrenaline, I race down the corridor, keeping my eyes wide for another clue. Likely she's farther down in machine access. I just don't know how much farther. Seren would have been smart to bring a comm with her, but she was only acting out of emotion when she rushed down here.

A toppled kiosk blocks the passage—a remnant of a former battle. I curse my lack of foresight in getting it cleaned up and double back to find a way around.

I duck into the centermost of the terminal rooms and power through it to a doorway connecting to a room on the other side of the level. My arm scrapes the doorframe as I run past it, making more noise than I want. It's doubtful anyone's here, but I can't be making mistakes like a recruit.

Still, Seren's not far. I can sense her. Or maybe that's just my wish. More proof would make it real. I'll risk breaking a little caution to find out. Being too safe is also failure.

A quick check of the corridor outside the terminal room and I'm back on track. But at this speed, both Daga and Seren would hear me from a level away. It doesn't matter. I'm desperate to find her before he does. With a renewed spirit, I spin around the last turn of the level.

And drop to a roll, my head missing the top of an old barrier by the breadth of my smallest finger. My sudden move runs me into a wall with a thump. I land on the deck hard, but I'm up in a second, hurdling the final barrier on the level and sliding down the ladder to one-twenty-four.

The backups of all the ship's systems are here, stored in tanks of self-sustaining bio-memory. I'm more concerned with all the potential hiding places on this level. Unless they burst, the tanks are harmless, triple-contained like the *Stratford*'s hull. Daga behind one of them wouldn't be.

As I choose a side of the level to travel down, I catch a flash of light and suck in a breath, dropping instantly. My pistol comes up, held steady as my finger touches the trigger guard. I go still, commanding my breath to slow, even as my heart pounds on the walls of my chest. And I wait.

The only way I'll beat Daga is to take him by surprise. The same way he killed Rhys. It's the one advantage I have alone—I can be as stealthy as he can—perhaps more so.

After a minute, I get up. It's obvious not even the air on this level is moving. Which means I'd better.

Then—something. Another clue? Only one way to know. I dig the toes of my boot into the deck and push off.

And catch my foot on a cable tray.

I yelp, my arms flying up to keep my balance. I can't. My feet leave the deck. For a moment, I'm flying. My body screams, tensing as I come down. This is going to hurt. Badly.

My hands and arms hit first, buckling under the impact. I tuck my head to protect it and twist, but my wounded shoulder smashes the deck. I gasp and shudder, my forward roll collapsing as I land flat on my back.

Pain burns through me as my vision whites out and my head spins. Bish! I'm totally open like this! A five-year-old could take me out. I need situational awareness. Now. I shove off the deck to sit.

And retch. Hard. My stomach threatens to release its contents across a tank's power module. I collapse back down onto the deck.

I turn on my side and curl my knees up to my chest as I wince. My hand covers my shoulder as the wound throbs. Is this it? Is this the one strike that ends me? I refuse to believe it, yet I've never felt this weak. Every muscle in my body aches. I can't move my arm without showers of needles driving into it. If I don't get help, I might not survive. Efa doesn't want to find out this way that she was right.

I fumble for my comm with a shaking hand, struggling to slip it over my head. After a moment of fighting with the brace, it hangs off my ear as the opposite side jams into my skull. I can't die. Not yet. Too many are relying on me. We're already short-handed. Soon we won't be able to manage the ship on our own. That's not an option. I grab the mic button and press it, gasping to catch my breath.

And let it go.

I might survive, but Seren won't. If I make the call, Efa will rescue me. And only me. Why she has such an inflated sense of my importance, I don't know. Any of the crew could be the leader. All they'd need is time to learn.

That's it. There's nothing more to consider. I came down here to rescue Seren, and that's what I'm going to do. I won't die. All I have to do is get up—it's not an impossible task. It's not. I've faced worse. Much worse. The only difference between then and now is I never feared death before. Now I have over four thousand reasons for living, and one of them is named Seren. And another, newly special to me. Her name is Fana.

I grit my teeth and push through the nausea to kneel, sliding my gun back in its holster. My body wobbles before I steady myself by pressing on the deck. I take a moment to catch my breath, then slowly rise, my shoulders pushing back as I come to my full height.

A moment of dizziness hits me. I throw my arms out, panic racing through my body. But then it's gone. It's nothing. A side effect from being laid out on the deck. I'm fine, and I will continue. I inhale and take my first step. Exhale and take the next. When the spinning doesn't return, I advance, increasing speed as I feel more myself again. Halfway down the edge of the level, I'm moving as I should: silent, quick, stealthy.

That no one was here to see my failure is a miracle and a disappointment. Daga would have ended me in an instant. No gloating, no speeches. Just action. And that would have been that. But Seren would have come to my aid instantly. She—

There! Seren's backpack!

I crouch, my weapons in my hands once again. A bit of un-steadiness holds me for a moment. So does my scan of the area—no traps. At least, none obvious. It's enough. I slip to the corner where she stashed it, jammed between a pair of ventilation ducts. Just down the adjacent side is the rail car. I grin. She's remembered her training well. This is her pull-back point. From here on out, she's expecting to be on assault. She can't be far. Maybe less than a few levels down.

Don't do anything stupid, little sister. Anything more than you've already done.

ARGUMENT

FANA

THE AIR ON LEVEL eight is stuffy as I return to the circle of chairs with the crew. Tegan shuffles next to me on one side, with Aidan on the other. She pulls a chair up and offers it to me, but I refuse it, motioning for her to take it instead. I'm not in a sitting mood.

If I was floating through life, high on Ceri's confession, just before I arrived, I've crashed hard looking at everyone's sullen expressions. I can guess why we're here. Why Efa called this meeting, and if I had a violent bone in my body, I might smack her for it.

We're waiting for her now. She and her boyfriend. I know his name, I just don't want to say it. I'll call him Mister Useless instead. He could have talked some sense into Efa and put a stop to this madness. Yet here we are, gathered for what looks like a trial for a neural network accused of going rogue when everyone knows the truth: that's impossible.

It's up to me to make sure everyone knows the truth about Raey. She may be guilty of poor judgment or acting out of fear, but she doesn't deserve to be executed for it. I've got to do everything I can to make sure that doesn't happen.

"Attention, everyone." Merek, the unbootable boy, raises his hands as he and Efa stroll toward the group. "Efa has something to say, and then we've got to vote."

"Where's Ceri?" Dru asks. "I didn't see her in the med bay."

Niah rolls her eyes and folds her hands behind her head as she leans back in her chair. Tegan catches it and frowns. I sigh. *Here we go.*

"Yeah," Tegan echoes. "If she's recovered, shouldn't she be running this?"

"Running what?" I ask, pretending not to know the answer. I want Efa to say it out loud.

She puts her hands on her hips and crushes her lips together as she glares at me. Let her. I don't regret causing her trouble.

"Fana, if you don't want to be here, I think we'll all understand," Efa replies.

I just cross my arms and stand firm.

"Ceri's gone down to retrieve Seren," Efa says, catching everyone's eyes. "It was her choice, and I'm sure you understand. She'd do that for any of you. Anyway, she's fine with us doing this without her here."

Mari and Beka share a glance, their eyes widening. Aidan raises a hand to his open mouth. I've a feeling that none of them knew any of that. *Good job, Efa.*

"What *are* we doing?" Tegan asks.

"Deciding the level of Raey's guilt and what to do about it."

Wait. That doesn't sound like a trial. At least none I've seen. Those were only drama vids, of course, but they must have had some truth to them. There was at least a choice between guilty or innocent that had to be made.

But I put that thought aside as another part of Efa's answer grabs my attention. Ceri must have had a lot on her mind to forget. I might have been part of that. Of course, it's a bit of a selfish thought.

"So you're not executing her?" I ask, because I want to be certain.

"No, thanks to you," Sayer growls, leveling a finger at me. "Your little outburst twisted everyone's thoughts in the wrong direction."

"Not everyone's." Tegan glares as she corrects him.

Sayer shakes his head. "I don't know why you're making me out to be the enemy. I didn't poison Dru and Beka."

So my tantrum was good for something. I bite my lower lip to hold back my grin. My emotional fits used to sway Raey, too. Most of them were real. I was upset, and she comforted me like I was a baby. Even when she knew I was faking it. I'm glad to see they still work.

"You're not the enemy," Efa says. "Far from it. And you know that. Stop making this about you."

Sayer's eyes go wide. "Like hell I am! And don't forget, I'm not the only one who thinks I'm right. Deryn and Beka voted with me."

"Whatever." She sighs. "We voted, and since the majority wins, we're not doing what you want. So we need another option. Anyone have any ideas?"

I blink. How did they jump to this part of the trial? Doesn't Raey get a chance to speak? To explain? Are they so sure about how evil she is, even when all she's done in the past month is take care of everyone?

"Wait, doesn't she—" I start.

"Keep her locked up in that closet until her crew gives us the pods," Mari suggests.

"Yeah, trade her for the pods!" Dru echoes.

"Send her back!" Aidan says. "The sooner we get her off the ship, the better."

"No, idiot!" Niah smacks Aidan's head with the back of her hand. "Who'll take care of you if you get sick?"

I should be thankful one person here besides me has some sense to understand Raey's value to the crew. That should count for something. But they're forgetting all of that in favor of releasing their anger. I can't really blame them. All they've known since their adults tore them from their pods is terror and uncertainty. I doubt they know what mercy is. No one here has ever shown them any.

Still, this conversation is making me jittery. Just because everyone considers her guilty shouldn't be a reason to choose some random sentence. I should speak up.

"None of those ideas are good enough," Sayer says. "We need to send a message to the *Devant* not to mess with us. Punishing her is the way we do that."

"What kind of punishment?" Merek challenges. "She's already locked up."

"Cut her hands off!" Deryn yells and gnashes his teeth. "And send them back to her commander!"

My jaw drops. *Whoa, way too extreme!* I take back what I was just thinking about their sense of compassion. There is none. But I can teach them. I just need a chance.

"Hold on!" I shout. "This isn't the way!"

"Yeah?" Deryn counters. "What is?"

"Aren't you going to give Raey a chance to speak in her defense?"

"Hell no," Sayer answers. "She doesn't deserve one."

I spin on him, heat rising inside of me. No way is he going to control this conversation. "Everyone deserves one, no matter if they're already assumed to be guilty."

Niah catches my gaze and nods to motion her support. Tegan does, too. I give them an upward curl of my lip to show my appreciation. *At least someone's on my side.*

Sayer pushes to his feet, his chair shrieking across the deck. Nearly everyone else follows. He steps up to me, his gaze lowered and his fists up, ready to strike me. My breath gets caught in my throat. The other crew members go still. And Efa, who's supposed to be running this, hasn't said a single word in the last five minutes!

"And what did Beka and Dru deserve?" Sayer demands.

I huff. "That's not an excuse!"

"Why don't you tell them that?" He circles me, and I start really wishing that Ceri was here to protect me.

The last day on Earth, before I moved into the *Devant* permanently, I was gathering the last of my things from my home when I got caught in the middle of a firefight. I hid under my bed and covered myself with whatever I could find. Weapons ripped through the walls, burning everything the beams touched.

And when it was over, I escaped, only to find that both sides had decimated each other. None were left, save for the ones who were still dying. There weren't even medical teams to help them.

I recognized a few of the faces. Some of them had said they were planning to go with us. But they couldn't. Not anymore.

But if I've learned anything from Ceri's training, it's to know when to retreat and when to hold firm. This is a time to stand and fight. I might not win, but I'm absolutely going to put up a hell of a fight.

"And what's your excuse for taking the enemy's side?" Sayer challenges.

That's the best he can do? Okay. He's had less time being alive than I do, plus I've had more happy moments in my life. That doesn't mean he's wishing for more terror in his. If anything, his aggressive support of Dru and Beka shows me how much he cares. I can appeal to that.

"Sayer," I say, my voice shaky. "Until recently, you've been living in a nightmare. Everyone here left Earth because we knew we'd never survive the horror that was happening there. Eventually, anyone who had half a brain and didn't want to die also left. But your custodial crew didn't go through that. They never understood why killing each other couldn't be the way to get what they wanted. Maybe they didn't care to know. But all of you suffered from that, and everything that they promised you was lost. I'm so sorry for what you've been through. Truly."

Dru, Beka, and a few others shift in their seats, sharing uneasy looks. Maybe this is the first time they've ever heard anyone put it to them like that. Maybe they're realizing how they're just prolonging their misery by doing to others what was done to them—exactly what I hoped they would realize. All I know is that it's got to stop.

Sayer shrugs with one shoulder. "What's your point?"

"When does it end, Sayer? When do you stop living the horror that someone else wanted you to?"

Efa seems deep in thought when I glance at her. But I think she's listening, even if she's not watching me. Merek, at least, has his eyes tuned on my next words. So do the rest of the crew. *I need to make my next words Ceri-level great.*

I reach out and wrap his hands with mine. Sayer goes stiff and frowns. I'll give him a point for not pulling away, even when my gaze connects with his. Everyone's really locked on us now. I see them out of the sides of my vision. Good. Time to make my point.

"Sayer," I say again, but with less shakiness. "Let's break this cycle of terror. Let Raey speak for herself, or let me do it. But let's end this bish and create something better so that when the colonists arrive on planet, they'll have what they've been dreaming about, rather than the hell all of us have been through."

Sayer's jaw goes slack as he stares at me, holding that way for a long moment. But afterward, he shakes his head and looks elsewhere. I can feel my hope slipping. That's the best I could do. If he can't understand that, then Raey's really in trouble.

"You are completely nuts," he says and pulls his hands from mine, turning away to sulk. Deryn watches him with a furrowed brow. So does Beka, even though her gaze has something sparkling in it now.

"I think it's a good idea," Merek says. I spin on him, my eyes wide, and he smiles at me. "Fana's got a point. We've got to do better than the adults."

"I'll second that," Niah says. "She just said the most intelligent thing I've heard on this ship all week."

"But we are doing better!" Efa protests, her face troubled. Likely somewhere in the back of her mind, I bet she realizes what I said is the right way to do things.

The rest of the crew gathers around me, nodding and looking relieved. I'm far from surprised. Okay, I am surprised. A little. How I put some words together in some sort of way that made sense is nothing short of a miracle.

Now all I hope is that they act on it.

"Okay," Efa says, the beginnings of a smile coming to her face. "If you've got something you want to say about Raey, we'll listen. I can't guarantee anything will change, but for the time that you're talking, we promise to do our best to understand."

I smile back and nod.

Ooh, Ceri would be so proud of me.

DEPTH

— • —

CERI

ONE-TWENTY-FIVE. THERE'S LITTLE BELOW this save for the engines and the fuel that powers them. This is the domain of engineers. Of people like Fana. I'm almost afraid to touch anything, for fear of affecting the delicate balance of systems she's created to keep the *Stratford* on course. That goes doubly so for firing my weapon down here. If I have a choice, I'll use my blades.

And after the hell Daga has put us through, I'll be glad to watch him bleed to death.

The good thing about this level, besides the near-absolute dark, is most of it is just pipes and conduit, twisted in a never-ending tangle devised by someone—an engineer—to make the best logical sense for the application. Every bit of turned metal and formed composite burns with heat-soaked coolants and environmental air, warmed to keep the absolute freeze of space out of the ship. But the inefficiencies of insulation reward this level with an abundance of sweltering heat. At least that's how Fana explains it. She might as well have been speaking another language.

I advance carefully, my pistol and blade out, through the maze of pipes, dipping and dodging through spaces built with little consideration for people. Save for occasional maintenance, what happens down here is better left to the machines. Humans are just vermin crawling through the framework.

My head bumps into a hot duct, and I double over, hissing out a curse, my hand rubbing the spot to erase the pain. Luckily, it never comes, and I'm back up and worming my way through the mechanized jungle. Perhaps the level wanted to remind me how I am an unwelcome guest here. I proceed with more caution than before, mostly because I prefer not to hit my head again. Though, this level is difficult—

A bright beam slices across my path. I drop behind an air pump, my body screaming to flee, but I force myself to hold still. That was too close. If Daga gets another shot, he won't miss again. He picked the right level for an ambush, but he's lost his advantage. I push up and scramble, racing to find cover before he gets a better angle on me. The nearest wall is a safe bet. That'll cut down on the number of directions he can attack from.

I gasp for air as I run, nearly blinded by the heat that smacks across my face. This is foolish. I need cover to catch my breath, or I'll faint before I'm safe.

There!

I dive into a small recess between two massive machines, stopping short to avoid touching them. Fana's still got the scar on her back from slamming into one. I care less about that than the scream I'll make as it melts my skin.

A shot hits a conduit two paces away, raining sparks on me. I press myself to the deck and go still. Even if a burning ember sears my face, I can't give my position away. I'm dead if I do.

Two more shots fly over my head, glancing off metal with a piercing whine. I inhale and hold it, hoping he hits nothing critical. Then I'll have to move. That's what he wants—me to move and shoot back, just like he taught me to. But I won't give him the pleasure of thinking he was a good teacher. He was, but better than he realizes.

Once the light from the sparks fades out, I move, my heart pounding as I slip down the wall toward the ladder and slide down it. Halfway down, I spin to the other side, dropping to a crouch when I hit the deck. My eyes make a frantic scan of the level, searching for cover.

It's easy. This level's the same as the one above it.

I raise my weapon and fire two shots through the ladder's port. It's enough. He'll see it. Now all I've got to do is wait and hope he takes my bait. He will. Daga can't resist fighting me as much as I can't wait to end him.

He better not have Seren. Though if he did, he would have said so, exposing his position in favor of negotiating rather than fighting with me. It might have been the right choice. My fighting skill is far better.

I swallow, my throat dry even in the thick air. Seconds move by. Perhaps minutes. I'm too focused on the ladder to count. And time doesn't matter. I will wait here forever if I get the opportunity to level my barrel at his heart. Even if I doubt he's got one.

Another edgy moment passes. I shift, wiping the moisture off my brow with my sleeve. The heat is pressing down on me, threatening to knock me out from exhaustion. I desperately want water. But I can't get distracted by a little thirst. No. It's not little. I feel like I'm losing consciousness.

Dammit, where is he? My pounding pulse won't let me keep still for much longer, and I can't just sit around while Seren's still missing.

That's it. I'm going.

The moment I break my cover, Daga fires, ripping a line into the deck of the landing. Flames shoot up from the composite flooring, throwing me back. What the hell? He'd start a fire just to push me from cover? Now I know he's out of his head, just like Rabbit was.

I fire three darts back at him and race down a passage underneath a massive piece of equipment, smoke burning my nose and lungs. Three paces down, I find a tight space and squeeze into it. There's no other option. I'll try to hold out here. If Daga's truly disturbed, soon enough, he'll make a mistake. Then I've got him.

Without warning, my eyes shut. Bish, how is fatigue getting to me already? I force them open and reach for my canteen. He'll hear it, but I don't care. Staying awake is far more critical.

After a moment, the smoke clears, and everything becomes as quiet as the whistle of the nearest filtration pump will allow. I grit my teeth and lean out, moving with as much caution as I can put in my shaky body. He's got to be on this level now, but I need at least a hint of his location. Something I can target, even if it's not a direct shot. I'll fire, and if a single spark burns him, it'll be worth it.

My eyes focus down the way I came, searching for any hint of movement. I push myself against the deck as flat as I can go. The slight temperature difference is a welcome relief, even if it's only a few degrees.

A beam tears down the walkway, blasting a pair of pipes. One ruptures, shooting superheated steam into the space. I spring to my feet and fall back, tumbling through a space under a duct. My arm brushes against a burning surface, and it scalds my skin. Pain shoots up my arm, and I bite down to stop myself from crying out.

Bish, he's close. I saw the shot erupt from his weapon. I reach out and tap the trigger of my pistol three times as my body tenses. My darts glance off the pipes and ducts, pinging as they rocket down the aisle. Daga fires back, his beam slicing across my refuge. I drop, panting hard.

Another shot comes from my right. I return fire and move, ducking through a system of conduits before turning and firing again. We trade another set of volleys before I reverse course, circling to the left to flank him.

He fires as I move, cutting into a vent on my right. Then he fires again. And again. *Bish, he just keeps coming!* I aim for his last position and shoot. It's a waste of ammo. I could run through every clip I had and still not hit him. I've got to retreat. He's trying to set me up for the kill, just like he did with Rhys. I could lose this fight without ever seeing him.

My body is dragging in this heat. I've got to pull back more. I've got to find a solid defensive position. But bish. I'm not here to play defense.

Another shot flies by my head. It's wide. Way wide. I pause. No way is he that bad of a shot.

Wait. Can he see me or not?

No. He's not trying to hit me. He's driving me back. Toward the ladder. He wants me to go down. To separate me from my crew. I won't let him, but with no way to target him, I'll just be sitting and waiting for him to burn a hole through my head.

Retreat. It's the only option.

I dash for the ladder, another shot striking the wall behind me. Hyuk, I'm just doing what he wants me to. But I'll get him back. Twice over. I may even make him beg.

Until then, all I can do is lose him.

I slip down the ladder. He knows better than to follow right away. He'll wait, and that gives me a chance to put distance between us. Maybe even drop another level—yes. I'll do that. He won't expect it. It'll give me time to gather my wits. I could even search for Seren. *Ancestors, I hope she's still alive.*

My feet dig into the deck the moment I land on one-twenty-six. I charge down a passage along the side of the level, skidding to a stop and changing course to race down the next aisle I see. My lungs are burning. My heart is pounding. Adrenaline is pouring through my body. The ladder is just ahead. I'm going to make it. I'll make it and get away from him.

But I don't.

Just before the ladder landing, I drop, sliding to a stop and rolling under a large spherical tank, then spin on my belly, raising my gun over my head to aim at the ladder, ready for Daga to make his appearance.

I'm far from stupid. The second he made it to this level, he would have put the landing in his sights. I'd be dead if I showed any part of me in that light. I could be wrong, but I'm not risking my life to find out.

And I just came up with a better plan, anyway.

Placing my gun back in its holster, I unbutton my shirt and slide it off my shoulders, leaving it on the deck just in front of me, then roll out from under the tank. I stay pressed against the deck, unmoving. Listening. Everything is near silent. I pull my blade from its sheath.

I rise to a crouch and pick my shirt up, resting the inside of the collar on the tip of my blade, then tense, ready to spring into action. If this works, it'll only be for a split second. I'd better get my aim right. And my timing.

This will either be the craftiest thing I've ever done, or the most foolish.

I pull my arm back and target a spot. *Good enough.* I exhale and calm myself. *Ready?*

My blade snaps forward, catapulting my shirt into the air. I spring up, taking three steps and launching myself into the air. My arms raise over my head. My body twists as I form myself into the right arc.

Two beams fire in quick succession. There's a flash and a puff of smoke. My shirt dissolves. The remnants float to the deck.

A second later, I'm through the ladder port, tucking my head in as the next level comes up fast. I touch and roll, wincing as the deck scrapes against my back. With a growl, I slip into the darkness, taking up my gun and putting the ladder in my sights.

But Daga won't follow. He knows I'd have him. He'll wait until he comes up with a new plan. And by then, I'd better have found Seren and be headed up.

REUNION

CERI

My back burns from where the deck scraped across my bare skin, but I push the pain away. It's only a minor annoyance, anyway. And once I find Seren, I can get Efa to fix me up back in medical. Her scolding will be far worse, I'm sure. Especially when I return without my shirt.

Fana would die to see me like this. I grin just thinking about the look on her face. Though, I'm not sure I'd be ready to bare myself in front of her. Even when every Tarakh girl has unclothed herself before the others, I find myself shying away from the idea. That's completely odd.

Focus, Ceri. There are far more important things to be considering. Like how to stay alive. Daga will get his plan together and be in pursuit again soon. He might even try to slip past me through the hull and attack from below. I've got to be ready for both possibilities. And I've still got to find Seren. There's a good chance she's here or on the levels below.

If she's alive.

One-twenty-seven offers little in terms of variety compared to the two levels above. The only difference is there's a monitoring station at the center. I head there, as I might find something useful. Like a med kit or a uniform. Or another weapon.

I'm doubting my choice to have taken only my blades and pistol. Either would end Daga with ease, but he's got me outgunned with that beam rifle he stole from one of the *Devant*'s agents. He's getting more skilled using it with every shot. It won't be long before he's using it exactly how he needs to.

Daga will get more aggressive now. He won't take another chance that I slip through his trap again.

As I enter the monitoring station, most of the screens are black, perhaps set on standby. I welcome the comfort of the dark, even if it makes searching the area a challenge. Still, this is a highly defensible area. If I wanted to stay here, all I'd need to do was secure the entrances before Daga comes.

But nothing of interest comes from my search. So I head, empty-handed, toward the ladder, hoping I won't need to descend much farther than the next level. At some point, I will need to make a stand against him, and the closer to reinforcements I can be, the better.

With a quick check of the landing below, I slip down the ladder, spinning to its back side as soon as my head clears the port. Daga would shoot me in the head just to watch my body crash onto the next level.

Movement down the platform catches my eye. Bish. Was that him? How'd he get here already?

No. Not Daga. A person for sure, though. I've seen that kind of blurry action too many times before to mistake it for anything else. But, if not him, then...could it be?

A lump forms in my throat as I rush toward it, allowing my steps to make just enough noise that any soldier would notice it. And I hope she does. We'd slip out of here and be headed up in the seconds that follow.

That sound. I suck in a breath and hold it. There's no mistake now. I'd recognize that shuffling gait anywhere. It's Seren. It's really her.

I snap my fingers twice in rapid succession. Seren's mouth opens as she drops into a defensive stance, her weapon coming up only to drop the second she spots me.

"Ceri!" she hisses, her eyes opening wide. A second later she motions me to follow her and spins, taking off toward the other ladder in a hurry. Foolish. She doesn't know Daga could be down there. Should I shout at her to stop? No. That'd be even more idiotic than what she's doing. I just have to move faster.

I burst forward, rushing to catch her. Speed's far from the issue. Seren's smaller and more agile. She slips between machines and ducts with relative ease. I'm getting closer, but not as fast as I'd like.

Seren slows before we hit the landing, diving into a space between two huge boxed systems that run through the floor. My brow tightens. What is she thinking? I grit my teeth and scan behind us before following.

"What—" Seren blinks at me, breathing hard. "Wh-where's your shirt?"

"Daga shot it." I glance behind me, checking once again for movement, then press a hand on her shoulder as I lower myself to the deck. "Get down."

"How are you here?"

"Not how," I reply. "Why. And you know the answer. Now, here's how we're going to get back."

Seren frowns. "Get back?"

"Yes, trust me." I raise a finger. "We drop to one-twenty-eight and catch the rail car. Daga might try to come from below, so we've got little time. We'll move down in an alternating cross pattern. That's one he doesn't know. It'll take him a moment to figure it out, and by then we'll be gone."

"But..."

I squeeze her shoulder. Of course she's scared. Me too. Still, that she's not just agreeing instantly with me is putting me off.

"No, don't worry. We'll make it," I say with a smile.

"No..." Seren sighs. "I thought you came down here to help me. I can't leave. Daga's still alive!"

My words evaporate from my mouth as it opens. Why I didn't expect this from her baffles me. Perhaps it was the vision in my head I had of Seren apologizing for her actions and begging me to save her that threw me off. Perhaps I was just hoping she was still the same person she was before, even when I knew she wasn't.

"You aren't up to that fight," I say, taking her by the shoulders. "*We* aren't up to that fight."

"But I hit him. Hard. On his right arm. I shot him before he could move," Seren says and grins. "You should've heard him cry."

"Yeah?" I raise my eyebrows. "Well, all it's done is make him angry. And now he knows we're both down here. Isolated. Is that how you plan a strategy? Huh? You might have scored a hit, but we've got an entire battle to win, and we won't do it by ourselves. Not against him."

"What makes you think he's that tough anymore? If he was still as good as he was before, I wouldn't have gotten a hit on him at all. He's weak! We can get him. You and me, Ceri. We can end this!"

I'd hug her if I wasn't ready to smack her first. Seren's taken a lot from me, but her bravery is all her own. I was never this defiant to my squad leaders. Or maybe I was. Niah had to put me in my place more than a few times. And she made sure I learned my lesson. I can still feel the sting of her discipline on my cheeks.

"We're not having a discussion in the middle of an active battle. Once we're in a secure area, we can talk all you want." I grab her wrist. "Now come on, we're running out of time."

Seren plants her feet and catches my eye. "I'm here until Daga is dead. Or until I am."

Fire courses through my body at her insistence. Or is it just stubbornness? Perhaps I've trained her too well. Whatever the reason, I won't accept it.

"Dammit, I will knock you out and drag you back by your hair if you don't move now," I hiss.

"No."

Bish. This girl.

I level my gaze at her and narrow my eyes. "Seren..."

She shuts her eyes and takes a moment to breathe. I take the moment to scan the area—still clear. When I turn back to her, her stance has relaxed. The defiance is gone, replaced by a confidence and ease I've never seen before. My lungs get tight, and I prepare myself to hear something that I know will shake me.

"Ceri," Seren begins. "We can't retreat. Daga will press his attack, and he'll either kill all of us or make us his slaves. I'm not going back to that. No adult will ever hit me or give me an order or hurt any of us. Ever again."

I sigh. "He won't make us his slaves, but we've got to prepare for a proper assault. Let's give him the respect he deserves and make sure that we've got the best opportunity to take him out."

I jump when Seren grabs my arms, moving to twist from her grip. But she holds on and gets close, maintaining her eye contact, and the tension releases from me.

"While you were recovering, I've been following him. Gaining intel. I waited almost an entire day before I took my shot, just to be sure." Her hands tighten on my arms. "I can tell, Ceri. He's not right in the head. And we've got another advantage: Daga thinks he's only chasing you."

I would want nothing more. Except I do: safety for my crew, above all else. Even if that means Daga gets to live. Revenge isn't everything. I could learn to tolerate him for their sake. Perhaps even strike a deal. It'd be no different from what I've tried to do with the monsters on the *Devant*.

Seren shakes my arms, her eyes open wide. "So? What do you say?"

My lips curve upward, and I pull her into an embrace. I could not adore her spirit any more than I already do. And I can take little credit for it. Really, I don't want to take any at all. Seren's become a force to be reckoned with. It's a shame Rhys never understood that. Perhaps he might have, if he was still alive. But he's not. Daga got him because I was careless. I won't be again. Daga will die, and it'll be done with more discipline and more patience than I've ever had before. We will secure every approach, double-check every weapon, drill every skill until I'm satisfied. Then, Daga will be ours.

Until then, we need to be safe.

Which is why, as Seren relaxes in my arms, I take her legs out, spinning her around as she drops to the deck. She fights me all the way down, squirming and kicking at my shins as she snarls. I'm on her in a heartbeat, covering her mouth as I remove her weapons and bind her arms behind her. Even then, she struggles to free herself. I have to lie on top of her until I can tie a bandage around her mouth. Only then does she stop, and I pull her up, keeping my arms about her.

"I know you hate me right now," I whisper in her ear. "But there's no way I'm going to let you get even a scratch. You're way too important to me, and I hope you know that. So now, we're going back up, reequipping, and doing as much training as we need to. Then, when the moment comes, I promise: you'll take the shot."

APOLOGY

FANA

THE CREW WATCHES ME as I pace across the level, racking my brain for the right words to begin my testimony. I don't know why I'm stressing myself out on an opening sentence. They're only words, just like whatever else I wind up saying. It doesn't matter what they are, as long as I make sense. I just need to get my point across. That's all I need to do.

Well, that, and figure out what my point is.

Despite my indecisive mode, everyone sits patiently, watching and waiting for me to begin. All except Sayer, of course. He would have been happier if I had kept my mouth shut. That's impossible. Raey's loyalties may be in question, but she truly cares for these kids. If she said she wouldn't hurt them, I believe her. And nobody's going to execute her. That'd be more than wrong. And, if for no other reason, I still love Raey.

"Alright," I begin, turning to face the crew. "Let's start with a few facts to put things in perspective, okay?"

I get a few nods and a few crossing of arms. I'll take it. It's better than them all tuning me out and deciding Raey is guilty long before I even open my mouth.

"First, we all know Raey took the risk of coming here to get me, but then she stayed—"

"Because you convinced her to!" Deryn shouts. Efa throws him a glare, and he ducks his head. At least he shuts up and lets me continue.

"Yes," I say. "I made her aware of the problems that the ship was having. And how all of you were at risk of getting sick. But it was her decision to stay. Remember that Commander Azazhi wanted her to bring me back as soon as possible, and it took two squads of security agents to get me back to the *Devant*. You've got to realize, Raey's always been about her mission, about putting people first and making sure they get the care they need. That, above anything else, is what motivates her."

"How can you be so sure?" Aidan challenges. "Like, weren't you in stasis since the *Devant* left Earth?"

As heat touches my cheeks, I stop my pacing and turn to face him, forcing the smile on my face to stay up. *Little brat.* How did he know about that? Oh, wait, did I tell everyone? *Bish.*

"Raey and Fana were in a relationship before they left Earth," Merek explains. Aidan's eyes pop open. So do mine. Why'd he bring that up? Not that we've made a secret of it.

What will they say about Ceri and me? *Is there a Ceri and me?* I can't wait to find out. Unless the answer is no. I'm really hoping it's not. Really, really hoping.

"Get on with it." Sayer yawns. "Some of us would like to get back to our day."

"Like you've got something better to do," Niah spits. "You'll sit and listen, even if she takes all day. Raey gets her fair chance."

"But it won't," I add.

Sayer rolls his eyes, then leans back in his chair and puts his feet up on the edge of Dru's chair. She frowns at him but remains silent.

"It's okay, Fana," Merek says. "You can take whatever time you need."

I smile and nod, then continue my shuffle about the level so I can get over my slight embarrassment. None of them better try to use my past, or Raey's past, against us. I might do the same to them. And I know plenty of rumors and secrets about these kids, thanks to them trusting me. Though they wouldn't any longer if I did that. *Now, what the hell was my point about all this?*

Right.

"Beka, how are you feeling?" I ask.

Beka shrugs. "Fine, why?"

"And you, Dru?"

"I'm okay." But suspicion lurks on the youngest crew member's face. "Why do you want to know?"

I clasp my hands behind my back and approach the two of them, though their looks are far from welcoming of me. I suppose I'd be the same way if I thought someone was trying to pull me into their gravity-well hell. Of course, I am.

"Don't you realize it was Raey who helped you get better?" I ask. "She did. And she's been helping our crew through plenty more since then."

"Helping? Is that what that's called?" Beka barks, leaning forward. "She and all those creepy doctors over there poked us with a bunch of needles and all sorts of other bish. What the hell was that all for, anyway? What did they take from me?"

"Blood samples are—"

"It wasn't just blood."

I blink as I catch all the nodding heads, my jaw going slack. What happened over there? Why didn't they tell me? I turn to Efa, yet she only shakes her head. Either a warning not to ask or she doesn't know. I suspect she does.

These poor kids. Don't they ever get a break?

"I'm...I'm sorry. I didn't know," I say, dropping my head.

"Now you get what kind of monster you're defending?" Say-er hisses.

"What?" My head's already shaking. "No! Raey isn't a monster! You've got to understand, she's got lots of experience, but she's just a med-tech. She has no authority on the *Devant*. If the commander or any of the senior medical staff ordered her to, she'd have to—"

"But that doesn't make it right, now, does it?" Deryn says.

My body shakes as I stare at him. Raey will die and it'll be my fault. It'll be my fault because I failed to defend her. Even the air on this level will deny that she deserves to breathe it. And if I keep floundering like this, the crew will start to question my loyalties.

Dammit. I know Raey's not a bad person. Why won't they believe me?

"Enough," Efa growls. "We said we'd listen and we will. Fana—"

"Forget this already!" Sayer snaps. "Raey deserves to be punished. That's all there is to it!"

"No!" I shout, shaking my fists in the air. "No! Raey's...You don't understand her at all! Everyone makes mistakes! All she's ever wanted was to give you the future all of you deserve! And this isn't it! This is absolutely. Not. It!"

Silence follows. So much so that I can hear my words continuing to bounce off the walls. Not that they deserve to last long. Not a single one of them has changed their minds about Raey. I can see it in their faces, lips pressed, eyes hard. They made their choices even before I opened my mouth. What a waste of time this was.

I sigh and drop into a chair. Maybe Raey should have defended herself.

Efa reaches out to touch my arm but hesitates. My shoulders droop. I could use the comfort and support, but I won't get it from her. She's too worried about everyone liking her as a leader. I turn away and face the far wall. It's the only thing not judging me right now. Including myself.

"You've got no idea about the planet you left behind," I say. "You think there were problems then? It's a hundred times worse than you could ever imagine it to be when we left. Why anyone stayed there is beyond any sense. Probably they're all dead by now. And they deserve to be, after all the damage they did."

Bish. Maybe I shouldn't have said that. With all the shifting around I hear behind me, they must all be thinking about the homes they left behind. Bright, joyful homes, I'll bet, with the sun shining high above on the greenest of grasses in their yard. They'll never experience that again. And they've learned to love only the darkness. The light just uncovers everything they rather keep hidden.

"We suffered a lot to get the *Devant* ready," I continue. "All of us were pulling double duty. I was supervising the installation of the ship's engines, and Raey was rushing to get the medical bays online while helping to look after the city of people who camped just outside the spaceport. All of them needed to be prepped for stasis, and that was taking forever. Then some bastard blew up half the town and killed thousands. Raey tried to save as many as she could, but we still ended up with plenty of pods that had no one to go in them.

"Sorry," I mumble. "You didn't need to know all that."

Why did I ramble like that? It won't change their minds. Now, as I hang my head, all I can do is picture Raey in her white medical gear, racing into the scene of the disaster. I screamed at her to put her mask on, fearing she'd inhale radioactive particles. Or worse, nano weapons. Raey risked her life for so many, she can't discern the difference between sides—or levels of entitlement. To her, everyone deserves to be healed. That selfless nature is why I fell in love with her. Ceri's like that, too.

"Yeah, what was your point, anyway?" Deryn asks, breaking the silence.

"Idiot," Tegan hisses. "Just shut up."

I stand, taking a breath before I glance their way.

And quickly shut my mouth to stop from gasping.

Dru's crying, and Aidan's rubbing a finger under his eye. Niah folds her hands into her lap and stares at the deck. Mari just looks lost, her gaze searching anywhere that's not at me or anyone else.

Whoa. Did I just do that?

"Thanks," Efa says and exhales deeply. "I'm sure Raey would appreciate you sharing that with us. Did you have anything else to add?"

Do I? How do I even find something else to say after that disaster? I might completely condemn Raey if I say anything more.

I just shake my head.

Efa nods and stands, Merek along with her. She turns to face the crew, making sure they're all paying attention before she continues, "Alright, I think you've all had a moment to think about everything Fana's said. Now, we'll vote. You have two choices to consider. Imprisonment is the first."

"And execution is the second," Sayer adds.

Efa tilts her head and narrows her eyes at him, but he just folds his arms and leans back in his chair, smug. *Jerk.* For someone who cares so much about the lives of the crew, he should understand that everyone's life is precious. Efa better not give in to his bish.

"And execution is the second," Efa echoes with a shake of her head.

No way. She can't be serious.

STAY

—— • ——

FANA

GREAT. AS IF THERE wasn't enough tension between all of us before. Now every member of the crew is tightly packed with a megaton of stress over this vote. Do they even realize the consequences of it? Even Sayer, who's been hot to bring a punishment down on Raey, has no clue what he's saying. I doubt he truly wants her dead, but it'd take someone pounding reality into his head for him to get that. Ceri would, but she's not here. Maybe Niah could, if she were feeling up to it.

I do my best to get her attention, but she's fixated on the wound just below her collarbone. If she's in pain, there's no way I'll get her to say something.

It doesn't matter. I don't even get the chance to try.

"All for imprisonment?" Efa asks, raising her hand. Four others follow. Merek, Tegan, Aidan, and Mari. Then, as she struggles to hold back a sob, Dru lifts her arm.

"So it's settled," Merek says.

The air that's been locked in my lungs slips out. *Oh, thank...whomever!* It doesn't matter. I'm just glad they were more reasonable than I expected them to be. They might talk about killing as if it were the same as taking a nap, but I've heard their conversations. These kids talk about life. And hope. And even love. Death is a quickly fading subject, and I am grateful for that.

"Hold on!" Sayer says, shooting up. "I didn't vote. And neither did Beka and Deryn! We deserve our chance."

Okay. Maybe not all of them are like that.

"There's three of you," Merek points out. "And six have already voted. I think you can figure out the rest."

"I didn't vote, either," Niah corrects in a raspy voice, then shrugs when everyone turns to her. "Sorry, it's hard to talk today."

"Then vote!" Sayer charges. If Efa and Tegan didn't roll their eyes, I would have.

Still, to her credit, Niah straightens up and locks eyes with him. "Imprisonment."

Sayer huffs and launches himself from his chair to stomp away. The entire crew sighs when he's gone. He'll be back, though. I'm not sure I'll be ready for that.

"You get a vote, too, Fana," Merek says. "I'm guessing you're voting not to execute."

As much as I can celebrate them not murdering Raey, a lump remains in my throat. That closet they've got her in is no place for anyone to be for long. Even my prison on the *Devant* was ten times larger, and that was still just a storage locker.

"I don't really think either option is right, honestly," I reply. "But definitely not execution."

"Anyone want to change their vote?" Efa asks. No one does. "Then we will keep Raey locked up until we all agree to release her."

I blink. Does Efa even understand what she just said?

"Wait," I say, holding my hands up. "You can't just create a sentence with an indefinite time frame!"

"An in-death-what?" Dru asks.

Tegan leans over and whispers in her ear. Dru responds by making her mouth into a big circle. Everyone else is less confused but more annoyed. Normally I'd be kicking myself for one of my outbursts with no thought put behind it. This time I'm confident I've spoken right. I think.

"Why not?" Efa tilts her head to look at me as she frowns. *Really? Does she not know?*

"Do you want to leave her with no sense of hope?" I shake my head. "That's torture!"

"Oh, come on!" Deryn throws his hands up. "It's not like we won't feed her or anything!"

"Yeah!" Beka says, slapping her hand on the armrest of her chair. "We'll be giving her better treatment than she was going to give me or Dru! Who cares how long she rots in a closet?"

My body droops. I was wrong about them being any level of positive. I suppose it's not so easy to get rid of that killer mindset. Most of these kids have had years to grow comfortable with the idea of ending someone's life. How they sleep with all they've been through is still a mystery to me. Bish. I still have nightmares about crossing between ships with no tether.

It doesn't matter. Raey may deserve punishment, but we were just talking about how we should be better than the adults. About how we won't treat anyone the same way. This is exactly the time for us to do the right thing. Hell, what happens if they forget she's in there?

"Remember," I say, catching as many eyes as I can. "Ceri was in that same closet for months."

Beka's eyebrows mash together, which isn't what I was hoping for. But Tegan grimaces and looks at Beka, studying her as if deciding what to say to the girl. I mean, I can't blame Beka for being angry. Heck, more than angry. But where does this false sense of justice end?

"It won't be like that," Efa says. "Ceri was a problem Chief Generys wanted to forget about."

"So were you," Deryn sneers. "Ow!"

His hand covers his cheek as he winces, whirling toward Niah as she glares at him. She crunches her hand into a fist, threatening Deryn with it before returning it to rest in her lap. *Whoa.* Ceri claims Niah's in no condition to fight. I seriously doubt that's true.

Still, as mean as Deryn's comment was, he didn't deserve that. Overkill again. And this from the eldest crew member, who's supposed to know violence solves nothing. Is this the only way they know how to solve their problems?

"What was that all about?" I ask.

"Chief Generys is Efa's mother," Merek explains.

"Was," Efa corrects. "As far as I'm concerned, my parents are dead."

Merek's face droops, and he brushes a hand down his face. Then he goes to her, wrapping an arm about Efa's shoulders. She leans into him a little but remains stiff, refusing to let go of whatever rage she's holding inside. Likely it's at her mother for abandoning her. I'd be all sorts of angry about that.

I think I'm getting it now. These kids need some serious therapy before they can let go of their shoot-first attitude. Of course, they just voted to lock away the one person who knows anything about mental healing.

"Listen," Merek says to me. "We haven't forgotten what Raey's done for us. We'll take care of her. And you can visit her if you want to."

Great. Thanks so much, Merek. I smile anyway, even as my stomach churns with the thought of Raey staring at the walls of a closet.

With that, most of the crew head out, leaving me with Merek, Efa, and Niah. I curl my top lip in, sensing I should take advantage of the sudden decrease in the number of opinions.

"What if there was a better idea?" I say.

Efa's brow gets tight. "What do you mean?"

"Well." I fold my arms and pace around the chairs. Better they don't see that I don't actually have an idea yet. "What if we could turn this to our advantage?"

Efa's frown deepens, and Merek adds his own to their reaction. I pick up my pacing to escape them for just a few seconds. Not that it helps much. My head's a complete blank, and when I try to come up with something, all I can think about is Ceri.

I've got this icky feeling she's not okay. Like something terrible's happened to her, and she's somewhere down in the lowest levels, hurt or wounded and unable to call for help. This Daga guy seems far deadlier than Captain Yelekal or any *Devant* security agent could ever be. He's turned most of these kids into the killers they are. What kind of butcher must he be?

She's okay. Ceri's okay. At least that's what I'm trying to convince myself. It's not working. All my brainpower's being used to come up with the plan that I'm currently failing to come up with.

Niah nods at me as I come back around and lock eyes with her. It's a single nod—slow, steady, and full of confidence. *For me?* Whatever, I'm glad to have all the support I can get, even if it's imaginary. My energy lifts just wanting to believe Niah's backing me up. Now I need to make her support worth something.

Ooh, wait. I've got it.

"We still need pods, right?" I suggest. "Stasis pods with the medical modules connected to them. That way, we can…"

I make a minor gesture toward Niah. Likely she saw it. And hopefully, she doesn't mind. It's for her, mostly. And for anyone else who might need one.

"Of course we do. And we're running out of time," Efa replies, biting her lower lip.

Merek makes a sound like something's caught in his throat and points a finger at me. "You think Raey has some value to the *Devant*?"

"Of course she does," Efa replies, frowning at him before turning back to me. "She's a med-tech. That kind of training and experience is always needed. I'm so glad we didn't vote to execute her. There's still so much I need to learn. I'm really hoping she'll still teach me while we've got her locked up."

Oh bish, I didn't consider that! Efa might decline my suggestion just on that basis! What do I do then?

"But." Niah coughs. "Is she valuable enough?"

Efa wrinkles her nose as she stares at Niah. I don't know if Efa's just concerned, or if she's trying to figure out what Niah meant. Maybe both.

Suddenly Efa's jaw drops, and she spins on me. "You want to trade Raey for the pods?"

My lips curve up. I'll never say she's not sharp. Most of these kids are. Okay, all of them are. Maybe that's because the ones who weren't are all dead. But Efa's face turns troubled as she considers my idea. *Yikes.* Maybe it wasn't good after all. Not that I can blame myself. It was all I could come up with quickly.

"It's a risk, for sure," Merek says. "And we'll probably have to agree to more than we did before, but if nothing else, it'll get the trade going again."

"How do we present it to Azazhi?"

"We tell him the truth," Niah replies. "We caught his crew trying to abduct ours, and if he wants her back, he'll resume the exchange."

Niah puts her legs up and leans back in her seat to fold her arms across her body and close her eyes. A breath escapes my lungs as I watch her struggle to rest. I'm grateful for her support. Too bad I won't be getting more of it. And Efa's still chewing on my plan. I pace again, wrapping my arms about me. She's going to say no. I'm sure of it. What do I do then? I've got nothing else. They'll keep Raey locked away until they can figure out what to do with her, and they won't try too hard. They've got better things to do.

I really wish you were here, Ceri.

"Okay," Efa says. "We'll try it."

I stop short. *Wait. What?*

Merek and Efa turn to me expectantly, and I shrink. What do they want me to say?

Efa's words break through my confusion, sinking into my brain as understanding hits me. I snap my mouth shut, and my lips slowly push up into a hesitant smile. Did they just accept my suggestion? They did, didn't they? I've convinced them.

They're going with my plan!

OPENING

—— • ——

CERI

"DO ME A FAVOR and keep quiet, unless you want to kill us both. Yeah?"

I watch Seren's face for a response, though all I get is contempt blasting from her eyes. I can understand, but I won't release her until we're back up on fourteen. With the rest of the crew. And safety. Then she can yell and scream all she wants.

Gripping a pistol in each hand, I peek from our hiding spot, scanning and listening for Daga. With the whir and clank of the machinery surrounding us, it's far from effective. We'll just have to stay sharp.

With a quick breath, I slip out, beckoning her to follow. Seren wobbles forward, bumping her shoulder on the edge of a machine before she can exit. She glares at me again, but I'm not to blame for her restraints. I remember all too well how she left me lying on the deck in medical. My hip's still sore from that fall. Though my bigger hurt is not a wound Raey or Efa could care for. Only Seren can make it better.

And she will, the moment we return.

"This way," I whisper. Seren shakes her head. I insist and she repeats her motion. Only a pistol aimed at her head gets her moving with eyes wide. If she was paying attention, she would have seen my finger was nowhere near the trigger. I was only making a point, which she missed. We'll discuss it later. Right now, we move. Fast.

With Seren in front, we slink down a passage loaded with rumbling machinery. Orange status lights illuminate the deck beneath our feet, and us. A tightness grips my chest—more than was already there. I'll relax once we hit darkness again. But only a little.

We duck our heads to enter an enclosed space beneath a massive tank. I can only imagine what's in it. Whatever it is, it's likely dangerous to humans. We won't be staying around to find out.

As we come around a turn, Seren stops and glances back at me, glaring again. Bish. She's right to. Just ahead, a mass of pipes and wires forms a web so tangled and complex, even little Dru would have trouble crawling through.

Seren drops her eyes, motioning to the bandage covering her mouth. With a sigh, I reach out and grab it, giving her a warning to keep quiet before pulling it down.

"The rail car's the other way," Seren hisses. "That's what I was trying to tell you."

Hyuk. This was essential time we just wasted. We can't afford to lose more.

"Go," I say with a nod. "Move fast."

Seren does a quick scan, taking a deep breath, then jets out from the dead end.

And dives for cover when a beam fires across her path.

"Keep moving!" I shout as I launch a hail of darts toward the origin of the shot. Seren groans as she tries to get up, but stumbles as she pushes off the deck with only her toes. I rush forward, hauling her up with an arm about her waist, then drop her on her feet and yank her after me.

Another shot strikes a wall close to our heads. Too close. My body screams to move faster. How did he reposition so quickly? I glance up, searching for movement. But there's no way he could climb over the equipment down here. Not that fast.

"Cut my restraints!" Seren cries. I consider—two of us would be a stronger defense—but there's no time to stop and do it. We're dead the moment we even hesitate.

"Keep going," I say. "I'm covering you from behind."

Daga's attack pounds a wire tray just over my head, spraying sparks into my face. I wince and throw a hand up to block it, but it's too slow. Seren keeps running. I fire five shots into the darkness, hoping in vain that I'm keeping him from shooting back. He's out there somewhere. If I keep firing, I'll hit him. Maybe.

Bish. Seren's too far ahead. And she's about to lose her cover!

"Seren!" I shout. She spins, jogging backward to search for me. No! What is she doing? I wave her on with a violent gesture. She gulps in a breath and swivels back around.

A beam strikes her right through her back.

I scream denial and charge as Seren's body convulses, her back arching and her mouth dropping open. Hyuk no. Not her. It's my fault. I let her go before me. She's defenseless. Why? Why the hyuk did I do that? I've got to get to her. Now. It's a stupid move, yet I can't stop myself. Daga will take me out the moment I'm in the open. I don't care. I dig the tips of my boots into the deck. Am I even moving? Everything is an effort, like running through water deeper than my head. I've got to get to her. I've got to protect her. Seren can't get hit again. I'll take one if I have to. Just not her. Not my little sister.

Seren's eyes defocus. Her body tilts to one side as her knees give out. I reach out to stop her from falling—I can't—I'm too far away. She collapses, head hitting the deck as her body thuds down, jerking once before going still. I cry out, yet I hear nothing. I keep racing toward her. Daga's ready for me. I know it and I don't care. Seren's shot. She's shot, and it's my fault. I refused to trust her to come back safely. I should have talked her into it. She would have listened to me. She would have.

Now she's on the deck. Seren's body is on the deck. Her unmoving body is on the deck.

Ancestors, no. Not Seren.

A flash on my right sends me diving as a beam flies over my head. I drop and roll, coming up on my knees as I cross Seren's body. My hands jam under her shoulders, and I lift, pulling her to me and shooting to my feet. Cover. We need cover. There's a compartment five paces away. We can make it.

Another shot passes by as I crash into the space and lay Seren down. I tighten my jaw and rip her shirt open. But I know what I'll see. I know how horrible it'll be. Niah got hit in almost the same spot. Twice.

"Hang on, Seren," I whisper as I cut her wrists free. "I'll get you out of here. You'll be safe. You'll be safe."

I jam a hand into my pants pocket and pull out every bit of medical gear I brought with me. First the cauterizer. She doesn't need it, but it'll stop any secondary bleeding. Then I stuff the wound with as many bandages as I can, sealing the hole in her back and on her chest over with sec skin. It'll hold for a while. It has to.

I turn my ear to Seren's mouth and listening for a sign of life—and sigh. She's breathing, but just barely. I press two fingers to her neck, right where it meets her head, and nearly burst into tears of joy. She's got a pulse, if weak. She'll live. Seren will live.

"That's what happens when you send a little girl to do your fighting for you, Ceri," Daga calls, his words echoing through the clusters of machinery.

I snap into action, snatching both pistols up and aiming out the gap in our hiding spot. He's close. All I need is to see him once, and then he's done. Forget letting him be. I'm ending him here and now.

"But that's enough!" I shout back. "You can't even kill a little girl, Daga! You won't be any match for me."

"You're forgetting I'm the one with the plasma rifle."

Good. He's only got the one. That's bad enough. Daga's skill with it has increased. I need to even things out, or he'll just keep attacking from a distance and pick us off one by one.

"Have to rely on distance weapons now, old man?" I taunt. "Come fight me with a blade if you want to see just how good I've gotten."

"And give up my advantage? No thanks." Daga chuckles. "Though I am impressed how you took out those soldiers. Where'd they come from? Another ship? How'd they find us?"

"There's no *us*, you bastard. The moment you show a hair on your head, I will end you!"

I check Seren again—no change. She won't remain that way. And Daga seems content to trade insults while he presses me for intel. Either I kill him or escape with Seren. Neither seems likely, but if I want her to survive, one of them needs to happen now.

And I want nothing else but for Seren to survive.

"Ah yes, that's right," Daga sneers. "The little squad leader thinks she can run a ship with her brats. Just how is that going for you?"

"None of your hyuking business."

"Aww, come on, Ceri. It's been lonely down here with no one to talk to. Why not have a chat with your old captain?"

"Go to hell!" I fire three shots through the opening of our shelter. They spark and ping as they glance off a platform rail. I shouldn't waste ammunition like that, but Daga is really grating on me. If I don't get out of here soon, he will talk me into fighting him. And I need little convincing.

Only my concern for Seren keeps me from charging out there and unleashing a storm of darts on him. Strange that she's got more influence on me wounded than she does battle ready. I'd much prefer to watch her bickering with Rhys as she held his hand. That's the Seren I wish I could see right now. If only it could be.

"Planning something, are you?" Daga challenges. He's moved positions. I'd better find the rail car before Daga gets an angle on me. Sooner than that, even. I need to be moving in the next ten seconds, or I better find a different way to escape.

I survey the area, searching for the way to the rail car that Seren mentioned. It can't be far, can it?

Okay. I see it now. It's along the wall, ten paces past the cluster of pumps and gauges. They're five paces away—if I move fast. Really fast. I'll need to make a distraction, throw Seren on my back, and run like hell. We might just make it.

"Don't try it," Daga warns. "You won't get past the pumps."

Bish. I'm too obvious.

"Why do you think that's my goal?"

"You forget I know you, Ceri. You used to be ruthless as a squad leader, but you've grown sentimental. Too much of that teenage desire to get all hot and heavy with a boy, I bet. Especially after you watched Generys' daughter fall for that Fahrasi." Daga spits. "Disgusting."

I hold back a laugh. *Boy? If he only knew.* Not that I care what he thinks of Fana. Daga only understands what fits into his world, and I no longer do. That could give me an edge. And with it, I'll cut through his attention and make an opening Seren and I will slip through. I just need to keep him talking.

That should be easy.

"That reminds me," I sneer. "Why did she leave you here? Did you become useless to her? Chief Generys had no interest in an insane murderer? Ha! You've got no one, Daga. Just like you deserve!"

I spot a target and raise a pistol, aiming just left of it. It's only a guess on where he is, but I hope the blast the transformer creates is disorienting enough to give us a chance.

"What?" I call. "No answer to that? Maybe if you hadn't gone crazy, you might have had a seat to a new world. But face it, Daga. You've always been a freak. And the passengers would never want a ship baby like you as a part of their colony."

Daga fires a shot. It hits the deck and dies in a small pile of embers. Not even close.

But mine will be.

I squeeze the trigger and launch a volley at him. They hit the transformer dead on, and it explodes, a ball of blue flame enveloping the box as bits of it shoot off in all directions. The boom it creates is even larger, pounding my eardrums as I grab a conduit to keep from crashing to the deck.

That's it. Go. Go now.

My pulse is pounding in my ears as I scoop Seren up, spinning her onto my back. I lock her arms around my shoulders and grab her legs. Then I'm off. We're at the pumps in three paces and headed to the rail car in two more. Seren's heavier than I remember. I gulp air and push harder. My arms and legs burn from the effort. Three more steps and we'll be there.

Daga's silent. That worries me. He could target us while we wait for the rail car. No. Why wait? I'll find a place to take cover. He won't get us. He's losing his chance. Maybe I got him with that explosion. Though I doubt it. He'll fire any second. He has to, or we're gone.

Or not.

Daga's welded the rail car entrance doors shut.

Hyuk.

SURETY

— • —

FANA

IT'S SILLY, BUT I want to hold Raey's hand. Just for remembrance's sake. Once the *Devant* reconnects their personnel bridge to our airlock on seventeen, she'll walk across it, and that will be the last I will ever see of her. My former lover, and friend, will disappear, and all I'll have left of her are some happy memories—and a bunch of really sad ones.

I reach out to her, but she only glances at me, an eyebrow raised. I falter and shy away, my hope for a warm farewell crumbling. *Well, that was really stupid of me.* I should've realized I can't have it both ways. And it's probably better that it ends like this. It'll hurt less. Maybe.

We only got the medical modules in trade for her returning to the *Devant*. I guess that was an acceptable exchange. Raey was always going back, and if we hadn't agreed to release her, we were getting nothing.

"This is bish," Sayer mutters as he stands with Efa and Tegan. "What kind of goodwill is this? They're trading her for the stuff we were supposed to already have. This was their plan all along, I know it."

"It wasn't. Azazhi wouldn't have guessed we'd find out about Raey," Efa replies and nods at me. "You can thank Fana for that."

I shrink at Efa's praise. Uncovering Raey's treachery was close to the last thing I'd ever want to be responsible for. Even now, when I understand why, it still stabs a blade through my heart.

"Not just Fana," Sayer spits back as he slaps his chest. "I was there, too!"

Efa rolls her eyes. "Yes, how could I forget? What exactly did you make Fana agree to so you'd help her?"

Sayer throws his hands up. "Nothing! It was all for the good of the crew. That's the truth."

But her pressed-lip glare says she believes otherwise. I'd almost forgotten about his request. Not that I had any time to make good on our deal. And I hope he's not expecting me to anytime soon. It's far from easy to reverse-engineer something even as simple as a beam weapon, though I probably could take a solid guess at what the internals are. Directed energy—

"Hey, heads up," Tegan says, pointing. "They're coming across."

Sayer's and Tegan's hands fly to their pistols before Efa waves them down. Four security agents come across the bridge, each pushing a cart loaded with containers. Based on their size, they're making good on their agreement. I can't think of any reason they wouldn't. It's my crew who's on the losing side of this deal.

As they arrive on our side, Efa taps the airlock override and slides the door open. Raey frowns as a burst of air from behind us rushes past, sending a chill down my back. *Negative pressure, how considerate of them.* They've lowered their environmental air levels so they don't blow contaminated air into our ship as everything equalizes. My ears pop in confirmation when it's done.

When the agents step onto the *Stratford*'s deck, they form a wall with the carts, leaving only a small space between the two middle ones just big enough for someone to slip through. They're also wearing full suits and masks. I'm not sure for whose protection that is, but they're clearly not taking chances on anything. Sayer's already eying the rifles on their shoulders.

For an uncomfortable moment, we're at a standoff, the agents behind their carts, hands gripping the straps of their rifles, and my crew staring back, bodies tense. Only Raey seems disinterested by any of it.

"Specialist Raey T'ena, step forward," the lead agent says, motioning for her to approach. Sayer moves behind her and, with a cautious glance at the agents, removes the restraints on her wrists.

A heaviness lands in my gut. This is it. This is goodbye forever. I wish I could send her off by telling her I forgive her, but I can't. I'm not ready to, and I know I'll hate myself for it later. If only I had more time. It can't happen, and that's so strange. After this point, I'll have nothing but time.

Raey turns to Efa. "Thank you. I know you had some influence here, and I'm grateful that you chose not to let me rot in that closet."

"And I wish you had made better choices," Efa replies, her face a mix of sourness and regret. "We could have protected you."

Raey's gaze drops to the deck as she nods. She'll miss Efa, I think. She was the only one of our crew who truly respected Raey. Everyone else tolerated her for the things she did for them. But Raey could never become one of us. She's an adult.

Oh no, Raey's looking at me. I suck in a breath and hold it. I'm not ready for this. What do I say? Does it even matter?

"I know you had something to do with this, too." The edges of her mouth curve up slightly. "Thank you for standing up for me. I won't forget it."

My lips tremble as I pound my brain to come up with something meaningful to say. But before I can think of a single word, Raey turns away and heads toward the agents. One of them keys their comm and speaks into it. As soon as she crosses through their barrier, they'll haul her back.

No! She can't! I haven't said a single word yet! Raey can't just leave. Not like this. We've shared so much. I need time to come up with something good. Whatever that is. This is the last thing she'll hear me say. It's got to be important. I need it to be important.

"Raey, wait!" I shout and dash after her. Everyone jumps, hands flying to guns.

"Fana!" Efa warns. "Don't get any closer!"

Raey stops, her jaw dropping open as she twists toward me and goes still. Raey's caught between a moment of confusion and happiness. My heart nearly bursts. *She's waiting for me!*

Now I've got to get back to words. If I can. I shouldn't have rushed at the agents like that. Ceri's tried to teach me battle awareness, and I sort of remember, but for those few seconds, all I could think of was Raey. I've only been learning combat tactics for a month. She's been in my head for years.

I come to stand before her, our gazes connecting. I inhale a shaky breath. I'll keep it brief, say whatever comes to mind first. That's best. It'll be from my heart, honest and pure. Then I can let her go, knowing she's heard my true feelings. That's the only way to say goodbye to the person who I was once ready to marry.

"Raey, I—"

The lead agent shoves her. Raey shrieks, her arms flying into the air. And before I realize it, arms wrap around my body and haul me up and over the barricade. Efa shouts something. But I'm still trying to understand why he pushed Raey. And why's Efa so angry?

Wait! No! No! They're taking me! *Someone help!*

"No!" I scream as I twist and writhe in the agent's grasp, my arms flailing about in a vain attempt to pummel him. But I'm already over his shoulder, being hauled away like a sack of trash.

"Shut the airlock!" Efa shouts. "Don't let them out!"

Dart guns scream into action. Beam weapons fire. Shots burn into walls with a sizzling hiss. Smoke fills the space. It's a screen!

"Fana!" Raey sobs from somewhere deep in the haze.

"Dammit!" Efa yells. "Where is she? Fana!"

Boots thunder around me. My stomach pounds into the agent's shoulder with every step. I can't let this happen. I can't let them take me.

With one last effort, I kick. My foot makes impact with someone's torso. A man grunts and falls away. I contort my body and slip from the agent's grasp. Then I'm on the deck—no, not the deck. It's the bridge between the ships!

I push myself up and stumble toward what I hope is the *Stratford*. Desperation is rushing through every pore of my body. I've got to get back. To Ceri. To the crew. They need me. I can't abandon them. I can't! With all the strength I have in me, I break into a run.

And crash into a retreating agent, bouncing off him and falling on my butt. His hand grips my shirt and yanks me hard. I fly up and land on my feet, coming face to face with the agent's mask. My mouth opens to scream.

A beam weapon fires through the smoke. It's diffused and useless. Darts follow. One glances off the agent's armor. He checks it, suddenly distracted.

I shove him away and run, but he grabs my arm and spins me around. My head snaps to the side as his fist meets my jaw. There's a flash before my eyes. Then black. My legs go weak and I collapse. I hit the bridge with a thud. Everything is spinning around me. Someone lifts me up and slams a helmet over my head. *No! Get it off! There's no air!* I gasp as my hands scramble to find the latch. A chilly breeze blasts me in the face. It's an emergency hood!

A boom shakes the bridge, and it falls out from under my feet. I go weightless. *Decompression!* They blew the bridge!

Then someone yanks me forward. It's freezing! My whole body's shaking beyond my control. Where am I? I thrash and twist to find a handhold. Or a foothold. Something. Anything to keep me from leaving the *Stratford*.

Ceri. Where are you?

The tug of gravity drops me onto my shoulder. I cry out in pain. Hands grab my limbs and slam me to the deck. It's warm, and I press against it, even as I struggle against my captors. The helmet gets ripped off my head. I shiver as the chill from it touches my skin. But warm air touches my face, and I open my mouth to suck it down. A scent lingers in it, familiar and...

Unwelcome.

"Let me go!" I scream, kicking and thrashing against two figures in black suits. They carry me out of the airlock and turn me upright until I land on my feet. I break my leg free and slam my boot into someone's knee. They cry out and drop, but I get a fist in my gut for my efforts. I retch and double over, the contents of my stomach threatening to erupt up my throat.

Someone presses down on my neck to keep me like that, as another binds my wrists and ankles, clamping the devices just a little too tight. I grind my teeth and push away the pain. No one on the *Stratford* would treat me like this. *My* crew would never hurt me.

It happened so fast, my head's still spinning over it. Was this their plan all along? What happened to Raey? Does she not matter to them? *No, that's not it.* They just wanted me more. But...why?

I shudder as a sob rushes through me. Everything I've done. Everything I fought for. Everything I've wanted. Gone.

Ceri's face comes into my thoughts. Her piercing eyes, the curve of her nose. The lushness of her lips. The softness of her cheeks. I squeeze my eyes shut as a pain stabs me through my chest.

And now to face what? Execution? Would Azazhi put his crew at so much risk just so he could kill me? It makes no sense.

The security agents grab me by my shoulders and flip me up. My head wobbles until someone grabs my braids and yanks my head forward. I wince and whimper, squeezing my eyes shut as I suffer through the pain.

When I open them again, Captain Yelekal's grinning face comes into view. He's looking at me like I'm some kind of prize he's just won.

"Welcome back to the *Devant*. Traitor," he sneers.

I spit in his face.

Then everything goes dark.

CASUALTY

CERI

With no other choice, I dash toward my last option—the ladder. Daga's expecting us to escape by climbing up to where we can access the rail car. That'd be my first choice, too. But heading down might offer the same chance, and I've no time left to consider. Seren's body is getting cold. I don't know how much longer I can keep her alive. And I have to. There is no future I see without Seren in it.

I know Daga as he knows me, and I'm sure my idea has crossed his mind, though downward to him could be a trap. It's not, unless he's sealed the doors for eighteen levels. That's doubtful. Daga always planned to take us out here. He just didn't realize what I'd do to save her.

Soon enough, he'll figure out I've chosen the harder option and give chase. I'd better be two levels down by then, though that's a dream. I'm hardly fast with Seren in my arms.

But there could be a way to help that.

I swing her legs to wrap around my waist and carry her like a child against my hip. It'll be easier to climb this way. Her arms hang loosely around my neck. Her face presses against my neck. There's breath there, and breath is life, though it's weak. I'd better hurry.

With most of her weight off my arms, I'm moving faster, ducking under pipes and squeezing through rows of conduit. I won't get two levels down, but I'll get a strong head start.

We hit the ladder and slide down, my feet planted on the sides as I hold on with one hand. But the deck comes up faster than I've judged it. My heels touch down first, and I stumble, toppling backward. My arms wrap around Seren, pulling her on top of me as I brace for the strike.

The air bursts from my lungs as we crash to the desk. I gasp for a breath, but it doesn't come. Seren moans, her head rolling to one side. Breathing or not, I've got to get up. Now.

Only when I sit up does my breathing return. But I'm wasting too much time. Daga could be on us any second. I grit my teeth and push up. My back aches from the impact. My legs strain with the effort to put us both back on two feet. By the time we're standing, I'm breathless again.

"Hold on, Seren," I whisper in her ear as I slide her back into position. "You'll make it. I promise."

I choose a direction, and we're off again, speeding straight across the level on a bridge that spans a massive sphere. I don't know what it is, and I've got no time to wonder.

A shot comes from the opposite side of the bridge, burning past my face—too close. I drop, rolling over on my shoulder.

Bish it all! There's no cover! And my gun hand is holding Seren. I could fire with my left, but why bother? That shot was just to prove he's got us. The next one will be deadly.

How'd Daga beat us down here? Did he know I'd do this all along?

"Thought you were clever, didn't you?" Daga calls. He's just ahead. The only way is back. And he knows it. I'll get a shot right through my spine if I try it. We're stuck.

Unless...

Daga fires again, striking the handrail by my head. I duck but realize how futile that is. But now I'm convinced: there's only one way out of this.

I swing my legs over the side of the bridge and glance down into the darkness below. No telling how deep it is. It's still better than letting that bastard shoot me.

My lungs fill with what could be my last breath, savoring it for just a second. Then, with a jerk of my body, we slip off and plummet into the depths.

The air rushes past us as we drop. Daga yells in frustration and I grin. We've denied him the chance to murder us, but I might have just done it for him. We're coming up fast on the top of the sphere. My body tenses. This will hurt.

I cry out as we impact and bounce. We slide down the side of the sphere, making contact. My arms wrap around Seren, and I tuck my head against her and hold on with all the strength I have. I fight the sphere's force that threatens to roll us over and straighten us out. The *Stratford*'s forward motion pulls us, and we slide across the surface, picking up speed. I've no control. We scrape against it, over and over, the friction barely slowing us down.

We're airborne once again. I cling to Seren as if she was life itself. No telling how far we've fallen. This next landing will be hard. Really hard. We must have fallen three levels by now. I hope not. We won't survive more than that.

Impact.

A railing comes up fast. My boots strike it, and we spin, slamming into the opposite side with my back. I bark in pain as we rebound off the rail and crumple to the deck. I curl up into a fetal ball as Seren slides from my grip.

"Still alive, then? That's impressive." Daga's voice floats down from above, followed by a beam of light. I grab Seren and shove us both into shadow, even as my body arches in agony. Not a second later, his light illuminates the spot where we landed. I sigh. Lucky. We were very lucky.

I find a spot to rest and pull Seren to me. Her breathing is ragged. I check her pulse, holding back a sob as I struggle to find it. *There.* It's there. But it's weak. Hyuk. My pain be damned. I've got to get her to Raey, and the only way to do that is to beat Daga to a level with rail car access. Right now, we've got a lead. I need to maintain it. He's already headed down after us.

Could I set up an ambush? End him before he finds Seren? Doubt fills my head. My body aches everywhere, and my head's pounding from that fall. If I face Daga head on, I'd better be in top form. I'm far from it. One wrong move from me and it's over.

And from what Efa said, he could just nick me with a blade and I could be done. Bish, after that fall, I might be dead already. Whatever. Only Seren matters.

With a deep inhale and a focus of my remaining energy, I lift Seren up and hobble to the next ladder. Who knows how many levels I'll need to descend to find rail car access. I'll go all the way to the engines if I have to. I'll do everything I must to save her. Seren won't die. Even if that means giving up my life.

Daga's footfalls ring out on the grating above—hyuk, he's close enough to spot us! I rise to the tips of my feet and slip closer to the ladder. We're almost there. Once we're down, I can power across the level to the next landing, giving up stealth in favor of speed. I just hope I can keep it up long enough. My lungs are on fire. So are my legs. But I've got more in me. I think. I've just got to dig deep enough to find it. This is the kind of moment I've been training my crew for. If I can't do it, how could I ever expect them to?

Almost there. Ten steps to go.

He appears out of nowhere, dropping a full level to land between us and the ladder. I skid to a stop and reverse course as Daga raises his gun. I weave and duck to complicate his aim, but at this distance, he won't miss. We're dead.

Daga laughs. "Too easy. Way too easy."

I cringe, expecting the shot. It never comes. No time to wonder why. I run faster, putting as much distance between him and us. Now the only way is back up. But where's the ladder? We fell nearly two levels and passed them by. I'll lose valuable time searching for them.

"Think it through, Squad Leader," Daga calls. "You're over-burdened. You can't outrun me carrying another person around. Even one as skinny as her. Are you sure she's even still alive?"

What? He didn't fire just so he could taunt me? Hyuk him. I'm going to unload every dart I have right between his eyes.

But I've lost his position. His voice sounds like it's coming from everywhere. He could be moving to cut us off from the ladder right now, and I'd never know.

Daga continues, "You know, this is the most fun I've had in a while. It'd be unfortunate if it ended so quickly. Why don't you put her down and come face me? You'll save her if you win. No chance if you don't try. Right?"

I slip into a slot between two power distribution boxes and put Seren down. It's long enough space to hide us both. But not forever. He'll wait us out if he has to, and he's got nothing but time. Seren doesn't have that luxury.

My fingers check Seren's pulse again, and panic fills me. It's so weak I almost miss it. Damn. I'm failing her, and Daga's the reason. Just running won't work anymore. What can I do?

"Come on, Ceri," he taunts again. "Blades only. Let's see if you remember everything I taught you."

I press my lips together. I better not regret giving away my position.

"Why are you doing this?" I shout. "Everyone's gone. You've got no reason to fight us."

"No?" Daga chuckles, but his tone turns dark. "You put me down here, Ceri. I'd be living a good life on some beautiful planet if it wasn't for you. Now, I was fine down here on my own. I even had a nice stash of supplies that the crazies left behind. But then you brought your brats down here to end me. For what? Protecting my territory from an invader? I've got every right to cut every one of you in two if I want to."

So he's the one who murdered the *Devant* crew member. And for what? Stepping on his territory? This is our ship now. He's the invader. Not that I'll get him to see it that way. Or capture him to face justice.

It also means he'll never allow me to save Seren. Our only hope of escape is to kill him.

And I will. I hyuking will.

With one last check on Seren, I slip out, blade at the ready. Its dark metal vibrates in my hand. I tighten my grip, but I can't stop the shaking. My entire body's trembling. I'm not ready for this. There's no choice. It's him or me. And Daga's got nothing to lose. I'm risking everyone and everything if I don't kill him. Seren. The crew. Our passengers. Fana.

"So what'll it be, Ceri?" Daga calls.

The moment I spot him, I drop into a crouch, my free hand sliding to one of my pistols. Maybe I could hit him from here. Two shots to the head, and it'd be over. I've done it before. Though now I regret it. Those Fahrasi kids didn't deserve death. Daga does. I could protect everyone with two taps on the trigger.

No. I can't take the chance of missing. And I might. The quiver in my hands makes it very possible. If I don't make sure he's done, there's no chance of getting Seren back to safety. Her only hope is that I end him for certain. And even as a hundred reasons of why I shouldn't race though my head, I rise and approach, gripping my blade in anticipation of sticking him with it.

"I'm here," I say and step onto the platform he's chosen for our last battle. I suppose it's appropriate—a space approximately five paces by five, surrounded by a waist-high railing with a console on one end. The rays of a single light fall down, illuminating the platform just enough for my eyes to catch even his trickiest of moves. And he will definitely deploy as many tricks as he can. So will I.

Tricks are all I've got left.

"Put your pistol there," he says and motions to the console, on top of which his plasma rifle lies. For a brief second, I consider grabbing it, but I'm less familiar with it than he is.

We're close now. It wouldn't be a problem to shoot him at this range. He's definitely watching for that, and in this small space, he could skewer me with his unsheathed blade before I could even aim my weapon at him. We've drilled for that. Over and over. Daga wouldn't be able to shoot me, either.

And the idea of watching him bleed is winning over my sense of justice.

With a grin, I make a show of pulling my gun from its holster and placing it next to his weapon. The second it's down, I spin to face him, not wanting my back exposed to him for long.

Daga leers as he takes in my shirtless body. "Well, you've become a woman now, haven't you? Sharp problem-solving with that one, by the way. Not that any piece of clothing will help you now."

I drop into a stance. "You'll have to hit me first."

"Oh, don't worry about that." He grins and flicks his blade as he mirrors my position. "You've brought me nothing but hell, Ceri, and I will make sure you feel every bit of suffering I've ever endured."

We face off, our gazes locked as we watch for the other to make the first move. He drops a little lower, recalculating his position. I slide a little to the right, my free hand moving back.

Daga lurches forward, his blade stabbing out. I dodge and slice at his arm. He spins, slicing at my head. I duck and slash at his knee. He reverses stance, switching his blade to his other hand. His dominant hand. Hyuk, why didn't I catch that?

I sweep at his legs, and he jumps, raising his blade above his head. My only choice is to roll and evade. Daga pivots and charges as I shoot to my feet. He's coming fast. I drop on one knee to counter—too late. Daga plows into me, and we both fly, crashing into the rail and to the ground. My body arches from the impact.

And Daga's blade slides into my side.

I scream, slamming my fist into his face. He grits his teeth and leans in. The blade sinks deeper. I gasp and dig my boot into his gut, my hand fumbling toward the pocket on my leg. He pushes harder, but I've stopped him. For now. It won't last.

"It's over, Ceri. Give up," he growls.

My brain screams with the pain, my vision going bright. I jam my hand into the pocket and rip Seren's pistol from it.

My shots are hasty. Random. I squeeze the trigger again and again. It's all I can do. He's got me, otherwise.

It's a miracle that one hits him.

"Hyuking brat!" he shouts, and pulls back, his hand covering his body just under his arm. I fire again. Daga roars as the dart pierces his thigh. He kicks at the blade sticking from my side. I roll away and take aim again, but Daga's gone, his rifle along with him.

Leaving me on the deck, writhing in pain.

Bish. I can't move with this blade in me. And if I remove it, I'll bleed out. My hand slides down to the cold steel in my side, just under my ribs. Warm blood seeps from the wound, but slowly. At least there's that. I need cauterizer, and lots of it. But I used all of mine on Seren. Battle dressing alone won't save me.

Maybe Seren's got some. I never checked. I just need to get back to her. If I can.

I grip the railing and then, slowly, slowly, pull myself up. My head spins. My legs will give out any moment, but I move, step by step, using everything and anything to keep me upright, until I get to Seren.

I slide down next to her, wanting to do nothing more than lie down—but not yet. The blade comes out first.

As careful as I try to be, the edge is sharp. I whimper as I pull, my body going tense with each micro movement. I gasp and pant, forcing myself to stay awake. But the pain is a small agony compared to knowing that I may not have enough time to save both of us. Still, I pull, the edge cutting into my flesh as the blade rings its final taunt.

Then it's out.

"Seren," I whisper. "I need your cauterizer."

I reach out to find her leg. It's colder than I remember, but I've got to help myself first. My hands dig into her pockets and pull out any bit of aid kit I can find, dropping it into and around my wound. The pain is pushing my eyes back into my head. It doesn't matter. I just need to live long enough to get her home. All that matters is her. Seren's got to live.

"Hey," I say, reaching out for her hand once I'm done. "Let's get you back, yeah?"

But the moment my fingers touch hers, my heart drops into a deep chasm. My ear covers her mouth and my fingers find her throat. Nothing. Absolutely nothing. My gut hollows out as I scramble to put my ear against her chest.

Nothing.

My eyes shut, fighting to keep the tears from overwhelming me. It's impossible. My eyes fill with so much moisture, I'm blinded. It doesn't matter. My weak arms wrap around her, and I hold her lifeless body in my arms. She's so cold. I rock her. Gently. With as much love and care as a big sister could.

But I can't call myself that. Not now. Not until I find the man who did this to her and remove him from this universe. *Daga.* Daga's to blame for this. Daga took my little sister from me. And I won't stop until I end him in the most panful way possible.

"Efa," I say into my comm. But my voice is hoarse and muddled from near-endless sobs. I sit up, take a breath, and clear my throat, hoping to sound anything but lost. "Efa, pick up."

"Ceri!" Efa replies in mere seconds. *"Where are you? We need you back here! We've got a serious problem."*

I pause as I reach for the last bit of sec skin to cover my wound. "What? What is it?"

"Listen, Ceri." Efa sighs into her mic. *"Fana's been taken. The agents from the* Devant *who came to take Raey stole Fana instead. They just took her and blew their connection to the ship. We almost got blown out the airlock."*

I squeeze my eyes shut. No. Just no. This can't happen now. Not now. I've got nothing left. No way to help. Fana's lost. She's gone. My soul is crumbling.

I suck in a ragged breath and remember Fana's smile. It took me so long to realize what it did to me. Even in this dark moment, it lifts me a little. But all I have of it now is this memory. Struggle as I might, I can't keep it alive in my head. I reach for it, and it floats away, disappearing into darkness. A sob wells up within me, and I gasp for another shakier breath. My face burns with the flow of new tears. In my desperation for solace, I recall the warmth of Fana's skin pressed against mine, sensing it as if she were here. I break as it, too, fades. Everything turns cold. So very, very cold.

My hands clench. Rage grows within me. Daga took my little sister, and Azazhi stole my happiness.

Now all I have left is revenge.

"Ceri?"

"Seren's gone, Efa," I say, squeezing my eyes shut as I swallow hard. "She's down on one-twenty-nine. Send someone to retrieve her. I'll make sure she's easy to find."

"Oh, Ceri. No!" Efa sobs, but quickly recovers. *"What about you? Are you okay?"*

My eyes drop to my side before I reply, "I'm fine."

"Okay. Good. Stay with her, then. I'll send Sayer and Tegan down to help you. Come back quickly. I really need your help up here."

"Sorry, Efa," I reply, my voice hardening. "I can't help. I'm going after Daga. He did this. He killed her. I won't allow him to live any longer."

"No!" Efa cries. *"Don't be an idiot! Ceri! Stay on the comm!"*

But I've stopped listening. I'm lost in trying to imagine Seren's bright eyes looking at me. My hand reaches up and brushes her hair back into place. She should look good for when she meets Rhys again. I want her to make him smile. I know she will when she sees him.

Then, with one last glance at her, I stuff my pockets with as much ammunition as will fit. I pull Seren's blade from its sheath and slip it into my boot. I'll take anything I can get my hands on. Anything that'll take Daga out.

This ends now.

HAZARD

— • —

FANA

THESE BASTARDS. THEY CAN'T find a better place to keep me than this closet? I still don't understand why they took me instead of Raey. And they knocked me out and dropped me in this storage chamber with just some padding on the deck for a bed. My head is pounding. I'm so dizzy, I can't even stand without getting sick. I don't know how I'll escape like this. And I *will* escape. I've got to get back to Ceri and my crew.

I scratch at the sore spot on my arm, covered by sec skin but still showing blood around the edges of the patch. I bet they stole it—my life's essence—those bloodsuckers. They wouldn't tell me why, but they rushed through the procedure, and now my entire forearm throbs. Raey would curse them out for such sloppy work.

Raey. By the look on her face, it was a complete surprise when the security agent shoved her. It was surprise for me, too. And everyone else who wasn't an agent. She's likely staring at four very compact walls, just like I am right now, wondering how this happened. They'll try to trade her again for something. That is, until those kids realize Commander Azazhi has no interest in getting her back.

Sorry, Raey, but you brought this on yourself. The crew of the Stratford *would have taken you in and welcomed you as one of their own if you hadn't betrayed them.*

A knock comes at the door. I tense and do my best to remember everything Ceri taught me about fighting. *Don't wrap your fingers around your thumb. Punch with your body, not your hand. Strike sensitive parts and run.* And if I can get a lucky hit in, I'll be running as fast as I can and hope I can stay on my feet.

"Chief Neridi?" a voice calls as the door opens. It's Taye! But what does he want from me?

His eyebrows rise as he comes in, but the medical mask on his face hides whether he's smiling or not. I'll take the chance and say he is, which is a good sign he's not about to torture me.

"Were you expecting another prisoner to be in here?" I ask, fully intending to bare my unhappiness at him.

He glances out the door before shutting it and turning his attention to me. Sort of. "What? Oh, no. I was looking for you," he replies.

"Yeah? Why's that?"

Taye sighs. "Hey, Chief, I know you've been treated poorly by the commander for doing what you thought was right. But ever since they brought those kids aboard, things have changed. We've lost a lot of good crew and have had to pull people from first shift to fill in. Most of them just went back into stasis a month ago."

I tilt my head. "Lost?"

"Yeah." He lowers his gaze. "Two doctors and three med-techs. A few from engineering—"

"Like who?"

"Dejen and Biruk. And you remember Selam from my team."

"Of course." I smile, remembering her first day on the ship. *Poor lady. She was so awkward.* But then it hits me: she's gone. "No! You can't be serious! What happened to the vaccine they were rendering?"

Taye shakes his head, dropping his gaze. "It didn't come fast enough."

"How many?"

"Twenty-five in total."

"Bish, Taye, that's like half the crew!" I slap my hand on the padding, and it makes a dull thud. Taye's eyebrows crash, and he watches me for a moment. *Huh? Oh. Right. I was just talking like the crew of the* Stratford. I was so shocked, it just came out. Taye must think I'm some kind of strange creature now. "I'm sorry," I add, doing by best to offer him a sincere smile.

Taye grips at his shirt. "Chief—"

"You don't need to call me that. Not anymore."

"I don't think I could ever not call you that. What you've done for this ship and its people. And then you went to another one and did it all over again. I've got too much respect for you. That's why I'm here. I had to tell you."

"Tell me what?"

"We're leaving. The *Devant* is accelerating to its standard cruise velocity, and we're leaving the *Stratford* behind."

My jaw drops. "W...what?"

But by the dip of his head as he avoids my gaze, Taye is telling the truth.

If my heart wasn't secured behind my rib cage, it would have fallen out and left an empty, gaping hole for Taye's news to flood into. The emptiness is already there, devouring any hope I might have had about a better life.

Hyuking hyuk! Why is this happening to me? What the hell have I done to deserve this? How pathetic am I? A day ago, I found out that the girl I've fallen hard for actually likes me back. But now I'll never see her again! And how did it come to be that both my lovers, past and present, are on the same ship and I'm not? And those kids! My crew who trusted me like a sister. My family is gone.

I pull my knees to my chest and bash my forehead on them. All I want is to bawl like some miserable little girl. I've got every right to. Nobody else on this ship is being denied the life they want. I hope they drop me into stasis and never wake me up.

"Chief? Are you okay?" Taye asks in that male *I care, but I'm completely clueless about how to help* tone. But he's not to blame. He may be the only friend I have on the *Devant* now.

"No," I reply. "I feel like hell." My hand slides across my stomach. It aches like someone injected air into it and it's blown up like a balloon. For all I know, it has.

"What can I do? Just tell me whatever you need, and it's done. I'm not the only one on this ship who still respects you, Chief."

My gosh, he's serious. And likely my only hope. Taye's senior crew now. If anyone can get me whatever I need to escape, it's the guy right in front of me. He's got access to, well, everything but Commander Azazhi's quarters, and I won't be getting out that way. There are plenty of other options, however.

Maybe my luck's not as bad as I thought.

"Taye, I can't stay here," I say.

"No, of course not."

I run my tongue across my teeth. *Yes, clueless, and still my only hope.*

"No, I mean, I've got to get back to the *Stratford*," I explain. "Now. Before we throttle up the engines."

Taye pulls at a strand of his tight curly hair, almost as if he wants to tear it out. *Now he's getting it.*

"Chief, that's impossible," he counters. "There's—"

I sit up. "You said whatever I needed. And that's what I need, Taye. Raey's still there. The commander left her and took me instead. She can't be alone. And the *Stratford*'s crew really needs me, more than this ship ever would. I've got to get back."

"Yeah, but I was thinking more like a way to make you comfortable. Or put in a good word for you with the commander so you could get a berth assignment. Something like that, you know? Not committing treason against my ship."

I press my lips together. Of course that's what he meant. It was me projecting my hopes on him that made me forget that. But I really wish he'd forget his fear of Azazhi so he'd agree to help me.

I smile at him. "It's not treason." *And that is a total lie.* "Even if you got caught, which you won't, no one will punish you. Not with the ship short on experienced crew. They need you, so the worst you'd get is a mark on your record. And since

Azazhi doesn't give a bish about regulations, your record is meaningless."

He shakes his head. "N-n-no. I can't risk my status. Sorry, Chief. Ask me anything else. Please."

Maybe I should just knock him out, take his security pass, and run. He'd be helping me, *and* he wouldn't get in trouble. I think I even remember how to do it like Ceri showed me. Not that I'd feel good about hitting Taye, but if this is the only way to escape, then I hope he'll forgive me.

Though I'd never find out because I wouldn't get to ask him. Ever.

"Baati would have helped me," I mumble, crossing my arms. "Just like he did before."

Taye frowns. "He didn't have a choice! He was following your orders. And why bring him up, anyway? Isn't it bad enough that your friends over there killed him?"

"We don't know who killed Baati, Taye. But I promise you, it wasn't one of those kids."

Taye's eyes go wide. "So there's a murderer loose on their ship? And you want to go back there?"

"Not *want* to. *Have* to. I'm not worried about some crazy adult. Staying here will kill me. For real. That's why I need your help, *Chief*."

He clenches and opens his hands. Then repeats it. And does it again. After a fourth time, he sighs and shakes his head, glancing away from me. "I already told you I can't," he says.

"You can if we bring Baati's murderer to justice." I spring to my feet, raising my hands before he can refuse again. "Think of it. We turn him over to you, and you can take the credit for negotiating the trade. Azazhi will see the *Stratford*'s crew didn't do it, and he'll have someone to bring to justice. What a morale booster that'd be, right? Then we resume the exchange, and everyone gets what they want."

Taye wags a finger at me. "You're forgetting yourself in that whole scenario, Chief. The commander brought you back because—"

"No!" I shout. "He didn't *bring* me back. That bastard abducted me! And threw Raey away in the process! And before any of that, he did this!"

Scar tissue had partially filled the hole in my hand. Raey had done her best with the technology available on the *Stratford*, but it would require a long nap in stasis if I wanted it to look normal again. And I do, though the hideous way it looks is a major benefit right now because Taye gasps and backs away.

"Fana, are you saying Commander Azazhi shot you in the hand?"

"Not him." I let my hand linger in his gaze a little longer before lowering it. "But he gave the order. You would have seen it the last time we met in engineering, but I was kinda busy rescuing the *Stratford* kids."

Taye shakes his fists, his forehead getting tight. I would smirk if I wasn't so angry right now. And I deserve to be. I've been taken from my home and left to rot in a closet.

"Commander Azazhi is a monster, Taye," I hiss. "You're getting that, aren't you? He didn't steal me back and nearly blow a hole in their ship because he needs my expertise. I'm just a pawn to him. A hyuking item. Something he can use as leverage so he can take every useful bit of colony-building equipment from the *Stratford*. And if he doesn't get that, he'll kill me."

Taye inhales as he drops his hands on his head and squeezes. Everything I've told him sinks into his brain. Good. Maybe I won't have to knock him out after all.

"So will you help me?" I plead.

He looks me straight in the eyes and nods. "Okay."

Finally.

EXPOSURE

CERI

I PRESS A HAND to my side as I slip off the ladder and plant my feet on the deck of one-thirty-five. My wound has become a throbbing dull ache now that I've packed it with the last bit of Seren's cauterizer. An old sec skin patch covers it, and that's already stained with the dark crimson of my blood. Unless I'm very lucky, it'll get worse when I battle Daga again. Not that I care. I only need to stay alive long enough to watch him die. Then, I will join Seren and Rhys in a place that is far better than here.

Fana will be sad to learn what happened, though maybe she'll never find out. None of us will ever meet her again, captive on the *Devant* as she is. Perhaps that's for the best. She'll be around familiar people and not reminded of the hell that killed those she cared about.

My heart aches thinking about her. Not just because I'm desperate for another chance to press my lips to hers and feel her warmth close to me. Her sharp mind, strong compassion, and even the adorable way she smiles all make up the person I've...yes...completely fallen for.

But I shouldn't have kissed her. That connection isn't something I can have. I'm a leader, and love is a distraction, no matter how wonderful it felt. And it was more amazing than I could ever expect. For the first time, I understand why Efa chose Merek and how her love for him nearly ended her.

Not that knowing will help me now.

I step across the deck, the very one that began this downward spiral. This is where Daga murdered Rhys and set everything that's happened in motion. I can't believe—

Bish! There he is!

My hand flies up. I tap the pistol's trigger five times in rapid progression. Five darts burst from my gun, racing toward him. I charge behind my attack. They won't hit, but I planned it that way. I want to be close when I end him.

The darts ricochet off every metal surface, spraying sparks over Daga. He cries out as I round the turn, vaulting into the air to pound the edge of my gun into his back. Daga growls and spins, catching me in the gut with his fist and knocking the air from my lungs. My arm swings out as I fire at his head. He drops and spins, attempting to sweep my legs from under me. I jump and twist, avoiding his attack but land hard, my face contorting with the pain.

Daga swings his fist down at me. I roll away. He strikes at me again. I kick my heel into his arm. His body twists, but he catches himself and punches, missing me by a hair's width.

I push away, shooting to my feet. Daga launches from his spot on the deck. His arm pulls back to throw a punch. But he growls as his wounded leg makes him stumble. I spring forward and catch him across the face with my gun. His head snaps to one side, and he goes down.

I'm grinning in bloodlust. I've got him now. It's all over. My gun comes up, aiming for his head. Two shots right through his eye, and I can return.

If only I was so lucky.

Daga's leg shoots out, striking me in the shin and knocking my foot off the deck. My balance vanishes. I throw my hands up to catch myself. Too late. I tumble, my arms shooting over my head.

He's on me in a heartbeat, pounding on my kidneys. I shriek and writhe, trying to get out from under him. His fist strikes the side of my head. Stars cross my vision as my pulse thunders inside me. Daga rips the pistol from my hands and jams it into my temple.

Bish. He's got me. I'm done, anyway. My body is withering by the second. It's the blood loss. Who knows how much I've lost? I gasp for a breath. I'm still living. Which means I'm not done fighting. But how do I get out of this? There's no way he misses.

"Did you really think you could kill me?" he hisses, and spits. "Now, after I end your brat ass, I'm going to hunt down the rest of your crew, and then I won't have to see another hyuking brat on this ship ever again."

My blood boils. I thrash and swing at his legs with my bare hands. Anything to hurt him.

"I hate you!" I scream with every ounce of my breath. "You hyuking bastard!"

He's too far back. But even as my body screams in terror, I won't give up. One more strike. One he'll feel for the rest of his life. I'll attack him with anything. Anything! I'll make him hurt one more time before he ends me. Bish! If only I had a weapon!

Seren's knife!

Daga chuckles. "The feeling's mutual, you damn brat. Say goodbye."

I twist hard as he fires. The dart glances off the deck. Daga loses his balance. I bend my leg just enough and grab Seren's blade, slicing across his calf as it slips from my boot. Daga shouts, recoiling from my strike. I slash at him again, but only get air. He aims again. I kick the pistol away and shove up.

His shot goes wide. I scramble away on my hands and feet, gasping for breath. Daga fires again—too close. I turn and launch myself at him, my blade chopping at his gun arm, missing by the smallest distance.

My shoulder hits him in the stomach, and we go down. The pistol drops from his hand. I swing my blade, slicing across his chest. Daga hisses and throws me off him. I fly into the corner of a filtration container and drop. He pushes to his feet and crashes into a duct before staggering away into the dark.

A hoarse cry escapes from my throat as sobs rack my body. My chest rises and falls with the pain of each breath. No. This isn't right. This isn't how I imagined it. I saw it all clear in my head—me standing over him as Daga took his last breath. Instead, I lie here, broken, while he gets away.

I was wrong to choose revenge. But Seren's death blinded me. I forgot everything but that, and now I've got nothing to show for my fatal mistake. Efa would smack some hard sense into me if she were here. And I would've pushed her to hit me harder, even while I was covering her back. We were a great team. But she chose love over hate. Why couldn't I do the same?

It was never in me to choose it. My solution is to shoot first. Now I don't even have a gun.

I push myself up onto my hands and knees, wiping at my eyes. The throbbing in my side has become a sharp burn. I can make it to the rail car. There's nothing else for me to do. If I die on my way up, at least I tried. At least I attempted something, because I've failed at everything else.

Bish, why couldn't I end him? Even now my hate for him riles my blood and pounds the pulse in my ears. That monster forced me to murder children! Kids my age. The mere thought of what I've done for him shakes every bit of my being. Killing him once wouldn't be enough to rid myself of every torturous moment under his boot. He deserves to suffer a hundred times over, just like all of us have suffered.

Yes. That's it. But it's not about revenge. It was never about that. I am here to protect my crew. Nothing else matters but their survival and that of our passengers. I do this so that they will endure.

Purpose warms my body, filling me with the strength to get up. I grab hold of a conduit and pull myself up. Daga can't be far. I hurt him good. And I will finish what I started, but this time, it'll be for the sake of the people on the *Stratford*. My people.

I press my hand to my side as I stagger down the walkway. Fresh blood soaks my dressing. It's no surprise. But all the damage I've taken has cut the time I have left down to nothing. I could collapse any minute, and I won't get up again. Every second I've got left has to count. That's the only way I protect everyone.

As I lumber into the dark, something on the deck catches my eye. Long and black, half hidden under the bottom of a filtration unit. I gasp and lurch toward it, straining hard to pick it up. My lips curve up when I do.

Daga's rifle.

A beep echoes in the distance. I pause, listening for more. Not the rail car, but what? Maybe down one level? Perhaps. Only one way to find out.

Using the rifle for support, I make my way to the ladder and slip into the shadow around the landing, listening for movement. But he's not there. Daga's not waiting in ambush. He needs to care for his wounds, or he'll bleed out faster than I will.

Another beep. What is that sound?

Strapping the rifle to my back, I descend, grunting with every movement. My legs shake under the pressure, and my grip on the rungs is weak. I focus on each motion, one at a time. The ship slips away, and now it's just me and the ladder.

Until my boot taps the deck on the level.

My head spins as I touch down. I grab the ladder to steady myself and shut my eyes. My heart is racing, even as my body gets heavy—no. *Not yet. Please. Just give me a little more time.*

After a minute of fighting for control, I shuffle down the corridor toward the source of the sound. As I get closer, the sound grows. I slip the rifle off my shoulder and aim it forward. Daga. It has to be Daga.

Three status lights glow unusually bright on the wall. I drop into a crouch as low as I can tolerate and waddle up to the lights. They're mounted on a control panel next to a door with a large port window in it.

My jaw goes slack. It's a maintenance airlock. And Daga's gone through it!

I take a breath and hold it, slipping toward the door and peeking through the port. He's not there, but the airlock's cycled. He's gone outside. What? Why? Does he really hope to escape me out there?

No. Not escape.

Daga knew I'd hear the airlock's status tones. It's a dare. A challenge to fight him outside the ship. But that makes little sense. We'd have thirty minutes of air. Less if we're breathing hard. Unless...

I smirk. It's to his advantage to be weightless. No pressure on his legs. He'll be able to stand, and other movement will be less effort for him.

And less for me, too.

Of course, I could just lock him out there. He'd suffocate, and that'd be it. But he must have realized that. Daga knows I can't just walk away now. Not without watching the life slip from his body. I need that ending. So does the crew.

I open the airlock's inside door, taking a moment to gaze through the outer porthole to the stars beyond.

It'll be the last time I do.

OPPORTUNITY

FANA

MY FORMER SHIP HAS fewer levels than the *Stratford*. Only twenty-seven, to be exact. Yet I always seem to find myself on the lower ones, as if this domain was created just for me. I like to think it was. That way, I can move through the ship without collapsing into complete panic.

Taye has helped me to return to my personal arena, sneaking me down passage after passage and down stairs—yes, stairs—to get to the one exit off the ship no one is likely watching: the cargo hold.

Taye slides the door at the bottom of the stairwell open and waits for me to hobble down the last steps, which I do in way longer than record time. I'm struggling to walk straight, much less descend. And even though Taye is taking a colossal risk in getting me down here, the least he could do is give me a hand down.

As desperate as I am to get back to the *Stratford*, the extended space walk that will get me there is shaking me to my bones. If Commander Azazhi is planning to accelerate back to the *Devant*'s standard cruise velocity, he's moved the ship far away from the *Stratford* to avoid any issues. As if the distance I crossed the first time wasn't terrifying enough. This time I'll be stretching both my air and propulsion supply to the limit. And I'll be doing it alone.

I can't let fear stop me. I must get back to Ceri and her crew. They're everything to me now.

"I won't be turning on the lights, for obvious reasons," Taye says. "So just go slow. I doubt anyone will be looking for you just yet, anyway."

I sneer. *Fine, if that's how valuable I am to them.* Though, I'm unsure. They wouldn't have made the effort if Azazhi thought I was worthless to him. He'd be thinking that right now if he knew where I was and what I'm about to do. There's no doubt Yelekal's agents would shoot me first before they did anything else. Not that it matters. My only choice is to return. I'll die if I stay here.

The *Devant*'s cargo hold is far less mysterious than the darkened levels of the *Stratford*'s storage areas. Theirs requires machines, manually operated by humans, to move things around, creating arbitrary piles of crates and boxes everywhere. And they've taken many of those to build defensible positions and secure areas to wage war from. This ship has aisles upon aisles of crates, stacked nearly to micrometers of perfection. But of course, the automated systems that run this hold only do as we've programmed them. I'd likely be bored to death if the lights were on.

"This way," Taye whispers when he doesn't have to and beckons me to follow. I glance around before the automatic light in the stairwell shuts off, just to get my bearings, then move. He frowns as he watches me, crouched down as I am. "What are you doing?" he asks.

"Trying to be stealthy," I reply.

"Why?"

I sigh and stand straight. "So no one sees me, dummy."

"Chief. You realize it's near pitch black, don't you?"

"Just go."

Taye sighs, and I'm glad for it. The sound he makes helps me to keep behind him. Otherwise I might get lost, and then I'd have to call out, and that's risky because someone could come down here, even though it's unlikely.

"Ow!" I shout and drop to the deck.

"Shhhh!" Taye responds. Then, "Are you okay?"

"No," I reply. "I just smacked into something really big."

"Don't move." The shuffling of his feet comes closer, and soon I feel him touch my head before he quickly retracts his hand. He taps my shoulder, then, and I get that he's offering to help me up. I reach out to search for his hand and take hold of it once our fingers touch. With a sharp jolt, I'm back on my feet—*whoa! Too fast!* The ship spins around me, and I cling to him so I don't land flat on my back.

"Sorry," I breathe. "I'm okay now."

"Are you sure?" he asks.

"Yeah, but what did I hit?"

"Likely a stasis pod." A resonant thump sounds when he finds the object and pats it. "Yep."

What are...Oh! These are the pods that should have gone to the *Stratford* and didn't because of poor Baati. Nothing much to do about that. At least they got sixty-one working units with medical modules now. Ceri won't be happy about it, though. She feels every death on that ship as if it was her fault. All she's ever done is fight to protect her crew.

It'd be a miracle if I could get the rest of them over there, but without convincing Azazhi to reconnect the ships again—which will never happen—it's impossible. I mean, given enough time, I might be able to design a solution that could be manufactured and assembled here, but no one will ever give me that luxury.

"Come on," Taye says. "It's not far to the locker and the airlock."

Both words make me shudder. The locker is where the EVA suits are kept, and the airlock...well, that's just the entrance to my nightmare. If I didn't need to stay sharp, I'd ask Taye to fill me with a bunch of relaxants so I don't freeze the second he locks the helmet on my head. My feet hesitate to move forward with each new step.

By *not far*, I suspect Taye meant not the entire length of the ship, which is, obviously, still far. The *Devant* isn't as long as the *Stratford*, but it is wider by a good amount, save for the aft of the ship where the engines are.

And we're walking across that expanse right now.

As we walk, or in my case, shuffle, I touch upon pod after pod. At least that's what I think they are. When I tap on them, they resonate like stasis devices, empty of their fluids or passengers. I haven't been counting, but there certainly seems like a lot.

"Hey," I say. "Just how many surplus pods are here?"

"Five hundred twenty-seven," Taye replies.

And I come to a complete stop. "Over five hundred? Are you sure?"

"Of course I'm sure. My team's the ones who transported them over, remember? I know nearly every unit and modification done to them."

Modification. Dare I ask? No. What matters is that Azazhi lied and held back almost the same amount of pods he said he would give us! And of course, he found a reason not to do that. Bastard. I doubt he ever intended to make good on his side of the deal.

The *Stratford*'s passengers could really use what they're owed. Bish, they could use every last one of these. What we were supposed to get would only cover the units that were about to fail. We need extras in case more go down, and given the age of the equipment, I'd say that's likely.

I sigh. There's no chance of the ships connecting ever again. Azazhi may be a tyrant, but he's a smart one. He'd never give Ceri the opportunity to overrun his ship to rescue me. And she would. I know she would. She almost did it before.

Oh, my heart's racing just thinking about being in her arms again!

"Hey," Taye says. "You went quiet. Are you okay?"

"Yes!" I wince at the loudness of my voice and lower it by a lot. "Yes. I was just wondering if there was a way to get these pods over to the *Stratford.*"

Taye snorts. "You've got no chance of that, Chief. Just be happy that we're getting you back there. Moving even a single pod across the current distance between the ships is impossible. You'd be more likely to make the *Devant* travel faster than the speed of light."

My forehead gets tight. *It's not impossible. Just difficult.* Taye's a brilliant mechanic, but he doesn't understand the physics involved. They're complicated, but I could make the calculations. And when he dismisses my thoughts like that, it really pushes me to try.

But I should forget it. Forget I'd ever said it and get my butt off this ship now.

Hyuk that.

"You know what, Taye?" I say. "I'm going to figure it out."

"Figure what out?" he asks, concern drifting into his voice.

I feel my lips turning up even before I answer. "How to get the pods across."

"Oh, no. No, Chief. That is a guaranteed way to get you recaptured. Or shot. And I just got done telling you there's no way."

"Thanks, Taye. Challenge accepted!"

Taye moans. It just makes me smile more. Of course, I've got a ton of things to measure before I can carry out whatever plan I come up with. And I'll need quite a few things. A propulsion system, a lot of cable or wire. And time, which I won't get more of. Once the airlock opens, it'll be a race to get all the pods off the *Devant* before Captain Yelekal and his agents arrive to arrest me. Or kill me.

"But you'll help me, Taye, won't you? If only to see this crazy idea work?"

"Listen, Fana." Taye comes close and puts his hand on my arm. Once he finds it. "You are probably the most skilled engineer I've ever known. And that includes the people who designed this ship. But this has almost no chance of working. I'm less concerned about getting in trouble than I am about watching you fail."

I grab his arms and turn him to face me. I think. This darkness is a pain. "I won't fail, Taye. I can't fail. There's no life I can imagine having if I'm stuck on this ship. The *Stratford* is where I belong, and I have to get there or die trying."

My pulse is pounding at the prospect of success. And from fear. But this is a problem I was born to solve. That it could end with me saving the day for the *Stratford*'s passengers while poking Azazhi in the eye only makes it that much sweeter. I need to take a big bite of this challenge sandwich as soon as possible.

Like right now.

Taye holds me back, squeezing my arms. Honestly, it's awkward, because most chiefs on this ship are way more formal with each other than this. Though, if there were ever a situation that made it okay, this would be it.

"There's no way I'll stop you from doing this, is there?" Taye asks.

"Taye, I hope you understand. There's no other option for me. If I want to live, I need to be there."

He squeezes my arms again and then backs away with a sigh. A moment of panic rushes through me. *Wait, is he going to turn me down? Does that mean I've got to solve this alone?* That's an absolute guarantee for failure. I really hope he gets just how critical this is for me. And for the *Stratford*'s crew.

"Okay, Chief. I'll help," he says. "And if you figure this out, I'll make sure your name goes down in the records as the most insane, and the most brilliant, engineer who ever lived."

Pure delight rushes through me, and I jump up and down like a kid getting their first ice cream. I knew he wouldn't let me down. Taye helped me before when he knew we were breaking regulations, and he's doing it once again. How could I be more grateful for someone like him?

"Taye, I could kiss you," I say.

"Yeah?" he replies, sounding uncomfortable. "Please don't."

EXCURSION

CERI

I PULL THE PRESSURE suit from its rack and unlock the seams, sitting down on the ready bench to prepare. It'll take me ten minutes to put it on, and in that time, who knows what Daga will be doing. Likely setting up an ambush. Not that there's any place on the surface of the ship to hide. But just so I avoid any potential for attack the moment I exit the airlock, I peer out the port and search for him.

It's clear, but I'm far from satisfied. He's out there somewhere, waiting for me. And Daga will take any advantage he can get after the damage I've done to him. Out on the hull, we'll be weightless, save for the constant force wanting to rip us from our magnetic grip and hurl us toward the nuclear furnace of the engines. We're not that far from them now, and a pressure suit is no protection from that inferno.

I try not to think about how these will be my last moments. Ever. I should be grateful for that, really. Hope has made me consider life through a brighter lens, and even though those happy moments were brief, I'm glad to have had the chance to experience them.

My feet slip into the bottom half of the suit. I bend down to lock it in place, gritting my teeth to bear the pain as the pressure on my side increases. It's only for a few seconds, but it hits me so hard I've got to clamp my hands on the bench for fear of falling off it.

If Daga wasn't as wounded as I am, I might call for support. But Efa'd take me out of the fight, and I can't have that. It would fill me with rage if someone else ended him, and the last thing I want is to die with anger in my heart against one of my crew. It must be me. Only me. With a single attack, I will end my suffering. And everyone else's.

I gasp as I raise my hands above my head, doubling over as agony burns into my side. The top half of the pressure suit falls from my hands and tumbles to the deck with a dull thump. Dizziness hits me hard. I collapse onto my side, panting. Bish, I'm in a bad way. All I can hope is that Daga's worse. It's the only way I beat him.

I cough out a laugh when I remember how I used to think that he cared about us. That somewhere deep beneath that harsh persona was a fatherly figure. What bish. Daga only cared about annihilating the Fahrasi so our faction could survive. Not that we Tarakh could have survived without the engineering expertise of our enemy. And that was the irony of the entire war: we would have lost everything the moment we had won.

With a grunt, I pick up the pressure suit top and slip it on as I remain sideways. When I sit up, the locks between the torso and the legs click into place. I reach for the helmet, hesitating only for a moment where my desire to avoid more pain over-shadows my will to finish this.

I grab the helmet from its shelf, my side throbbing hot, warning me not to overextend. I gulp in a breath and move it until it's above me, then lower it onto my head, hoping my side doesn't erupt in agony.

Thirty seconds to double-check the seals, check the oxygen mixture, and rest a moment, even as my life slowly drains from me. It's alright. There's still time enough to fight. And die.

My hand lifts to tap the airlock cycle control, hovering over the button for two seconds so I can whisper a prayer. *To my Ancestors, give me the strength to end this now. Mother and Father, please forgive everything I've done, though I hope you never find out. My dear crew, may this bring you peace for however long you may live. And to Fana, wherever you are, don't dwell on me for long. Move on, and may you find happiness, as I cannot be the one to provide it.*

I tighten my jaw and tap the button. The status light turns amber, and the muted hiss of air being removed from the chamber buzzes around my helmet. I should take this time to reacquaint myself with the plasma rifle and make sure I can fire it with gloves on. It'd be mostly worthless to me if I can't. I shuffle to where I left it, put a hand on the bench, and lean down to pick it up.

The airlock spins across my vision. My knees buckle. I drop, crashing on my side, my helmet slamming into the bench. Bile forces its way into my mouth. My lips smash together to hold it in, noticing the tang of blood mixed within it.

Hyuk. There's not enough air left in the chamber to take my helmet off. But I can't see. I can barely breathe. And I'm about to vomit.

I slump onto the deck and shut my eyes. It'd be so easy just to drift away. Fade into nothing and that'd be the end. I can't. While my heart beats, I still lead this crew. There's too much for me to do before I let the dark take me.

My hands press on the deck, and I focus my will to get me back to my feet. I grip the edge of the bench, set my jaw, and push. My muscles strain. My body shakes. I grit my teeth and reach down inside me for more strength.

But it's not to be.

My legs give out. My fingers slip off the bench. And I collapse to the deck once more.

Hyuk. This can't be the way it ends. I can't fail my crew like this. Seren can't have died for nothing. And I've set the airlock up so Daga can return, stepping over my lifeless body as he makes his way into the ship to murder my friends.

My hand moves to key the comm mic. One call would be all I needed. One call and I'd be saved. It'd be so easy. Efa would come to rescue me. Sayer would take care of Daga. Raey would heal me. My crew would be free. I would live on. Maybe even find happiness in something new.

I press the button. Static fills my ears. They're listening. All I have to do is speak. Two words would be enough. Two words and it'd be over.

So I lift my finger off the key switch and cut the signal. This might end with their help, but the torment would live on inside me. And I don't want to suffer any longer. Not when I've got a responsibility to my crew and passengers.

And Fana.

Even if it's impossible. She deserves our effort to try. She belongs on this ship, with the people who care about her. My end would be peaceful if I knew they'd go after her. But to make that happen, I've got to get up. Now.

With my lungs expanding, I suck in as much oxygen as I can. Then, focusing on the face of every crew member, I roar and thrust down on the deck. My hand latches to the bench. I lift off the deck. I'm almost up. My feet are flat on the deck.

And my legs go soft.

"No!" I shout, my hand flailing out to grasp a handhold. The door latch. The wall. Anything to keep me from falling. I grab the rifle and use it to push me along toward the outer hatch. I can stand outside. All I have to do is make it there.

I hit the hatch release and lean into it, the spinning in my head and the weakness in my legs threatening to drop me out the airlock, where I'll float away. All I can do is steady my breathing and focus as best as I can. Daga is no better. And neither of us have experience fighting outside the ship. This will be as even as it gets.

With a tight grip on a handle just inside the outer door, I step out, the magnetic locks on my boots powering on. As much as I want to stare out into the forest of stars, I can't. Daga is the only target I need to see.

I twist to reorient my body, sucking a breath in between my teeth as an ache rips into my side, smacking me back to alertness. I shiver as if I could feel the chill of space through my suit. But I welcome it. I will take anything that will keep me sharp.

Pushing myself up to stand, my feet locked to the black metal of the ship's hull, I lift the rifle to my shoulder and sight down the barrel as I scan the area, searching for Daga.

And find him.

He's made it farther than I expected. A hundred paces at least, his boots sliding across the hull. He's headed forward, making his best effort to get to the upper levels. But why?

To slip into another airlock and escape me, perhaps. Well, he won't.

I power the rifle on, take aim, and fire. The beam flies past his head, close enough for him to take notice, then disappears into the blackness. I grin as he freezes and turns, cautiously.

I've got his attention now. What happens next is up to him.

EMANCIPATION

FANA

"Okay, what do we need first?" Taye asks.

"We need light."

Taye huffs and clicks on a palm light, shining it on the deck so as not to damage our eyesight. The little device is powerful enough to illuminate the surrounding cargo hold for about eight meters around us. As my eyes adjust, I take in the half-dozen stasis pods I can see without squinting. The way they're pressed together only hints at the sea of units I'm wading in. I inhale slowly. This is going to be a significant task.

No, really. It'll take some serious time if I can't gather up enough equipment to make this work.

"Now we need about a kilometer of tether and something that goes bang," I say.

"This isn't the armory, Chief," Taye replies as he examines the side of a pod. "Nothing explosive down here."

"Nothing that's *designed* to be explosive," I correct. "You know reactive compounds as well as I do."

"Yes, and you know we don't keep those kinds of things down here. Try again, Chief."

I roll my eyes. Not that Taye is looking at me. He's too busy doing something I should be doing—searching for anchor points on the pod frame. He's right, though. Anything caustic, unstable, or radioactive is in a smaller hold that's isolated from most everything else on the *Devant*. So I'll have to find something else to power my crossing or risk entering a highly secure area to get what I need, and that won't work. Yelekal's agents would be on me in seconds.

"You got another light?" I ask.

"No, but"—Taye turns the light on row after row of storage racks—"I'm sure you'll find one there."

As if I didn't know that. I grumble and head toward the nearest rack, but I can tell just by the size of the crates I should look elsewhere. This is already wasting time. I have 526 connections to make between stasis pods, and multiple more to whatever devices I find to propel this super-elongated train to the *Stratford*. And I'll need an equal number of them for the other devices I'll use to slow down my winding transport.

No doubt someone would notice a kilometer-and-a-half-long stasis pod snake blasting out of the *Devant*'s cargo hold. One of the junior crew might even believe we've got a hangar belowdecks, and actually, that's not a bad idea, once all the cargo is off-loaded. I'll have to share that idea with Taye later, before I leave. If I can.

Though what I'm staring at right now just may be the way I manage it.

"Taye," I hiss. "Get over here!"

He pads over, his eyes big as he looks at me expectantly. I nod to a collection of tall composite fiber cylinders, and he lights them up. Their dark exteriors suck in most of his palm device and offer little in terms of a hint about their function. But I know. And as Taye gets closer, his forehead collapsing into wrinkles, so does he.

"Air tanks, Chief?" Taye shakes his head. "There's nothing combustible in them. They're just fourth-level backup pressurized—"

I grin as his jaw drops open.

"How many do you think you'll need?" he asks, still staring at the tanks.

I bite the edge of my lower lip and consider. "Now that's a good question."

The trick will be to get this massive train moving, though if we turned the gravity off on this level, I'd need a lot less force to do so. We could emergency blow the airlock, too, for a nice kick, though that'll get Azazhi's attention on me in less than a second. He'll retrieve his pods and leave my lifeless body behind. No, just a brief flicker of the artificial gravity—which will make everything in here float for a bit—should do fine.

The key problem comes when I've got to decrease my velocity or risk punching a huge hole right through the *Stratford*. This is a massive amount of weight I'm taking with me. Once it gets going, it'll take a huge amount of energy to stop it. And it has to stop.

"Alright, let's check the pressure in these tanks."

Taye inhales. "Are you sure you've got time for this?"

I only clench my teeth as I duck under the shelf and peer at the closest gauge. Good, this one's fully charged. Just to make sure, I check a few others. All of them are as pressurized as the day we rolled them onto the ship. I'll consider myself lucky and use the time to calculate how many of these tanks I'll need to turn my plan into reality.

"Say, how much do you think one of those pods weighs?" I ask.

"With no fluids and nobody in it?" He pokes a finger into his cheek as he glances at the nearest one. "Likely as much as Captain Yelekal."

I snort. He's probably not far off. Though *probably* won't get me there. I need an exact number, or I could be way off in figuring this out.

"It's got to be in the manifest," I say. "Go look it up for me, would you?"

"I don't have to go anywhere, or have you forgotten we all have these?" Taye reaches into his side pocket and pulls out his data tablet. My mouth drops open. That thing's got a light on it! *How dare he keep that from me!*

I had forgotten about them, actually, since mine is over on the *Stratford*. It'd be a bad idea to use it here, anyway. The moment I powered it on, it'd announce itself to the *Devant*'s data network, and then I'd fail to escape again. I could spoof a different login, but that'd take time I don't have.

"Give it here, then!" I hold out my hand and shake it. Taye frowns but does as requested.

No sooner than it's in my hands do I call up the ship's cargo manifest and search it. I'm extremely tempted to log into the command program and look up when the *Devant* will accelerate, but I really don't want to learn I'm out of time.

"Decent guess," I say as the data comes up. *Okay. Got what I needed.* Now to crunch some numbers and see if I'm completely dreaming about how possible this will be.

First, mass per pod times number of units. Add in…hmm. I'll need to check the weight of the tanks and tether, too. Then take the pressure and convert that to a force measurement…a little guessing here, but it should be okay. Finally, I get my distances and velocities together, and—

I gasp. "No way in hell!"

"What?" Taye drops to a crouch beside me and scans the calculations until his eyes go wide. "We don't have anywhere close to five hundred tanks!"

Adding that many tanks would require an equal number of tethers and would add a massive amount of weight and complicate the setup to a level of impracticality. And someone would catch me in the act before I even made half of the connections!

My shoulders droop. I knew this would be tricky to pull off, but this is…this is impossible. Even if I cut the acceleration by a factor of ten, I'd still need more tanks than the *Devant*'s outfitters would have ever considered loading onto the ship.

I close my eyes and lean my head back on a tank, lacing my fingers behind my head as I run the numbers again. But it's useless. It's just too much weight to move.

Sayer will be the toughest to tell. Out of the entire crew, he'll take it the hardest, though I worry about Ceri. Unlike Sayer, she'll keep her disappointment inside, and I couldn't bear to watch her stay silent when I know she'll be blaming herself for it.

"Do you really need them all?" Taye asks.

My eyes pop open to look at him. "Huh?"

"Do you really need all 527 pods, or would, say, a hundred work?"

He can't be serious. Did he even think before he asked?

I pound my hands on my thighs. "No! We'd be sentencing our passengers to death if we can't replace their units! And more could go bad anytime!"

"Well, how many, then?" Taye throws his hands up. "If a hundred wouldn't work, would two hundred?"

I stand and rub my eyes with my palms. Maybe I've slipped into some alternate reality where everyone's an idiot. Whatever it is, I don't really want to deal with it right now.

"Two fifty?" Taye adds.

"No! I can't consider that!"

"Fana, you've got to, or you'll have to wake them up."

"Wake adults up on that ship? No way in hell!"

Even as I say it, I know Taye is right. We won't let harm come to anyone else, even if they're adults. But the idea of anyone trying to force their will on my crew burns a hole right through me. Not after all they've suffered through and all they've fought for. Their sacrifices can't be for nothing.

I sigh and pick up Taye's tablet again, thumping out a new set of calculations with my thumbs as Taye watches, his eyebrows crashing together. But the results aren't good enough. So I try again, chewing on the inside of my cheek to distract me from thinking about just how many units I'm leaving behind.

"So?" he tries after a minute, in a decidedly softer tone than before.

I hand him the tablet. "At least 247. And that's pushing it, but I won't cut the number any lower. This is what I'm doing, whatever the risk. You're still helping me, right?"

He smiles and puts a hand on my shoulder with a squeeze. "I'll start cutting the tether to suitable lengths."

"You found some already?"

Taye nods. And I hug him.

Taye jumps but returns the embrace once he's relaxed enough to remember to do so.

"Thank you, Taye. You're saving a whole lot of people, you know."

"Two hundred forty-seven, to be exact, right?"

"More like 4,123." I smile when he pulls back to look at me with a curious gaze. "Don't forget the *Stratford*'s crew, which, by the way, includes me."

It takes hours for us to put it all together, during which we hide from *Devant* crew members three times. But once it was all done, it was a sight to behold. Nearly half a kilometer long, coiled around a central spoke like a snake. We both suit up, and I secure myself to the lead pod, straddling it as if I was riding a horse. And I don't know how to do that. The only horses we had were virtual.

"Okay," Taye says through his suit's comm. *"Once I open the airlock doors, I'll release the artificial gravity. You'll know when that is."*

Sure as hell, I will.

And then, after all this time of feeling normal, my stomach tightens. I imagine myself hurling through space—at a modest velocity of seven meters per second squared—with nothing, absolutely nothing, to retrieve me should my crazy contraption fail. And there's a serious chance of that.

"Ready?" Taye asks.

"No," I reply through the comm, perspiration dotting my forehead and face. "But do it anyway, before I change my mind."

"Copy that, Chief. Counting down in three. Two..."

I frown when he stops counting and turn to find out what happened. But Taye is just staring at me, a soft smile on his face, made tender by the orange-yellow light inside his helmet.

"What happened to one?" I demand.

"I'll miss you, Fana," he replies. *"You're a real inspiration to me."*

A warmth spreads through me. "Aww, Taye, no need to get all—"

"One."

I scream as the lock opens and the gravity powers down. Before I can protest, thirty tanks of compressed air open their valves with a tremendous *whoosh* that blows dust through the hold. I jerk as the pod rockets forward. *Oh bish, what am I doing?* My hands grip the cable. I press myself to the pod, desperately wanting to shut my eyes. I can't. I've got to ensure I'm on the right vector. My heart is pounding. My knees are shaking.

And then, I'm in space.

SHOWDOWN

CERI

Daga would be wise to surrender. I've got him targeted, and I won't miss. Though I doubt he'll give up so easily. Really, I'm hoping that he doesn't. There is no universe where Daga gets off easy from the pain he's inflicted on the children of the *Stratford*. If the other adults were still here, they'd get the same. Then again, this would be a very different situation if they had remained.

There'd be a lot more kids still alive, for one thing.

Daga raises his hand, slowly. I tense. There's something in it—a weapon? I can't see from this distance. He pauses at his hip. My finger touches the trigger.

A flash. Bish, he's got a pistol! Mine. I suck in a breath and fire, but my aim's off. The shot's wide. I move to dodge his shot and hope I've moved fast enough.

No. I've moved too fast.

As I plant my foot to stop, I skid across the hull and nearly crash down an inlet. Bish! That's why he's moving slowly. If I don't do the same, I'll launch myself off the ship! But I'm not used to this. I can't fight slow. It makes no sense.

He slides toward me, taking advantage of my awkward attempt to recover, and fires again. I drop to the deck as quickly as I dare, hoping my timing is right. With the mass of stars behind him, it's nearly impossible to detect his shots. I'll never hear the pistol fire, either.

I go flat on the hull and fire twice. One shot bounces off the dark metal and speeds into space. The other is just wide. I've never had to fight at this distance, and I'm quickly realizing I'm bad at it. So is he.

At least so far.

Daga's closing the space between us faster than I'm ready for. I push up and skate toward him, firing twice for effect, hoping that slows him, but he keeps coming straight at me. I should've known better—he's too well acquainted with my tactics. Every time I aim, he fires, and I'm forced to move.

My breaths come faster as I rise, binding moisture to my helmet's visor and narrowing my vision. I press myself to get calm before I use too much air. Or go blind. There's no time to make an adjustment to the suit's internal environment, certainly not in the middle of a duel.

Daga's barely ten paces away. I take aim. So does he. We slide in opposite directions and fire, circling each other in a death spiral as we close in. His steps seem weak, unsteady. Good. I outmaneuver him. Just for a second. It's enough. I tap the trigger.

Got him now.

With an impossible twist, Daga evades my shot. I let off another beam. It rockets past him and burns into the hull. Hyuk!

He aims his gun at my head. My body screams to run. Daga fires.

But he's out of ammunition!

He throws his weapon at me—it's just a distraction. In a heartbeat, he's flying toward me, arms out. I pivot to evade. Too late.

I grunt as his helmet impacts my gut. My body bends under the force, and I topple, my boots still locked to the hull. Daga grabs my shoulders and forces me down. His knee goes into my side. I wince and punch him in the leg. His body jerks, and he twists off me to crash onto the hull.

We lie flat, side by side, staring up at the stars and catching our breaths. One of us will find the resolve to move first, and whoever does will have the advantage of the first strike. That could be me. All I need to do is lift my body, and I'll have the shot.

Hyuk, where's the rifle?

I snap my head, about to search for it. It must have flown out of my grasp when Daga hit me. But where is it? Did it float off?

There it is! Just ten paces away. But Daga spots it, too. We lock gazes as I tighten my muscles, preparing to shoot forward. He watches me, his hands set on the hull and his body coiled to launch. At this moment, we've never been more alike. Both of us should be unconscious from our wounds. Yet we're unwilling to give in to our pain. Not while the other remains alive.

I shove off the hull, disconnecting my boots as I kick to boost my speed. But Daga grabs my leg and slams me down. I gasp as I hit. Bish, he's climbing past me. I slam my fist into his side, and both of us fly backward. My boots magnetize themselves on the hull, stopping me from flying away. I stand. Daga's up, too, closer to the rifle than I am. I race toward it, but he'll get there first. Should I retreat? Where? Back into the airlock? No. I won't make it in time. But how can I beat him to it?

I unlock my boots and sprint forward. It's a stupid plan—the moment my foot floats too high, I panic and lock them down again. I've lost time. Daga's three paces from the gun. I'm two behind him. It's too late. He's got me. *I'm dead. I'm dead.*

My heart pounds in desperation as my hand grips Seren's blade. It's my last weapon. I pull it from its sheath and skate forward. He's bending down to pick the gun up, spinning toward me as the rifle comes up. I dodge right and swing, striking the barrel of the weapon and knocking it away. It comes out of Daga's left hand but stays in his right. I press my attack, pivoting to bring the blade in front.

We collide, the rifle barrel glancing off my helmet and the blade catching on his suit's seal, twisting my wrist back. I drop and jam my shoulder into his chest. He loses his balance and flails his arms out. The rifle fires, sending molten metal up from the hull. I dive away, stabbing the blade down to slow my movement.

My side screams in agony, but I force myself up and shoot forward. I've got to stay close. I've got to keep him from aiming. It's the only way I survive.

Daga sets his feet, regaining his balance. I switch my grip on the blade and spring forward. His rifle's coming back around. He sets the stock on his hip. I swing. He aims. There's a flash.

I throw my hands up and cry out. We lock gazes again. He's grinning as if he won. My throat gets tight as I back away. Did he shoot me? Am I dead?

A puff of gas escapes Daga's suit. Warning lights flash inside his helmet. His eyes go wide as his hands race to find the hole and cover it. The rifle floats free from his grasp. I gasp, my brain screaming for my body to move. I shoot my hand out and grab it, swing it up to my shoulder, drop to one knee.

And fire.

The bloom of flame that erupts off Daga's chest forces my eyes to squeeze. I can feel the heat through my suit. Daga's body convulses and goes limp, his head drooping. A second after, his arms float up and hang suspended. The rest of his body follows, rising off the hull. A chill races through me. My jaw slackens as I rise to stand, staring at his unmoving body.

Did...I...do it? Is he gone?

I won't wait to find out.

I plant my foot and kick, connecting with his gut. Daga's body doubles over and launches off the hull. He's headed aft. To the engines.

Then, as if our spirits were connected, my knees give out, and I collapse. My body's tugged down by the motion of the ship, and I come to rest on the hull. Weightlessness takes my arms and lifts them to float. My life force is draining from me, seeping down into the ship where it will join my Ancestors and all the soldiers—the children—who died before me. Yet I'm smiling. For once in my brief life, a sense of peace washes over me. I have no worries. This moment couldn't be more perfect.

So I get to gaze out into the universe again, after all. It still stirs my soul, just like the first time I experienced it. The infinity that I see fills my mind with so much possibility, I can't keep it all straight. It's fine, though. Let the next generations of crew contemplate it and choose their future. I've done what I've set myself to do.

I suppose I should at least let Efa know what I've done. She'll be glad for it.

"Efa, come in," I call through the comm, my voice raspy and weak. She'll notice. No avoiding that.

"Ceri! What's your status?" Efa's voice is pitched high, desperation already creeping in. *"Tegan and Sayer found Seren. Now Sayer's coming back up, but Tegan wants to give you support. I'm sending Merek, too. Where are you?"*

"I got him, Efa. I got Daga. He's gone. For certain this time. I sent him into the engines."

"Into the engines?" Efa gasps. *"Wait, are you out on the hull? Do you need help? I'm sending them there now."*

The edges of my lips curve higher. She cares about me, so very much. I am lucky to have such a dear friend. It would be good if we could have this conversation face to face. To say a proper goodbye. Then she'd know my reasons. She'd see the acceptance in my eyes, and she'd understand.

"Don't worry about me, Efa," I say. "I'm okay. Really."

"Like hell you are! We're coming for you, so don't be a hyuking bish about it! Now where are you?"

I don't have the strength to battle with her over this. Even as she talks with me, she's organizing a rescue team. They've got more important things to do, like ensuring our passengers get to where they're going.

"It's over, Efa," I croak. "I did everything I could. Let me rest. Just promise me you'll get Fana back. The ship needs her, and that means you do, too. Everyone's in your hands now. And you're more than capable. You'll take care of them. I know you will."

"No!" Efa cries. *"No! You don't get to say that! Not after you saved me! You can't! We need you! The passengers need you...And Fana needs you, too!"*

I'm drifting off. My eyelids are growing heavier by the second. Okay. I'm ready. All I need to do is say goodbye and I can close them forever. It'd be such a relief to let go.

"Ceri! Talk to me!"

I smile. "Don't worry, my friend. I'm not in any pain. Just tired."

"Ceri," Efa whimpers. *"Please...hold on. I can't...I can't do this on my own."*

"You can. You're stronger than I ever was. And you taught me how to feel love, when I thought I never would. Or could. I'm so grateful for that. I hope you get to have children, Efa. As many as you want. They'll be amazing, I'm sure."

I think I'm babbling. Words are pouring out of me, out of order. My body is numb. And cold. I wish someone was here to hold me. But I chose this, and I accept it. My body relaxes as my head slowly turns to one side. The stars seem brighter now. One in particular, brighter than the rest, twinkles at me. Perhaps that's their star. The sun of our passengers' new home.

They'll make it there. I'm sure of it. All our efforts have made it possible. And maybe, just maybe, on the first night on their new planet, when the dark sky still twinkles with a billion lights, they'll look up at it and remember how they got there.

"Can't you just tell me where you are?" Efa's meek voice floats into my head as my eyes close. This girl. She'll never stop trying. That's how I know I've nothing to worry about.

"In a better place. That's where I am," I whisper. Then, with my last breath, "Thank you, my friend. I love you."

Efa screams, shouting at the crew to move their asses. Merek says something to her as boots scramble behind them. Somewhere in my mind, I chuckle. All this, for me? When will they realize that in the scope of the universe, I'm not important? Nothing matters but the continuation of life. We've done our best to guarantee it happens. That's all we can ask of ourselves.

And as I drift away into nothingness, I'm glad I could do just that.

SACRIFICE

— • —

FANA

I'M FLYING. OR, MORE accurately, hurtling through space at a fairly unimpressive velocity toward a faint but glowing light. Speed doesn't matter, really, as long as I arrive at my destination. It's the *Stratford*, and as long as it doesn't change course or accelerate, I'll make it. In fact, it's the only thing I'm sure of.

There's likely to be some serious chaos on the *Devant* until they realize the cargo hatch opened rather than blew off. I hope Taye evades any direct connection to my escape, though I'm not too worried. It'll take Azazhi and the senior crew time to figure out what happened, and Taye should have plenty of time to detach himself from any suspicion. I'm really glad he helped me. There's no way I could've done it on my own.

But now, for better or worse, here I am.

From the moment I launched, I've kept my eyes shut. Mostly. I've had to check my positioning and direction, but I could use the reflection in the stasis pod's canopy to do that. The first time I looked toward the *Stratford*, my head spun so hard I nearly vomited in my helmet. After that, I clung to the top of the pod like I was a baby hanging on my parent's back.

I mean, anyone would consider what I'm doing completely stupid, and it is. I've only got four air tanks to maneuver with up front here. The rest are at the end of my pod train, their valves facing forward. They've got to stop me from crashing. And that's just one of the thousand things that could go wrong with this foolishness.

Oh, hell. I really need a distraction.

I check the gauge on my air supply—and instantly regret it. It's already down to sixty percent. *Bish.* I can't be worrying about breathing when I'm trying to land a massively long and heavy object. Maybe it could be enough, but after my last excursion to the *Stratford*, I'm not up for taking chances.

But at the moment, there's little I can do besides kill myself with worry. Perhaps I can try to enjoy the view for once. Like, really, really, try.

I open one eye and watch the stars slide across the pod's canopy in a distorted arc. But it's less interesting than I hoped. *Do I dare?* My other eye opens a crack. Then a little more. I raise my head. The muted light of the universe touches my retinas. *Okay, this is much better.* I let my eyes fully open and take in the enormity of what I see. It's—

Static bursts through my comm. I scream and jerk. My feet lose their hold on the pod. I scream again and yank hard on the tether wound around my hands. My pulse pounds hard. *Hold on, Fana. Hold on.*

"...hold on. I can't...I...do...my own."

I freeze. That's Efa! Can she hear me?

"Efa!" I call. "Come in! It's Fana! Are you receiving me?"

My comm reverts to picking up only the background noise of the universe. That might be interesting, but not when I'm making a ship-to-ship transfer with no space vehicle and a very limited amount of propellant. Or control.

I'm five minutes out, so maybe I just got lucky. Even if I can make out the *Stratford*'s shape now, their comms weren't designed to reach this far. Still, Efa's voice was full of something. Fear? I sure hope not.

"Efa," I try again. "Pick up. Let me know if you can hear me."

"*...my friend...love...*"

I suck in a huge gasp. Was that Ceri just now? Her voice sounded so weak. *Yes. It absolutely was.*

Chills run down my back. Why would Ceri be talking about love with Efa? Especially when she sounds like she's hurt. She'd never get all mushy out of nowhere. Not unless—

No, Ceri can't be wounded. Not again.

"Efa! Please! Pick up!"

A rush of static hits my ears, and I wince. It's still too far for a clear transmission. That won't stop me from trying. Or her.

"*...F...Fana...you? Wh...location...*" From what I hear, she sounds like she's in a total panic.

"Efa! I'm on my way to the *Stratford* right now! I'm targeting the cargo hatch on ninety! I've got a huge cargo to deliver! You're going to love it!"

But all I get back is silence. It won't be much of a delivery if I can't get it inside the ship. And the timing has to be perfect. Once I slow down, I'll lose the lead I planned so I could meet the *Stratford* on its vector. And I've got no way to catch up with it.

"Fana! Fana! Are you reading me?" Efa's voice comes in so loud I mute the comm, my ears ringing. I reset the volume and drop it to a reasonable level. She must have switched to the ship's system, which also means the *Devant* can hear her. I'll have to risk it. I'm too far along my trajectory now.

"Efa, it's Fana," I call. "Can you get a few of the crew down to ninety, like, now?"

"*What?*" Efa squeaks. "*Why? No. No. I can't spare anyone. I'm sorry. Where are you?*"

I blink. Why is she turning me down?

"Listen, I'm on my way from the *Devant* with 247 stasis pods. They'll be ours, but I need to secure them to the ship, or they, and I, will be lost in space."

I swallow hard at the thought. I didn't make half my fingers bleed just to fail at the last possible moment.

Efa sighs. "*Oh, hell, Fana. Why now?*"

"Huh?" Did she not just hear the part about me getting lost in space?

"*Listen. The entire crew's suiting up. Ceri's somewhere out on the hull. She and Daga had a fight, and now...*" Efa chokes up and my stomach tightens. "*Fana. Ceri could be dead.*"

The air rushes out of my lungs. But breathing is not a concern of mine anymore. If Ceri is really dead, I don't even want to take another breath.

"*I'm really worried, Fana. She was saying some strange things. And now I can't get her back on comm.*"

No. This is not fair. Not fair at all. Why is the universe punishing me? Why am I not allowed to be happy? And Ceri. Her promise of a better life gets taken away? And her only future is to sacrifice her life for the sake of thousands of people who won't ever know what she did for them.

I don't accept that. Not at all.

All I want to do is find her. Find her now. But I'm stuck here, putting along at the pace of ice melting in space. The three minutes I've got until I arrive at the *Stratford* are a million years longer than I can wait. The pods still need to get inside the ship, and my air supply is down below thirty percent.

But my heart aches. It aches so badly, thinking that I may never talk to her again. Or see her smile. Or kiss her.

Hyuk this. I'm jumping off the moment I'm in range of the ship. If the pods crash, they crash. I don't care. I just want to see her. I need to see her.

No. That's wrong. She risked her life for her people. Ceri would tell me any sacrifice she's made is worth it. She had a mission, and she took it on with not a single doubt about what she was doing.

Oh, Ceri. Please. Please be alive.

"Fana?" Efa queries.

Bish, I wish I had Taye's tablet. Calculations are flying through my head. I do my best to keep track of the numbers, but I don't have every measurement. I've got to make a few big guesses, and that's dangerous. Not as dangerous as riding a stasis pod through space with little control, though what I'm considering right now is way more insane.

But I have to. I'll be empty without her. Ceri risked everything to save me. She deserves for me to do the same for her.

"Fana? Are you still there?"

"Have one of the crew open the outside airlock door on ninety and leave it open," I reply as I shift to take up my makeshift control unit. "They won't have to stay. Just make sure it stays open."

"Okay, but what are you planning?"

"I'll find her, Efa. I promise. Have everyone ready."

My forward tanks may just have enough air for this. Maybe. As I make my fancy maneuver, the *Stratford* will be sliding by, and I can't miss. I'll crash on the hull if I have to, though that'll destroy most of the pods. As it is, the first few will get damaged. But I can't have it both ways. And if I sacrifice a few pods to save Ceri, it'll be more than worth it.

"Deryn's opening the airlock and going out there to search for her," Efa says. *"He'll be nearby if you need support."*

"Better he's not," I reply. "I can't guarantee this will work."

"What...are you planning?"

Sorry, Efa, can't talk now. I bite down on my lower lip and tap the controls, aiming more forward on the *Stratford* than I'd planned. I'll need the extra time and the extra margin of error. My piloting experience is limited to the one time I got to sit at the controls of a shuttle. I get the theory but have no practice to back it up.

This will be hyuking amazing if I pull this off.

Another tap on the valve release and the pods roll, curving into the ship as I fight to keep calm. I'm quickly getting nauseous, but I can't spot Ceri if I keep my eyes closed. My utter fear will just have to deal. This is for Ceri.

My pod train coils around the *Stratford*, fairly close to what I hoped. Maybe I can get closer to the hull. Just tap the controls—*No. Don't overcorrect. That'll mess it up.*

I scan the black exterior of the ship, straining to notice anything out of the ordinary. Though, even at this distance, it'll be hard to spot a human on a skyscraper-long ship. Ceri had a battle. Maybe there are signs of that.

Oh bish, what if she's floated off?

Then I see it. A speck of orange, way closer to the engines than I'd expect anyone to ever be. I recognize legs...and arms. They're just hanging in space. My chest tightens. It's Ceri. It's got to be Ceri.

I just hope she's alive. I will thank every god, spirit, deity, or holy person who's ever existed if she is. *Just please, please, please, let her be.*

"Found her!" I shout, my mouth spreading into a wide smile. "I found her! She's just outside of an airlock on the bottom section of the ship!"

"One-thirty-six!" Sayer shouts. *"It's got to be one-thirty-six! There's only one airlock down there!"*

"Everyone, get down there now!" Efa barks. *"Go! Go!"*

Okay. I did as promised. Now to land this train.

My finger covers the valve release as I take a wild guess at how much air remains in the four maneuvering tanks. All I need is one solid blast to put me into the airlock, but I might not even have that left. This is really the reason we spend so much time in the design phase. Not that I had time. Any longer on the *Devant* and I'd be stuck there permanently. Or executed.

An alarm sounds in my helmet. *Oh bish! Not again!* My air supply is almost out! I may have to rush this more than I expected to. No. I definitely will.

With no time left, I hit the button and brace for the rapid deceleration. But it doesn't come. My forehead gets tight. I tested all the connections. I was sure it would work. Everything else has. Maybe something came loose during launch? I lean forward to check the cabling.

And nearly get tossed off the pod.

I scream as I flop over the front, dangling by the strap around my left wrist as the pods continue to slow.

Idiot! Of course it'd take a second! The tethers have to become taut again in the opposite direction they were traveling! Now I'm the front bumper of a vehicle that weighs several thousand times my weight, and if I don't move, there won't be much left of me to remember.

My suit continues to shout warnings in my ears as I flail my hand to catch the strap I was holding. It's too far away. I'll have to climb up to reach it, but I need the strap to get up there!

Forget it. I don't have time for this. I'll control the pods from here, then disconnect before I get squashed and float in after the pods.

Yeah, this'll never work. I'm doing it anyway.

I hit the maneuver tanks. The pods arc toward the ship. They jerk as they scrape across the metal of the hull. The airlock is coming up. I grab the tether connection, take a breath.

And release.

The pods overtake me and crumple into the airlock. I enter a second later, flailing out to grab a tether and wrap it around the first thing that seems solid.

Then bump into the airlock wall.

Leaks. Check for leaks in the suit!

I peel myself from the wall of the airlock, my hands racing across the thin layers. They make these things durable. I think. I hope. I've got no air left to lose.

"Everyone, this is Tegan. Merek's found her. Repeat, Merek's found her, but she's unresponsive."

Panic seeps into me. My skin goes cold. This had better not have been for nothing.

"Get Raey," I say. "Get her now."

CONCLUSION

—— • ——

CERI

"I THINK SHE'S STILL alive!"

Fana's words float through my mind as if she was next to me. But that's impossible. Fana's imprisoned on the *Devant*. And I'm dead. Yet, I sense touch. Someone's hands, perhaps. It's difficult to tell. The feeling is distant. Elusive. When I focus on it, it evaporates into nothing.

I'm not sure what I expected death to be like. Certainly not this state of nonexistence. Maybe it'd be a moment where I met my Ancestors. They would welcome me and take me to their place of rest, or I would join with them in some other way. I don't know. My parents never taught me much about that sort of thing. They believed little in it, though they had strong faith in this expedition. Enough to make me a believer, too.

As much as I try, I can't form thoughts beyond each passing moment. Memories come to me, drift away, and I've no recollection of what they were. I only know they existed. Do I? Or am I just a memory? What is this I'm experiencing? I just seem to float along through...what?

Wait. What was that? Did someone call my name? Is that what I have to do? Find my Ancestors? How do I move?

Another connection from somewhere. I feel...shaking? Movement? No. What was I trying to do before this? I'm dead, aren't I?

"She's lost a lot of blood. There could be damage to her liver and intestines. Surgery's the only option. But I've never done an operation like this. This is not part of my qualifications."

Raey's voice. I heard it clearly. Something's happening. A warmth forms in my side. It's getting warmer—no. Hotter. It burns. It aches. I scream to escape it. I can't. It's consuming me. I must get away. I must.

Pain. I feel pain.

"She's gaining consciousness!" Fana shouts. "Ceri! Ceri! Can you hear me?"

Everything fades away. I'm returned to placid nothingness. Relief washes over me. I would smile if I could. Maybe I am, and I can't tell. Could this be it? The moment where I meet my Ancestors? I can't wait. I have so much to tell them. Seren could be with them. I hope so. I really want to see her again.

"We're losing her!"

Efa's voice now. I'm sure of it.

Whoa! What the hell was that? Everything scrambled, then went bright. The afterimage remains. It's not clear. Fear is coming over me. What is this? I just want to rest.

"Again! Do it again!" Raey shouts.

Is this a memory? It's too real. Whatever happened, I don't want to experience it a second time. It's punishment. Payback from the universe for killing children. I deserve it, but it was so intense. And I—

"Clear out!"

No. Not again!

Brightness explodes across my vision. I gasp, my body tingling with the shock of their assault.

Wait. My...body? Am I alive?

"Ceri." A hand goes behind my head. Efa's. "Ceri, can you hear me?"

Awareness returns. I have hands. Arms and legs. A head. They're all so heavy. My throat is raw. There's something in it. Someone's holding my hand. But I've got no middle. No gut. No chest. It's like they're not there.

"Her pulse has stabilized," Raey says. "But the machines are keeping her alive. It's unlikely she'll remain conscious for long."

"Ceri, squeeze my hand if you can hear me," Efa says.

I try.

"Did she?" Fana asks, her voice some distance away. "Did she?"

"A little."

So I live. If it can be called life. I'm enslaved to machines that breathe for me. Keep my heart beating and my lungs moving. Probably feed me and urinate for me too. I am dead without them. Maybe I should be. I don't want to exist as a parasite to a machine, but I fear I will have no say about it. I doubt I can even speak. And they'll keep me alive, just so they won't have to mourn me. Just so they can feel good about saving my life, when they never even asked me if I wanted to live.

I said goodbye, though it was far from what I'd imagined it to be, and I've pictured it many times since waking from stasis. It was a near guarantee, submerged deep in that bloodbath, that we'd be dead before long. We even looked forward to it. And then Efa met Merek, and dying became something to avoid.

Still, I did what I promised I'd do. My crew and my passengers are as safe as they will ever be for the next three hundred years. Then, once they reach their destination, it'll be on them to survive. What reason do I have to live beyond now, sentenced to a medical bed like this? No. It's senseless. I refuse it.

But my opinion won't matter. Even if I could tell it to them, they'd reject my plea and try to convince me I'll heal, when they know I never will.

Someone strokes my hair, running their fingers through what must be a completely tangled mess. Still, it's soothing. Their touch shows how much they care for me. And in that is a trap. Soon, I'll start feeling guilty about wanting to die, and I'll convince myself to fight for their sake, when all I'd be doing is prolonging my suffering.

"We're here for you," Fana whispers. "Everyone is. Just rest, okay? We'll take care of the ship. Don't worry."

A weight presses on me. Poor Fana. Even while she comforts me, I can only feel regret. What could have been if we could have had our time together? I don't want to consider it. The desire to live, just to be near her, will come. But it's wrong. There is no moment in this life where I will ever get to kiss her again.

"Ceri, we have to decide something," Efa says. "It concerns you, so I want you to hear it."

"Hear what?" Fana asks.

"Come out with me," Raey says. "Let Efa tell her alone. It'll be up to them to decide."

"Decide what? Hey! Don't touch me! Okay. Okay. I'll go. For now. I'm coming back once they're done talking."

Bish. Leave her alone. Isn't she suffering enough?

"Listen." Efa's voice is closer to my ear. She must have sat down. Or kneeled. "I know what you're thinking, Ceri, and I'm not upset. Not any longer. But we both know, right now, you're far from living. It's not just the wounds Daga gave you. Your body's had it, Ceri. All those years of fighting have caught up to you, and without an actual doctor, there's not much we can do. I tried to warn you, but, as usual, you bish-head, you didn't want to listen."

My hand tightens as much as it's able. Efa responds by squeezing it back. I listened, though. I heard every word she said and the distress behind them. There was nothing I could do about it. I had to fight him. He had to die.

"Still, you saved us all," Efa continues, rubbing a thumb across my hand. "Again. No one could have done what you did. You've sacrificed so much, and there's no way to show you how grateful we are for that. Not that you'd accept it. Jerk. But there might be a way to make things better for you."

I try to shake my head, but if it moved once, I can't tell. She has to let me go. I won't be their burden. Didn't Efa see how much Niah hated to be cared for? I won't live like this. Not even for a day.

But how can I tell her that with this mess of a body I'm in?

Perhaps sensing my discomfort, Efa brushes my hair back behind my ear. I tilt my head into her touch, connecting with her the only way I can.

"Fana's back, Ceri," she says. "She escaped the *Devant* and brought pods back with her. A lot. Your girl really came through for us. Now she's out there tearing her braids out because she wants to be with you. I'll let her in, but we've got to figure this out first, okay?"

I can hear the smile on her lips. Does she know? Or just suspect? In my semiconscious state, I may have said some things I'd be embarrassed to admit. It hardly matters now. If Efa cared anything for Fana, she'd lock her out of this room and tell her to forget about me. Not that she ever would. I could never forget her, either. Not for a second.

"So here it is. Raey thinks you could heal in a stasis pod. One of the ones that Fana brought with her. Now, we don't know how long it'll take, so..." Efa goes quiet for a moment, and her unspoken words become clear to me.

While I recovered in the pod, everyone would grow older. Efa could be the same age as my mother when I woke again. Little Dru could be twice my age. And Fana...

Fana could be just like Raey.

"Niah's already asked to be the first to go in as soon as we can connect the new pods. And I'm sure you'd agree, it's the right thing for her. She deserves to see the new world. Bish, we all do, but someone's got to run the ship. I'm planning on doing that. So is Merek. Everyone else has to decide, too, though I think they'll follow what you started."

I'm not sure I could make that decision. To live, that is. What's the difference between dying and waking up to see all the people I care about have lived their lives while mine was frozen in time? My life is over. How can I choose to go on when there's no way forward?

"Think about it, Ceri," Efa whispers into my ear. "Please? No matter how long it takes. It would make me so happy to see you on your feet again. Forget about the years. You've got a chance you didn't have before, thanks to Fana."

Efa strokes my hand as she holds it, and we stay that way for countless minutes. Time becomes meaningless. I forget about my unfortunate condition and simply enjoy being with my friend the way we used to be. Though moments like this were few, they were crucial for our survival.

"I should let Fana see you," she says finally. "I'm causing her all sorts of anxiety, keeping her away like this." Efa chuckles. "Bish, she's got it bad for you."

I squeeze her hand once again, as hard as I can. Likely that's not hard at all. But she notices.

"And one more thing, my friend. Since you didn't give me the chance to say it before," Efa drawls. "I love you with all my heart, and I don't want you to suffer anymore. I'll do anything I can to stop that from happening. Anything. Got it?"

Efa presses her lips against my cheek, holding it there for a second. One kiss will have to suffice for the many she used to shower me with. It's enough.

And with that, she's gone.

"Ceri?" Fana says meekly as she enters. "Can you hear me?"

I move my hand—at least I think I do—to answer her. Fana inhales and rushes to my side, taking my hand up and pressing her cheek to it. Seconds later, drops of moisture slide across my fingers. I would stop her tears if I could. For now, I can only accept them.

"I'm sorry," Fana whimpers. "I'm so sorry, Ceri. If I was here, I could have helped you, and maybe you wouldn't be like this now. I know I couldn't have stopped you from doing what you did, but I would have been there for you. I swear I would have been there."

She rests her head on my chest, her body heaving with each sob. Bish. She can't do this. I strain to embrace her, but my arms just won't move.

The pain returns. The ache. The hurt. But it has moved from my side and into my heart, and this is by far a harder pain to endure.

Oh, Efa, why did you let her back in here?

"Raey told me they want to put you in stasis," Fana says, sniffling as she lifts off of me. "It'll work, Ceri. The pods from the *Devant* are the best humanity could design. It'll heal you, just like it did for me. Be confident in that.

"I know you're worried about it. About the time it'll take. No one knows how long that'll be. The pods weren't meant to be medical devices. That's just a side effect of the technology, even if it's a good one. It was seventeen years before they woke me up. I was fine long before then, but they didn't need me. They shouldn't have waited. Raey really missed me, just like I'd miss you. Horribly. But if I knew I'd get to see you again, recovered and whole, I could wait. I could wait forever for you."

I gather every bit of strength I have and force my eyelids open. Everything's blurry. A dark form hovers above me, swaying slightly. It's her. That's all I need to know.

After a few minutes, or what seems like that long, my sight clears. Fana looks down at me, her mouth and eyes drooping. What a sad state I've put her into. I'd do anything to make her smile again, but what can I do?

Except say yes.

Our eyes connect then, and the fear in hers shakes me. I am helpless to comfort her, yet I can still do something—I can give her hope.

I do my best to nod, though I've no idea if I've succeeded, until Fana smiles and laughs through her tears. The success of my efforts reaches me, and I realize, even in this reduced state, I am still capable of so very much.

Fana loves me. So, for as long as I live, I will fight to bring her happiness.

ABANDONMENT

FANA

As I leave the medical bay, I'm filled with a sense of a new beginning. And just like all new beginnings, this one is a little scary. It's the unknown that frightens me. Like any future—it's uncertain, but it offers great promise. For the first time since I arrived on the *Stratford*, there's a buzz of excitement about the crew. We've recovered from all but the most minor problems. The ship is perfectly on course, and everyone is learning new skills at an amazing rate. There's little any of us could ask for.

Save for Ceri being whole again.

Raey and I need to talk about that. Now, before Ceri enters stasis. I don't want her in there any longer than she has to be. For her to wake up seventeen years from now would be absolute torture. She's got to be around her crew while they're still young, or she will suffer from the loneliness I felt. I won't let that happen.

I find Raey and Efa down the hall in Ceri's office, though I suppose it's Efa's now. It still looks the same, of course. The large crème-and-white-framed desk that belonged to the former chief still hogs the back of the space. Behind it is a mass of waist-high cabinets under a countertop full of composite fiber printouts and stationary knickknacks. And along the side wall is a cot that Ceri brought in here but almost never used, preferring her old nest in the girls' barracks. Efa sits cross-legged on it now, frowning at Raey, who leans on the edge of the desk, her hands resting on each side of her. They both turn as I enter.

"She'll do it," I say, coming to a stop just a few paces inside the door.

Efa's face brightens. "Great! Let's get her prepped."

"Wait." I hold up a hand. "Before we do anything, we're going to agree right here and now that she's only in there until she's fully healed. Then we pull her out immediately."

Efa presses her lips together. She wants Ceri and me to be together, but she doesn't want to promise me anything. She's not familiar with just how advanced these pods are, so I can't blame her. Efa will learn, though. I'm just hoping she learns before we put Ceri in one of them.

"Fana," Raey begins with that tone of hers that signals a lecture. "Medical recovery during stasis isn't an exact science. We don't—"

"—know how long it takes," I finish. "You know how aware of that I am already."

"Yes, which is why making any promise right now would be foolish."

"Except we can all agree on what I'm asking for because I'm not putting any time limits on it. All I'm asking is for her not to wake up to a crew she no longer knows. Is that so unreasonable?"

I must have made my point with Efa, who lowers her gaze as her face turns pained. Raey sighs and does her best to smile.

"I'm glad you made it back, Fana," she says.

I'll take that as her giving up and use whatever small bit of maturity I've collected not to press her more. It's a win for me, however small.

Aidan rushes in, his chest pumping as he forces himself to breathe. When he spots Efa, his mouth opens as if to say something important.

Then shuts when he sees Raey.

He and I haven't spent that much time together, but I've never known him to be overly dramatic. Whatever's bothering him is likely going to be a serious issue. And likely it'll be something I'll need to repair.

"What is it?" I ask.

Aidan's wide eyes swing between all of us as he pants.

"Everything okay?" Efa tries.

"The..." He glances at Raey again, and now my stomach is getting tight. "The *Devant*..."

"What about it?" I demand.

"It's...gone."

The color drains from Raey's face. Bish. I should have warned Raey. Maybe I selfishly wished she'd stay around. Well, my wish was granted, and I'm a total jerk for keeping the possibility of it to myself. I guess Azazhi decided messing with us was more trouble than it was worth, even to retrieve the stasis pods. Though he was always about his own survival rather than everyone else's.

Efa frowns. "What do you mean?"

"I mean, it's gone!" Aidan shakes his head. "Dru was looking out of the fore port on two, and she saw it get bright and shoot away so fast she couldn't track it. We tried calling them, but they don't answer."

Efa stands. "Show me."

"Don't bother," I say, and they snap their gazes at me. "Taye told me they were leaving. That was supposed to be with me on board, of course. Though, now that we have a moment, I have to say I'm really glad I wasn't."

Efa folds her arms. Raey's eyebrows clash. All I can do is shrug.

"Sorry," I say. "It's my fault for not bringing it up. There were other more important things going on, you know?"

Raey sinks onto the desk, her gaze dropping to the deck. So she still had some hope she might return to her ship. *But really? As if the agents abducting me wasn't enough of a hint?* Azazhi must have decided she was expendable when he first allowed her to remain on the *Stratford*.

Poor Raey. It's like no one wants her. Except we were ready to welcome her until she betrayed us. I mean, I totally get she was trying to save her crew. Only they're not her crew anymore. Raey's stuck here now, just like the rest of us.

And maybe that calls for a reconsideration of her status.

"Uh, Efa, can I talk to you for a moment?" I smile as I clasp my hands behind my back. Raey connects her eyes with mine, searching for the meaning behind my request. I reply with a brief nod, and it clicks.

"I'll, uh, go check on Ceri," she says, eying Aidan with an expectant glance. He nods, and a second later, they shuffle out and head to medical.

Efa motions for me to join her on the cot. I smile but decline, moving to take up the spot Raey was just occupying. It seems appropriate, as I've now become her spokesperson for the second time. It's a position I'd prefer not to have, but no one else knows her as well as I do, and no one else would do this for her.

"I know what this is about," Efa says, pulling her knees up as she leans back on the wall. "And I can't say what you're about to ask will be easy to grant. But since you're up there in the rankings just behind Ceri for the amount of amazing things you've done for us, I think you're allowed to make difficult requests."

I chuckle and fold my arms in front of me. "Thanks, I guess. But I'm not expecting anything unreasonable."

"Unreasonable when it comes to Raey, you mean." Efa grins as my jaw goes slack, sticking out a toe to tap my leg. "You're *Stratford* crew now, Fana. Get used to digs like that."

"What about Raey?" I counter. "Is she *Stratford* crew now, too?"

Efa's heavy sigh is my answer, though I suspect I'll get more of an explanation, and as Efa tilts her head and wraps her hands around her knees, I ready myself to hear it.

"No one will just forget what she's done," Efa says. "You know that. Sayer will give us all sorts of trouble if we let her roam free around the ship. He still wants to execute her."

"But she's got skills we really need. I mean, how much has she taught you already? I doubt that's even half of what Raey knows. And her experience is even more valuable. We won't do well if we don't have a medical technician."

"But you're forgetting, now that we've got the pods you stole from the *Devant*, we can wake up medical personnel when we need to."

I grumble over Efa's point. It's true, we've got an option that we never had before. The adults have skills and knowledge we don't. And they'd be more familiar with this ship than I am. Still, if everyone's having issues with Raey, they definitely wouldn't want to create some kind of chain reaction by upsetting the balance we've got now.

"You'd really wake up an adult?" I ask. "That'd be a bad idea."

Efa shrugs. "They're just passengers, and they'd want to take care of us. Bish, my parents are here. They'd help us if we asked them to. So would a thousand others. And none of them ever betrayed us."

"But they could."

Efa levels her gaze at me. "What are you saying?"

Yeah, what am I saying? If I want to convince her, I better make a strong point here. And if I do it right, Raey could become my ally in getting Ceri back on her feet as soon as possible. It's selfish, but I really don't want to be alone for seventeen years. Not after I just found the one person in this universe who wants to be with me.

"We've got a stable situation right now. We know what our problems are, and we've got clarity on how to solve them. All we've got to do is the work. And we absolutely can do it. Raey won't betray us." I duck my head. "Again."

"And?"

"Well, for one, she's got nowhere else to put her loyalties. We're the only ones to take care of her now. And she cares about this crew. I know she'd want to do her part."

Efa folds her arms. *"And?"*

Wow, she's hard to convince. "Do you know why engineers work within a specific set of limitations?" I try.

Efa shakes her head.

"It's so we don't have to worry about unknown variables or other problems we can't solve. It makes designing things way easier. We've got a crew. We know what they can do and what they can't. Even if some of us don't trust her, we still understand what she's capable of. If we wake up a bunch of adults, it'll complicate what we have. Maybe even destroy it."

She chews on her lower lip, considering. And taking way longer than I might hope to do so. My body gets tight watching her. Is this such a big thing I'm asking for?

No. But I can hardly be patient. Raey deserves freedom, and she'll appreciate it if we give it to her. The more we can relearn to work together, the better it'll be for everyone. It'll take time, but the crew will forgive her, even if they never forget. People change. They've got to learn that.

Right now, though, I really wish Efa would get the point I'm trying to make.

"Let me talk with Merek and Sayer," Efa says. "If I can get them to agree, the rest of the crew will go along."

Oh good. She does get it. I nod and hold back my smile. "Okay."

She pushes herself off the cot and stands, reaching out to squeeze my hand. We share a smile, even as something keeps me from feeling at ease. Everything seems like it's headed in the right direction, so why can't I be happy about that? Of course, I'd be ecstatic if Ceri were okay, but something else is bothering me. There's this strange twist in my stomach, and I'm not sure why.

"Hey, but let's not wake up any adults for now, right?" I ask, in case that's it.

Efa smiles. "Don't worry."

Except that I do.

EPILOGUE

— • —

EFA

WE DIDN'T SAY GOODBYE to Ceri. We said goodnight. Having dosed her into a medical sleep, we laid her into the last of three new pods cleared for service. Fana bawled when we lowered the canopy. So did Dru. Even Sayer rubbed at his eyes a few times when I spoke about how we'd see her again and have the chance to tell her everything we've done. It would be as if no time had passed at all.

I struggled to hold back my emotions in that moment. I'm leader now, and as much as I wish I wasn't, I've got to be strong for the crew. That's what Ceri would've done. Still, when Raey engaged the stasis control, I had to turn away while Merek covered for me. And once we were alone, I let my tears flow while he held me.

A few days later, as we pushed ourselves to create a regular schedule, Merek, Sayer, and I met with Raey as she and Fana went through the new pods to certify them for use. Then we'd begin transferring passengers out of the failing units. I don't know how that'll work, but I'll have to trust Fana and Raey on that.

"Confirmed, 231 all test out. Plus, the other 62 we received prior makes 293 pods available. The rest that Fana brought are only good for parts," Raey says. "She's taken Beka, Aidan, and Dru down to the repair shop to help her disassemble the units and organize them into subsections."

"That's more than we need!" Merek cheers and takes me by the shoulders as he beams. I'll be celebrating, too, as soon as the entire job is done. Then we can think about the rest of our lives on this ship.

"How long will it take to move everyone over?" I ask.

Raey shrugs. "Well, we need to double-check and make sure we're moving only the people we really need to. Even with restasis, there's a risk. It'd be better to leave people where they are. I'm sure we'd all prefer not to wake a bunch of people up who suddenly have a medical emergency."

"What do you mean?" Sayer says, frowning. "We turned out alright."

"True. Children's bodies are more adaptable. Adults take longer to wake up, and there are more risks involved."

Unease hits me as Raey's words make connections in my mind. *Wake up. Adults. A bunch.* I was only talking in what-ifs when I suggested it to Fana, but now it's becoming a strong reality, I'm not so sure I'm okay with it. I attempt to catch Merek's gaze, but he's too focused on Raey. I poke him to get his attention, and when he jumps, Raey and Sayer also turn to me.

"Are you concerned about something?" Merek asks.

"Aren't you?"

"Should I be?"

I sigh and roll my eyes. *Of all the times for him to be stupid.* "We're going to be waking up a bunch of adults! Don't you see the issue with that?"

"They're just passengers." Merek shakes his head. "None of them will want to be awake for very long."

"And what if they do?"

"Wait." Sayer steps in front of me to get closer to Raey. "If adults want to stay awake, can't some of us return to stasis, then?"

My hands clench, and I resist the urge to punch Sayer in the back. But if he's thinking about sneaking out of the duty we all agreed to, I will knock his teeth out. It's bad enough we're short four people in a crew of fourteen—fifteen if we include Raey. The custodial crew was forty, not including families. And all they had to do was maintain the Stratford. Not rebuild it.

"Absolutely," Raey replies. "The Devant doesn't have a generational crew. We just staggered rotations, and while that meant some of us would be old by the time we arrived, we would all get to live the remainder of our lives on the new planet. In fact, other than Commander Azazhi and his senior staff, the rest of us would retire the moment we set our feet on Asteria."

I should have known this would happen. Ceri's in stasis less than a day, and there's already a challenge to my leadership. Of course it'd be Sayer.

"No!" I shout. "We are not doing that."

"Hey." Merek rubs my shoulder. "It's okay. He's just asking a question."

My eyes narrow at him. He doesn't get to play peacekeeper today. Sayer needs to fall in line, or Merek and I will have to fight him again the next time he goes against us.

"No, he isn't." I thrust a finger at Sayer's chest when he rotates to face me, locking eyes with him. "Are you?"

"It's not a bad idea, Efa." Sayer's placating tone only stirs me up more. "Wouldn't you like to live on a new planet?"

"No one is living anywhere if we don't ensure this ship gets to its destination! All of us agreed to make that happen, Sayer. Did you forget?"

Sayer's open mouth and raised hands won't get him any-where with me. Every time he challenged Ceri, I was there, watching him. I won't give him even a sliver of a break. It'd be nice to have some support, though. Like from the man I love.

I pound Merek's arm. He yelps but gets my hint and levels his gaze at his friend.

"Let's just get everything stable before we decide something like that, yeah?" Merek suggests. "We've had some serious mo-ments, and now we're ready to really set things in place. Once we're satisfied, then we can discuss rotating shifts."

"All of you have done so much to protect the passengers of this ship," Raey says. "You all deserve a rest. We could at least give those we wake up the option of remaining awake for a while."

"Hey," Sayer snaps. "Just because we agreed to let you free doesn't mean your opinion is equal to the rest of us."

"She's trying to support you, if you didn't notice," Merek says. "And it's a reasonable suggestion."

I gasp and pull away from him, my mouth hanging open as I stare, disbelieving the words that came out of his mouth.

Merek takes me by the shoulders, that same gentle smile on his face as the first time he kissed me. Now I'll remember it as the look he betrayed me with while I was struggling to lead the crew.

"It'll be alright," he says, rubbing my arms. "We're all in this together. The ship and all the passengers will get where they're going. If we can, too, that'd be wonderful. I want to have a life with you, Efa. A good life. One where we get to enjoy moments as often as we battle through them."

I rip myself away from his grasp and glare at the three of them. They might not realize it, but they're standing together as they face me. Three against one. I've lost this argument, the first of my time as crew head. I hope it's the last, though I know it won't be. Ceri needs to heal quickly, or we're all in trouble.

"I better not regret this," I say.

Books by Marc B. DeGeorge

The Stratford Saga

A Universe Upon Us

A Universe Against Us

The Universe Before Us

The Air Born

A Call to the Sky

A Challenge for the Sky

A Crisis in the Sky

Origin Story

The Starship Sneak
The Reckless Rescue
The Traitors' Trial
The Conspiracy Clash
The Deadly Discord

About the Author

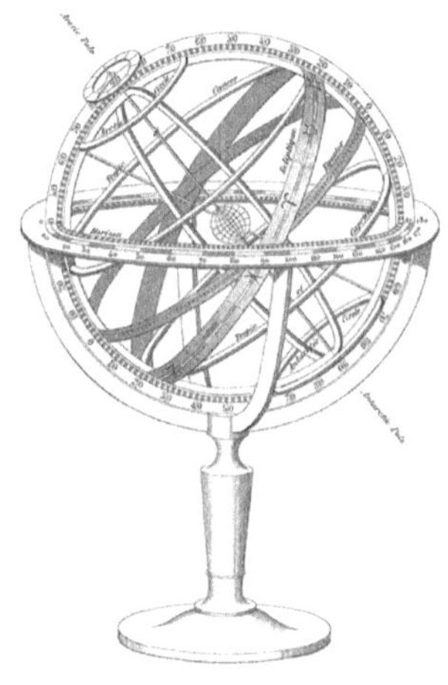

Amazon bestselling author Marc B. DeGeorge has always wanted to be an astronaut, but since he failed his mission at Space Camp, he now writes science fiction stories with a human focus. In his spare time, Marc works a full-time job for a major manufacturer of professional audio equipment and has taught audio technology at the college level. He's also been studying the shamisen for over sixteen years and performs regularly around the Eastern US.

amazon.com/Marc-B-Degeorge/e/B09LDCNVHV/

facebook.com/MarcBDeGeorge

instagram.com/marcbdegeorgeauthor/

g goodreads.com/author/show/22081012.Marc_B_DeGeorge

www.ingramcontent.com/pod-product-compliance
Lightning Source LLC
Chambersburg PA
CBHW061210190726
48288CB00001B/134